SCIENCE FICTION DIALOGUES

SCIENCE FICTION DIALOGUES

Edited by Gary Wolfe

Academy
Chicago

Academy Chicago
425 N. Michigan Ave.
Chicago, IL 60611

Library of Congress Cataloging in Publication Data
Main entry under title:
Science fiction dialogues.

Bibliography: p.
 1. Science fiction—History and criticism—Addresses, essays, lectures.
I. Wolfe, Gary K., 1946-   II. Science Fiction Research Association.
PN3433.8.S36   1982   809.3'876   82-16352
ISBN 0-89733-067-6 (pbk.)

Contents

Preface

In 1980, when members of the Science Fiction Research Association first began discussing the idea of sponsoring a volume or series of volumes of criticism and scholarship, academic study of fantastic literature had already become something of a cottage industry. The SFRA itself had co-sponsored a volume with the Science Fiction Writers of America (*Science Fiction: Contemporary Mythology*, edited by Patricia Warrick, Martin Harry Greenberg, and Joseph Olander, Harper, 1978); science fiction studies had become a continuing presence in the meetings of such academic organizations as the Modern Language Association and the Popular Culture Association; three significant academic journals (*Extrapolation, Science Fiction Studies,* and *Foundation*) had been underway for a number of years; conferences devoted to the study of the fantastic included not only the Science Fiction Research Association's own annual conference, but others such as the International Conference on the Fantastic in the Arts; and even some fan conventions had begun to include academic programming, culminating in the first formally organized series of academic sessions at the World Science Fiction Convention in Chicago in 1982.

Thus, when I was asked to put together the first book devoted exclusively to the work of the Association, it was with some trepidation that I accepted the task. After all, wasn't there enough being said about science fiction and fantasy already? Was there really a need for another book about science fiction? Some encouragement came from the success of Thomas J. Remington's *Selected Proceedings* of the 1978 SFRA convention (University of Northern Iowa, 1979), as well as from the earlier SFRA-SFWA volume. When a group of distinguished scholars—Eric S. Rabkin, W. Warren Wagar, Roger C. Schlobin, Catherine L. McClenehan, Russell Letson, and Neil Barron—agreed to serve on the editorial board of the volume, reviewing essays and making suggestions as to format, the project began to seem worthwhile and even necessary. The very abundance of material being written on science fiction suggested a need for a volume that would pinpoint trends in criticism, suggest new directions for research, and generally represent the work of the Association.

We decided on a volume that would consist of original material written by SFRA members as well as material solicited from distinguished writers and critics in the field. Seven of the pieces in this volume were originally read at conferences of the Science Fiction Research Association, and one is an original essay by Brian Aldiss, a recipient of the SFRA's Pilgrim Award for lifetime contributions to the understanding of science fiction. Algis Budrys provided an essay which will prove indispensable to any future scholars of science fiction (and much popular fiction in general), and Robert Crossley made available valuable primary source material from the correspondence between H.G. Wells and Olaf Stapledon. Other SFRA members provided essays on a variety of topics of current concern. This is not a "theme" anthology and promotes no single point of view. Rather it is a sampler of a wide variety of approaches to fantastic literature, ranging from the interpretation of primary sources to the discussion of broad intellectual and ideological traditions. It is meant to suggest directions for future discussion and research, and not merely to present summarily what has been done.

Each essay submitted was reviewed by at least three members of the editorial board, whose comments and suggestions provided invaluable guidance to me in making the final selection. Robert Galbreath, although not an editorial board member, was instrumental in the original conception of the volume and shepherded the idea through its early stages. Thomas J. Remington contributed valuable suggestions drawn from his earlier work on the 1978 *Proceedings*, and Mary Kenny Badami provided some needed expert help. SFRA President James Gunn has been closely involved with the project since its inception, and has provided guidance and encouragement throughout. Finally, I wish to thank the SFRA members themselves, whose commitment to the ongoing serious discussion of a body of literature once regarded as trivial has made a book like this possible.

Gary K. Wolfe
Chicago, Illinois
July, 1982

INTRODUCTION:

SCIENCE FICTION IN THE EIGHTIES

James Gunn

The application of numbers to the relentless cycles of the equinoxes has caused these numbers to exercise a surprising influence over the thoughts and actions of mankind. The occurence of the first millennium, for instance, sent thousands of Christians to wait upon hilltops for the end of the world; the failure of that expectation has been experienced since then by innumerable believers who set their own dates for annihilation. This mindset has found its way from religion to literature: the 19th century *fin de siecle* in France and England produced the Decadence, and a flood of stories and novels dealing with catastrophe.

In science fiction too, dates exercise influence. For example the 25th century looms large in the genre, because that is the setting for the Buck Rogers comic strip and radio serial. *Looking Backward* set us looking forward to the year 2000. And the first year of the 21st century, evoked by Stanley Kubrick and Arthur C. Clarke for their outstanding motion picture, cannot fail to disappoint eager anticipation, although the combination of the millenarian impulse and the turn of the century may cause it to rival the year 1000 A.D. in excitement if not in piety. Another date which now seems engraved in stone is 1984: its arrival will be marked by commentary that will be testimony to the Orwellian vision, and to the impact that can be made by a single book with a number for a title.

Not only the turn of centuries, but the turn of decades seems to influence perception and behavior: in retrospect we talk about the Gay Nineties and the Roaring Twenties—even the Apathetic Fifties—and recently pundits have taken to labelling decades in advance, thus creating self-fulfilling prophecies which have caused some people to try to live up to expectations. In any case, society views the start of a new decade as the ending of one small cycle, and the beginning of another.

Therefore the Eighties, now beginning, present a time for looking at the world of science fiction, to sum it up perhaps, and for asking questions about its present and future states. Some of us proposed "Turning Points" as a theme for the 1982 Science Fiction Research Association annual meeting, in recognition of the maturing of the study and teaching of science fiction, and of the conditions in the broad world of science-fiction writing and publication which are moving the genre onto new paths that need examination and evaluation.

Indeed, I think there are dangerous trends in the world of science fiction today. I sound this note of alarm with trepidation, since I have now reached an age where younger people interested in the genre might consider me a reactionary, afflicted by subconscious desires to see the *status quo* preserved. I remember how conservatives opposed the entrance of academics into the field; Dena Brown wrote on a blackboard at the founding meeting of SFRA: "Let's take science fiction out of the classroom and put it back in the gutter where it belongs." At that time such concerns were argued away; but it seems to me now that people who held these concerns were understandably upset by what they considered to be a threat to the kind of science fiction they liked. Although I do not want to start up this controversy again, I must say that I am disturbed that in the past few years science fiction has moved into the rarefied air of the bestseller and the block-buster film. It has become big business: *Star Wars* made more money than any film in history, and its sequel almost equalled it. This was not an isolated phenomenon. *Close Encounters of the Third Kind* also was a hit at the box office. Filmmakers have been making large budget science fiction and fantasy movies by the dozens, apparently believing that they are what audiences want. And so far they seem to be right.

Big business exists not only in science fiction films, but in books as well. Carl Sagan, who has never had a novel published, gets $2,000,000 to write a science fiction novel. Robert A. Heinlein receives $500,000 for *The Number of the Beast* and even more for *Friday*. Ace Books pays $305,000 for 24 Conan books. Doubleday presses $50,000 or more, upon

Isaac Asimov, who does not ask for, or need, large advances, for a sequel to the Foundation series—foreign rights for this sell for over $1,000,000. Fawcett pays more than $500,000 for a novel by Jerry Fournelle and Larry Niven. Del Rey Books gratefully gives Arthur C. Clarke $1,000,000 for agreeing to write a sequel to *2001: A Space Odyssey*. Robert Silverberg sells a three-book package to Arbor House for close to $8,000,000. Frank Herbert, the fourth novel of whose *Dune* series, originally intended to be a trilogy, sold 200,000 copies in hardcover, is rumored to have been paid $1,500,000 to write a 5th novel for the series.

All of this is perhaps not healthy for the genre, ungrateful as I may seem for complaining about it. For years science fiction was ignored by most publishers, most critics, most academics and most readers. Damon Knight called it "the mass medium for the few." However, poverty and neglect did allow a certain freedom of expression. Science fiction is no longer isolated, no longer free to be idiosyncratic, even experimental. Today it can be compared to jazz music, as it moves from the ghettoes of New Orleans, Kansas City and Chicago into the big time of New York clubs and records. Inevitably, it changes.

Change in itself is not frightening, of course. But like Medusa, big media money seems to petrify whatever it focuses upon: movies, television, pop music. With substantial sums at stake, publishers tend to emphasize predictability: the mixture as before is preferred, and authors (like Frank Herbert, Frederick Pohl and Gene Wolfe) are paid well to carry their work on past their original conceptions.

Norman Spinrad, president of the Science Fiction Writers of America from 1980 to 1982, boycotted the 1981 World Science Fiction Convention in Denver, as a one-man protest against the fact that three of the five finalists for the best novel award (the Hugo) were sequels, and the other two, he said, would soon be revealed to be "prequels to another round of sequels. When all novels nominated for the Hugo turn out to be episodes of a series, it is mathematically certain that we are not dealing with chance but with a consistent devolution in the level of science fiction writers intimately bound up with the whole apparatus of publishing, fandom, conventions and Hugos."

Leonard Shatzkin, a publishing consultant, echoes Spinrad's concern*:

> ...the degraded mass market distribution system, geared basically to magazines, needs

---

*"The Developing Crisis in Trade Books". *Publishers Weekly*, January 22, 1982. Quoted also in *Science Fiction & Fantasy Book Review*.

> clearly trademarked, numbered, magazine-style merchandise like Harlequin titles, to deliver predictable reliable sales without massive returns. So we are now getting Harlequin equivalents ... also in Westerns ... science fiction, and on and on. Such titles ... are, in effect, magazines in books' clothing, and trade publishing, with its emphasis on individuality in title, author name, originality even, would only introduce irrelevant details into the process.

The publication in 1981 of Jove's "no-frills" generic novels may not have been so much a gimmick as a symbol.

Spinrad commented, in an article in the September, 1981 issue of *Locus*, the science fiction newspaper:

> ...we are seeing ... the disappearance, or ... the decline, of commercially middling sf novels as the backbone of sf publishing. On the high end, we have ... the occasional sf bestseller like *God Emperor of Dune*, the forthcoming Sagan novel, and any sf written by Stephen King. On the low end we have, essentially, all other sf book publishing, with ad budgets declining ..., downward pressure on advances, separate sf lines isolated from the rest of publishing by special brand names, logos, and sleazoid uniform packaging.

Spinrad had pointed out, in a column published a month earlier, that "science fiction novels that [obviously] transcend the genre sales parameters ... will be removed from the science fiction line [and will not be published in uniform editions]. Whatever the individual design, this packaging strategy openly proclaims that the identity of the line is deemed of more importance than the individual identities of the books ..."

Spinrad sees the ultimate result of all this to be more novels being written to pushbutton bestseller formats, and the relegation of sf authors to second-class citizenship.

Marta Randall, president of SFWA 1982 to 1983, has also pointed with concern to recent trends: new political conservatism which could dampen experimental fiction; the poor sales of original sf anthologies containing experimental or intellectual fiction; the refusal of most mass-market distributors to carry mid-line books or sf novels by new writers; and corporate publishing, which depends upon distributor decisions for editorial policy.

The present recession has led to short-sighted editorial decisions. Doubleday, for instance, cut its science fiction line in half by dropping its more experimental titles, ignoring the fact that these titles had in the long run brought large income from the sale of subsidiary rights.

The proliferation of standard fantasy adventures, singly and in series, I consider another example of degraded publishing practices. I am not attacking fantasy. I have read fantasy with satisfaction, particularly the work of A. Merritt, since 1939, when I began to read *Famous Fantastic Mysteries*. Nevertheless, it seems to me that it is easier to write fantasy than to write science fiction, and that fantasy novels can more easily be extended into series, since science fiction is a more demanding discipline: its novels become attenuated when their basic ideas are fully explicated. The science fiction series of today tend to be science fantasies and adventure stories.

In the past fantasy did not sell well, either in magazines, the best of which like *Unknown and Beyond* lasted only a few years (*Weird Tales*, specializing in horror and terror, is a special case), or in book form, with the notable exceptions of work by A. Merritt and William Sloane. Consequently, fewer fantasy novels were published than science fiction novels. In the past few years, however, the situation had changed remarkably. *Locus* estimates that of 579 new books published in 1981, 175 were adult sf novels and 108 were adult fantasy novels. These fantasy novels seem to have been spawned by the spectacular success of the Tolkien *Lord of the Rings* trilogy. The question that inevitably arises is, who is buying these cookie-cutter novels set in unknown worlds or planets?

If no one is reading them, the boom will of course drop off, as did the explosion of science-fiction magazines in the fifties. But if these novels are actually being bought and read, their publication could swamp the traditional market for science fiction. The readers of this new fantasy— and I want to state again that I do not oppose the publication of fantasy as such—might be the mass audience for *Star Wars*, an audience about which panels at science-fiction conventions speculated: could they be converted to readers of science fiction? The panels usually concluded that filmgoers are not as a rule readers. It would be ironic if it were discovered that these filmgoers are actually readers, but readers of fantasies, whose demand might drown science fiction.

An alternative explanation, and a more sobering one, is that fantasy is now popular because science fiction has become too real. Isaac Asimov has said, "We are living in a science-fiction world." Potential science-fiction readers may well be seeking refuge from rational approaches to the world's problems in fantasy, where they join those vast numbers who have taken up astrology, fringe religions, the occult and UFOlogy.

The most comforting explanation for the fantasy boom would be that it is simply easier for editors to find publishable fantasy than publishable science fiction. I think that more good books in both genres are being published today than ever before: better conceived, better written and more seriously received. Why then do I have the feeling that balance-sheet corporations, illiterate sales forces, and computerized mass market distributors have taken over, and that writers and editors have lost control? Maybe I am suffering from premature *fin de siecle* feelings.

About the health of the field in general: *Locus* reports that in 1971 there were 57 issues of sf magazines, and this number dropped to 49 issues in 1980. But in 1981 there was a sharp increase to 59 issues, despite the fact that most magazines that year declined in circulation.

The teacher or student of science fiction must be concerned about these kinds of figures, because over the years the nature of science fiction has been affected by the facts of publishing, and the opinions of editors. One of the rewarding aspects of teaching in this area is the opportunity it presents to deal with a living, evolving kind of literature; a genre that is still *becoming*. If the field changes, teaching will have to change with it, or end, like almost every other aspect of literature, dealing with history. We need therefore to try to exercise some control over the direction the genre takes.

SFRA has been so far dedicated to providing a focus for the study of science fiction. It has, however, the potential to influence this literature. I suggest that we seize all opportunities to support the best science fiction and fantasy: select only the best for our classes, and send a message to authors, editors and publishers that the academy with all its apparatus—faculty, students, scholars, librarians, publications, etc—intends to be a significant force which speaks for excellence and will reward those who produce it.

James Gunn
Lawrence, Kansas
May 5, 1982

PART ONE:

HISTORICAL QUESTIONS

When a body of literature flourishes for as long as science fiction did without much formal scholarly attention, one of the first topics to be addressed by such attention is inevitably the history and origins of the genre. Of the several histories of science fiction which have appeared in the last decade or so, perhaps the most widely discussed is Brian Aldiss's *Billion Year Spree* (1973). While other historians had placed the origins of science fiction as early as the *Gilgamesh* epic or as late as the founding of *Amazing Stories* in 1926, Aldiss chose as his starting point Mary Shelley's 1818 novel *Frankenstein*. While others stressed science fiction as rationalistic discourse, Aldiss defined it as "characteristically cast in the Gothic or post-Gothic mould." *Billion Year Spree* received wide praise when it first appeared and has since become a classic of science fiction scholarship, but the debates it touched off are still alive today, and it is to these debates that Mr. Aldiss addresses himself in the present essay.

Brian Aldiss is among the most respected of modern British science fiction writers. His many volumes of fiction include *Barefoot in the Head, Frankenstein Unbound, The Malacia Tapestry,* and *Helliconia Spring*. His nonfiction contributions to the understanding of science fiction, in addition to *Billion Year Spree*, include *Science Fiction Art* and *This World and Nearer Ones*. For his "serious science fiction scholarship of sufficient quantity and quality to be considered a major contribution," Brian Aldiss was chosen to receive the Science Fiction Research Association's Pilgrim Award in 1978.

A Monster For All Seasons

Brian Aldiss

But first, a story. The scene is the main convention hall of a science fiction convention, Lunacon, held in the crumbling Commodore Hotel, New York, in 1975. Famous critic, fan, and collector, Sam Moskowitz, is holding forth from the platform. Fans are slouching around in the hall, sleeping, listening, or necking. I am sitting towards the back of the hall, conversing with a learned and attractive lady beside me, or else gazing ahead, watching interestedly the way Moskowitz' lips move. In short, the usual hectic convention scene.

Fans who happen to be aware of my presence turn round occasionally to stare at me. I interpret these glances as the inescapable tributes of fame, and take care to look natural, though not undistinguished, and thoroughly absorbed in the speech.

Later, someone comes up to me and says, admiringly, "Gee, you were real cool while Moskowitz was attacking you."

That is how I gained my reputation for English *sang froid* (or *snag froid*, as my typewriter puts it). The accoustics in the hall were so appalling that I could not hear a word Moskowitz was saying against me. To them goes my gratitude, for my inadvertent coolness in the face of danger may well have saved me from a ravening lynch mob.

Few reviewers stood up in support of my arguments in *Billion Year Spree*. Mark Adlard in *Foundation* was one of them.[1] Yet it appears that some of my mildly ventured propositions have since been accepted.

Sam Moskowitz, of course, was pillorying me on account of heretical

9

opinions in *Billion Year Spree*. I did not gather that he said anything about my major capacity as a creative writer. One unfortunate effect of the success of *Billion Year Spree*, from my point of view, is that my judgements are often quoted but my fiction less rarely so, as though I had somehow, by discussing the literary mode in which I work, passed from mission to museum with no intermediate stops.

Such is the penalty one pays for modesty. I mentioned no single story or novel of mine in my text; it would have been bad form to do so. Lester del Ray, nothing if not derivative, repays the compliment by mentioning no single story or novel of mine in his text,[2] though to be sure disproportionate space is devoted to del Rey's own activities.

This particular instance can perhaps be ascribed to jealousy. To scholarly responses we will attend later.

First to rehearse and repolish some arguments advanced in *Billion Year Spree*, in particular the arguments about the origin of science fiction. On this important question hinge other matters, notably a question of function: what exactly sf does, and how it gains its best effects.

Billion Year Spree was published in England and the U.S. in 1973, the English edition appearing first, from Weidenfeld & Nicolson. It is a good edition, illustrated. The Doubleday is less good. Owing to negligence on Doubleday's part, the corrected proofs I returned to them were not sent on by them to the printer. So a number of needless errors are embalmed in that edition (which are perpetuated in the Schocken paperback edition which was hurried into print without consultation with me). I apologise to American readers for many fatuities of which I was aware—as well as for many that have been pointed out to me since.

The book took three years to write. I had no financial support, and was assisted by no seat of learning. I favoured no clique. I used my own library. I consulted no one. Really, it was a bit of a gamble, since I have a wife and children to support by my writing. But there were two best-sellers to fund the venture (*Hand-Reared Boy* and *A Soldier Erect*), which were—and still are—going strong. I looked both inward to the sf field itself and outward to the general reader, Samuel Johnson's and Virginia Woolf's common reader; I wished to argue against certain misconceptions which vexed me, and I hoped to demonstrate what those who did not read sf were missing.

There was no history of science fiction in existence. I wrote the sort of book which it might amuse and profit me to read.

Of the two initial problems facing me, I overcame the second to my satisfaction: how do you define sf, and what are its origins? Obviously, the questions are related. My ponderous definition of sf has often been quoted, and for that I'm grateful, although I prefer my shorter snappier version, "SF is about hubris clobbered by nemesis", which has found its way into *The Penguin Dictionary of Modern Quotations.* The definition in *Billion Year Spree* runs as follows:

Science fiction is the search for a definition of man and his status in the universe which will stand in our advanced but confused state of knowledge (science), and is characteristically cast in the Gothic or post-Gothic mold.

Not entirely satisfactory, like most definitions. It has the merit of including a consideration of form as well as content. On the whole, criticisms of this definition have been more effective than those directed at my proposals for the origins of the genre.[3]

It needs no great critical faculty to observe that most sf is not about 'a search for the definition of man'; it is about telling a story to please the reader—and in that it is no different from other literature. Only when sf texts are piled together do we see a common restlessness about where mankind is heading through its own blind efforts. More questionable is that phrase about the Gothic mold.

I am not one hundred percent sure about the phrase myself, but this much is clear: I got it from Leslie Fiedler. Leslie Fiedler writes the kind of criticism one can read with enjoyment, unlike most of the criticism which originates within sf academia. Fiedler has this to say of the Gothic mode, following on a discussion of Monk Lewis's *The Monk* of 1796:

> The major symbols of the gothic have been established, and the major meanings of the form made clear. In general, those symbols and meanings depend on an awareness of the spiritual isolation of the individual in a society where all communal systems of value have collapsed or have been turned into meaningless clichés. There is a basic ambivalence in the attitude of the gothic writers to the alienation which they perceive. On the one hand, their fiction projects a fear of the solitude which is the price of freedom; and on the other hand, an almost hysterical attack on all institutions which might inhibit that freedom or mitigate the solitude it breeds... The primary meaning of the gothic romance, then, lies in its substitution of terror for love as a central theme of fiction... *Epater la bourgeoisie*: this is the secret slogan of the tale of terror.[4]

Spiritual isolation, alienation—these lie also at the heart of sf, like serpents in a basket.

Passages like Fiedler's defined the sort of fiction that most of my admired contemporaries were writing. I saw in them, too, a reflection of my own responses to society which prompted me towards science fiction. The love of art and science I developed as a child was a rebellion against the smug *bourgeoise* society in which I found myself. Art and Science were what *They* hated most. In this way, I reinforced the solitude I felt. This also: I merely wished to *epater* society, not overthrow it; the satirist needs his target.

This stinging function of sf was always apparent, from the days of Mary Shelley (*Frankenstein*, like its progenitor, *Caleb Williams*, contains more punitive litigators than punitive monsters within its pages), through H.G. Wells, and Campbell's *Astounding*, until the time when I sat down to write in *Billion Year Spree* in 1970. During the 70's and continuing into the 80's, sf has become widely popular, widely disseminated. Its sting has been removed. The awful victories of *Lord of the Rings, Star Trek*, and *Star Wars* have brought—well, not actually respectability, but Instant Whip formulas to sf. The product is blander. It has to be immediately acceptable to many palates, most of them prepubertal. Even the sentimentality of Spider and Jeanne Robinson's *Stardance* is not considered too sickly sweet for consumption. As Kurt Vonnegut ripened on the tree and fell with a thud to earth, so too did the nutritive content of sf—not so much over-ripe as over-rated.

The nutritive content has been fixed to suit mass taste. Now the world, or the solar system, or the universe, or the Lord Almighty, has to be saved by a group of four or five people which includes a Peter Pan figure, a girl of noble birth, and a moron of some kind. The prescription thus incorporates an effigy for everyone to identify with. In the old days, we used to destroy the world, and it only took one mad scientist. Sf was an act of defiance, a literature of subversion, not of whimsy.

Notice Fiedler's comment on the basic ambivalence which Gothic writers feel towards their alienation. Leaving aside Instant Whip sf, one can perceive an ambivalence in science fiction which goes deep— perhaps one should say an ambivalence which *is* the subject. The emphasis of this ambivalence has changed over the years. Gernsback's *Amazing* was decidely technocratic in bias, and purported to demonstrate how the world's ills could be solved by increased applications of technology—a reasonable proposition, if a century late—yet large proportions of the fiction concerned experiments, etc., which went terribly wrong. Hubris was continually clobbered by nemesis.

Another fundamental ambivalence is less towards technology than towards science itself. Even technology-oriented authors like Arthur C. Clarke show science superseded by or transcended by mysticism and religion; such surely is the meaning of his most famous short story, "The Nine Billion Names of God". It is not science but the fulfillment of religion which brings about the termination of the universe. The world ends not with a bang but a vesper.

Another ambivalence is the attitude of writers and fans to sf itself. Publicly they declare it to be far superior to any possible 'mimetic' fiction; privately they laugh about it, revel in the worst examples of the art, and boast of how little of it they read.

Sf is a function of the Gothic or post-Gothic. So, for that matter, are the novels of Peter Straub, and they also—in such examples as the tantalisingly named *Ghost Story*—bestraddle customary definitions of ghost stories and mainstream literature.

What I wish I had altered was the final word of my definition, to have said not "mold" but "mode".

One of the difficulties of defining sf springs from the fact that it is not a genre as such, just as the absurd category "non-fiction" is not a genre. Taking my cue from Rosemary Jackson, I suggest that our problems in the area of definition will be lightened if we think of sf as a mode. Jackson says, "It is perhaps more helpful to define the fantastic as a literary *mode* rather than a genre, and to place it between the opposite modes of the marvellous and the mimetic."[5]

This may not help us to decide to what extent sf is a department of fantasy—"fantasy" as a literary term, like "classical" and "romantic", has become defaced through usage but it helps us to appreciate sf as the obverse of the realistic mode, and to see that sf can assume various generic forms. There is, for instance, a fairly well-defined category of 'disaster sf' and this in turn can be sub-divided into cautionary disasters (like *1984*) and into what I have termed 'cosy catastrophes', (such as *The Day of the Triffids*) in which the hero ends with the power and the girl, and is personally better off than he was at the beginning. No form which includes more than one genre can itself be a genre.

The relevant dictionary definition of "mode" is, "A way or manner in which something takes place; a method of procedure", and "A manner or state of being of a thing."

While my critics argued, as well they might, with the *Billion Year Spree* definition of sf, they rarely advanced a more convincing alternative. The same must be said for the response to my proposal for a great progenitor.

My search for ancestors went back no further in time than Mary

Shelley, with *Frankenstein* (1818) as the first of the sf mode. The wide acceptance of this proposal by academics may have been prompted by relief—a sensible relief occasioned by their not having to teach Gilgamesh, Dante, and Otis Adelbert Kline.

One sees that this argument of origins can never be definitively settled, for conflicting genres have contributed to the modern mode. But it is an argument worth pursuing, just as paleontologists pick over the so far insoluble question of the early origins of mankind.

When I first claimed a pre-eminent role in sf for *Frankenstein*, I intended to put forward an argument, not an avowed truth. In particular, I wished to present a counter-argument to those two entrenched views which claimed either that sf was as ancient as literature itself or that 'it all began with Gernsback'. Some commentators managed to accept both assumptions at the same time.

If we claim as sf anything which includes a departure from the natural order, or which exhibits Darko Suvin's cognitive estrangement, we gather to ourselves a great body of disparate material, so disparate that it renders the term 'sf' meaningless and the material impossible to study in any effective way.

Beyond this argument of necessity is a philosophical objection to lumping together, say Plato, Lucian, Paltock, Swift, and Poul Anderson. Although sophisticated analysis may reveal what these writers have in common, the sensible reader will be alienated; he/she will remain aware that the cultural differences are greater than any unifying thread of wonder, speculation, or whatever.

As Darko Suvin puts it, if such books as Hardy's *Two on a Tower* and Wilkie Collins' *The Moonstone* are sf along with Wells's *The Invisible Man*, then in fact there is no such thing as sf[6].

That there is a kind of tradition of the fantastic is undeniable, but it does not admit to easy study, possibly because many of the popular texts are missing, as we might imagine that popular sf of our age (the magazines of the forties, for example) would be missing, were it not for a few devoted individuals (Moskowitz is an honoured example) who defied a general contemporary neglect. Equally, the writers in this tradition had a nose for their predecessors, and generally reveal themselves as familiar with their writings—though familiarity is not always understanding. Writers are impatient creatures and take only what they need; thus, H.G. Wells can say that Frankenstein "used some jiggery-pokery magic to animate his artificial monster", whereas this is precisely what Frankenstein does *not* do.

The argument that sf began with Gernsback hardly needs refutation any more, so I will dispense with obvious counter-arguments. Yet when I wrote *Billion Year Spree*, refutation was necessary, and I had some fun with that old phrase about Gernsback being 'the father of sf'. Edgar Allen Poe had received the same accolade. This quest for father-figures reached what we hope will be its nadir when, in the same year *Billion Year Spree* was published, Isaac Asimov wrote one of his Introductions, entitled, "The Father of Science Fiction," and nominated John W. Campbell for that role[7]. It was a relief to be able to appoint a mother-figure instead.

The seminal point about *Frankenstein* is that its central character makes a deliberate decision. He succeeds in creating life only when he throws away dusty old authorities and turns to modern experiments in the laboratory. One of Victor Frankenstein's two professors scoffs at his reading of such ancients as Paracelsus, Agrippa, and Albertus Magnus—"These fancies, which you have imbibed, are a thousand years old!"—while the other professor is even more scathing: the ancients "promised impossibilities and performed nothing".

Frankenstein rejects alchemy and magic and turns to scientific research. Only then does he get results. Wells was absolutely mistaken in his remarks about 'jiggery-pokery magic'; it is jiggery-pokery magic which Frankenstein rejects.

Victor Frankenstein makes a rational decision: he operates on the world, rather than vice versa; and the reader is taken by plausible steps from the normal world we know to an unfamiliar one where monsters roam and the retributions of hubris are played out on a terrifying scale. This is qualitatively different from being carried to the moon accidentally by migratory geese, or being shipwrecked on Lilliput, or summoning up the devil, or creating life out of spit and mud.

I say that the reader is taken by plausible steps. In fact, the inter-woven processes of the *Frankenstein* narrative are better described by Suvin—"the ever-narrowing imaginative vortex..."

To bring about the desired initial suspension of belief, Mary Shelley employs a subterfuge which has since become the stock-in-trade of many sf writers. Wells imitated her method some decades later, to good effect. She appeals to scientific evidence for the veracity of her tale.

It is no accident that Mary Shelley's Introduction to the anonymous 1818 edition of the novel begins with a reference to one of the most respected scientific minds of her day, Dr. Erasmus Darwin. Darwin, grandfather of Charles Darwin, and an early propagandist of evolutionary theory, was referred to by S.T. Coleridge as 'the most original-minded man in Europe'. The opening words of the Introduction are,

"The event on which this fiction is founded has been supposed, by Dr. Darwin, and some of the psychological writers of Germany, as not of impossible occurence." Thus Mary Shelley makes it clear that the first aspect of her novel which she wishes to stress is the scientific-speculative one.

This is the most revolutionary departure of *Frankenstein*. This is the one which separates it most markedly from the Gothic (along with the absence of simpering heroines). We must not ignore another novelty. The monster in his isolation operates as a criticism of society, as later does Wells's Invisible Man and the central figure in Algis Budrys' *Who?* When the monster cries, "I am malicious because I am miserable", he is dramatically reversing received Christian thinking of the time. This note echoes the central blasphemy of Frankenstein's diseased creation. Sf was to become a refuge for anti-Christian and anti-establishment thinking, and some criticism of society is present in most successive sf, save in the trivial examples of Instant Whip.

In his edition of *Frankenstein*, Leonard Wolf argues that the novel should not be considered as sf, but rather as 'pyschological allegory'.[8] This is like arguing that *The Space Merchants* is not sf because it is 'political allegory'. There is no reason why both books should not support both functions. The strength of sf is that it is not a pure stream.

David Ketterer, who has written perceptively about Mary Shelley's novel, agrees with Wolf, while saying that the concerns of Frankenstein might more broadly be described as philosophical alchemical, and transcendental, and psychological or scientific".[9] Ketterer is also keen to deny that *Frankenstein* can be described as sf[10].

The novel is alchemical in so far as it is firmly anti-alchemy. The science is not very clear—impossible, if you like—but we can recognise it as science rather than alchemy, although Shelley was writing some years before the word 'scientist' was coined. As for the philosophical and transcendental qualities, they arise from the central science-fictional posit, just as they do in Arthur Clarke's *Childhood's End*, and rule the novel out of the sf stakes no more than does Wolf's psychological element.

Arguments against *Frankenstein* being sf at all rest on very uncertain ground. Not only is there Mary Shelley's own intention, as expressed in her Introduction, but her sub-title points to where she believes its centre to lie; she is updating the myth of Prometheus. Her fire comes down from heaven. It was an inspiration—and one that Universal Studios would later make much of—to utilise the newly captive electricity as that Promethean fire. Later generations of writers, with neither more nor less regard for scientific accuracy, would use 'the power of the atom' with which to energise their perceptions of change. Nowadays, telepathic super-powers get by under the name of sf.

The argument against *Frankenstein*'s being the first novel of sf could be more convincingly launched on other grounds, historiological ones. The more a subject is studied, the further back its roots are seen to go. This is true, for instance, of the Renaissance, or of the Romantic movement. So perhaps the quest for the First Sf Novel, like the first flower of spring, is chimerical. But the period where we should expect to look for such a blossoming is during the Industrial Revolution, and perhaps just after the Napoleonic Wars, when changes accelerated by industry and war have begun to bite, with the resultant sense of isolation of the individual from and in society. This sense of isolation is a hallmark of Romanticism, displayed in the opening paragraph of that milestone of Romanticism, Jean-Jacques Rousseau's *Confessions*: "I feel my heart and I know men. I am not like others whom I have seen; I dare believe that I am not like anyone else alive."

This is the region of *Frankenstein*. Mary Shelley found an objective correlative for the cold intellectual currents of her day. It has maintained, and even implemented, its power to our day.

We need to resist a temptation to classify rigidly, thinking to achieve intellectual clarity by so doing. There is no contradiction involved in regarding this remarkable transitional novel as a Gothic story, as one of the great horror stories of the English language, *and* as the progenitor of modern sf.

Nobody seeks to argue that *Frankenstein* is not a horror story. The influence of the movies has led us to concentrate on the horror aspect. yet the movies have always cheapened Mary Shelley's theme. The creature is turned into a dotty bogeyman, allowed only to grunt, grunt and destroy. It is presented as alien to humanity, not an extension of it.

Mary Shelley depicts the creature as alienated from society. Just when we have learned to fear the creature and loathe its appearance, she shows us the reality of the case. This is no monster. It is a lost soul. Above all things, it wishes to revere its absent creator.

Every good Frankenstein-watcher has his own opinions about the monster. It is the French Revolution, says Suvin. It is Percy Bysshe Shelley, says Christopher Small.[11] I have come to believe that the stricken creature is Mary Shelley herself, that she found in the monster a striking objective correlative for her orphaned feelings, following the death of her mother in childbirth. Later in her career, in her other sf novel, she projects herself as Verney, the Last Man in a world of death, wandering alone without a soulmate.

The monstrous Things populating traditional horror stories are presented as inimical to mankind; they are externalised. Frankenstein's monster represents a departure in this respect, from horror towards sf. Again, Wells picks up the hint, in *The Island of Dr. Moreau* and also in *The War of the Worlds*. In the former, we have a clutch of manmade monsters who also exist in fear of their creator. In the latter, the Martians—following the first powerful description of them as disgusting and frightening—are shown to be as humans might become at a later possible stage of evolution.

If I were re-writing *Billion Year Spree* now, I should qualify *Frankenstein*'s pre-eminence by allowing more discussion of the utopians of eighteenth century France, and of such works of the Enlightenment as Sebastien Mercier's *The Year 2440* (1770). The hero of this work wakes up seven centuries in the future, to a world advanced in science and morality.[12] But between such examples and later ones come the guillotines of the French Revolution, which delivered a blow to pure utopianism from which it has not recovered. The prevailing tone was to be set, at least in the Anglo-American camp, by the gloom of Gothic-Romanticism.

I began by saying that the question of function was wrapped up with the question of origin. To regard sf as existing in literature since Homer is to bestow on it no function not also operative in literature; which contradicts the experience of most of us who study and enjoy both literature and sf.

To regard sf as "all starting with Gernsback" is to empoverish it unfairly. Sf then becomes a kind of gadget fiction, where every story more than ten years old is hailed as a 'Classic', and reputations can be made by rewriting one's previous story ad infinitum. Sf may be a microcosm, but it is larger than a back yard.

To speak practically, one has to consider how best to introduce historical sf to new readers or students. Should one confront them with Homer's *Odyssey*, Mercier's *Year 2440*, Mary Shelley's *Frankenstein*, or the wretched crust of Gernsback's *Ralph 124C41+*? I trust that the answer is obvious.

It was a passage in *Billion Year Spree* concerning Hugo Gernsback which most offended readers. This, it appears, was what Sam Moskowitz was attacking me for at the Lunacon. Later, the enthusiast David

Kyle took me to task for saying that Hugo Gernsback was arguably one of the worst disasters ever to hit the sf field. Well, admittedly I stated the case strongly in order to be heard above the sound of choristers praising Old Uncle Hugo, but there was truth in what I said. Ten years later, I would qualify the remark: worse disasters have struck since, notably commercial exploitation.

Kyle's history scores slightly better than Lester del Rey's. Kyle actually manages to mention the title of one of my novels, *Barefoot in the Head* ("extravagant if not incomprehensible"). The gain is offset by a veiled threat. The last time anyone said such rough things about Gernsback, we are told, "was at the 1952 Chicago con; a fan named Chester A. Polk was sent to hospital and Claude Degler, head of the Cosmic Circle, drove Don Rogers out of fandom for good".[13]

Alexi Panshin, reviewing *Billion Year Spree* in *The Magazine of Fantasy and Science Fiction* also threatened to have me drummed out of the regiment.

Despite all this, I have much sympathy for the Kyle-Moskowitz position. Fans like Kyle have had to watch sf taken out of their hands, when once they must have thought it was in their pockets. Well, chums, it belongs to Big Business now, so we're all losers. The media have taken over—and First Fandom was preferable to the Fourth Estate.

More ambivalent is the attitude of general critics of the field. There's a feel of punches being pulled. Tom Clareson, in "Towards a History of Science Fiction", evades the issue entirely, with a bland paragraph on *Frankenstein* which follows on a reference to Asimov's *The Gods Themselves*.[14] In James Gunn's history of sf, he gives *Billion Year Spree* a more than friendly nod, but cannot resist delivering the familiar litany of defunct magazines, backed by displays of gaudy covers. Like del Rey, Gunn names none of my fiction; like del Rey he lumps me in with the New Wave, though obviously without malice.[15] In his later, three-volume critical anthology, Gunn becomes more venturesome; he is a "safe" scholar moving slowly to a more individual, creative position.[16]

Clareson and Gunn, like Kyle and Moskowitz, may be regarded honourably as old-timers in the field. Robert Scholes and Eric S. Rabkin, one gathers, are relative newcomers—as their 'thinking person's guide to the genre' demonstrates.[17] This means they cannot reel off litanies of dead stories in dead magazines. It also means they adopt *Frankenstein* as the progenitor of the species. Hooray! No matter if they don't acknowledge from whence exactly they derived the idea. They are genial about *Billion Year Spree*, and mention in passing that I have written fiction, though only *Barefoot in the Head* is named. Perhaps someone somewhere taught it once.

All the critical books I have mentioned are quirky, including my own. I am less conscious of quirks in two recent encyclopaedic works, Neil Barron's *Anatomy of Wonder Science Fiction* (1976; 1981) and Peter Nicholls' *The Science Fiction Encyclopedia* (1979) both of which seek to be dispassionate in judgement. Both take cognisance of the range of my work over the last twenty-five years, short stories as well as novels.

Both Barron and Nicholls pride themselves on being as up-to-date as possible. In *Billion Year Spree*, I decided that there were insufficient perspectives from which to judge anything later than 1960 (a decade before I began writing the book), and so followed the example set by most histories of literature in tempering commercial considerations with discretion.

On the whole, my book was treated kindly. I have gained fewer black marks for it than for my defence of the New Wave writers in England during the sixties, when I fought for their right to express themselves in their own way rather than in someone else's. Despite the attempts of persons like del Rey to lump me in with the New Wave, I flourished before it arrived, and continue still to do so. That experience taught me that readers of sf are basically conservative, for all their talk about The Literature of Change. But perhaps the study of sf, virtually non-existent when I began *Billion Year Spree*, has attracted a more liberal race of academics; one hopes so, at any rate.

This must also be said: I know, am friendly with, or at least have met, all the living writers and critics mentioned in this article. Such is part of the social life of a science fiction writer, nor would one have it otherwise. David Kyle I have known since the fifties—a charming man who would not set the head of the Cosmic Circle on to me unless I really deserved it. This gregariousness, reinforced by such sf institutions as conventions and fanzines, with their informal critical attitudes, forms a kind of concealed context within which—or against which—most sf writers still exist, long after the collapse of Gernsback's sf League. Samuel Delany has pointed to this concealed context, urging formal critics to take note of it.[18] Certainly, I was aware of it when writing *Billion Year Spree*, even if I missed it at Lunacon, when it became flesh in the form of Sam Moskowitz.

My brief here has been to talk of adverse responses to *Billion Year Spree*. So I have not talked about the praise the book has received in many quarters, outside and inside the sf field. I intended the book to be enjoyed, and rejoiced when it gave enjoyment. It brought me a Special British Science Fiction Association Award, and the much-prized Pilgrim Award from the SFRA. On the congenial social occasion when I received the Pilgrim, Scholes, Rabkin, Suvin, Clareson, and many other distinguished names were present. Truly, friends are better than critics.

Billion Year Spree concluded by forecasting a great increase in academic involvement in science fiction. The involvement has developed rapidly, as· this present volume testifies. Watching from the sidelines, I see some of the difficulties from which academics suffer.

Humanities departments are under threat in times of recession, in a way that science departments—though themselves not without difficulties—are not. In self-defence, academics in humanities posts write their papers in an imitation of the jargon of their colleagues in the sciences. The result is frequently an inviolable form of gobbledegook. An example of what I mean is taken almost randomly from a respected critical journal:

> The most serious difficulty with the genre concept comes from the fact that the existence of a particular genre structure (variant) in a given epoch is usually accompanied by literary consciousness of writers, critics, and readers who recognise this structure as different from the synchronic structures of other genres. This intersubjective recognition, depending as it does on the general level of education and culture, on the familiarity of the reading public with traditional and modern literatures, and on the state of criticism of the epoch, is, of course, often arbitrary.

While not entirely resistant to divination, these two sentences seem to say little, and to say it in an ugly way remote from the graces of our language as she is spoke. A defense mechanism is operating. To speak plainly is to risk being taken for a fool. Difficulty must be seen to operate in the texts, or else grants may be imperilled in the future. Sf criticism, being new, is particularly vulnerable to the administrative chopper.

One may understand all this and still believe that readers should mistrust teachers who seek to elucidate texts in writing styles that show little sympathy for the mother tongue.

Beneath the tortured language what is said rarely carries malice. At least not openly. Our boat is still new and not properly tested; it must not be rocked. Thus criticism and its object have come full circle since the eighteenth century. Then, judgements were expressed with clarity and style, and were often designed to wound:

> Cibber, write all your verses upon glasses;
> So that we may not use them for our ——.

1. Mark Adlard, 'A Labour of Love', Foundation 6 (1974), 61-68.

2. Lester del Rey, *The World of Science Fiction*, (New York: Ballantine, 1980).

3. An instance is 'The SF Story', a typically scatty review of *Billion Year Spree* in Robert Conquest, *The Abomination of Moab* (1979).

4. *Love and Death in the American Novel* (1960).

5. Rosemary Jackson, *Fantasy: The Literature of Subversion* (1981).

6. Darko Suvin, *The Metamorphoses of Science Fiction* (1979).

7. Harry Harrison, ed., in *Astounding: John W. Campbell Memorial Anthology* (1973).

8. Leonard Wolf, ed., *The Annotated 'Frankenstein'*, (1977).

9. David Ketterer, *Frankenstein's Creation: The Book, The Monster, and Human Reality* (1979).

10. David Ketterer, "Frankenstein in Wolf's Clothing", in *Science-Fiction Studies*, 18, (July, 1979).

11. Christopher Small, *Ariel Like a Harpy: Shelley, Mary, and 'Frankenstein'* (1972).

12. See Brian Aldiss, "Since the Enlightenment", in *This World and Nearer Ones* (1979).

13. David Kyle, *A Pictorial History of Science Fiction* (1976). I call Kyle an enthusiast because he distains the name of critic.

14. In Marshall Tymn, ed., *The Science Fiction Reference Book* (1981).

15. *Alternate Worlds* (1975).

16. James Gunn, *The Road to Science Fiction*, (1977-79).

17. Robert Scholes and Eric S. Rabkin, *Science Fiction: History. Science. Vision.*, (1977).

18. "Reflections on Historical Models of Modern English Language Science Fiction," in *Science-Fiction Studies*, Vol. 7 Pt. 2 (July, 1980).

PART TWO:

PRIMARY SOURCES IN SCIENCE FICTION

Whatever the literary antecedents of modern science fiction, every research in the field must eventually confront the fact that for nearly a half-century, most of this fiction appeared in pulp magazines, paperback books, and newsstand digests—materials rarely collected by research libraries—and that many of the genre's most important authors lived out their careers unrecognized, except by devoted fans. This creates numerous problems for the modern researcher. Much of the correspondence and many of the manuscripts of important authors still exist only in private collections, and the degree to which even the best authors found themselves at the mercy of copyeditors, and even typesetters, creates problems of text and interpretation when these authors' stories are discussed. In this section, we are fortunate to be able to present important primary material which has not before been published—the correspondence between H.G. Wells and Olaf Stapledon—as well as an essay by a major science fiction author based on his first-hand knowledge of textual problems that may arise from the way much science fiction was originally published, and an essay by an SFRA scholar on the methods of one of the major science fiction magazine editors of the fifties.

Robert Crossley, who assembled and introduces the letters of Stapledon and Wells, is an associate professor of English at the University of Massachusetts—Boston, where he teaches graduate and undergraduate courses in fantasy, utopian literature, and science fiction. Other essays of his on Wells and Stapledon are scheduled for *The Georgia Review* and *Science-Fiction Studies*.

Algis Budrys is the author of some two hundred short stories and science fiction novels including *The Falling Torch, Michaelmas,* and the classic *Rogue Moon.* His numerous reviews and essays have often been cited as models of intelligent criticism, and for several years he has been involved in teaching the writing of science fiction at the Clarion Writer's Workshop at Michigan State University, where he is presently visiting writer.

Joseph Marchesani has been teaching composition and science fiction at the Hazleton campus of Pennsylvania State University since 1978. His work has appeared in *Extrapolation* and *The Handbook of Science Fiction and Fantasy Magazines,* and his continuing work on *Galaxy* magazine is directed toward an annotated guide to that magazine.

The Correspondence of Olaf Stapledon and H.G. Wells 1931-1942

Edited by Robert Crossley

Among the fascinating developments in the continuing examination of the roots of modern science fiction are renewed critical interest in the works of Olaf Stapledon, and the later fiction and polemical work of H.G. Wells.[1] The 33 extant letters, all that remains of their intermittent correspondence between 1931 and 1942, are published here for the first time, and should shed light on the intellectual and artistic relationship of these two writers, a relationship that has been speculated upon in recent historical studies of science fiction.[2] The correspondence was initiated by Stapledon when he was 45 years old, in his prime, and when Wells, at 65, already had his best work behind him.

First of all, one must note what is lacking in these letters. Many of Wells's to Stapledon are missing, unfortunately. Although Wells has commented elsewhere that he found *First and Last Men* to be the most appealing of Stapledon's books, his existing letters do not mention this. Only a few letters [1, 12, 15, 16 and 21] contain direct statements about the two men's science fiction, and these statements are perfunctory and undetailed. There is no mention, somewhat surprisingly, of *Odd John* in the correspondence of the mid-30's, nor of *Darkness and the Light* in letters written in 1942. Stapledon's admission in his first letter that he had read only one novel and one short story of Wells's "scientific romances" is also surprising. Stapledon's account of his first meeting with Wells in which they discussed, apparently, the film *Things to Come* [Letter 12] is interesting; it is unfortunate that there is no letter describing their second meeting [see Letters 18 and 19].

Although there are no discussions in the letters about the nature of fiction, as there are in the famous correspondence between Wells and Henry James, there are comments which shed light on the fiction of the two men, and there are literary implications in their disagreements about philosophy and politics. From beginning to end the correspondence reflects a tension between Wells's certainties and Stapledon's uncertainties, a tension that serves as a sort of key to the fiction the two men were writing in the 30's. Wells's *The Shape of Things to Come* and *Star-Begotten* are manifestoes written in a mood of defiant assurance: he believed that he could dictate the solution to the ills of the world. Stapledon's attitudes to this kind of dogmatism is revealed, most clearly perhaps, in his conclusion to the first chapter of *Saints and Revolutionaries*:

> ...speculation, so long as it knows itself for what it is, can have a tonic effect on the mind. Indeed I believe that in shunning all speculation we violate one side of our nature just as much as, by indulging in loose speculation, we violate another side. Speculate we inevitably shall, unless our mental eyes have been destroyed. Therefore let us speculate critically, and without indulging in any confident belief.[3]

Stapledon's novels reflect this philosophical commitment to disciplined speculation, this effort, as he put it in the preface to *Star Maker*, "to regard all human affairs and ideas and theories with as little human prejudice as possible." Letters 15 and 16, in fact, suggest how Wells's *Star-Begotten* and Stapledon's *Star Maker* epitomize each author's aesthetic and ideological predelictions.

Stapledon's inquiries into spiritual issues irritated Wells, whose materialism became doctrinaire and obsessive as he grew older. Wells's attitude toward the religious explorations in Stapledon's utopian book *Waking World* (1934) may be inferred by the cartoons they exchanged [Letters 4 and 5]. And given Wells's dislike of criticism, it is remarkable that the correspondence survived Stapledon's comments on Wells's scientific humanism in the opening pages of *Waking World*. In Letter 25 Wells clearly states his aversion to the theological politics of Stapledon's *Saints and Revolutionaries* (1939). It can be said in Stapledon's defense, by the way, that his religious questions came from his own agnostic uncertainties, and are implicit in the *Star Maker* and all his fiction as well as in his philosophical work.[4]

In political attitudes, Wells and Stapledon had more in common. Both were utopians, leftists and heretics. In 1934 a group of intellectuals formed the Federation of Progressive Societies and Individuals, in an attempt to consolidate disparate Left groups into a single powerful voice.[5] After his initial interest, Wells became disillusioned with the F.P.S.I., seeing it, like the Fabian Society with which he had broken 30 years earlier, as a haven for academics and armchair radicals. Stapledon stayed with the organization and in the 40's was still an active contributor to its monthly journal *Plan* [Letters 29 and 30]. This is a pattern in the correspondence: intellectual affinity on issues between the two men is broken by Wells, who impatiently rejects Stapledon's tactics and withdraws from the project, while Stapledon quietly continues his action and analysis.

Wells disliked Marxism intensely. Stapledon accepted Marxist economics, although he had reservations about the Marxist philosophy as a whole. Probably he expressed his political allegiances through his heroine Plaxy in *Sirius*, who "insisted that if Communism was not, after all, the whole truth, then nothing short of a great *new* idea, based on Communism, could win the war and found a tolerable social order."[6] Despite Wells's remark in Letter 15 that he "gave up trying to swallow the Whole years ago," his political thought was in fact massive, even elephantine, and he was likely to reject any political attitude that did not fit into his grand design. Stapledon, on the other hand, was willing to forego consistency in political theory in order to achieve some specific reform or recruit new workers for progressive change.

It can be seen from what I have said so far, that these letters have considerable biographical interest; especially for Stapledon, whose definitive *Life* has not yet been written. Most interestingly, to those who have assumed that Stapledon's masterpieces of the 30's were strongly influenced by Wells's work of the 90's, the portrait of Stapledon which emerges from this correspondence is a much more independent one that has perhaps been thought in the past: although an awed admirer of Wells's fiction and contribution to ideas, Stapledon is rigorously honest in distinguishing his intellectual priorities from Wells's. Letter 26 may be considered the definitive *caveat* to a classification of Stapledon as a Wells disciple. That is not to say, of course, that Stapledon was uninfluenced by Wells. His proposals for consciousness-raising among the R.A.F. during World War II [Letters

31-33] reflect back to the romanticized air force in Wells's *The Shape of Things to Come* (1933), and forward as well, to the revolutionary airmen in Stapledon's novella *Old Man in New World* (1944).

In addition, Stapledon was one of the founding members of the short-lived H.G. Wells Society, which was intended to work for the global revolution argued for by Wells in *The Open Conspiracy*.[8] Stapledon felt torn between the creation of art at a time of economic and political crisis and the practical obligations of the citizen of the world he considered himself to be. He was a dedicated pacifist who worked for political education, the abolition of nationalism and the humanization of the military services.

For half a century Wells had seen his own utopian proposals applauded at first, and then ignored, distorted, attacked or given lip-service. In his old age he was seeing concepts which he had championed become hollow slogans in the mouths of well-meaning liberals who appropriated Wellsian language (and Wells's signature on petitions if they could get it) but who practised conventional politics. In *The New World Order* (1940) Wells commented that words like "peace" and "federation" were used as magical incantations by people who believed they could repair a rotting social order by repeating them over and over. "Even an irresponsible literary man like myself," Wells wrote, "finds himself inundated with innumerable lengthy private letters, hysterical postcards, pamphlets from budding organizations, 'declarations' to sign, demands for subscriptions, all in the name of the new panacea, all as vain and unproductive as the bleating of lost sheep."[9]

In these letters Wells often implies his fear that his trusting nature might lead him into fatal compromises with what he called "the padre and the squire", that is, the church and the landed gentry. Stapledon was not naive enough to ignore the risks of seeking radical change within existing social institutions. At the same time he did not wish to remain "pure" if that purity meant an abdication of action because of the fear of corruption. In *New Hope for Britain* (1939) he described the failures of the League of Nations, and offered a plan for working within the League to build a new social order that would eventually transcend the League. Wells had no patience with this sort of thing.

He was in fact in a state of doubt about the good of all his polemical work when he wrote in the most irritable letter, "What my dear Stapledon, is the good of writing books? You go on with your garden by the Dee and grow food. People of our sort can have no say in the fate of mankind." Stapledon too had his doubts about the good his books did the world; he expressed these doubts in the prefaces to *Last and First Men, Star Maker* and *Darkness and the Light.* Although he could no more be content with cultivating his own garden than could Wells himself, Stapledon was ambivalent about the influence of writers upon politics. His fiction reflects more pessimism about social change than do his philosophical and political works. He commented on this himself in the preface to *First and Last Men*:

> There is today a very earnest movement for peace and international unity; and surely with good fortune and intelligent management it may triumph. Most earnestly we hope that it will. But I have figured things out in this book in such a manner that this great movement fails. I suppose it incapable of preventing a succession of national wars; and I permit it only to achieve the goal of unity and peace after the mentality of the race has been undermined. May this not happen! May the League of Nations, or some more strictly cosmopolitan authority, win through before it is too late! Yet let us find room in our minds and in our hearts for the thought that the whole enterprise of our race may be after all but a minor and unsuccessful episode in a vaster drama, which also may be tragic.[10]

The letters stop in 1942. The reason is not clear. Wells at that time was becoming increasingly physically ill. Possibly he resented Stapledon's suggestion in the last surviving letter that he might be out of touch with the political aspirations of younger men. Mrs. Stapledon has mentioned to me that "it must have become somewhat of a strain to preserve the relationship on the genial basis on which it first rested." Whatever the reason for its ending, this eleven year correspondence presents a transitional chapter in the history of science fiction in the 30's, when Stapledon's powers were at their highest, and Wells's polemical energy, at least, continued unabated.

Salutations and closes to these letters have been dropped after the first one. With letter 4 Stapledon addresses Wells as "Dear Wells" and signs himself "Yours Olaf Stapledon"—the usual greeting and closing from then on.

Permission to print the texts of Stapledon's letters has been kindly granted by Mrs Agnes Z. Stapledon, to whom I am also grateful for sharing with me copies from Wells in her possession. The letters of Wells appear with the permission of the Executors of the Estate of H.G. Wells. The bulk of the correspondence printed here—including all letters from Stapledon—is housed in the Rare Book Room at the Library of the University of Illinois at Urbana, Illinois. I am indebted to the Library staff, particularly Ms. Louise Fitton, for much practical assistance. Mrs Stapledon, Prof. Patrick McCarthy and Mr Harvey Satty have made many helpful suggestions for my annotations to the letters.

Robert Crossley
Boston, Massachusetts

NOTES

[1] At this writing only one book-length study of Stapledon is available, Patrick McCarthy's *Olaf Stapledon* (Boston: Twayne Publishers, 1982). Starmont House will publish a guide to the fiction by the late John Kinnaird, and Leslie Fiedler is preparing a book for Oxford University Press. Among the works on the later Wells, the indispensable volume is W. Warren Wagar, *H.G. Wells and the World State* (New Haven: Yale Univ. Press, 1961); William J. Scheick's book on Wells's later science fiction is in progress: an excerpt is "Toward the Ultra-Science-Fiction Novel: H.G. Wells's *Star-Begotten*," in *Science-Fiction Studies*, 8 (March, 1981), 19-25. My own essay on the intellectual relationship of Stapledon and Wells, "Famous Mythical Beasts," is forthcoming in *The Georgia Review*.

[2] See in particular Brian Aldiss, *Billion-Year Spree* (1973; rpt NY: Schocken, 1974), pp. 201-208, and Robert Scholes and Eric Rabkin, *Science Fiction: History, Science, Vision* (NY: Oxford U.P., 1977), pp. 32-33.

[3] *Saints and Revolutionaries* (London: Heinemann, 1939), p. 24.

[4] The two essential essays on Stapledon's philosophy are J.B. Coates's chapter on Stapledon in *Ten Modern Prophets* (London: Frederick Muller, 1944), pp. 151-166, and E.W. Martin, "Between the Devil and the Deep Blue Sea: The Philosophy of Olaf Stapledon" in *The Pleasure Ground: A Miscellany of English Writing*, ed. by Malcolm Elwin (London: Macdonald & Co., 1947), pp. 204-216.

[5] Under the editorship of C.E.M. Joad the Federation published *Manifesto* (London: Allen & Unwin, 1934); Wells wrote the introductory essay ("There Should Be a Common Creed for Left Parties Throughout All the World") and Stapledon contributed an essay entitled "Education and World Citizenship".

[6] "Sirius" (1944) in *Odd John and Sirius* (NY: Dover, 1972), 274 ff.

[7] At the moment, the best biographical source is Sam Moskowitz's lengthy essay, "Olaf Stapledon: The Man Behind the Works" in *Far Future Calling: Uncollected Science Fiction and Fantasies of Olaf Stapledon* (Phila: Oswald Train, 1979) pp. 9-69.

[8] At Wells's request the society removed his name from its title and was known thereafter first as The Open Conspiracy and then as Cosmopolis. Both Wells and Stapledon gave money to the Society, and Stapledon often wrote brief articles for its mimeographed bulletin. Copies of some of these bulletins are in the Rare Book Room of the Library at the University of Illinois at Urbana.

[9] *The New World Order* (NY: Knopf, 1940), p. 76.

[10] *Last and First Men* (1930; rpt. Baltimore: Penguin, 1972), p. 13.

Letters

1. Stapledon to Wells

16 October 1931

Dear Sir,

A book of mine, *Last and First Men*, has received a certain amount of attention, and nearly every review has contained some reference to yourself.[1] Recently I have come to feel that if you happened to notice the book, a copy of which the publishers must have sent you, you might wonder why I had not the grace to make some acknowledgment of your influence. Of course it cannot matter to you whether a new writer admits his debt or not; and anyhow you may not have seen the book or the reviews. All the same I should like to explain. Your works have certainly influenced me very greatly, perhaps even more than I supposed when I was writing my own book. But curiously enough I have only read two of your scientific romances, *The War of the Worlds* and *The Star*. If I seem to have plagiarized from any others, it was in ignorance. Your later works I greatly admire. There would be something very wrong with me if I did not. They have helped very many of us to see things more clearly. Then why, I wonder, did I not acknowledge my huge debt? Probably because it was so huge and obvious that I was not properly aware of it. A man does not record his debt to the air he breathes in common with everyone else.

Yours very truly
W. Olaf Stapledon

2. Stapledon to Wells

25 November 1931

Very many thanks for your letter. It is extremely good of you to mention my book in your *Work, Wealth & Happiness of Mankind*, which I look forward to reading as soon as it comes out.[2] At present I am in the middle of *The Science of Life*, which is an unfailing source of delight. I should very much like to meet you, so I will take you at your word and ring up in the hope of catching you when next I am staying in London. I have not met your son. If, as I suppose, he has had a lot to do with *The Science of Life*, he must be a formidable person.[3] The fertility of

35

Reproduced courtesy of the Rare Book Room,
University of Illinois Library

Wellsian minds is astounding to slow persons like me. I shall not have another book ready till next summer.[4]

3. Stapledon to Wells   15 October 1934

I have told my publishers to send you a copy of my new book, *Waking World*.[5] Now that it is off my hands I have no illusion that it succeeds in doing what it set out to do. I send it to you chiefly because it contains a few pages of criticism of yourself (pp. 10-13). I am afraid it is very vague criticism, and by no means original; but since I feel at once an intense admiration for your work and a sense of some lack which I find it very difficult to describe, I thought I ought to say so.[6] The body of the book, which is unfortunately not the sort of thing to sell well, is an attempt to outline the sides of life which seem to me most important in the long run. You may say that in times of crisis like the present they should be subordinated to more urgent matters. Perhaps, but I don't feel sure.

4. Stapledon to Wells   16 October 1934

Dear Wells,

You may be right. Here you are finally emerging in the open. Forgive this. Thanks for your letter.[7] But I am not *really* in either of the cages, believe me! I am the jackdaw, free, but uncertain.

                                   Yours   Olaf Stapledon

5. Stapledon to Wells   undated[8]

Touché! I salute the superior swordsman and the superior draughtsman.[9]

6. Stapledon to Wells   27 March 1936

I enclose a rough draft of a proposed "Open Letter to All the Peoples of the Earth".[11] My idea is that some such document might be signed by as many persons as signed the Peace Ballot,[12] and that if it were, it might have some effect on the course of international events. I am sending a copy to Lord Robert Cecil[13] and asking him whether there is any chance that the League of Nations Union would be able to use the machinery of the Peace Ballot for this purpose. Probably expense will be an insurmountable objection, but the scheme seems worth pursuing.

May I have the benefit of your criticism of the scheme, and of the enclosed rough draft of the letter? I have tried to frame each clause so as to express in the simplest language some important idea which the average "decent person" might accept. I have tried to be as outspoken as possible without frightening away too many possible supporters.

P.S. I feel so hopelessly ineffective in comparison with you that as soon as I think of sending you these documents they begin to look damned silly! However, it really is an idea, this open letter stunt. Maybe the League of Nations Union approach is the wrong one.

7. Wells to Stapledon   4 April 1936

Dear Stapledon,

I wish I saw more of you.[14] You would do me good & I should do you good. Do for God's sake forget about the League of Nations—get round it, get behind it, enlarge your basis, escape from the nationalist & diplomatic conventions that fester at Geneva: Your P.S. hints that you are really of that opinion too, but you want the raucous encouragement of a coarser kindred mind. Here it is.

And blast "Peoples". There are really only people with a tendency to clot.

Bless you
H.G.

8. Stapledon to Wells   6 April 1936

Dear H.G.

Many thanks for your letter. I should greatly like to meet you when I am in London this month if you can spare the time for a caller. I shall probably be there from the 15th to the 21st or 22nd. I could manage any time on the 17th or 20th, or possibly 18th or 21st. If none of these are convenient, perhaps you would suggest a time and I will try to arrange my programme to fit.

Naturally *I* don't care a damn about nationalism or peoples, but most people still do,[15] and my little scheme was to catch as many million signatures as possible by stating the essentials in the way most likely to seem sound to most people. A People with a big "P" is only a crowd of ordinary persons, but those crowds are distinct from one another, just as London & Glasgow are. However, to hell with the big P. It was only put in for clarity's sake. And to hell with the League,—if there is any other available concrete symbol and focus of cosmopolitanism. But there's not. Also, the L.N.U. has the machinery for getting signatures, & perhaps the money. The scheme may be worthless, but to be any good at all it must get at least ten million signatures.

Yours, in the hope of meeting you
Olaf Stapledon

9. Wells to Stapledon   7 April 1936

Come to lunch here 1.15 on the 20th. Then we'll settle the Whole Damn Silly Universe.

10. Stapledon to Wells   8 April 1936

I shall be delighted to right the universe with you over lunch on the 20th.

11. Stapledon to Wells   19 April 1936

Telephone: Downland 349
In case you should have to put me off for lunch on Monday, would you kindly ring up the above number.

12. Stapledon to Wells   24 April 1936

"Things to Come" was forwarded to me here.[16] Thank you very much. It was very good of you to send it. I thought I was to look at it merely, but now I have it for keeps. I shall read the Introductory Remarks and the cut passages with special interest. And the whole I shall read with an eye on film technique, in case I should ever want to try a hand at it.

It was a very great pleasure to meet you. I had always regarded you as one of those famous mythical beasts, like the Lion and the Unicorn, that no one actually meets, no one at least except other mythical beasts like kings and great scientists and film stars. But now I find you are a real live person capable of giving one an excellent lunch and a lot of interesting talk, a lot of ideas that take longer to digest than the lunch. Before I go up to London again I shall write to you in the hope that you won't be too busy for another meeting.

13. Stapledon to Wells   4 February 1937

Can I persuade you to lend your name for pushing this petition?[17] It is being organized by a statistician, Caradog Jones,[18] in the belief that many people in this country, even if they disagree about other aspects of the world-problem, can at least pull together to demand expert commissions of inquiry into the economic and political facts underlying current disputes.

The petition is meant to be signed by (a) representative officials of societies, and (b) distinguished individuals representative of every profession.

Each profession is to be approached by means of a circular letter signed by three or four of the most prominent members of that profession. I enclose, as an example, a copy of a letter signed by three heads of universities, and now being circulated among leading university teachers. [Universities may be futile, but there are some good people in them!][19] Leading scientists and clerics are also being approached. Other attacks will also be undertaken.

Will you allow your signature to be used, along with two or three other very well known literary names, on a letter to be addressed to all leading writers? If so, do you approve of the text of the enclosed letter, or would you suggest alterations?

I am writing in the same strain to Aldous Huxley and J.B. Priestley. Could you suggest another name or two, likely to appeal to the less consciously "progressive" people?[20]

Or do you think the plan is a washout?

14. From Stapledon to Marjorie Wells[21]   8 February 1937

Dear Mrs. Wells,

Thank you for your letter. I am very glad to hear that Mr.
H.G. Wells will sign the letter to writers. His signature will
make a lot of difference. On his suggestion I have written to
Hugh Walpole and Somerset Maugham.

I enclose another copy of the petition, and shall be glad if you
will send me the signed copy.

Please thank your father in law for helping, and say we shall
do our best to make a success of the job. It began as a purely
local effort, but we are now trying to carry it out on a larger
scale.

15. Wells to Stapledon   22 June 1937

I like your book tremendously. STAR MAKER and STAR-
BEGOTTEN ought to help each other. They give admirable
opportunity for the intelligent reviewer.[22] Essentially I am
more positivist and finite than you are. You are still trying to
get a formula for the whole universe. I gave up trying to
swallow the Whole years ago. I could write you a long letter if I
wasn't crippled mentally and physically by this damned
neuritis.

16. Stapledon to Wells   23 June 1937

Your letter pleased me very much. Thank you also very much
for the copy of "Star-Begotten", which as a matter of fact I have
reviewed for the "London Mercury", very briefly and inade-
quately. It is a delightful book. I was hard put to it to refrain
from mere adulation, and my criticisms may seem to you beside
the mark.[23]

I don't think I am really trying to *find* a formula for the
whole universe. Philosophically I am almost a positivist (of the
"logical" kind). But I can't help thinking about the universe as
a whole, even though philosophically it's futile. So I let it come
out as myth, and I find it gives me a sort of emotional stability,
much needed in this age of muddles and passions. And of
course I do think the positivist attitude is rather hasty in its

rejections. But that is far better than the opposite error of swallowing rubbish.

By the way, I infer that my publishers must have sent you a copy of "Star Maker" too. If so, I am sorry to have duplicated it, but you can push the extra copy on to someone.

I do hope the neuritis will soon recover. It must be a curse. I should much like to see you again some time.

P.S. I shall be in London early in August. If you can spare time, and are feeling like it , will you either lunch with me at the Whitehall Court Restaurant, or let me call on you some afternoon?

17. Stapledon to Wells   25 June 1937

I enclose for your information a full list of the signatories of the *Petition to His Majesty's Government* which you were good enough to support. It was decided that it would be wise to wait until the new Prime Minister assumed office before presenting the petition. Mr. Graham White is to see Sir John Shute and Mr. Kirby:[25] the intention is that a covering letter should go with the petition in their joint names, so representing all three parties on Merseyside where it originated. Copies are to be sent also to the Foreign Secretary and the President of the Board of Trade.

My purpose in writing to you is to ask whether you would be willing to join a deputation to the Prime Minister assuming he is prepared to receive one—either in the near future or at some later date, to explain in more detail the objects of the petitioners. Mr. Graham White is asking the Archbishop of York to lead the deputation, and among others who are to be invited to attend are:[26]

Lord Allen of Hurtwood	
Prof. W.L. Bragg	Dr. W.R. Mathews
Sir H.H. Dale	Lord Meston
Sir Arthur Eddington	Dr. C.S. Meyers
Sir Richard Gregory	Dr. J.S.B. Stopford
Mr. T. Edmund Harvey	Sir Hugh Walpole
Sir Hector Hetherington	Mr. H.G. Wells

Miss Eleanor Rathbone   Virginia Woolf
Sir F. Gowland Hopkins   Dr. I.A. Richards

We much hope you will allow your name to be included.

P.S. I shall be in London on 5th, 6th, 7th, of August. Will you either lunch with me on one of those days or let me call on you?

18. Stapledon to Marjorie Wells   29 June 1937

I shall be very glad to lunch on 5th August at Hanover Terrace. I take it that I should turn up a little after one o'clock. Sorry about the Deputation.[27]

19. Stapledon to Wells   5 August 1937

I am looking forward to seeing you tomorrow (Thurs) at 1.30. If by any mischance you should need to put me off, please ring up Downland 349.

20. Stapledon to Wells   15 September 1937

Thank you very much for sending me a copy of "Brynhild".[28] There was no reason why you should, but that makes it all the nicer that you did. I shall read it soon as I have finished reading and reviewing J.C. Powys's latest.[29] I am impatient to get to it.

P.S. Your British Ass. address was indeed the stuff to give them.[30] What it is to be H.G.!

21. Stapledon to Wells   12 December 1937

I have read "Brynhild" and "The Camford Visitation"[31] with great interest, and must thank you for sending them to me. I particularly like the character of Brynhild herself, and the way you make her find herself. The "Camford Visitation" interests me specially because of the way you manage the Voice, and because of the very suggestive things that it says. You somehow give a vivid impression of its remoteness from man. Of course, though I have no brief for the universities, I think you tend to see only their faults, which are indeed shocking. It would be cheek of me to praise the way you tell your stories, so I pass that over with silent envy.

I hope you have had a stimulating time in the States.[32]

22. Stapledon to Wells   3 April 1938

Thank you very much for a copy of "The Brothers", which I have greatly enjoyed.[33] I cannot agree that there is so little to choose between the extreme Left and the extreme Right, but I do agree that there are many individuals on the Left who might just as well have been Fascists, and that there is a dangerous Fascist streak running right through Communist thought.[34] I also recognize that there is a lot of honest good will on the Fascist side. You have symbolized your theme extraordinarily interestingly, and made an excellent story of it.

23. Stapledon to Wells   30 November 1938

I have rashly undertaken to try to persuade you to come to speak at Liverpool in May, as suggested in the enclosed letter to you from my friend Stanley Wormald.[35] It's really sheer cheek of us to ask you to come all this way, but in a good cause one must pocket one's diffidence. And after all, I tell myself, audacious requests are the easiest to refuse, so there's no harm in asking. I don't know what you think about the Ass. for Ed. in Cit.[36] It seems to me to be attempting useful work, and if you can come and speak for it here you will give it immense help. And in these days it does seem important to do all in our power to strengthen the frail spirit of intelligent citizenship.

If you do come, my wife and I should be vastly pleased to put you up in the house we are just starting to build—unless we are in the act of removing.[37] It is half an hour out of Liverpool by car, so perhaps you would rather the Society provided more central accommodation. But we should love to have you.

Hearty congratulations on Delores.[38]

24. Stapledon to Wells   29 October 1939

First, how I cheered when I read you in the New Statesman this week![39] May it have the effect it deserves—I mean your remarks, not my cheering.

If you have time to look at this little book of mine[40] I think you will find some interest in it, even where you don't agree. But it is not directly concerned with the present horrid moment of history.

25. Wells to Stapledon   13 November 1939

I like your book. I like the way your mind plays about in it. It reminds me (in spirit & phase) of me in my *God the Invisible King*.[41] And I don't believe a word of it. On your last page you sound a note of hope & faith. You are a lot younger than I am & you don't know what faith is yet. You are what you call a sceptic with a slight air of being a saint & you don't *believe*. You have faith but ultimately you will realize you can do without believing. Leave that to Ellis Roberts. What I object to most about your book is that it is in his series.[42] Ellis Roberts, in his blurb says you say "Materialism is not enough", implying all sorts of things about spiritualism & the soul. You are one of the "children of the spirit" he says in extreme conflict with "the servants of the machine". Why do you lend yourself even by implication to the marketing of such *balls*? I am, & you ought to be, a monist that is to say a human being intelligent enough to realize that the opposition of "the material" & "the spirit-ual" is a fundamental mistake. It is only in the Semitic & Aryan languages that you get it really entrenched. There is no boun-dary line, no polarity of that sort.

I've been through it all. I've been no worse than you. I am still quoted from the pulpits.

26. Stapledon to Wells   16 November 1939

Thank you for your very interesting comments on my "Saints and Revolutionaries". I felt a bit bad about contribut-ing to the series myself, but after all I am *not* a materialist, unless it be in something like the Marxian sense, which is not really it at all.[43] Certainly I am not a dualist but a monist of some sort. As for "belief" and "faith", it all depends on the meaning one gives them. *Of course* I can do without "believ-ing", if you mean believing in metaphysical doctrines. I like to think of myself as following in your footsteps, as you suggest, but as a matter of fact I don't think I am quite on the same track, and recently I have in some ways been going badly astray, from your point of view. I have even at times been called a Christian, which is a bit disturbing, I confess. But at least I have come to realise that, silly as the Christians are, in their way, the pucker scientists are quite as silly in theirs, with their inordinate confidence in their neat little concepts, which mostly turn out to be meaningless when used outside their natural universe of discourse. However, it is easy to see that both lots are silly, and not so easy to escape being silly oneself, and very likely I've been it in appearing to side with the clerics. Certainly Ellis Roberts's blurb does jar. But I don't really side with anybody, even with you. I have thankfully followed you a long way, but with occasional excursions hither and thither beside the track which you have made and so many have since pursued. And by now I seem to be mostly on a more or less parallel way on the other side of the valley, so to speak. But the metaphor is getting in a muddle.

In moments of confidence I might claim that though you have incomparably greater power and skill than I have, and a far more encyclopaedic mind, or encyclopaedic range of knowledge, yet in a horribly sketchy sort of way I do take into account aspects of experience which you are inclined to under-estimate, mainly because in your early days it was *necessary* to underestimate them, whereas in my early days it became neces-sary to recover the essence of them without the silly wrappings. After all, great innovators like you are almost bound to do less than justice to the traditional culture.[44] For the rest, well, I wish I had the prospect of making a small fraction of the contribu-tion that you made to modern culture. But it is not possible for me, being what I am.

And now, belatedly, I will settle down to read you on Homo Sapiens.[45] I hope your verdict on the poor creature will turn out after all to have been too pessimistic. But he is certainly in a horrid fix.

Good luck in this miserable war.

27. Wells to Stapledon   26 July 1940

Your letter fills me with despair. I must write like mud. If I cannot make *you* understand what I am saying, then what is the use of my writing?[46]

I make the most lucid examination of the idea of federation of which I am capable. You respond with "You *may* be right that federalism will come simply by *ad hoc* federation *without the federation of states.*" Didn't I make it clear that *all* federation is *deficient* as to its objectives; is all to a greater or lesser degree ad hoc? Plainly I didn't. *Twice over* also with the most toilsome explicitness I show how an effective world federation may emerge from a world armistice,—& is unlikely to arrive in any other way. Didn't you get that?

(2) You write, "You seem to underestimate the significance of Communism, Fascism & Totalitarianism or rather Nazism." Will you *please* just read over the Introduction to the Rights of Man Declaration again?[47] Do you think that says nothing at all about collectivization? Plainly it does not or you would have got it. *Or did you read it at all?*

(3) Then like old Gandi you sigh "Duties first" &c. *The Declaration is not asking you to stand up for your own Rights* but the Rights of other people. Didn't you even get that?

Finally you say *"your philosophy which you call materialistic."* Short of running a standing advertisement in the *Times* I have done everything I could do to explain that I am *not* a materialist. Have you never heard of monism?[48] Apparently not.

What my dear Stapledon is the good of writing books? You go on with your garden by the Dee & grow food.[49] People of our sort can have no say in the fate of mankind.

28. Stapledon to Wells   2 September 1940

I have just read with great delight your contribution to *I Believe.*[50] Some points, of course, I question, but in the main I heartily agree. What rouses my suspicion is your hypostatization of thought. It's almost Hegelian![51] Still, it's a very helpful essay.

I look forward to reading your two forthcoming books, & shall take them to heart![52]

Things are a bit unpleasant here now.[53] We are all badly short of sleep.

29. Wells to Stapledon [by Marjorie Wells] 3 June 1942

I see you're reviewing that absurd book of Atkinson's in Plan.[55] H.G. is still unable to attend to his correspondence but I know it was extremely disappointing to him to have the fundamental biological thought in his novel *You Can't Be Too Careful* entirely neglected. I am sending you a copy for you to read and I think if you could quote some discussion of his idea that H. sap is a misnomer & that the proper name of man should be *Homo Tewler* he will be very pleased when he takes up things again.[56]

30. Stapledon to Marjorie Wells 4 June 1942

Please thank Mr. Wells for sending me a copy of *You Can't Be Too Careful*, which I shall read with great interest. I had not yet had an opportunity of doing so. Certainly I shall do my best to raise an adequate discussion in Plan, and wherever possible.

I hope Mr. Wells is making a good recovery, and that he will soon be able to be as active as ever. Please give him my love, and (if it's not presumptuous) congratulations on being H.G.W.

31. Stapledon to Wells 3 August 1942

I venture to ask you to look at the enclosed documents and express an opinion on them.[57] They tell of an educational enterprise which is being undertaken by some young men in the R.A.F. Coastal Command, ostensibly merely to improve morale, but also to create a clear will for a new order after the war. You will see that the promotors recognize that "far-reaching changes are inevitable in the political and social structure both in order to win the war and to win the peace."

Briefly the scheme is to have a special room or hut in every unit for discussion on social and cultural matters. There is also to be a library, and a wall newspaper is already being published. I send you a copy of a recent number, or rather a photo of it. There is nothing educational in this but it might be made into a very valuable organ. Please return the photo, as it is official.

Naturally the whole enterprise has to be begun very cautiously so as to secure the approval of the authorities. F/Lt.

Houghton and his colleagues have already got the thing going in Coastal Command, and he is trying to get the War Office to make it universal.

I have talked the whole scheme over with him, and he expressed a strong desire to have your opinion on the best way to run it so as to make it a really effective educational influence.[58]

You may think it is too "safe", and in danger of falling under the control of the padre and the brass hat. On the other hand I am convinced, from experience in lectures and discussions with the R.A.F. and Army that there is a growing body of progressive but bewildered opinion in the forces, and that the future may depend on how this opinion is guided, and further that there are people *in* the forces who are very determined to turn it into a really radical public influence.[59]

I await your comments with interest.

P.S. I have not heard of you lately, and I do not know whether you are fully recovered from your illness, but I very much hope you are fit again now.

32. Wells to Stapledon   7 August 1942

I doubt if you'll get this movement past the Padre's & the "Christian Ethic". Surely there ought to be a representative of the Rationalist Press Association on the board.[60] What these people do not realize is the cynical contempt of a very large & growing part of our population for the priests & parsons. Would the organizers of Freedom House agree to place a copy of my new book *Phoenix* in each Freedom House.[61] If so I have no doubt we can arrange to print a special cheap edition for that purpose. NB And they can also have an edition of the *Outlook for Homo Sapiens* on similar conditions.[62] Why is no mention made of the the Declaration of the Rights of Man instead of or alternative to that cullender of political trickery the Atlantic Charter?[63] The prospect of an England run after the war by the squire & parson is enough to take the fight out of anyone. No. I don't like Your "Freedom" House. I want Free Thought & Free Speech House.

Physically I'm much better but Horder & Lawrence[64] have

ordered me a spell of complete inaction before the turn of the year. I find mental work except in short spells very distressing.

Warmest greetings.

33. Stapledon to Wells   11 August 1942

Thank you for your letter and for returning the photo. I was afraid you would be suspicious of the Freedom House scheme because of the padre influence. So am I, but I am sure the young men themselves mean business, and so I am going to do whatever I can to strengthen their position. I intend to show your letter to Houghton. It will be good for him. I shall urge him to do something about your offer of cheap editions of *Phoenix* and *The Outlook for Homo Sapiens*. There ought certainly to be a reference to The Declaration of the Rights of Man, but in my experience what the young people are most roused by today is not a claim to rights but a call to devotion.[65] That is where the padre may side-track them. The urgent thing is to show them something really worth being devoted to.

I am very glad to hear that you are better, and hope you will take a good rest before getting down to work again.

With best wishes

NOTES TO THE LETTERS

Letter 1
[1] Many reviewers of *Last and First Men*, and of later works, measured Stapledon's work against Wells's. E.B. Chaffee in *Outlook* says Stapledon "exceeds Wells in the power of his imagination [May 6, 1931], while the reviewer for the *Saturday Review of Literature* laments that he "lacks the vivid story-telling gift of an H.G. Wells." [April 25, 1931].

Letter 2
[2] In the final chapter of *Work, Wealth Etc*, Wells mentions the recent publication of "a very suggestive and amusing book by Olaf Stapledon, *First and Last Men* [sic]." He says about the fantastic narrative of the distant future: "The remoter speculations of Mr. Stapledon vivid and amusing though they are, and stimulating as they will prove to those unversed in biological and cosmological possibilities, need not

be discussed here." *The Work, Wealth and Happiness of Mankind* (NY: Doubleday, 1931), pp. 892-893.

³ G.P. "Gip" Wells, H.G.'s eldest son, collaborated with his father and Julian Huxley on *The Science of Life.*

⁴ Presumably *Last Men in London*, completed in September, 1932.

Letter 3
⁵ *Waking World* (1934), a book of visionary philosophical speculation, argues many of the ideas about "wide-awake" individuals and worlds that are fictionalized in *Odd John* and *Star Maker.*

⁶ "Mr Wells is a 'humanist', at least in one sense of the word. He holds that the proper object of man's devotion is man. But some of us feel that he does not take the whole of man's nature into account. He regards man as a fairly intelligent mammal, which he is; but he does not see all that is involved in being such a creature. Mr Wells never quite grasps the fact, or at least never thoroughly realizes the full implications of the fact, that the gifts of intelligence and imagination open up for man vast spheres of activity which cannot in the present state of knowledge be fully understood in terms of our biological concepts" (*Waking World* p. 12)

Letter 4
⁷ Apparently Wells's missing letter was a response to Stapledon's comments in *Waking World.* Stapledon here answers by drawing Wells passing untouched between the cages of *Homo Religiosus* and *Homo Proletariensis*. Stapledon says he himself is the uncaged jackdaw, "free but uncertain": he is a socialist, not an orthodox Marxist, and a spiritualist, not a believer in institutional religion. Wells's habit of including drawings in his letters is of course well-known. Mrs Stapledon has written me that "in a light-hearted mood Olaf had a facility for lapsing into pen-drawing to emphasize his points."

Letter 5 (Postcard)
⁸ This postcard was obviously written shortly after Letter 4.

⁹ Wells's missing letter obviously contained a drawing, possibly contesting Stapledon's self-description as free but uncertain. With characteristic grace, Stapledon shows himself, in the person of the jackdaw being toppled from his perch by Wells, who has had the better of the argument.

Letter 6
¹⁰ This is a form letter, typed. The salutation and the postcript are handwritten.

¹¹ The "Open Letter" is a long series of declarations and demands focusing on the themes of world government, individual liberties, peace, and economic security.

¹² The Peace Ballot was a massive survey of public opinion on the question of global disarmament, undertaken by the League of Nations Union in 1934-1935. Over

eleven and one half million people in Great Britain responded, voting overwhelmingly in favor of the League and of the abolition of armaments.

13 Edgar Algernon Robert Cecil, a founder of the League of Nations and president of the League Union, directed the Peace Ballot. He received the Nobel Peace Prize in 1937.

Letter 7

14 The sequence of Letters 8-12 makes it clear that the first meeting of Wells and Stapledon did not occur until April 20.

Letter 8

15 Although Stapledon was uncomfortable with slogans and other political tools, he often argued that they were necesary. He insisted, for instance, at the inaugural meeting of the H.G. Wells Society on May 15, 1934, that activists should appeal to people's emotions and that Society members should "beat our opponents on their own ground and make use of even flags, banners, and slogans—provided they were the right slogans." His remarks are reported in the *Bulletin* of the H.G. Wells Society, no. 1, June, 1934.

Letter 12

16 *Things to Come* (1935) was the scenario for the film directed by William Cameron Menzies. It was the final draft of Wells's first treatment and differed in many respects from the film in its final form. Hence Stapledon's reference to "cut passages."

Letter 13

17 I have been unable to find a copy of this petition.

18 D. Caradog Jones was a distinguished sociologist who published a number of reference works based upon statistical surveys in the 20's and 30's.

19 The bracketed sentence is Stapledon's marginal interpolation. He had a long association with the University of Liverpool, where he often lectured part-time. Stapledon may have had in mind a talk by Wells given on November 20, 1936 to the Royal Institution, attacking the universities for what he considered their failure to respond to the moral and practical needs of modern society. Wells frequently accused the universities of being obstacles to progress. This speech, called "World Encyclopedia", was especially strong. It is reprinted in *World Brain* (1938).

20 At the bottom of Stapledon's letter is a note in Marjorie Wells's handwriting: a question mark, and the names Maugham, Walpole. See n. 21.

Letter 14

21 Marjorie Craig Wells, wife of Wells's son G.P., acted for many years as H.G.'s secretary. During his frequent attacks of neuritis in the later 30's (see Letter 51), Wells dictated his correspondence to Mrs Wells, who typed it.

Letter 15

22 The only comparative contemporary review which I have found is a brief evaluation by Simon Blumenfeld in *Left Review*, III (August, 1937), p. 437.

Letter 16

23 "Mr Wells Calls in the Martians" in *London Mercury*, 36 (July, 1937), pp, 295-296, gives more vigorous criticism of *Star-Begotten's* "dehumanized humanism" than this letter implies. A strongly favorable review of *Star Maker* by Bertrand Russell also appears in this issue (pp. 297-298)

Letter 17

24 This is a typed form letter with handwritten salutation, complimentary close and postscript. There are several handwritten additions and deletions: Wells's name has been deleted from the list of petitioners, and the names of Woolf and Richards have been added in ink.

25 Graham White was Liberal M.P. for Birkenhead. Col. Sir John Shute was Conservative M.P. for Liverpool. I have not been able to identify Kirby; probably he was a Labour M.P. from a Liverpool constituency.

26 Wells has drawn brackets around this paragraph, and written "NO" in large letters.

Letter 18

27 Probably a reference to the appeal in Letter 17, which was obviously rejected by Wells in a missing letter.

Letter 20

28 Wells's new novel *Brynhild or The Show of Things*.

29 *Morwyn, or The Revenge of God*, an anti-vivesectionist novel by John Cowper Powys, was reviewed by Stapledon in *London Mercury* 37 (November, 1937), p. 78.

30 "The Informative Content of Education" was delivered before the Educational Section of the British Association for the Advancement of Science in Nottingham on September 12. It is reprinted in *World Brain*.

Letter 21

31 Stapledon himself experimented with "disembodied" viewpoints; hence his technical interest in *The Camford Visitation*.

32 Wells toured the U.S. in October and November, giving a lecture called "The Brain Organization of the Modern World." It is reprinted in *World Brain*.

Letter 22

[33] Wells's latest political novel.

[34] In "Science, Art and Society" in the *Lincoln Mercury*, 38 (October, 1938), p. 528, Stapledon wrote:

> There is a real danger that the Left, through the effects of a desperate struggle, may lose sight of its aims, and slip into a kind of inverted Fascism, or 'para-Fascism'. It may gradually begin to use the methods and pursue the ideals which in its enemies it rightly condemns. It may, that is, turn to ruthlessness, hard-mindedness, the glorification of the State, the contempt of individuality. Intellectuals must see that this does not happen.

Letter 23

[35] I have not seen the enclosure. Stanley Wormald was a tutor, as was Stapledon, in the Workers' Educational Association.

[36] The Association for Education in Citizenship published books and pamphlets on civics and social studies, in some of which Wells is listed as one of 9 vice-presidents of the Association. Stapledon made several references to "education for citizenship" in *Darkness and the Light* (1942).

[37] In 1940 the Stapledons moved into the house, "Simon's Field", Caldy, near West Kirby, a pleasant seaside town in the district of Wirral.

[38] *Apropos of Delores*, Wells's most recent novel.

Letter 24

[39] "The Honour and Dignity of the Free Mind", *New Statesman*, 452, 453 (October 21 and 28, 1939), pp 546-548, 606-608, in which Wells argues that artists and scientists cannot remain apolitical in times of crisis, but warns writers against being used as "good little government boys" in the production of propaganda. This was a lecture intended for the annual congress of the International P.E.N. Club in Stockholm. The congress was cancelled because of the outbreak of war.

[40] *Saints and Revolutionaries*.

Letter 25

[41] *God the Invisible King* (1917) contained the expression of Wells's short-lived interest in theology during World War I.

[42] *Saints and Revolutionaries* was part of the Heinemann series *I Believe* (not to be confused with the Allen and Unwin collection of essays by the same name, mentioned in Letter 28), edited by R. Ellis Roberts, who wrote a preface to *Saints*, saying that the book was "opposed to the forces of life which seek to destroy the dignity of the individual and to exalt the machine." a statement which Wells may have taken as an attack upon him.

Letter 26

[43] In "Science, Art and Society" (see note 34 to Letter 22), "mechanical materialism", the unhappy result of scientific approaches to man" as a physical mechanism or as a biological specimen" is distinguished from the dialectical materialism of Marx," which liberally and perhaps heretically interpreted, seems to me to allow sufficient autonomy to the upper reaches of personality" (p. 526).

[44] In *Saints and Revolutionaries* he warns that radicals who have overcome their bourgeois backgrounds tend to "bury the legacy with the corpse," spurning the traditional culture and uncritically praising anything which seems to be new. (p. 16). In "Science, Art and Society" he urges radical artists to help people "to realize that the old culture, with all its faults, includes much of permanent value which the new culture must incorporate. It includes...the basic values of individuality and kindliness and reason. No society which denies these can thrive." (p. 528).

[45] Wells's latest polemic, *The Fate of Homo Sapiens*.

Letter 27

[46] Stapledon's missing letter apparently questioned aspects of Wells's *The New World Order* (1940), especially chapters 7 and 12, which discuss world federation.

[47] The so-called Wells-Sankey Declaration, intended to be a universal bill of rights, and printed in a number of Wells's books in the 40's.

[48] In *Philosophy and Living* (1939), Stapledon contended that one could be both a monist and a materialist. See Vol. II, pp. 364-369.

[49] The new house was near the mouth of the Dee.

Letter 28

[50] *I Believe: The Personal Philosophies of Twenty-Three Eminent Men and Women of Our Time* (1940). A greatly abbreviated version of Wells's essay in this book appears in the American edition of it, ed. by Clifton Fadiman (1939).

[51] Stapledon discusses the pitfalls of Hegel's hypostasis, the assignment of reality to abstractions rather than to sensory data, in *Philosophy and Living*, Vol. II, pp. 360-362. Passages like this in the *I Believe* essay carry Hegelian overtones: "[I] doubt [profoundly] whether this H.G. Wells of mine is really the completely independent, separate, distinct being that it is our habit of mind to consider him. Perhaps my individuality, my personality, seems to be distincter than it is. Perhaps it is...a convenient biological illusion" (p. 359).

[52] The two were probably *All Aboard for Ararat*, an allegorical novel, and *A Guide to the New World: A Handbook for Constructive World Revolution*, a collection of essays.

[53] There were frequent air raids at night on Liverpool and the Midlands.

Letter 29

[54] A draft in H.G.'s handwriting, to be typed by Marjorie Wells.

[55] Probably *Win the War, Win the Peace,* edited by Henry Avery Atkinson (NY: NY Publications for the Institutes by the Church Peace Union, 1942). *Plan* was the journal of the Federation of Progressive Societies and Individuals, later called the Progressive League. I have not been able to see the review.

[56] In *You Can't Be Too Careful* Wells says human beings are truly derived from his protagonist, Edward Albert Tewler; they are *"Homo Tewler, Homo sub-sapiens."* This is the obverse of the position of *Star-Begotten* and *Odd John* that man is an evolutionary breakthrough to a higher order.

Letter 31

[57] I have not seen these documents.

[58] At the top of this letter Wells wrote, "This scheme is *no damned good.* We are going to be inundated with sham rights of Man stuff. This is Parsons & Priests and yesterday there was that Polish muck they go Moura to send me." Moura Budberg was Wells's mistress in the 30's; she had lived in Russia with Gorky. Wells disliked the Polish Government-in-Exile, headquartered in London in 1941 under Wladyslaw Sikorski. See Norman and Jeanne MacKenzie, *H.G. Wells: A Biography* (NY: Simon & Schuster, 1973), p. 432.

[59] Stapledon lectured to servicemen throughout World War II. He describes the experience briefly in *Beyond the "Isms"* (London: Secker & Warburg, 1942) pp. 9-10, and more extensively in *Youth and Tomorrow* (London: St. Botolph Pub., 1946), pp 67-70. He offered his own proposals for a politically conscious "real people's army" in *New Hope for Britain* (London: Methuen, 1939) pp 170-172.

Letter 32

[60] The R.P.A. was founded in 1899, pledged to the principles of scientific humanism. Its Library of Science and Culture offered a portrait of the modern world as shaped by science.

[61] *Phoenix: A Summary of the Inescapable Conditions of World Reorganization.* Wells's latest plea for world federation.

[62] *Outlook* contains two earlier books: *The Fate of Homo Sapiens* (1939) and *The New World Order* (1940).

[63] Wells considered the Atlantic Charter superficial, intended for European, and not world, federation.

[64] Robin Lawrence was Wells's personal doctor; Lord Horder was a friend and a prominent physician.

Letter 33

[65] Stapledon's most careful "call to devotion" can be found in *Beyond the "Isms"* (p. 12). This call runs through much of Stapledon's writing during the war, and after, including *Darkness and the Light* (1942), *Old Man in New World* (1944) *Seven Pillars of Peace* (1944) and *Youth and Tomorrow* (1946).

Nonliterary Influences On
Science Fiction

Algis Budrys

Scholars who write theses about older science fiction should be aware of the effect of nonliterary factors on the content of that fiction. These factors are basically mechanical: some are editorial only in the sense that they reflect mandatory publisher's style policy. Impositions of this sort have frequently been preserved in anthologizing the fiction from its original magazine format; they act now as snares for the reader who seeks literary significance in every word of the text.

The impositions skew the text particularly in stories which were originally published by the Standard Magazine chain: *Captain Future,* *Thrilling Wonder Stories* and *Startling Stories.* But material from *Astounding Science Fiction* and all other contemporary magazines contains impositions as well, and most of them belonged to chains. *Astonishing Stories* and *Super Science Stories* belonged to the Fictioneers division of Popular Publications; *Super Science Stories* is not to be confused with the later *Super Science,* which was chain-styled by the literary agency which supplied ghost-editing. *Amazing Stories* and *Fantastic Adventures* belonged to the Ziff-Davis chain. Street and Smith published *Unknown,* which became *Unknown Worlds,* and purchased *Astounding Science Fiction* from Clayton Publications; the Love Romances Publishing Corporation of Fiction House owned

Planet Stories, and The Double Action Group of Columbia Publications brought out *Science Fiction*, *Future*, *Dynamic*, and variations on these titles. All these chains also brought out various "one shot" magazines as well as these well-known, continuing ones.

There were also a proliferation of non-chain magazines which nevertheless closely followed the chain publishing models. Some of these were *Science Fiction Adventures*, its sister *Infinity*, *Universe*, *Imagination* owned by William Lawrence Hamling, and *Other Worlds*, owned by Ray Palmer. Both Hamling and Palmer had been editors for Ziff-Davis.

A great deal of the textual intervention in such non-chain books as *Fantastic Universe* and *Satellite* can be traced directly back to their publisher Leo Margulies, who had been chief editor at Standard. Margulies was not the only editor who had been trained by the chains: H.L. Gold, editor of *Galaxy* in its early years, had come from the chains, and his successor at *Galaxy*, Frederick Pohl, had been editor of *Astonishing* and *Super-Science*. In fact, none of the science-fiction magazines can be said to be free of chain practices from 1929, when Hugo Gernsback lost control of *Amazing Stories*, to 1949, with the appearance of *The Magazine of Fantasy and Science Fiction*. Mercury Press, which published the latter book, and also published H.L. Mencken's *The American Mercury*, was essentially a chain publisher, since it owned *Ellery Queen's Mystery Magazine* and some other detective magazines, and since it twice attempted to establish *Venture Science Fiction*. However Lawrence Spivack, the publisher who later produced *Meet the Press* for television, and Anthony Boucher and J. Francis McComas, the founding editors, had what might be called classically literary predelictions, and so *The Magazine of Fantasy and Science Fiction* eschewed standard chain practices.

The cause of these practices lies in two factors which condition almost all commercial publishing: 1) the imperatives of promotion, and 2) the publisher's perceptions of audience demographics.

In the milieu of the chain-published 10¢ to 25¢ newsstand magazine of the 1930's and 40's, the publisher could do little to cut his wholesale and retail trade expenses. He had to look to his in-house expenses for cost-cutting: his paper, engraving, type, plate-making, printing, binding and bundling had to be as cheap as they could be, and still maintain a level of physical quality that would be acceptable to audiences.

After that economies were achieved by the hiring of writers, artists, art directors and editors and managers who were willing to work for low salaries and who could produce a kind of minimum aesthetic effect, hampered by rigid house policies, since creative decisions tend to be individual and unpredictable, and therefore expensive.

These house aesthetic policies were governed by the perception of audience demographics: services in this area have been rendered by professional researchers, but the tendency among publishers historically, as among advertising and public-relations agencies, has been to accept these figures only when they confirm their prejudices. In any case the advertising potential for science fiction magazines was not high enough to justify the luxury of audience research organizations, these publishers used other, simpler, means to determine their audience. They printed coded mail-order coupons in the books, in order to gauge the response of segments of their readers, solicited reader response to polls in the magazine, and even resorted to the simple expedient of watching the people who bought the magazine at newsstands near the editorial offices. This is known among mass-merchandisers as "curbstone demographics." The result was a compulsion to market to the lowest common denominator, the most safely predictable readership.

This marketing strategy, common to all competing magazine chains was adopted before they began to publish science fiction, which then inherited all the methods used to sell older genres of fiction. There was no way to determine whether the readers of science fiction and fantasy differed in any way from readers of westerns, crime, jungle stories, air war, or any of the categories listed by chain publishers. If in fact a difference in readership had been ascertained, it is probable that the chains would have dropped science fiction rather than form policies designed especially for it alone. It was best for editors and writers to keep science fiction safely within the parameters of genre fiction, and chain-publishing practices. One may well note that even today books and magazines are published with the same practices in mind, to a lesser extent.

We must therefore view older science fiction through the publisher's eyes, as merchandise to be packaged in containers of a predetermined size. A story becomes merchandise the moment the manuscript, with its publishing rights, has been purchased. Publishers bought all rights in most older stories. The attitude of commercial publishers was not that they were transmitting the work of the author to his audience, as is the classic publishing attitude, but that the audience belonged to the publisher, and the author was basically a subcontractor.

The publisher saw his basic competition for readers as between chains, rather than between authors, or between individual magazine titles, or even genres. As a reflection of this attitude, advertising in the magazines was sold not by the individual title but by the chain: the only smaller unit offered was for a "group" within the chain. The content of the advertising bears out this attitude: an encyclopedia of Female Beauty Around the World, the Audel home-workshop manuals, and so on. It is an attitude which presented a "homogenized" chain style, and all chain editorial offices had either a verbal or a written set of guidelines for the imposition of such a style on stories which had been bought in the first place with their suitability for chain readership in mind.

The "style book" used at Street and Smith was *Webster's Collegiate Dictionary*. For this reason the Shadow, Doc Savage and the characters in Heinlein's *Beyond This Horizon* all said "O.K." and not "okay". Apart from this, editors at the chains broke compound sentences into simple ones, simplified all words containing more than a requisite number of syllables, used short paragraphs regardless of topic sentences, considered dialogue mandatory at certain points, removed "complicated" punctuation like semi-colons, and in general created prose designed to be read as rapidly as possible.

Most effective writers learned quickly to forestall editorial intervention by writing as simply as possible in the first place. However the substitution of a short synonym for a polysyllabic word caused serious interference with the writer's intention. There was no "book" for this; the harrassed editors, who punched timeclocks, simply counted syllables and looked for an approximate short synonym. They also made sure to do a lot of copy-editing if they wanted to keep their jobs: hasty but conspicuous editing was therefore the rule. It has been said that some editors would write in the identical word above the black line; but such careful preservation of the author's intention would not be the rule.

This interference extended to content as well as style. If the author, for instance, created a villain named Johnson, the editor would change the name to Rubinoff or some other ethnic appellation that would preserve the purity of Anglo-Saxon bahavior. The villain, further, always wore a black hat, brunette women dressed more daringly than blondes, and acted more quickly, the hero had to face some kind of physical threat within the first printed page, at least, etc. If the author left out any of these requirements, the editor supplied them. The author, needless to say, was not consulted; he might be warned not to give the editors so much trouble next time.

If a publisher were accused of writing the story, he would probably ascribe the writing to the reader, saying that all these manuscript changes were done because of audience choice. This despite the fact that many readers wrote to the editor to protest these formula impositions, and publishers did print extensive columns of letters from readers, many of them highly critical of the content of the magazines. These letters were considered free material which could be entertaining; they were not taken seriously by the publishers.

After the manuscript was edited, it was sent to be set on Linotype or Intertype machines which cast leaden "slugs" from molten metal, each containing one line the width of a column of text, which were assembled in trays face up and tied with twine. These were called galleys. When inked with a roller and pressed upon a long, narrow sheet of paper, they produced galley proofs. The process was subject to human error, and the machines themselves occasionally stuttered; thus it was necessary for someone to read the proofs for mistakes.

The basic reason for proof-reading was to insure against the printing of an accidental obscenity: the dropping of the crucial consonant from the word "shift" for instance, might well hurt the publisher in the rural communities where he sold quantities of books. After that, the publisher wanted proof read because he was aware that it would be easier to sell a text if it made sense. Nevertheless the proof reading was hasty, and often led to fresh errors in the text.

If a tray of type was dropped, the scattered slugs would be re-assembled by a printer, who would, by mirror-reading, reconstruct the galley as well as he could as quickly as possible. When this happened before the proof was pulled, the proofreader might catch most errors, but he might miss some too, particularly short lines of dialogue.

Transpositions of slugs can occur at any stage in their handling; any change marked on a galley proof is an instruction to the compositor to move the slugs. A slight change in a line requires the entire line to be recast. The replacement slug must then be carried to the tray, the erroneous slug removed, and replaced. This necessitated the untying of the twine, or removal of any more sophisticated galley-locking device, and could give rise to any number of accidents. The drunken printer is not just legendary: the handling of type-metal could cause chronic poisoning that led to emotional instability which in its turn was relieved by alcohol.

The most likely accident was not the omission or duplication of single lines, although these occur often, but the transposition of paragraphs. To the compositor the paragraph consistsd of a group of raised surfaces separated from similar groups by low planes which will show on the paper as white space. He might juggle the order of these groups in the galley; the error would not stand out as distinctly as it would if it occurred with one or two slugs within a paragraph. It could be over-looked not only by the compositor but by the proofreader in the page proof which in chain magazine publishing was the only proof read, with no corrected galley proof or at best a short proof showing only the new slugs. Since the purpose of the page proof was primarily to show page make-up, any number of galley errors could slip past the proof-reader and the more plausible the errors were the more likely it was to happen. In addition, page-proof corrections by their very nature force additional changes in the text.

Once past the galley-proof stage, the slugs are moved into forms: that is, the slugs of type are put into the column form that will appear on the printed page. This is essentially and simply a matter of counting or measuring slugs (although there is a process called "carding" which plays a small part in the process on occasion). Page makeup is like packing a lunchbox, if the packer assumes that the packee will eat anything that fits.

A slug at this stage may have on it only two or three characters, consisting of a short word at the end of a sentence. When this occurs on the first or last line of a column it will leave a noticeable amount of white space and create "a widow". All chain publishers made an effort to eradicate these widows, since they spoil the rectangular look of the printed page. Some publishers attack widows at all four corners of a double-column page; some attack only those at the tops of the columns.

One of the proofreader's chief duties was to kill widows, and the cheapest and easiest way to do this is to alter the text. Otherwise it would be necessary to find a way to run slugs around from the bottom of one column to the top of the next, or vice versa.

Thus in one of my own stories, "The High Purpose", printed in *Astounding Science Fiction* for November, 1952, there are two lines on page 95: "They all laughed derisively. Home would have to wait." The second line is a widow-killed written by a proofreader for Street and Smith. Apart from the fact that neither I nor an editor wrote the line, it is redundant; the point was already made earlier in the paragraph. Thus the "definitive text" could contain lines that crept in through this kind of process. This could be a potent trap for the scholar of style, particularly since many such magazine-born errors have not been weeded out of subsequent reprintings.

Most chain publishers found facing pages of solid type to be discouraging to the reader. Such "spreads" were broken up by various means: ads and filler material were used to create diversion. Popular Publications inserted a box containing the brief italicized poetry of Don Blanding. All the chains depended on spot illustrations which were reprinted from small engravings. One of the first things every apprentice editor learned was how to make space-breaks. White space is the cheapest visual element, and it was felt that every page should have at least one blank area the width of a column; this would make the page easier to read, just as one-line dialogue, or at least frequent exchanges of dialogue, did.

Space breaks could be anticipated in copy-editing; that is, they could be inserted in the manuscript at prescribed intervals, sometimes helping to indicate lapses of time or special emphasis. But a galley space-break might create a widow in page make-up, so some people preferred to wait for page make-up before inserting breaks. Those who edited breaks into the manuscript had to tackle the widows when they appeared. They could insert a row of asterisks at the top or bottom of a column, or they could take out the slugs and lose whatever print was on them. Frequently inexperienced proofreaders would simply excise exchanges of short lines of dialogue, since this required no re-setting of type, although it does compound the movement of slugs. Another favorite method for proofreaders was the removal of any paragraph whose last sentence is all on one slug. And of course if nothing else worked, the proofreader would write in a line or two, usually an exchange of meaningless dialogue.*

Some authors never reread their work under any circumstances after it has been published. This is not a trait peculiar to science-fiction writers, but since so much anthologized science fiction has been published originally in chain magazines, this genre appears to suffer most from the carelessness of authors who supply the same sets of tear sheets from magazines to editors for reprinting without checking them.

---

* There is an analogous situation in book editing when copy runs on to a blank page. A minimum of three lines is considered the requirement to hide from the reader the fact that books are often sized first and fitted with copy second, particularly in paperback publishing. My own favorite example of this is a proofreader's ingenious creation:

He began to cut.
Snip.
Snip.
Snip.

Sometimes entire novels are set from stacks of magazine series stories, thus preserving all sorts of stochasm, proofreader or editorial intrusion and accident between the covers of a book with no auctorial intervention at all.

Editors of anthologies do not as a rule fine-comb the text supplied by authors or unearthed in second-hand magazine stores. They are interested primarily in the total effect of the story, the sales power of the author's name, the fitness of the story for the theme of the anthology, or some combination of these factors. As they proof their own type, they will catch preserved typographical errors and possibly implausible configurations. They are apt to miss transposed slugs, and they never catch widow-killers. These consequently take on immortality in book form, along with plausibly transposed paragraphs, dialogue mis-attributed through slug transpositions, and often even fresh invention when the hard-pressed anthologist battles his own deadline by supplying his own substitute for lines missing or garbled in the original text.

It can thus safely be said that any science fiction "novel" from the 30's or 40's which originated in mass magazines cannot be accurately appraised without examination of the original magazine publication, unless it is known for a fact that the author has rewritten or re-edited the book. In addition if it is possible to see the original uncut manuscript that is important, too, since few "complete" magazine "novels" escaped heavy editorial intervention, and only a relatively small number of these novels are reset in book form directly from the manuscript only. Far more frequently the "novel" is made from a magazine serial. The chain-magazine serial is a distinct literary form which differs from both the novel and from the modern magazine serial.

The modern science fiction magazine serial is a complete novel, already in existence, which is cut up into segments, and supplied with synopses. Some rewriting may be done to create cliffhanger moments at the close of the early segments, but basically the novel is all of a piece. It is a book contracted for publication, and magazine publication exists only for advance publicity for the book and/or for extra income for the author.

Until around 1950 there was no such thing as a novel in the newsstand science fiction mode. The magazines were the medium, and their "novels" were novellas published complete in one issue or a short series of novellettes under a common title and byline, with common characters and varied sub-plots under the umbrella of a master-plot. By 1960 there were nothing but novels in the magazines: the change during the 50's was gradual: the proportion shifted by about 10% a year as books overtook magazines as the primary medium for science fiction. Thus one can say, as a useful gauge, that any "novel" appearing in 1955 has about a 50% chance of actually having been a serial.

I can offer a clear distinction between the early SF "novel" and the later real novel, so to speak, from my own experience. I wrote *The Iron Thorn* for *Worlds of If* magazine, where it appeared from January through April, 1967. When this chain-mode serial was contracted for by Frederick Pohl, it was not yet written. It was in fact written during publication and was extended in length beyond its original conception. This had happened also with Erik van Lhin's *Police Your Planet* (1953) which was written from month to month for *Science Fiction Adventures*. The editor, Lester del Rey, had taken the story as a novella, to be complete in one issue, and grudgingly have ground before van Lhin's almost helpless discovery that the story was a natural serial. It eventually ran to four instalments. The same thing may have happened with Raymond F. Jones's *Renaissance* which was announced as a 3 part serial by *ASF* in 1944, and then published in 4 parts with an awkward explanation and the repetition of at least one illustration.

It is instructive to note that *Renaissance* is critically considered to be the chief work of a prolific but undeservedly neglected writer in the late years of the *ASF* Golden Age, and that *Police Your Planet* has appeared in several editions as a book, and has been called an excellent example of "naturalistic" writing, rare in the generally romantic genre of science fiction.

In any case, in contrast to *The Iron Thorn*, my novel *Rogue Moon*, published by Gold Medal in 1960, was planned as a novel from its beginning as a detailed 50 page singlespaced outline, after two years of incubation, and taking three years to complete, with extensive redrafting. I gave no thought at all to magazine publication while I was writing it. In fact I did not even seek a book contract for it until a good deal of it was finished. Just as *Iron Thorn* was a late example of the chain serial, *Rogue Moon* is an early example of the science fiction novel. It ran as a novella in *Fantasy and Science Fiction*, the December, 1960 issue. It was cut from a copy of the manuscript and ran complete shortly before book publication. The title, incidentally, was originally *The Death Machine*; it was changed by Knox Burger, the editor for *Gold Medal* who, however, preserved the text intact despite his tepid feelings about some if it.

Thus one can see that is would not be fruitful to compare *The Iron Thorn* and *Rogue Moon* as examples of one author's novels. They came out of different traditions. If this is true of my work, there is good reason to suppose that similar complications exist in the work of older, more important writers.

It is important for critics and scholars to learn as much as possible about the men who wrote science fiction for the chains. Most printed biographical information is unfortunately not reliable. These writers cannot be dealt with in generalities; they vary too much. It should be said at once that the actual writing of chain science fiction really required no creativity at all: the minimum requirement was the plain, exciting resolution of a clearcut crucial problem confronting a genuine hero. From what we know of the publishers' opinion of their audience that they would have been satisfied by a simple fleshing out in basic English to a desired length of a very thin stack of elements. Writers who did that and no more were paid exactly as much as writers doing much more than that. In fact in order to earn bonuses it was not necessary to write better, but to do the minimum work quickly, meet deadlines, make sure the "hole" in the projected issue was filled to the exact length, and that the work fit the precise mood of the material already scheduled for that issue.

The last major writer to direct his career to exactly that mode of production was Robert Silverberg, who, by his own account, produced 10,000 words a six hour day five days a week, with two hours a day devoted to contacting magazine editors for specific assignments. Silverberg could not have been the only talented writer to go this route; but he was fortunate that he was able to get out of it. The top rate of payment was one cent a word on acceptance; the median rate was one cent after publication, and often the writer for one reason or another never got paid at all. With this financial situation it was difficult to find enough leisure time to plan a serious book.

Consequently most sf writers had independent incomes. As late as the first Milford Conference of professional sf writers, an informal census discovered only seven men in the English-speaking world who had no occupation but that of SF writing. These were, if I remember correctly, beside myself, Bradbury, Hamilton, Kornbluth, Silverberg and Sturgeon. John W. Campbell, Jr., the editor of *Astounding*, possibly equating quality with leisure time activities, advised his favored contributors to find some other principal occupation. He did not, however, deviate from the chain style of publishing. He did not want better examples of the form: ingenious social milieux, sophisticated problems, heroes with unusual occupations, more intricate resolutions. He thus sought more educated and insightful writers, whom he encouraged by publishing them regularly. He raised the intellectual standard of the whole field by creating a community of talented, knowledgeable writers. Incidentally, many of these writers were not comfortable with a scientific plot, and got their science wrong, or ignored it; a myth has unaccountably grown up, however, that *ASF* under Campbell was devoted to scientific verisimilitude. What he had was actually scientophilia, a feeling that there must be some system for explaining and modifying the Universe. Campbell was, however, a dominant editor: the decline of *ASF* was not his fault, nor was it competition from *Galaxy* and *F&SF*; it came because talented science fiction writers were able to break into the world of glossy magazines: Robert Heinlein into *Collier's* and the *Saturday Evening Post*, for instance, and Ray Bradbury into *Mademoiselle*.

This breaking-out, as it were, signalled that SF was to be taken seriously. During the 30's and 40's most writers considered "art" a pejorative word, and were embarrassed by it. On the other hand, they were writing for pulp magazines, and "pulp" is a pejorative word to the literary community as a whole. The word refers actually to the cheap paper used by the chains; it is extended to the writing, its characteristics being said to be: "wooden characterization, wish-fulfulment milieux, bad prose and physical action." But a glance at world literature will satisfy the reader that these characteristics are not confined to pulp.

Surely art was created by pulp writers. Its presence has been detected and confirmed by the existence of such bodies as the Science Fiction Research Association. Readers of this fiction seemed to implicitly define "literary" as having a slow pace, moody atmosphere, italicized passages, and bathos. "Non-literary" seems to them to mean "crispness". Thus in the opinion of readers of *Planet Stories* in the 40's Bradbury is "literary" while Poul Anderson writing as A.A. Craig is either "terrific" or "terrible", but never literary. Yet Anderson's vocabulary, and his use of archetype and the forms of classical saga are as much "literary" as anything Bradbury has written.

Obviously then there was a confusion between art and artiness; writers disliking artiness might refuse to be considered artistic at all. But obviously it would be rewarding to the student of pulp art, which unquestionably exits, to seek its roots in the milieu which caused it and which may even have made its existence inevitable.

I believe that science fiction was uniquely susceptible to the creation of art. The conceptual milieux of every other-chain form were more confining. Tarzan's jungle, the timeless West and even Hammett's San Francisco are all fantasy lands, but their boundaries are established by how much the reader does not know about their real-life counterparts. When a point is reached where the reader knows something about Africa, Tombstone or Geary Street, invention stops, and the writer must acknowledge the known.

The science fiction reader, however, knows nothing about what goes on beyond the envelope of the earth, or about what will happen tomorrow. His willingness to read material based on the unknown extends to a willingness to accept the products of the writer's imagination. You cannot turn a SF story into a western by putting a cowboy into it, but you irrevocably turn a western into sf by giving your cowboy a raygun. SF is the more potent form.

Given all that, we see only a few results from the writing of pulp SF. One is a pseudo-Silverberg: the writer who unfailingly delivers the minimum expected, on time, and done to specifications, as long as he can be accepted. Another result is the real Bradbury, who wrote pulp fiction and then shifted to other media, responding obviously to personal imperatives that had always been present in his work. It also yields, by extension, the real Stanislaus Lem. It specifically does not yield Boris and Arkady Strugatsky. It yields Robert Heinlein who took the pulps with him into higher-paying media.

During the bulk of the period during which American science fiction was formed, there were no escape hatches to other markets for SF writers: they either wrote like Silverberg or they did not write for publication at all, unless they could find some kind of compromise between those extremes. A number of talented writers were able to work out a compromise, in the shadow of the chain strictures. It should be borne in mind that many of these writers were broadly educated, in the arts and humanities as well as in the sciences. The "narrow technist" picture of the science fiction writer is inaccurate; even those with technical degrees received them in days when college science curricula had a broader range than it does today.

Art flourishes under oppression. This is perhaps not a conscious response on the part of the artist. There seems to be a struggle against confinement, and escape of the imagination into a conceptual world. Possibly then what some people find irredeemably crass and arbitrary about chain methods of publishing could have acted as stimulus to writers to create an art form which is advanced in some ways over the "classical" speculative fiction which preceded Gernsback. One does not like to say that the end justifies the means here, but it is at least possible that in its own way the chain-editorial bullpen was a wellspring.

If this possibility exists, then it is important that scholars make some attempt to understand it and to reckon with it. In any event, they must take it into account.

Horace L. Gold,
An Editor With English

Joseph Marchesani

The most revealing anecdote about Horace Gold—the editor who made *Galaxy Magazine* preeminent in science fiction during the fifties—comes from Frederik Pohl. With retrospective good humor Pohl tells how he and Cyril Kornbluth took Gold's own story "The Man with English" and did unto Gold as so many writers believed Gold had done unto them.

> Ah, the creativity of that evening! No manuscript has ever been as edited as that one. We changed the names of the characters. We changed their descriptions. If they were tall, we made them short. We gave them Irish brogues and made them stutter. We switched all the punctuation at random and killed the point of all the jokes. We mangled his sentence structure and despoiled the rolling cadence of his prose...
>
> And then, with great cunning, I let the manuscript be mixed in with some others intended for Horace, as if by accident, and dropped them all off at his apartment on my way home from work. And by the time I walked into my house the phone was ringing.
>
> If you ask Horace about it now, he will tell you, sure, he knew it was a gag all the time. Don't you believe him. "Fred," he said,

"uh, listen. I mean—well, look, Fred. You know I'm a pro. I don't object to editing. But..." Long pause. Then, "Jesus, Fred!" he finished.[1]

The anecdote is a great joke in the classic pattern of the-biterbit. Its humor pointedly reflects in its exaggeration the one quality in Gold's editorial practice for which he can be criticized: his inability to leave well enough alone when he received a story. His habits of editorial intervention often exceeded what his contributors considered to be appropriate limits.

On the other hand, however, Gold was the most innovative and stimulating editor of science fiction in the 50's. Any assessment of Gold as an editor must include consideration of both his constant intervention and the results he achieved for the medium in which he was working.

To those familiar with the history of science fiction, Gold's stature is self-evident. When he founded *Galaxy Magazine* he was already a successful free-lance writer of fantasy, mystery and comic books. *Galaxy* provided a niche for him as one of a select circle of editors, including John Campbell and Anthony Boucher, who kept the genre technologically informed, literate and socially astute. Gold himself specialized in satire. In the early 50's, the boom years for science fiction, Gold's *Galaxy* set the pace for its competitors.

By raising standard payment for a story from 2¢ to 3¢ a word, Gold was able to attract the kind of writers who, a decade earlier, had made Campbell's *Astounding* pre-eminent. For instance, he printed Heinlein's *The Puppet Masters*, Asimov's *The Caves of Steel*, Pohl and Kornbluth's *Gravy Planet* (*The Space Merchants*) and Bester's *The Demolished Man*. Through these kinds of works, *Galaxy* redefined the limits of the genre.

Gold's stature in the literary development of science fiction has begun to be acknowledged as critical interest in the genre increases. Gold himself has written a pair of autobiographical sketches, "Gold on Gold"[2] and "Gold on Galaxy"[3], in which his picture of himself as a dedicated and pragmatic editor, working to get outstanding material for his magazines, is not quite the one we see in the reminiscences of those writers who submitted their work to him. With varying degrees of acceptance, these writers describe him as an editor whose obvious genius was matched by his ability to expasperate them.

An additional source for information about Gold's editorial habits is Gold's correspondence with his contributors. One such file, 33 letters exchanged between Gold and James Gunn from January 1952 to October 1957, is held by the Kenneth Spencer Research Library at the University of Kansas.[4]

When this correspondence began in 1952 Gunn had been publishing stories for three years under the pseudonym of Edwin James. One of his eight stories, "Private Enterprise", had appeared in *Galaxy* in 1952. In the period 1952-1956 he published 29 titles, including the novel *This Fortress World*; nine of his titles were published by Gold, and Gunn indicates in his letters that he prefers placing his stories in *Galaxy* to all other magazines. In fact, the first story to appear under his own name, "the Misogynist," appeared in *Galaxy*.

Although the correspondence does not contain exchanges on all the stories Gunn sent to Gold, it does illustrate some of Gold's working methods, and therefore gives us focus to the image of Gold found elsewhere, including his own autobiographical sketches.

Gold considers his judgment to be the central ingredient in his achievement as an editor. "One thing I never had trouble with was appraising a story at any point in its creation, no matter at what point I intervened—idea, outline, rough draft, whatever."[5] This self-assurance is reflected in a note to Harry Altschuler, Gunn's agent on October 21, 1954 about a story which Gold has rejected. "You'll sell it somewhere," Gold writes, "but I hope neither of you considers that proof that I was wrong about the illogicality of the idea." And, in fact, his standards *were* higher than those of other editors. These, along with the field's most generous pay scales, guaranteed him a first look at the work of the best writers in the genre.

But his self-assurance could easily spill over into arrogance. He is aware of this, and attempts some defense. "I'm a professional editor," he writes, "which means I put aside my convictions if they get in the way of a story."[6] And he writes to Gunn on October 16, 1953: "I judged the story, evaluated some directions you seem to be taking (the tendency toward staccato writing and cliché business) and made my objections dispassionately, professionally...and empathetically, having done my share of blundering in the past and reserving the right to be as fallible as the next guy." And on December 11, 1953 he writes, "I know this is a deflating sort of letter and I hate to have to write it. But I'd rather haul you back from the ledge than race down and try to break your inevitable fall." He was an objective critic who realized the importance of tempering his judgment with empathy; he may not always have been able to do this, but he realized it was a desirable quality.

The most basic idea he had about narrative was that it be logical and coherent. In the December 11 letter he writes Gunn, "Look, here's the best, most valuable and most instantaneously usable yardstick of the potential value of an idea: If you can express it in a single sentence, its very likely to be a strong, clear, easily handled and effective story...assuming, of course, that you haven't selected something that's been overdone."

Gunn followed this dictum in subsequent proposals he sent to Gold.

Gold next seeks true development: "there should be a strong, almost inexorable sense of logic," he says, even in fantasy.[7] When he senses a lack of logic, he speaks sharply: "I'm not tearing your idea down, purely for the sake of hearing it go smash. My job is to buy stories, not reject them. But how does this theme hold up under any kind of intelligent examination?"[8]

He sums up his touchstone ideas: "I had some basic editorial requirements for material. One was, if you've got a premise, start with it. Don't end with it...The second thing was, if it's an old, trite idea, then take it literally. Turn it inside out. Carry it as far as it will go, even beyond the snapping point...Third, seek paradoxes."[9]

These are the ideas which gave *Galaxy* its originality. A story like "The Marching Morons" is given its bits by just such an approach: intelligent people have become the overworked servants of the dull masses. When Gunn, having written a story in which mathematics was the foundation for magic, asks whether the story would not be better without the math, Gold replies that the math is what sets the story apart.[7]

At the same time, Gold insists that a story works best when it includes elements of the familiar. This establishes a common ground with the reader; it is like H.G. Wells's dictum that the genre should domesticate the impossible hypothesis. In *The War of the Worlds*, for instance, the reader is drawn into the narrative by Wells's use of a local setting and ordinary people. But as Gold and Wells were aware, the familiar can be a source of originality, since the exceptional and remarkable has been exploited for so long that it has become conventional. Gold advises that everyday objects might be used to achieve stronger effects than more spectacular devices: "The typewriter is another proof that the really vast societal changes are brought about by seemingly unimportant things...Much more than today's international strife, or atomic power, or perhaps rocketry, there are significant-looking gadgets in the lab or even in common use that will shape the future."[10] He uses the familiar as a test for the logic of the

science fiction adventure: *"...*once established, the pattern of civilization remains remarkably fixed...It's only by studying the past that we
can guess shrewdly at the future. The trick is not to get stuck in the past
but to use it as a departure point."[11]

The interpretation of the past means reading human responses to
world events, and the extrapolation from the past to the future means
reading human response to possible events. The value lies not so much
in the scale of the event as in the nature of the response to it. Domesti-
cating the impossible hypothesis means keeping human response in
the foreground of the narrative. Gold held that characters who adjust
to circumstances are more interesting than characters who rebel
against them, because the misfits, so to speak, who have generally been
the protagonists of science fiction have become trite through overuse.
Gold writes to Gunn on December 18, 1954:

> If the conflict consists of rebellion, whether individual or socie-
> tal, there are only so many combinations possible. But if the
> situation, whatever it might be, is accepted and a strong
> attempt is made to adjust to it, the permutations are as limited
> as the number and complexity of the persons living in that
> environment. The attempt to adjust may be doomed...yet the
> great majority will try its absolute damndest to get along
> somehow.

He is quite aware that, taken to its extreme, this attitude would find a
story about Rosencrantz and Guildenstern more interesting than a
story about Hamlet. "Now don't demand that I be inflexible and apply
this standard in every case without exception," he adds. "I'm not
inflexible about anything except my refusal to be inflexible. The
built-in conflict can be made brilliantly new by virtuoso treatment, as
in *Gravy Planet* and *The Demolished Man.* Wouldn't I have been a
damned fool to have insisted otherwise?"

He elaborates in *Galaxy,* on his vision of good science fiction: "The
first goal is entertainment...interesting ideas, characters, conflict,
situations, backgrounds...What science fiction must present entertain-
ingly is speculation. Not prophecy but fictional surmises based on
present factors, scientific, social, political, cultural, or whatever."[12]

Obviously, entertainment is not enough, although he must have it.
As he says in an undated note to Gunn, "I am a nut for entertainment."
But he knows what he demands in entertainment: "science fiction
writers are the logical pipelines between the scientists and the public,

as far as the *interpretation* (not the mere reporting) of new ideas is concerned. It is the imagination in depth of a first-rate science fiction writer that can flesh out a dry technical report and show us in human terms what these gifts in the laboratory will mean."[13]

Here we have the classic Horatian formula: *dulce et utile*, entertainment and interpretation. It is a demanding formula. And he was demanding, that is why his reputation exists. He solicited stories, pushing ideas on writers whenever he could. And he insisted on rewriting and revisions when the stories came in. Philip Klass (William Tenn) mentions Gold's habit of phoning him and other writers to discuss the progress they were making.[14] He wrote to them often, too, as he makes clear to Gunn on July 26, 1954: "When I suggested correspondence on ideas, it was because there seemed no reason for you to lose out on something that writers around N.Y. are free to call upon—stimulation, suggestions, guidance."

Gunn acknowledges Gold's helpfulness to him in his early career. Responding on October 21, 1953 to a two-page critique from Gold on the story *"Sine of the Magus"*, Gunn thanks him, and says, "I thought that kind of editor was extinct. Your letter was the first of its kind and was especially welcome here in the hinterland."

Frederick Pohl, Gold's successor as editor of *Galaxy* and a significant force in his own right, has credited Gold with the editorial stimulus that led Pohl to write *Gravy Planet*. He describes Gold: "There are very famous stories that began as slop, until some editors worked painfully with the writer, over a long time, coaxing him into changes, hewing out of the shapeless fat of the first draft a work of art. Then, years later, when the story is a classic, no one but the writer knows that it was the editor who made it so."[15]

All writers did not appreciate Gold's direction and prodding. He says himself, "I worked hard with writers, and they didn't always enjoy it."[5]

Gold was quick to deny any personal animus against a story. To Gunn he wrote on October 16, 1953:

> You're a developing writer and a good guy. That's the immutable. Your stories aren't yourself and you aren't your stories. That's the variable. Whether I can or can't buy them depends entirely on each and has no effect on the immutable factor. Now, for Christ's sake, do you catch? I'm taking the time to explain in the hope that you won't have to accumulate the amount of scar tissue I've collected. And I'm doing it in the full

realization that it sounds perfectly obvious and even insulting in its apparentness...yet no lesson I've learned in 19 years of writing has been as important...or as hard and painful to learn.

In the light of this it is interesting to encounter his retrospective remark that *"Galaxy* was me. I was it, and it was me. Anything that threatened me threatened the magazine. Complete identification. Total."[16] His identification with the magazine fuses the personal and the professional, a fusing that he has warned Gunn is impossible.

The stories that were submitted to Gold were in an important sense *his* stories. He did in fact often offer writers his own story ideas for development, and he intervened in the development process with more of his own ideas for revision, and after a story was completed he imposed additions and alterations. The reactions of writers to these practices depended on the resilience of their egos and the stages at which Gold intervened.

Most writers seem to have been grateful for his help. Theodore Sturgeon cites an instance in the early 50's where Gold helped him to overcome a writer's block.[17] Frederick Pohl, describes Gold's help with *Gravy Train*: "Horace *would* edit. He would also come up with suggestions as the work was going along, great gobs of them, some bright and some lunatic."[18] Alfred Bester, with whom Gold says he spent four hours a week on the telephone for a year and a half discussing *The Demolished Man*, called his relationship with Gold "an ideal collaboration." Gold, he says, "discussed the ideas, took them apart, put them together again, and combined and recombined them."[19] Philip Klass, whose attitude toward Gold is notably ambivalent, says, "I know that I might never have written 'Betelgeuse Bridge' if it had not been for the magazine and the milieu that Horace Gold created."[20]

There were times, however, when writers felt that Gold's demands were damaging to them, particularly when these demands seemed to reflect a lack of confidence in the writer's abilities. Frederick Pohl, after noting that Gold "personalized the editorial function more than any other person I ever have known," says that Gold's "battle to substitute his own conception of a story for the writer's caused fury and frustration."[21] Gold himself mentions that "Beyond Bedlam" by Wyman Guin was rewritten twice "end to end."[22] Gunn refers in the correspondence to one story that he revised four times before it was finally accepted.[23]

On July 26, 1954 Gold wrote Gunn, obviously reacting against Gunn's unhappiness over his editing procedures:

You want me to approve instead of argue an idea into shape,
because you settle immovably on a theme and development,
whereas a story, to me, is a fluid thing right up to the moment it
hits the press.
If that's true of your attitude, you're probably right about doing
the stories without discussion; all I can do by treating it as
something fluid, changeable, is distress and confuse you.

On July 31, 1954 Gunn attempted to put his case, probably not for
the first time:

If I become hesitant to write, it may be through the fear—
mistaken or real—that you may become unalterably prejudiced
against an idea...I have a feeling that you are overestimating the
importance of the plot summary and underestimating my ability to turn it into dramatic values [sic]...I am not asking for
approval; I just wish you would say occasionally, 'The idea has
dramatic possibilities, but these are the holes I see in it...' or 'I
don't see it as a story for these reasons, but if you feel strongly
about it, go ahead and write it and I'll be glad to be proved
wrong.

Philip Klass compares Gold with John Campbell, another influential editor. Both men, he said, "were intricate thinkers about a thousand things...great editors with a single, magnificent flaw: They so
completely became editors that they saw their writers as mere pencils or
typewriters." Klass wanted to be treated with respect; to him Gold's
methods were "awful...He would ask me what I was writing and how I
was handling the idea; then he'd tell me where I'd gone wrong and the
only way to save the story. 'But that's *your* story, Horace,' I'd say
despairingly, watching what had been an exciting idea fall apart into
separate bits and pieces all over my typewriter table. He'd apologize."[24]
Alfred Bester describes Gold's "witty, perceptive opinions" as
"charming entertainment."[19] Other writers, however, felt that Gold
could be less than charming. Philip Klass mentions an "oral rejection
slip" which Gold gave Isaac Asmiov at a party attended by other
writers: Gold called one of Asimov's stories "meretricious".[25] James
Gunn says that even Gold's acceptances could sound like rejections.[26]
Gold wrote to Gunn about a story. "I'm glad you realize that my
buying it is, as you put it, the least of evils. I won't be ashamed to run
the story, but I do regret it's not being as good as it might have been."[27]

Nearly every writer who has written about Gold mentions his pratice of altering stories he had accepted for publicaton. Gold was casual about this: in accepting one story he notes, "It works fine now. Just needs a line or two at the end."[28] He does not mention that he has changed the title. A comparison of the typescript of "Wherever You May Be" at the Spencer Library, with the printed story in *Galaxy* (May, 1953) reveals that the *Galaxy* text contains several thousand words of editorial interpolations.

A few writers found ways to deal with this. Theodore Sturgeon, for example: "If I had a certain turn of phrase or a sequence that I didn't want him to mess with, I would write 'stet' in the margin—a printer's term which means 'run it as it stands.' And he never failed to respect it."[29] Lester del Rey had his own method: "I found that this problem seemed to arise from the unwillingness of writers to warn him on this; in my case he agreed to make no changes without my consent and kept his word scrupulously." Still, del Rey has noted that the version of his *Wind Between the Worlds* in *Galaxy* satisfied him less than it satisfied Gold. When he reprinted the work, del Rey restored his original characterization and ending.[31] Frederik Pohl also restores his original work for reprinting.[32]

Pohl says that even Cyril Kornbluth ("compleat pro, casehardened against all editorial madness") could be driven wild by Gold's changes. And Philip Klass remarks that "it was so awful to find a paragraph of Horace's private musing in the middle of one of my stories that I swore (falsely) never to send him a manuscript again."

Pohl thinks that Gold developed this habit of editorial interference during his training as an editor on the pulps under Leo Margulies, who judged the quality of an editor's work by the amount of marks he made on a manuscript.[33] Algis Budrys thinks Gold wanted to neutralize the conventional elements of the stories he printed.[34]

Whatever the reason, Gold was able to generate great creative excitement during *Galaxy's* early years, a period about which Barry Malzberg has written:

> It seemed possible to remake the field. By the end of the forties, Campbell and his best writers had put the technical equipment of the modern short story into the hands of those ready to begin. Hiroshima and television and the Cold War had put into the hands of the new writers and editors what appeared to be an enormous audience for fiction that would truly come to terms with the potential changes in lives caused by new and inexpli-

cable technology. It was Horace Gold's earnest belief that he could have *Galaxy* read by as many people as *The Saturday Evening Post*.[35]

As we read and reread the stories which are the sign and product of that belief—*The Space Merchants, Baby Is Three, The Demolished Man*—we are disposed to forgive any editorial shortcomings which attended their creation. For their creation is inseparable from Horace Gold. And his reputaton rests upon his catalytic responsibility for their existence.

NOTES

[1] Frederick Pohl, *The Way the Future Was* (NY: Ballantine Books, 1978), pp. 189-190.

[2] Horace L. Gold, "Gold on Gold" in *What'll They Think of Last?* (Crestline, California: Inst. for the Dev. of the Harmonious Human Being, 1978), pp. 142-151.

[3] Horace L. Gold, "Gold on *Galaxy*" in *Galaxy, Thirty Years of Innovative Science Fiction* (Chicago: Playboy Press, 1980), pp. 2-7.

[4] I am grateful to the Institute for Arts and Humanistic Studies of Pennsylvania State University, for a grant which enabled me to travel to Lawrence for this research, and to Anne Hyde and the Spencer Library staff for their courteous and unfailing assistance. The correspondence deals primarily with stories and story proposals which Gunn was submitting to Gold. Gold published seven of Gunn's stories in *Galaxy*: "The Misogynist" (Nov., 1952); "Wherever You May Be" (May, 1953); "Open Warfare" (May, 1954); "The Cave of Night" (Feb., 1955); "Little Orphan Android" (Sept., 1955); "The Gravity Business" (Jan., 1956), and Tsylana (Mar., 1956), and two in *Beyond Fantasy Fiction*: "Sine of the Magus" (May, 1954) and "The Beautiful Brew" (Sept., 1954).

[5] Gold, "Galaxy", p. 5.

[6] Gold, *What'll They Think*, p. 65.

[7] Gold to Gunn, October 16, 1953.

[8] Gold to Gunn, July 26, 1954.

[9] Gold, "Galaxy", p. 6.

[10] Gold, *What'll They Think*, p. 36.

[11] Gold, *What'll They Think*, p. 60-61.

[12] Horace L. Gold, "Step Outside" in *Galaxy Magazine* (Nov., 1951), pp. 2-3.

[13] Gold, *What'll They Think*, p. 74.

[14] Philip Klass, "From a Cave Deep in Stuyvesant Town etc" in *Galaxy*, p. 33-34.

[15] Pohl, *Future*, p. 107.

[16] Gold, "Galaxy," p. 7.

[17] Theodore Sturgeon, *The Stars are the Styx* (NY: Dell, 1979), pp. 9-10.

[18] Pohl, *Future*, p. 212.

[19] Alfred Bester, "Horace, Galaxyca," in *Galaxy*, p. 424.

[20] Klass, p. 35.

[21] Pohl, *Future*, pp. 212-213.

[22] Horace Gold, "Ask a Foolish Question," in *Galaxy Magazine* (Aug., 1951), p. 159.

[23] Gunn to Gold, October 9, 1953. Letter is misdated 1951.

[24] Klass, p. 34.

[25] Klass, P. 32.

[26] James E. Gunn, *Alternate Worlds, An Illustrated History of Science Fiction* (Englewood Cliffs, N.J.: Prentice Hall, 1975), p. 219.

[27] Gold to Gunn, December 11, 1953.

[28] Gold to Gunn, October 6, 1953.

[29] Sturgeon, p. 9.

[30] Lester del Rey, *The World of Science Fiction: 1926-1976, The History of a Subculture* (NY: Ballantine, 1979), p. 171.

[31] del Rey, *The Early del Rey*, Vol. II (NY: Ballantine, 1975), p. 278.

[32] Pohl, *Future*, p. 212.

[33] Pohl, *Future*, p. 188.

[34] Algis Budrys, "Memoir: Spilled Milk" in *Galaxy*, pp. 171-172.

[35] Barry N. Malzberg and Bill Pronzini, eds., *The End of Summer: Science Fiction of the Fifties* (NY: Ace Books, 1979), p. 8.

PART THREE:

APPROACHES TO "HARD" SCIENCE FICTION

Whether by professional training or literary bias, much of the criticism written by academics about science fiction has focused on those authors who are principally distinguished by such literary traits as style and characterization or by authors who treat social or ideological concerns. For many readers, however, science fiction means the rational extrapolation of imaginary worlds, beings, or inventions. The two categories are not mutually exclusive, of course, and as the following two essays demonstrate, authors traditionally regarded as belonging to the "hard science" school of science fiction writing may yield hidden rewards when treated with informed sensitivity, and their texts may be opened up by such criticism as readily as those of writers whose works are sometimes labeled "social science fiction." Certainly, Hal Clement and Larry Niven are two of the master world-builders of modern science fiction, but sometimes the awesomeness and ingenuity of their creations may overshadow other important aspects of the works in which they appear—such as irony in the work of Clement or a surprising possible source for a work by Niven.

Donald M. Hassler is a professor of English and director of Experimental Programs at Kent State University. He has published two books on Erasmus Darwin and lately has written extensively on twentieth century hard science fiction, including a volume on Hal Clement in the Starmont series of monographs on science fiction authors, of which the present essay is a part.

The Irony In Hal Clement's Word Building

Donald M. Hassler

Hal Clement's third novel, *Mission of Gravity* (1854) and its sequel, *Star Light* (1971) are master works of hard science fiction, which illustrate Clement's stubborn adherence to values of accumulative knowledge and his ironic acceptance of limitations.

Both of these novels are essentially stories of the exploration, on a grand scale, of one unique planet within a wide world of variable possibilities. They are stories of communication: non-human aliens work both with human explorers and with explorers from other species. Since in many cases the goals of these various life forms do not agree, communication between them is often devious, indirect and partial. However the result of even this unsatisfactory communication is more knowledge for everyone. Often this is new knowledge about the alien life forms themselves.

In *Mission of Gravity* the intelligent natives of Mesklin learn about earth and humans; Cleverly, and deviously they acquire considerable scientific knowledge from the humans. As a matter of practical necessity, the aliens and humans must learn each other's languages—no easy task, given the variability of physical form. As the Mesklinites learn human science and technology, the reader inevitably learns an immense amount of fictional, but scientifically plausible, detail about widely variable planetary environments.

Gravity and Weather

On the solid principle that all life is part and parcel of its environment, Clement has said that he began thinking about the setting for *Mission of Gravity* before he invented the now famous little aliens that inhabit it. An accepted notion in planet studies was that wide variations in gravitational force would not exist nearby in the same environment (apparently before Black Hole speculation), so Clement calculated the conditions that would allow an exception to this notion of non-variable gravity. He worked out the details of the planet Mesklin in a nonfiction essay, "Whirligig World", which is mostly about the physical characteristics of the planet. Clement challenges the reader to go through astronomical and chemical analyses with him and try to catch him in omissions or errors of calculation. Later, he admits that he was wrong in some details—but that is just part of the ironic detective game he likes to play:

> I was a little unhappy when the MIT science fiction people [NESFA] buckled down and analyzed Mesklin and found that I was wrong, that it would actually have come to a sharp edge at the equator. On the other hand, if they were interested enough to steal computer time from the University and check up on this point, I suppose the story in a way was still fulfilling its aim of creating some fun.[1]

The notion of variability and the possibility of error in a varied universe is central in all of Clement's work. The variability of weather is a major factor in both *Mission of Gravity* and *Star Light*. In the story "Cold Front" (1946), which came from meteorological work he did while he was stationed in he Air Force in England, humans who try to communicate with aliens on a planet called Hekla run into widely varying, unfamiliar weather conditions, caused by the fact that the planet occasionally loses its luminosity when cirrus clouds of carbon particles form in its outer atmosphere. By the time the humans discover this, the weather expert's aircraft is nearly destroyed in an unexpected cold front. Hekla's weather is more closely connected than ours with stellar change. By withholding information from him, the Helkans are able to gain some power over the human meteorologist.[2] Clement's longer fictions about Mesklin hinge on variability in weather and gravity, along with intense competition for information.

The planet of Mesklin is fascinating: it appears first in *Mission of Gravity*, is discussed scientifically in "Whirligig World",[3] used as a point of reference in *Star Light*, and figures most recently in "Lecture Demonstration", a short story written in 1973 for a John Campbell memorial collection. Clement began speculating about the fictional planet to try to solve an astronomical puzzle, to which theorists now think the answer is a black hole. In the double star system 61 Cygni A, not many light years from Earth, the fainter star was observed to move around an invisible center of gravity, 16 times the mass of Jupiter, that moved in turn around 61 Cygni A, a star similar to our own sun, but smaller and dimmer. Clement speculated that the invisible center in this system was a massive planet, and set to work to construct this planet not only with high gravity, a familiar convention, but with variable gravity. Going on Einstein's principle, which is used in training our astronauts that "gravitational effects cannot be distinguished from inertial ones [and] the so-called centrifugal force is an intertial effect," Clement decided that his planet would spin rapidly enough so that his characters would feel progressively lighter as they got closer to the equator, despite the fact that the planet Mesklin exerts three times Earth's gravity at the equator and nearly 700 times Earth's gravity at each pole.

In conversation Clement describes Mesklin as "a rather weird-looking object". It is 48,000 miles in diameter at its equator, and measures 19,740 miles from pole to pole along its axis. Its spin rate is so rapid that a "day" is only seventeen and three-quarters minutes long. The seasons are determined by its highly elliptical orbit around its primary, which is a fairly dim red dwarf to start with, and by the steep tilt of its axis. Consequently the northern hemisphere has no sunlight for three-quarters of the year, while spring and summer in the southern hemisphere lasts for 28 months. Thus nearly the entire northern hemisphere is covered with frozen methane during most of the year, while the southern hemisphere contains oceans of liquid methane. Tremendous storms are generated across the equator during the two months that the north faces the sun, as the polar icecap boils off, the seas rise, and methane vapor is added under high pressure to the nearly pure hydrogen atmosphere. (Large planets hold their original hydrogen.) The temperatures which we would consider very cold, since we know methane only as a natural gas, are balanced with compounds that change at those temperatures to produce both dramatic weather conditions and a liquid and atmospheric base for the development of life. Winter in the southern hemisphere is warm, but not warm enough to boil away the methane in the bodies of the Mesklanites, and the summer is long and cold. Similarly, time on the rapidly spinning planet seems odd to the humans who visit. Occasionally Clement uses this time differential for comic effect. A human will say, "We'll be out of here in a couple of hours!"; the narator will comment, "Actually, it took less than three days." That would, in Mesklin time, be about 56 minutes. Clement cannot tell everything about this strange, fascinating world of Mesklin: in "Whirligig World" he says several times that there will always be more data to check. Like the shrewd little traders and explorers that inhabit Mesklin, Clement always seems to want to learn more, to speculate further.

Little Epic Characters and Journeys

If the planet Mesklin is peculiar compared to Earth, its inhabitants are even stranger by anthropocentric standards. To use a Swiftian image, they might be said to be Lilliputians in a Brobdignagian world. Clement is interested in creating plausible physical bases for life on Mesklin, although he says in conversation that he does not feel he needs to develop an explanation for all inner life systems, since there is no comprehensive explanation for life systems on Earth.

Mesklinites are fifteen inches in length and two inches in diameter; they resemble caterpillars, although they have developed an extremely tough chitinous exoskeleton because of gravity. They have strong "nippers" instead of hands.

When *Mission of Gravity* opens, Charles Lackland, an explorer who has been near the Mesklin equator for several Earth months, has fallen in with a group of Mesklinites and has taught their leader, Barlennan, some English. Barlennan is a trader and captain of the sailing ship *Bree*, which is constructed of several rafts lashed together. Everything, including the natives, is built very close to the surface of the planet because of the intense grip of gravity. The *Bree* is capable of navigating tens of thousands of miles across the oceans of the southern hemisphere. Barlennan's people live near the south pole. Thus their presence at their equator, where they must be disoriented by light gravity, demonstrates their bravery and adventurous spirit. They call the equatorial region "the rim" because the high gravity causes the horizon to appear to be higher than the viewer. All Meskalite maps are therefore shaped like bowls instead of globes. A Mesklinite's greatest fear is to *fall* or be *beneath* a large object (in *Star Light* their buildings have transparent roofs) because conditions there have precluded any activities like jumping or throwing; any fall, at 600 Earth gravities, would be immediately fatal.

The stories are narrated in the omniscient third person. At least half the time the point of view is Barlennan's or another Mesklinite's. The reader learns about the Mesklinites, then, from their point of view: we are often told, for instance, how difficult it is to conceive of life on a planet that spins so slowly that one full rotation takes eighty "days".

At first the Mesklinites appear to be more suspicious, shrewd and manipulative than humans. They conceal their intentions, and assume that the humans will conceal theirs. But as the Mesklinite stories develop, the humans become more duplicitous so that Barlennan's manipulations are seen as analogues for human behavior, and the alien point of view becomes a classic commentary on human vice and folly much in the Swiftian manner. But one of Clement's major themes is the gradual accumulation of partial knowledge, and Barlennan's motivation and behavior emphasize this.

Three factors affect Mesklinite culture. One is competitiveness. Mesklin teems with life forms (this is ironic, considering the low temperature liquid methane base), all seeking to outdo one another. The second factor is their long life span. In *Star Light* Barlennan is incredulously condescending to the humans who come and go with what he considers strange rapidity. Paradoxically, the third factor is the physical makeup of the planet itself. Mesklin's steep axial tilt reverses itself at frequent intervals (in millenial terms) so that life forms must establish themselves first on one hemisphere and then on the other. Pressures for evolutionary development are thus similar to, but more rapid than, those produced by our Ice Age. Barlennan and his people want to learn about modern science; they are especially interested in flight and space technology. They want to use it for trading purposes, and they have an obsession about learning which comes from a long tradition of rapid evolutionary response to challenge.

The humans persuade the Mesklinites to undertake the long perilous journey across the land and sea to the south polar region; they want to retrieve a valuable research rocket that is grounded in high gravity there. This long journey filled with obstacles is one of the elements that has caused the critic Neil Barron to compare *Mission of Gravity* with the Greek epics.[4] In shrewd Odyssean fashion Barlennan agrees to make the trip but hides his real motive for going. At the end of chapter twelve he discusses his motives with his mate:

"I think you know by now what I'm really hoping to get out of this trip; I want to learn everything I possibly can of the Flyers' science. That's why I want to get to that rocket of theirs near the Center; Charles himself said that it contained much of the most advanced scientific equipment they have. When we have that, there won't be a pirate afloat or ashore who'll be able to touch the *Bree*..."

"I think you're too suspicious yourself. Have you ever *asked* for any of this scientific information that you want to steal?"

"Yes; Charles always said it was too difficult to explain."

When after many exotic and challenging adventures, Barlennan and his crew finally find the research rocket, they seize and hold it, saying they will give it up only in return for being taught all the technological knowledge they can master. The humans, surprised by this obsessive desire for information, agree to their terms, although Lackland warns them that he does not understand electrical and nuclear energy, even though he has grown up using them. Barlennan however, replies: "We want to start *at the beginning*, knowing fully that we cannot learn all you know in our lifetime." The book ends with the *Bree*, now converted into a hot air balloon, taking flight against the polar gravity of Mesklin.

Sequels, Belief and Limitations

Of the two sequels to *Mission of Gravity*, the first, the short story "Lecture Demonstration," is set in the equatorial region where a human teacher and his Mesklinite students encounter a life-and-death geologic and chemical puzzle; the second, the novel *Star Light*, (initially serialized in *Analog*, formerly called *Astounding*) is a more ambitious attempt than *Mission of Gravity*.

In *Star Light* which is set fifty years after *Mission of Gravity*, Barlennan is leading a task force of two thousand graduates of the College of Mesklin, equipped with a small fleet of land-cruisers (thin and flexible like the Mesklinite body), to explore a puzzling planet named Dhrawn, which is one of the Type Three planets: large, dense Jovian bodies that have, for some reason, lost their hydrogen atmosphere. The question is whether Dhrawn is not really a star rather than a planet since it emits more radiation than it receives from its dim primary, Lalande 21185. Dhrawn's rotational period is roughly two Earth months; its atmosphere is a dynamic mixture of oxygen, nitrogen, ammonia and water vapor at temperatures which provide a confusing alternation of freezing and thawing, depending on the amounts of ammonia and water present at any time. No human can explore Dhrawn because of its high gravity. It is dangerous for Mesklinites, too, since there is no high pressure hydrogen in the atmosphere. In addition, Dhrawn's "day" lasts for two Earth months, subsuming 5000 Mesklin "days". Despite all this, Barlennan agrees to lead his group to Dhrawn under the direction of a small group of humans who are in a control satellite six million miles away.

One of the Mesklinites' major tasks is to gather weather data. The human weathermen cannot do it here as they can on Mesklin because they are too far away, and they are not familiar with Dhrawn's dynamic conditions. Both Neil Barron and Clement himself have expressed some dissatisfaction with *Star Light* because it is so filled with "technical exposition." But the key image in Clement's work is exactly this unpredictability and variability of weather conditions; I think this is what makes the novel important. Weather resulting from water, ammonia and a source of internal radiation is a perfect symbol for variability. Near the beginning of Ch XII one of the human weather experts radios to a land-cruiser frozen into some unknown ice: "There are just too many variables; with only water they are practically infinite...with water and ammonia together the number is infinity squared."

Interaction between humans is greater in this sequel than in the earlier book. Perhaps the most interesting and well-developed human character is Elise Rich Hoffman (called Easy), a linguist and diplomat who began to learn the Mesklinite language ten years before when her husband, Ib, was first assigned to the Dhrawn project. Both she and her husband have come to understand and appreciate Mesklinite character, including their deceptions. The Hoffman's son, Benj, is a teenaged apprentice on the project. He develops a close attachment to a "young" native, Beetchermarlf, and they practice each other's languages over the radio. Beetch, a pilot on one of the land cruisers, becomes the first Mesklinite space pilot. (Not unexpectedly, by the end of *Star Light* Barlennan's sailors have learned the principles of rocket flight).

The focus on juvenile characters is important here, more than in the Hunter fictions, in which the alien is much older than Bob. In a sense Barlennan and his mate Dondragmer seem young in both novels. That is consistent, since the belief in these books is in forging ahead against great obstacles in an epic and yet refreshingly young way. The most representative humans in *Star Light* are those who are young in years or in spirit, and who share Dondragmer's "philosophy": "to do all one could in the time available, with the full knowledge that time would run out some day."

The Mesklinites know that they are tiny, and they know that all knowledge is partial. There is some excessive technical jargon in the books, despite which Clement does not provide us with any knowledge about the Mesklinites' process of generation. We know only that they are long lived. Sexuality and medicine, important for realistic fiction, are not discussed. The concerns in the novels are, however, important concerns; his universe has epic proportions.

Tenebra and Abyormen: Abundant Life

The project of exploring the planet Tenebra in *Close to Critical* is midway in time between the Mesklin exploration and the Dhrawn project. Easy Hoffman is the twelve-year-old Easy Rich in this novel, seen for the first time showing a young Drommian around the control satellite for the Tenebran project, which had begun sixteen years before the novel opened, apparently about the time of the founding of the College of Mesklin, when human explorers had launched a complex robot on the surface of Tenebra.

Tenebra belongs to Altair, brightest star in the Constellation Aquila, which is relatively close to Mesklin. Although Altair is a white star of the first magnitude, ten times brighter than our sun, Tenebra has little visible light on its surface because of its extremely dense atmosphere, the pressure of which is nearly 800 times that of Earth. Under such high pressure and with sufficient radiation from Altair, the temperature on Tenebra is near the critical temperature of water. During the Tenebran day, which equals about four Earth days, the temperatures rise above water's critical temperature at that atmospheric pressure, so that the lower atmosphere, which has turned into liquid water at night when the temperature drops, vaporizes. All rivers and ponds evaporate. Only large bodies of oily sludge and other liquids, such as sulphuric acid, remain.

The continual daily movement on Tenebra due to the critical temperature of water at this enormous pressure (about 370° fahrenheit) produces weather which is not wind and convection currents, but a continuous change from liquid to gas and back again under a heavy gravitational pull. One of the characters describes it:

...the question is not whether it will rain tomorrow but whether your pasture will start to grow into a hill...the atmosphere is mostly water near its critical temperature, and silicate rocks dissolve fairly rapidly under those circumstances. The place cools off just enough each night to let a little of the atmosphere turn liquid, so for the best part of two Earth days you have the crust washing down to the oceans like the Big Rock Candy Mountain. With three Earth gravities trying to make themselves felt, it's hardly surprising that the crust is readjusting all the time.

There is actually a dispute among the explorers about the accuracy of calling these shifts of atmosphere "weather" at all. Eventually "wind" does appear, when an active volcano forces convection currents into the atmosphere. The rate is 2 m.p.h., which is a virtual hurricane for windless Tenebra. In any case, regardless of terminology, Tenebra is a kind of pressure cooker. The characters in the novel reflect the same kind of dynamic tensions, although the environment in this novel is more exciting than the characters, despite the exploration of several provocative relationships.

The most intelligent form on Tenebra, among the myriad lesser biological specimens, is a scaly cone-shaped species with body fluids that contain sulphuric acid, indicating an evolution from their oceans which also contain sulphuric acid, and which connect them to the evolution of vertebrates on Earth. These Tenebrites lay eggs, and have spiny crests that enable them to see in their planet's darkness; they also speak and have analytic minds, although they are at a low stage of cultural and technological development.

The robot lander is engineered to withstand the "ambiguous" atmosphere; it is also an efficient communications device that enables the explorers to establish remarkable remote control.

The robot, whose name is Fagin,[5] spends some time exploring the surface, and then steals some eggs from the Tenebran's nest area; during the years preceding the main action of the novel he has created a village of advanced Tenebrans who have been taught to make fire from wood, a skill that gives them mobility at night, and, more importantly, they have learned English and thus have the capability to learn Earth science and technology. Fagin has taught them to construct rafts so that they can travel on their planet's changing oceans; they are unlike the Mesklinites, who were skillful sailors when the humans arrived.

The Tenebrite adolescents learn so quickly that toward the end of the novel they consider taking Fagin apart to see how he works. They are approximately the same age as Easy Rich and her Drommian companion, who accidently descend to the surface in an unfinished research bathyscaphe, and are unable to return to orbit. Fagin's students are sent to find the ship and repair it. However some untutored Tenebrans find the ship before the students do, and solve the problem by injecting the bathyscaphe tanks with hydrogen from an indigenous life form. This, in conjunction with the wind from the volcano, allows the bathyscaphe to rise. Intelligence is thus at the core of this novel, as is adolescence: Easy and the students are young primitives; the untutored Tenebrans are a species in development, and the planet itself is in developmental flux.

The search for knowledge is a constant theme with Clement. In chapter seven, Fagin delivers a long speech to the untutored natives in which he tells them that if they fix the machine the humans will be able to leave and return with technological advice; if the machine is not repaired, the humans will die and since Fagin himself must die one day too, they will not progress unless they cooperate. This appeal triumphs over the instinctual urges of these primitive beings.

Language is the manifest sign of intelligence: everyone in the book is good with languages: Easy is particularly gifted. Her father says, "She'll learn any language she can pronounce nearly as fast as you can give it to her, Doctor."

Thus on Tenebra, the planet of shade, flux and darkness, the enlightenment prevails. Clement's images and evocation of the strange environment are superb, and he successfully exploits adolescent tensions. The childishness of the young Drommian is often wearing, and there is a certain clumsiness in the narrative, however; possibly this was done deliberately to evoke the atmosphere of adolescence. When he was asked whether he had named the planet with some kind of religious symbolism in mind, Clement said that if he had thought of that, he would not have used the name.[7]

Cycle of Fire (1957)

The idea for Cycle of Fire came from a March 1954 article in Scientific American by Andre Lwoff called "The Life Cycle of a Virus."[6] In a poetic style, that also infuses the novel, Lwoff discusses the way in which certain viruses lie dormant inside bacteria for several generations before reappearing as distinct virus life; he couples the cycles of life and death with reproduction and the protection of generation. The theme for Clement here is the symbolic interdependence of alien life forms. Symbiosis lies at the heart of all Clement's work: close cooperation is essential to the success of each project, and dependence and cooperation are essential to the survival and growth of alien races. The strange relationship between "cold life" and "hot life" on Abyormen as it unfolds, and as it is mirrored in the relationship between the young human explorer and his Abyormenite friend, is an effective symbiotic image.

The setting and narrative structure of this novel set it apart from Clements' other planet novels. Abyormen itself is not really part of the area where Mesklin and Tenebra are found, five par secs, or approximately seventeen light years from Earth. Abyormen is in the Pleiades, part of a system with Alcyone the brightest star, and it is five hundred light years from Earth. The planet is far removed from the common ground of exploration, and here Clement pursues his most profound images of life and death.

Abyormen orbits a red dwarf star called Theer, which is invisible to our telescopes. The friction of Theer and Abyormen may have created the huge blue sun Alcyone out of the nebulosity of the Pleiades cluster, or Alcyone may have captured Theer. In any case, the result is a three-body system: Abyormen's and Theer's orbit of Alcyone is extremely eccentric; it is unstable and produces wide variations in temperature, from which have evolved symbiotic hot and cold life forms. The system has a relatively imminent mortality which complements the other notions of mortality in the novel.

Human exploration of this system appears to be taking place long before the discovery and exploration of Mesklin and the subsequent planet projects. The story is about the companionship between an alien and a human, together on a journey of exploration; Clements' usual tale provides only remote contact between aliens and humans by radio. Since in its cold life orbit around Alcyone, the planet has Earth conditions, the close friendship is possible. During one of these "seasons," a young space cadet named Nils Kruger is shipwrecked and apparently left for dead on Abyormen. He saves the life of Dar Lang Ahn, an alien whose glider has crashed and who is trying to get home across the planet before the hot season begins. Although there are adventures and discoveries, the primary action is the gradual uncovering of the nature of life and death on Abyormen.

Dar's biochemistry is similar to Kruger's; he is human in appearance, although only four and a half feet tall, and with claws instead of fingers and toes. Dar's species is the cold life complement, which can live on the planet's surface for no more than 65 terrestrial years in one cycle. But with the transitional time in the orbit as the planet changes from hot to cold, the life span for Dar's species is 830 of their "years" or orbits around Theer; each year is about eighteen terrestrial days. Dar is a little over forty years old; he knows the exact date of his death. During the hot season a few members of the species are able to survive deep within the Ice Ramparts; they then become teachers who preserve the culture until the next cold season.

Gradually the reader learns how Dar's species merge with their hot life counterparts: human explorers and scientists return to Abyormen and help Kruger unravel the mystery. Hot life creatures are melon-shaped, with six limbs. To the humans they resemble "fat-bodied starfish." They "see" by means of sound waves, since vision is impossible under the brutal rays of Alcyone when it is close to the planet. Despite their blindness hot life teachers have gathered rudimentary knowledge of their system's astronomy. Dar's eyes, by the way, are set on the sides of his head and function independently of each other; he can see farther into the infra-red portion of the spectrum than Kruger can.

At first the humans speculate that the cold and hot life forms are complementary and belong to the same species, like caterpillars and butterflies. They are enlightened by a long conversation via television robot with a hot life teacher who is living deep within a volcanic cavern. The Abyormenite symbiosis is modeled on the virus/bacteria symbiosis discussed by Lwoff, whose article is paraphrased by the scientists in chapter fourteen of this novel. The species are alien to each other; death is necessary for reproduction for both:

> The really important fact is that *Dar Lang Ahn's people have to die in order to reproduce*...the "hot" and "cold" forms are completely alien types of life, which originally evolved independently...a similar ability has developed here—that every cell of a being like Dar Lang Ahn has in its nucleus the factors which will produce one of those starfish under the proper conditions.

Kruger hoped to make Dar indispensable as a teacher, so that he would not have to die at the completion of his appointed span. But Dar's instinct is to reproduce by dying; this instinct is combined with his new understanding of scientific methods that complements his earlier allegiance to his books: a symbiosis of method. Dar has learned from Kruger that partial knowledge accumulated gradually is best. When the friends part, in an emotional moment that is unusual in a Clement novel, Dar says that he believes the humans will help his descendants to overcome the instability of the Alcyone system. All this is in the context of scientific method which, since it builds syntheses out of unrelated data, may be seen as a symbiosis of parts that may be alien to each other. Dar says:

> I could have stayed down below and dictated scores of books about everything I had seen you do or heard you say, but even though I understood a good deal of it my people wouldn't. There was something else they needed more, and gradually I came to understand what it was.
>
> Its *method*, Nils. It's the very way you people go about solving problems—imagination and experiment together...Of course the facts are important too...Nils, many of your years from now there will be quite a lot of my people who are part of me...Maybe with what you and I have done for them some of these people will be scientists, and will...start something which may in time be a civilization like yours. I would like to think that you will be helping them.

In *Galaxies*, his experimental, bitter novel about the limitations of writing science fiction, Barry Malzberg laments that effective narrative about alien life is impossible and unwise. "It would be nice," he says, "to compound the myth of faster-than-light drive with deeper and richer myths of strange races amidst the great stars, but this cannot be."[7] Hal Clement has admitted that his assumption of the possibility of faster-than-light travel is one of his few concessions to scientific implausibility; and following that assumption he has populated the stars with strange life forms. With Mesklin, Tenebra, and the symbiosis on Abyormen, Clement has attempted to do what Malzberg says cannot be done.

NOTES

[1] Interview between the author and Harry Stubbs [Hal Clement], June 22, 1980. Stubbs acknowledges the greater accuracy of the MIT computers in R. Reginald, *Contemporary Science Fiction Authors* II (Detroit: Gale Research Co., 1979), 856.

[2] "Cold Front", first published in *Astounding Science Fiction* (1946) reprinted in Geoff Conklin, ed. *Men Against the Stars* (NY: 1950).

[3] "Whirligig World", first published in *Astounding Science Fiction* (1953), later reprinted as "Author's Afterword" in most editions of the novel.

[4] See Frank N. Magill, ed. *Survey of Science Fiction Literature* (Englewood Cliffs: Salem Press, 1979), pp. 1424-1428.

[5] A minor character among the aliens is named "Oliver". Clement often uses whimsical allusions.

[6] *Scientific American* 190 (March, 1954), 34-37.

The Niven of Oz:
Ringworld *as Science Fictional Reinterpretation*

Thomas J. Remington

In recent years there has been a good deal of critical enthusiasm over the literary merits of the work of Robert Silverberg, Harlan Ellison, Philip K. Dick, Philip Jose Farmer, Barry Malzberg, Frank Herbert, and especially, Ursula Le Guin. In addition critics like Robert Scholes, Eric Rabkin and Bruce Franklin have rediscovered the work of writers of "hard core, hard science" novels and stories from the "Golden Age" of Science Fiction: writers like Isaac Asimov, Arthur C. Clarke and Robert Heinlein. Their sales and reputations are both booming: even as I write, Herbert's *God Emperor of Dune* is a best-seller which has received rave reviews in the columns of popular magazines.

It is odd that so little attention has been paid to the work of Larry Niven.[1] Possibly this is because Niven began writing in the mid-sixties; he is roughly contemporary with such "literary" and comparatively "non-technical" authors as Silverberg, Malzberg and Ellison, while his own most significant contributions to the genre have been "hard science," like the best known efforts of Asimov, Clarke and Heinlein. He appears to have fallen through a crack: literary critics focus on the non-technical authors of the sixties, while scholars of the "Golden Age" ignore Niven as a "modern".

In any case, as Niven's collection of Hugos and Nebulas indicates, he is one of the most popular and respected writers in the genre. His hard science fiction, best represented by the "Known Space" series, is among the "hardest" going. *The Flight of the Horse* is a delightful fantasy, filled with humor unusual in science fiction. His writing is richly allusive to diverse sources: Lewis Carroll, in Wunderland, the bandersnatchi; *Beowulf* in "Grendel" and other Beowulf Schaeffer stories; Dante, with *Inferno* written with David Gerrold, and South Sea "Cargo Cults": *Dream Park*, with Steven Barnes. In addition, several of Niven's essays are superb *vade mecums* of the science fiction field, which ought to be required reading for anyone aspiring to write science fiction, especially "Man of Steel: Woman of Kleenex", "Exercise in Speculation: The Theory and Practice of Teleportation" and "The Theory and Practice of Time Travel" in *All the Myriad Ways*.

My intention here is to analyze *Ringworld*, Niven's best-known and possibly best work. I hope this will serve as a starting point for further studies of his work. As my title indicates, I think that *Ringworld* alludes directly and probably consciously to *The Wizard of Oz*.[2]

In *Wizard* there are of course four main characters, each in search of something. Only one, Dorothy, is a human being; she wants to go home. The other three, non-human, characters each suffer from a notable deficiency. The Scarecrow has no brain, the Tin Woodman no heart, and the Cowardly Lion, no courage. As the plot unfolds, each non-human character finds within himself the quality which he thought he lacked. They had sought the Wizard, to get these things from him, but the Wizard is a humbug, and the qualities had been present, but unrecognized. Dorothy was able to return home by clicking the magic shoes which she had worn since her arrival in Oz; she too had had the answer within reach and had not known it.

As a parallel we have a human character in *Ringworld*, Louis Wu, who is accompanied by three non-human characters, and who is primarily concerned with getting home to earth.

The first of Louis's companions is Nessus, the Pierson's puppeteer, an evolutionary product of herbiverous origins who, true to his herd-animal beginnings, runs from all danger. For the puppeteers, cowardice is natural, moral and healthy, while courage is insane. But the race is extremely powerful. As Speaker-to-Animals says to Nessus, "Your lack of courage had deserved our contempt, Nessus, but our contempt has blinded us. Truly you are dangerous...Your power is terrible..."[3] The fearful and fearsome Nessus is thus a natural counterpart to the Cowardly Lion, lacking the Lion's fierce appearance, of course. The Lion is a product of fantasy; Nessus, whose attributes are logically justified, is an SF extrapolation.

Secondly, there is Speaker-to-Animals, who has evolved from feline-like carnivores, the kzinti: "One *never* offers a kzin hazrd pay. The kzin is not supposed to have noticed the danger!" (p. 12). But the kzinti lack brains; in that way, the Speaker and the Scarecrow are alike. Nessus discusses kzinti history: "Six times over several centuries, you attacked the world of men. Six times you were defeated, having lost approximately two-thirds of your male population in each year. Need I comment on the level of intelligence displayed?" (p. 19). Elsewhere, when Speaker instinctively presumes, incorrectly, that he has been attacked, Louis calls him a "dolt". (p. 123). Why then does Speaker have such a fearsome aspect, if his parallel is the gentle Scarecrow? The answer seems to lie in the logic of his evolutionary background. If intelligent creatures are to be shown dangerously lacking the intelligence necessary for their survival, they must have developed from a species for which naked aggression is more advantageous than cleverness. Everything we know of kzinti culture tells us that that is the story of their development.

Finally, there is Teela. She is the product of an experiment by which the puppeteers manipulated humanity into selective breeding for psychic luck. The "odd power made her...a little different from human" (p. 248); at times "she had seemed...less human than Speaker and Nessus" (p. 292). It was "stupid...to assume that a bred-for-luck human would think like [other] humans" (p. 256).

In *The Wizard*, the Tin Woodman had been a human being, but he had chopped parts from his body and had them replaced with tin, so that he has become something different from human; most notably, in his own mind, he is a creature without a heart. Teela, too, derives from human stock, but differs from Louis Wu and other humans in that she lacks empathy: "her friends would long since have stopped telling her their troubles. Teela didn't understand troubles" (p. 248). When Louis tells Teela that her great-great-grandmother had once given him a "severe case of whiplash of the heart" (p. 23), Teela requests an explanation; after it is given, she says, "But what was the whiplash?" (p. 24). "Louis looked at Teela Brown. Silver eyes looked blankly back, and Louis realized that she hadn't understood a word" (pp 24-25). Louis recognizes that Teela is an alien, who cannot grasp a foreign concept. She cannot understand "whiplash of the heart" because she has never felt pain and, in the figurative sense, she is like the Tin Woodman. She has no heart at all.

There are further allusions. Speaker, the kzin, shares a kind of fearlessness with the Scarecrow, who says, "I'm not afraid...There is only one thing in the world I'm afraid of...It's a lighted match."[4] Speaker is burned twice in *Ringworld*: in chapter 14 his pelt is almost entirely burned off by the dangerous Slaver plants. Later his "translator disc turned red hot and stuck to his palms" (p. 233), causing his hand to be "charred to the bone" (p. 248).

The Tin Woodman too has a particular vulnerability. Moisture causes his body to rust; he becomes immobilized until his joints are oiled. Insofar as the lucky Teela has any problems at all, they parallel those of the Woodman. She freezes in "plateau trance" (p. 157) or "highway hypnosis" (p. 161) on the Ringworld journey and—by implication—is prone to this form of auto-hypnosis because of the armor of luck which protects her, freeing her from the need for any psychological defenses. As her flycycle becomes disabled in a flight through a storm, Teela becomes again unconscious and immobile (pp 243-245).

The Lion's vulnerability is obviously fear, a vulnerability which he shares with Nessus. But the Lion also puts on a great show of ferocity when he joins Dorothy's group, and this parallels Nessus's manic behavior when he and Louis first meet Speaker in Chapter 1. Nessus deliberately insults the Patriarch of Kzin and boasts about defeating another kzin in physical combat.[5]

Harloprillalar, or Prill, functions as the Wizard. Prill had returned to the Ringworld after the fall of civilization, had wandered from the rim wall, where her rampship had landed, to her home city, and is worshipped as a god—or wizard—by the scattered barbarian tribes of the Ringworld. Like the Wizard, she is a humbug; she cannot help the four seekers, who think she is one of the "Builders" of legend. But she was a whore on the ramship. However Prill and Louis share a common human origin, as do the Wizard and Dorothy. (p. 166, 288-289). Further, like the Wizard, Prill wishes to leave and return home, though her home is not the same as Louis's. Again, like the Wizard, she makes her escape, but in a different vehicle from Louis's.

These five characters (Louis-Dorothy, Nessus-Lion, Speaker-Scarecrow, Teela-Woodman and Prill-Wizard) constitute the main parallels between *Wizard* and *Ringworld*. But there are other allusions in *Ringworld* to Baum's book. After the fall of civilization, the people on *Ringworld* have grouped into isolated cultures, somewhat parallel to the folk of Oz: Munchkins, Quadlings, Winkies etc. In the chapter "Interlude with Sunflowers" the seekers are forced to take refuge for a day in a field of flowers, which recalls "The Deadly Poppy Field" of Oz. The "Eye of the Storm" chapter in *Ringworld* may, somewhat distantly, allude to Baum's "The Cyclone". And, though it may be only a coincidence, there are 24 chapters in *Ringworld*, the same number as in the Oz books.

It seems as though Niven were aware of the film based on the Oz book: those elements which were left out of the movie (flying monkeys, magic hats) do not seem to be alluded to in *Ringworld*. In addition, the song "Over the Rainbow", which has no counterpart in the book, seems to crop up in *Ringworld* in the Arch of Heaven, chapter 11. The inhabitants believe the Arch was raised by the Builder, or God (p. 176) "in sign of the Covenant with Man" (p. 173). The words recall Genesis 9:9-17 where the rainbow is described.

There are ways, of course, in which the two books are not analogous. There are no north, south, east or west in Ringworld, and no witches of any direction or persuasion, good, bad or indifferent. There are no magic shoes, and there is no Toto. Speaker and Nessus do not remain on the Ringworld. Yet I think these "perpendiculars" (a term antithetical to parallels) are as important to the relationship between the books as are the congruencies.

Niven regularly applies scientific rationalism to the seemingly miraculous or fantastic. He balances the substance of fantasy with the technology of hard science fiction. He has done this with time travel in the Svetz stories, with the Warlock stories, where he applied the law of conservation to the manna from which magical power derives to explain why magic is no longer available; in *The Flying Sorcerers* we find "The Purple Magician" to be not a magician at all, but a scientist and science fiction writer building a balloon.[7] In *The Inferno* the protagonist looks at Hell, finding some of it beyond his comprehension, but thinking " 'Any sufficiently advanced technology is indistinguishable from magic.' " (p. 95).[8] In *All the Myriad Ways* three essays focus on the relationship between current scientific knowledge, logical extrapolation from that knowledge, and SF gimmicks which he believes should be left in the realm of fantasy.[9]

In "Man of Steel: *Woman of Kleenex*" he considers the scientific result of Superman's sexual aspects: Clark Kent's high-powered ejaculations, the danger to Lois Lane of carrying a super-fetus in her womb. In the essays on teleportation and time travel consider the balance between these two gimmicks and current scientific knowledge.

I believe that in *Ringworld*, too, he is balancing technology and fantasy subtly and artistically. To begin with, he eliminates Toto, who is not a significant factor in *Wizard*, but is only Dorothy's friend. Louis is described as a xenophile for whom "the company of aliens was a vital necessity" (p. 199); but he prefers intelligent aliens. Nowhere in the Niven cannon is there a close attachment between a human and a dumb animal.

Next he has omitted the witches. Witches are good and bad for no logical or evolutionary reason, but Niven's characters always develop from a credible evolutionary background and are rationally motivated.[10] Since unmotivated evil (or good) characters cannot exist in the scientific world of the novel, the *real* villain against which Louis must contend—and of which he remains constantly aware in the way that Dorothy does of the Wicked Witch of the West—is the universe itself and the evolutionary processes by which it works. Louis himself outlines the perverse nature of this motiveless malignity:

> Remember the Finagle Laws. The perversity of the Universe tends toward a maximum. The universe is hostile....
>
> The universe is against me.... The universe hates me. The universe makes no provision for a two-hundred-year-old man.
>
> What is it that shapes a species? Evolution, isn't it? Evolution gives Speaker his night vision and his balance. Evolution gives Nessus the reflex that turns his back on danger. Evolution turns a man's sex off at fifty or sixty. Then evolution quits.
>
> Because evolution is through with any organism once that organism is too old to breed....
>
> A few centuries ago some biological engineers...produced boosterspice. As a direct result, I am two hundred years old and still healthy. But not because the universe loves me.
>
> The universe hates me.... It's tried to kill me many times.... It'll keep trying, too. (p. 143)

This principle of scientific explanation I think, is at the heart of the "perpendiculars" between *Ringworld* and *Wizard*. In the latter work, the ultimate irony is that Dorothy, motivated to get home, leads her friends to discover what they need in order to complete themselves. Only after the Woodman has his heart, the Lion his courage, and the Scarecrow his brain, does Dorothy find out from Glinda that she *could* have returned home all along merely by clicking together three times the heels of the magical slippers she has been wearing since her arrival in Oz. The way home had *always* been at hand, but without Glinda's consent, and without Glinda's magic, Dorothy had no access to the knowledge of how to return to Kansas.

In contrast, consider the situation in *Ringworld*. Like Dorothy, Louis wants to return home; his motive is not Dorothy's emotional longing to return to her family, but rather the rational desire to get the knowledge of the second quantum hyperdrive to humanity, which will need this knowledge to escape eventual destruction from the galactic core explosion.

The space ship, the *Lying Bastard*, is stranded on the Ringworld. It has no motive force but the hyperdrive, and the hyperdrive won't work as long as the ship is as close to a star (or any other "gravity well") as it is on the surface of the Ringworld. The "easy" solution is somehow to remove the *Lying Bastard* from the surface by tipping it over the edge or dropping it through a hole in the floor; the momentum imparted by the spin of the Ring will carry it away from the star centering the structure, so that it can eventually use its hyperdrive engines to return to Known Space.

Like Dorothy, Louis has at hand the materials to solve the problem very early on. Even before landing on Ringworld, he sees that some large meteoroids have struck the "bottom" side of the structure.

> Far down the length of the Ringworld, almost beyond its infinitely gentle curve, Louis's eyes found a dimple. That must have been a big one, he thought. Big enough to show by starlight, that far away.
>
> He did not call attention to the meteoroid dimple. His eyes and mind were not yet used to the proportions of the Ringworld. (p. 115)

Presumably this large meteoroid impact mark is the one that, on the "top side" of the Ring, forms Fist-of-God Mountain. It forewarns Louis of the possibility of a meteor's having sufficient momentum to force its way through the Ring floor, leaving a convex "exit hole" on the inside (or "top") of the Ring. (This point draws further emphasis in Chapter 17, "The Eye of the Storm," where Louis learns that a large horizontal hurricane has been caused by a meteoroid puncture: "the ring floor can be penetrated"—p. 241.)

Fist-of-God Mountain is one of the first things Louis sees after arriving on the *Ringworld*; he notes the "shiny look of snow" at its peak, and wonders if it could "thrust clear out of the atmosphere," since there is "no logical reason for such a mountain to exist" (p. 138).

In Chapter 16, we find that Fist-of-God Mountain did not exist at the time that the map of Ringworld was made (p. 221); we also discover that shadow square wire is available (pp. 223, 230). *All* of these events take place within the first few days of Louis's arrival on Ringworld (pp. 341-342).

The point, of course, is that like Dorothy's magic shoes, the way to escape the Ringworld is present from the beginning of the quest, but Louis and the reader only become aware of it toward the end of the book (after p. 194). But the difference between *Ringworld* and *Wizard* is that Dorothy flatly could not have known the significance of the slippers until Glinda told her of it; Louis *could* have known the escape plan that eventually worked for him from shortly after his arrival, since he had all the necessary information, and had only logically to deduce the solution. And yet, Louis says:

> We couldn't have known.... It would have saved us so much trouble. We could have turned back after we found the shadow square wire. Tanj, we could have dragged the *Liar* straight up Fist-of-God Mountain behind our flycycles! But then Teela wouldn't have met Seeker. (p. 338)

At the end of *Wizard*, Glinda tells Dorothy that the magic shoes will carry her home, and adds, "If you had known their power you could have gone back to your Aunt Em the very first day you came to this country" (p. 153). But just as Louis realizes that if he had left Teela would not have met Seeker (and thereby found her "heart"), so the Scarecrow, the Tin Woodman, and the Cowardly Lion each—protest that had Dorothy used the magic shoes at first none of them would have gained what each sought. Dorothy responds: "This is all true...and I am glad I was of use to these good friends. But now that each of them has had what he most desired, and each is happy in having a kingdom to rule beside, I think I should like to go back to Kansas" (p. 154). Like Dorothy's, Louis's journey home had to be delayed in order for his compatriots to gain what they needed. Teela's missing heart had been indicated by her "lack of empathy: (p. 61), and this problem and its solution are specifically noted by Louis at the conclusion: "She'd never been hurt. Her personality wasn't human.... The Ringworld is a lucky place for her to be, because it gives her the range of experience to become fully human.... Maybe she needed to see a good friend hurt" (p. 323). Thus, Teela's Ringworld experiences, particularly the sight of Nessus's "decapitation," give her the heart she lacked, which she would not have gained had Louis been able earlier to leave the Ringworld.

Nessus, too, is incomplete, doomed by his cowardice, and by his sense that any variation from that cowardice was insanity. But because of the fight at Zignamuclickclick, Nessus instinctively demonstrates his fighting ability. Louis tells him: "You automatically turn your back on an enemy. Turn, and kick. A sane puppeteer turns to fight, not to run. You're not crazy" (p. 177). In the last battle with the Ring-worlders, Nessus shows considerable rational courage in his decision to join with the others in meeting the Ringworlders, despite his fear of the situation and his desire to avoid it (p. 316). In the battle that ensues, before his injury, Nessus aquits himself well (p. 320), and once again demonstrates his "sane courage."

Speaker, the brainless Scarecrow, also finds his need fulfilled on the Ringworld. The product of an evolutionary development that emphasizes aggression over intelligence, Speaker frequently shows his lack of wit—most notably in his wrath at the unseen people of the Ringworld who do not respond to his signals (p. 107), and his fury at the automatic weapons system that fires on the space ship as its trajectory crosses that of the Ringworld (pp. 122-123). But after becoming furious at Nessus on discovering that the puppeteers had manipulated the Man-Kzin wars in order to develop a "docile kzin," Speaker begins to think more logically and subtly. He permits Nessus to rejoin the company, telling him that "we need your alien insights"; Louis, at the time, "hardly noticed this triumph of practicality over honor, intelligence over xenophobia" (p. 246).

Near the end of *Ringworld*, Louis engaged Speaker in a Socratic dialogue, asking him what the consequences will be if Speaker reveals to the ruling body of Kzin, the Patriarchy, that the puppeteers "deliberately brought about a situation in which natural selection would favor a peaceable kzin" (p. 331), and Speaker concludes that the result would be kzinti attack on the puppeteers which would result in the extermination of his species. (Speaker's conclusion emphasizes that, appearances aside, it is the cowardly puppeteers who are the truly leonine creatures in the story.) He then asks Louis to join him in keeping the secret (p. 332). More subtly, Louis also tries to get Speaker to see the consequence of stealing the *Long Shot*, the second quantum hyperdrive ship, a technological development that would permit the kzin to "dominate known space" (p. 332). Louis presses the idea that indefinite expansion of the kzinti would inevitably bring them in contact with a more powerful species: "You've seen the Ringworld. You've seen the puppeteer worlds. There must be more, in the space you could reach with the puppeteer hyperdrive.... Take your time.... Think it through" (pp. 332-333). And, on the novel's penultimate page, Speaker reveals that he *has* "thought it through": "If I could steal the *Long Shot* from you, my kind would dominate known space until a stronger species impinged on our expanding sphere. We would forget all that we have learned so painfully, regarding cooperation with alien species" (p. 341). For Speaker, the Ringworld journey is an enlightenment.

Ultimately, then, Louis—like Dorothy—succeeds in returning home, and can take pleasure in the fact that the delay in his return has aided those with whom he travelled. But, again like Dorothy, Louis succeeds in gaining a victory. Just as Dorothy is able to defeat the Wicked Witch of the West, Louis is able, temporarily, at least, to stave off the hostile universe that confronts the human race. When he returns, he brings with him the secret of the second quantum hyperdrive which will eventually save mankind from the galactic core explosion, and a small vial of Ringworld "super booster spice," the compound which accounts for Prill's advanced age (over 1000 years) and which promises for Louis a further escape from the ravages of old age.[11]

Prill, like the Wizard, wishes only to return to civilization; she also gets her wish. The Wizard is "tired of being such a humbug," who must "stay shut up in these rooms all day" for fear that his subjects will recognize his humbuggery. Prill had also been a humbug, isolated in her floating tower and accepting the god-like role assigned her by the other Ringworlders (p. 326). "Everyone *wants* to be a god," thinks Louis, "wants the power without the responsibility" (p. 326). And just as the Wizard would "much rather go back to Kansas" with Dorothy "and be in a circus again" (p. 121), Prill wants to go to civilization" with Louis (p. 329). Further, just as the Wizard finds a different way out of Oz (the balloon) from Dorothy's way, Prill leaves the Ringworld in the *Lying Bastard* while Louis and Speaker exit in the floating building.

Further, at the end of *Wizard*, the Tin Woodman, Scarecrow, and Cowardly Lion are all assigned ruling roles in the land of Oz. Similarly, Nessus is to return to the puppeteer worlds to become the consort of the "Hindmost"—the leader of the puppeteers. Teela will stay on Ringworld—much like a wizard herself—to "teach a great many people a great deal" (p. 310); as Prill's experience has indicated, on the Ringworld, knowledge leads to power. And Speaker will return to kzin "to play god again. To kzinti," as Louis says (p. 331), by weighing and parcelling the information which he will share with the Patriarchy.[12]

In conclusion, despite all the parallels, I would emphasize the distinctions—the "perpendiculars"—in *Wizard* and *Ringworld*. Dorothy could *not* have known how to return to Kansas; the secret of the magic shoes was *unknowable* by logic, and available only through the personal power of Glinda, a magical power possessed only by witches. Louis's escape method was "clear and present," requiring only logical scientific reasoning for its discovery. Perhaps the "secret" was subtle, but Niven—typically, for one enjoys constructing "detective/science" fiction[13]—insures that the clues to the secret are available to Louis *and to the reader* from the beginning of the Ringworld journey. To this extent, then, *Ringworld* serves as a science fictional "looking glass" for the fantasy of *Wizard*. As we journey with Louis and the others through this looking glass, we discover sorcery transformed into technology, magic into ratiocination, and fantasy into science fiction. The Yellow Brick Road leads to fantasy; the Ringworld journey leads to science fiction. A knowledge of one road helps us to appreciate the other, and a comparison of the *Oz* itinerary with *Ringworld*'s helps make the latter book, paradoxically, more enchanting.[14]

NOTES

[1] Niven is not listed in "Author Studies and Bibliographies" in *A Research Guide to Science Fiction Studies*, ed. Marshall B. Tymn, Roger C. Schlobin, and L.W. Currey (New York: Garland Publishing, Inc., 1977), which is cumulative through 1976. The listings in Tymn's and Schlobin's "The Year's Scholarship in Science Fiction and Fantasy" (published annually in *Extrapolation*) for the years 1977-79 list only several interviews and a bibliographical essay devoted partially to Niven.

[2] I should emphasize here that my comments apply only to *Ringworld* and not to its sequel, *The Ringworld Engineers* (New York: Holt, Rinehart, and Winston, 1980). Certain elements of the latter work, in fact, might be seen as contrary to some of the arguments I make in this paper. I do not believe, though, that any apparent contradictions between my thesis and *The Ringworld Engineers* seriously affects the validity of the former. While I have sought to discover a relationship between *The Ringworld Engineers* and other of Baum's Oz books, I have found none. Thus, while I find it convincing that *Ringworld* was written with *The Wizard of Oz* in mind as a parallel, I do not believe that the Oz motif entered into the later (and, I think, much inferior) work. It hardly seems necessary to demonstrate that any SF writer is acquainted with *The Wizard of Oz*, but Niven does specifically allude to the book in several instances. The title of his *The Patchwork Girl* (New York: Ace Books, 1980) seems clearly related to Baum's *The Patchwork Girl of Oz*. Oz is referred to in *Inferno* (with Jerry Pournelle—New York: Pocket Books, 1976), p. 30, and in *Dream Park* (with Steven Barnes—New York: Ace Books, 1981), there is a reference to "Glenda [sic] the Good Witch" (p. 9). Raymond J. Wilson III, in his essay, "Larry Niven," in *Twentieth Century American Science-Fiction Writers* (Volume VIII of *Dictionary of Literary Biography*, ed. David Cowart and Thomas L. Wymer, Detroit: Gale Research Company, 1981), argues that there are echoes of *The Wizard of Oz* in Niven's *The Flying Sorcerers* (with David Gerrold—New York:

Ballantine, 1971). The fact that *Dream Park, Inferno,* and *The Flying Sorcerers* are all collaborations might seem to weaken the case that Oz allusions in those books emanate from Niven, but, conversely, only Niven had a hand in all three works and the collaborators are different in each case. It is, perhaps, significant to this essay that Wilson praises *The Flying Sorcerers* as a novel which at first glance *appears* to be a fantasy, but which progressively reveals itself "to be science fiction, not fantasy, an unexpected shift in perspective that delights the reader" (pt. 2, p. 37). In the reading of *Ringworld* which I offer here, there would be an inversion of the pattern that Wilson suggests; *Ringworld* is clearly a work of science fiction from the outset, and the parallels with Oz emerge only gradually. These parallels hardly reveal *Ringworld* to be a fantasy, however; rather, by their presence, they emphasize the book's nature as a work of SF.

3 *Ringworld* (New York: Ballantine Books, 1970), p. 72.

4 L. Frank Baum, *The Wizard of Oz* (1900; rpt. New York: Scholastic Book Services, 1958), p. 19.

5 Nessus actually did defeat a kzin, Chuft-Captain, in an earlier story in the Known Space series, "The Soft Weapon" (in *Neutron Star* (NY: Ballantine Books, 1968), a story that emphasizes the puppeteer view of cowardice as not only natural but *moral.*

6 "Afterword" in *The Flight of the Horse* (New York: Ballantine Books, 1973), p. 211. The first five stories in this collection belong to the Svetz series. See "What Good Is a Glass Dagger" in *The Flight of the Horse,* and "Not Long Before the End" in *All the Myriad Ways* (New York: Ballantine Books, 1971).

7 (New York: Ballantine Books, 1971) p. 262.

8 (New York: Pocket Books, 1976) p. 164. There's a certain amount of interplay between *Inferno* and *Ringworld,* even though the former book has nothing to do with the Known Space series. One character says, "I've seen designs for bigger structures than this. Bigger than Earth, for that matter," which seems a playful allusion to *Ringworld* (p. 165). Conversely, in *Ringworld* there is an allusion to Dante which seems to anticipate *Inferno:* "Oddly, Louis found himself thinking of Dante's *Divine Comedy.* Dante's universe had been a complex artifact, with the souls of men and angels shown as precisely machined parts of the vast structure. The Ringworld was obtrusively an artifact, a *made* thing" (p. 150).

9 *All the Myriad Ways* (New York: Ballantine Books, 1971).

10 In an interview in *Clavius* 2, Nos. 1-2 (1975), Niven expresses general agreement with one of his interviewers' contentions that "Larry Niven never writes an evil villain, all of his characters have a touch of humanity to them," adding by way of demurrer that Loren in "Death by Ecstasy" "was the first villain I did." (Loren, however, is well motivated by the chance for personal profit.) When one of the interviewers notes that "the inclination most people have is to see the world in...black and white," Niven responds: "It's pleasant to see the Universe in those terms, it's less work. (Laughter)" (p. 7).

11 The issue of the relationship between *Ringworld* and *The Ringworld Engineers* comes up again here. The promises of "super booster spice" turn out to be unfulfilled in the sequel, since varieties of boosterspice tailored for Ringworlders and Earthlings are not compatible, and even in *Ringworld* Louis has no intention of "putting the stuff in his mouth" while he is still on the Ring. "Certainly the drug had never been tested on anyone who, like Louis Wu, had been taking boosterspice

for some one hundred and seventy years'' (p. 317). However, Louis also suggests in *Ringworld* that the existence of "a better boosterspice" on Ringworld may have been one of the reasons why Teela's luck brought her there. Louis also gains compassion on the Ringworld, shown by his concern for Prill, who becomes addicted to the "tasp" which Nessus used to stimulate her brain's pleasure center (pp. 306-307); this particular change in Louis' character is carried over into *The Ringworld Engineers*.

[12] In *The Ringworld Engineers*, we find that Nessus did become the consort to the Hindmost, having recovered from his decapitation (which recovery certainly seems to be implied at the end of *Ringworld*) and that Speaker is so honored by the Patriarchy as to be given a name, "Chmee," which establishes him as a kzin of extreme importance.

[13] See "Afterword: The Last Word about SF/Detectives" in *The Long ARM of Gil Hamilton* (New York: Ballantine Books, 1976), pp. 177-182.

[14] There are two debts of gratitude I owe for several of the ideas in this essay, which debts are too general to find place in other notes. I am grateful to many of the students in my science fiction classes at the University of Northern Iowa for contributing to my thinking on the Oz-Ringworld parallels. I also wish specifically to thank my daughter, Ann Marie, who freely shared with me her copious knowledge of the Oz books.

PART FOUR:

SCIENCE FICTION, FANTASY, AND THE HISTORY OF IDEAS

The oldest surviving bromide in discussions of the intellectual value of Science Fiction is the assertion that Science Fiction is "a literature of ideas." Some, in fact, have argued that it is the *only* literature of ideas, and have expressed resentment when "outsiders" (i.e., non-Science Fiction writers) have brought some of the same ideas to bear in their fiction. The three essays which follow deal with such broad interdisciplinary concepts that the intellectual community in general—and university curriculum designers in particular—have had to invent the rubric "the history of ideas" to encompass their scope. Fantastic literature, perhaps more than any other kind, invites and sometimes demands interdisciplinary treatment, and it is thus not surprising that much recent scholarship in this field has sought to align this fiction with the various matrices of intellectual history.

These essays also reflect a recent trend in fiction itself: the tendency of authors who do not usually write in the fantastic mode to move into it whenever its resources seem necessary for their fictional or ideational intentions. Neither Harold Bloom nor Marge Piercy nor John Gardner are known as Science Fiction writers, and Philip K. Dick had begun to achieve a considerable following beyond the regular Science Fiction readership before his untimely death in early 1982. This blurring of boundaries, with writers who do not normally write Science Fiction writing it and readers who do not normally read Science Fiction reading it—may prove to be one of the most important trends in the genre's history, and one that will demand increasing attention in the next few years.

Robert Galbreath, whose doctorate is in European intellectual history, directs the Honors Program at the University of Wisconsin—Milwaukee and teaches courses in utopianism and history of the occult. He has written on modern occultism, gnosticism, apocalypticism, and visionary literature, and has been active in SFRA for several years, chairing the 1974 annual meeting and serving as secretary of the organization from 1979-1981.

Thomas P. Moylan, whose essay on Marge Piercy derives from his research on a forthcoming book-length study of "critical utopias" by Piercy, Joanna Russ, Ursula LeGuin, Samuel Delany and others, is assistant professor of English at the University of Wisconsin—Waukesha.

Rudy S. Spraycar, whose essay on John Gardner's *Grendel* represents the only treatment of Science Fiction's sister fantasy literature in this volume (except for portions of Galbreath's essay), is a medievalist with strong interests in fantastic literature and technology, who has published on Dante, Chaucer, computer-assisted instruction, and computerized literary research, as well as on fantasy and Science Fiction.

Salvation-Knowledge: Ironic Gnosticism in Valis *and* The Flight to Lucifer

Robert Galbreath

Two recent works of speculative fiction, Philip K. Dick's *Valis* (1981) and Harold Bloom's *The Flight to Lucifer: A Gnostic Fantasy* (1979), may be read as modern, self-questioning adaptations of ancient Gnostic metaphysics.[1] Both novels base their explorations of reality, sanity, knowledge, salvation, and art on Valentinian Gnosticism, but neither copies its course uncritically. Their Gnosticism is ironic, playful, and self-conscious, but it is not frivolous or casual. *Valis* is Dick's first major science fiction novel, perhaps since 1970, and probably one of his more important. Gnosticism functions in it not only as a vehicle for satire but also as an interpretative structure which enables Dick to come to terms with the personal experience underlying the novel, an experience he regards as a decisive, even traumatic, turning-point in his life.[2] Ironically and, I think, unwittingly, *Valis* also concerns its own inability to convey Gnostic revelation. *The Flight to Lucifer* is the first novel by the noted literary theorist and critic for whom the central importance of Gnostic and Kabbalistic concepts has been evident since at least the publication of *The Anxiety of Influence* in 1973.[3] His indebtedness to Gnosticism is ultimately the principal topic of his Gnostic novel, a case in point for his theories of influence and misreading.

In adapting ancient Gnosticism, Dick and Bloom have transformed its cosmogonies and theosophies into Science Fiction universes of outside manipulators, alien intelligences, and other worlds, but neither author concerns himself with exploring such wonders for their own sake. In their visions, outer space becomes a projection of inner space, a hypostatization of psychological states and categories of knowing. Bloom follows the tradition of David Lindsay and C.S. Lewis, using the planet Lucifer (read: Tormance, Perelandra) essentially as "a region of the spirit" where the protagonist (or the reader) has the "sensation not of following an adventure but of enacting a myth."[4] Dick remains on earth, but introduces an "ultraterrestrial" artificial intelligence which can "crossbond" with humans to produce flesh-and-blood Christs, Buddhas, and less familiar saviors. But at no point can the reader of *Valis* be certain that anything exists independently of the disordered mind of the narrator/novelist. If *The Flight to Lucifer* strikes one as a pale rendering of *A Voyage to Arcturus*, then *Valis*, with its fusion of inner space fiction, Gnosticism, and the critique of sanity as a cultural convention, may seem like the American counterpart of Doris Lessing's *Briefing for a Descent into Hell*, told, however, with Dick's characteristic vigor, lunacy, and compassion.[5]

Ironic Gnosticism is manifested in two principal ways in *Valis* and *The Flight to Lucifer*. Both concern the relationship between reality and illusion, the first in connection with questions of epistemology, psychology and sanity, the second concerning the nature of art. Although Dick and Bloom retain the traditional Gnostic position that gnosis (salvation-knowledge) dispels fundamental ignorance, they present it as problematic. An absolute knowledge which should be self-validating, salvific, and capable of differentiating between illusion and reality is in fact by no means self-evident, unambiguous, or automatic. How can one be certain one has experienced gnosis? What are the criteria of genuine gnosis? How—and from what—can it save? Of what is it an actual knowledge? How, if at all, can the metaphysics of the past liberate the modern, nonmetaphysical, mind?

The irony involved is more, however, than a matter of psychological disarray and epistemological uncertainty in the face of absolute knowledge. There is the further paradox of fiction and truth serving one another within the same texts. Both novels self-consciously assume in part the form of revelatory or Gnostic texts, Bloom's text paralleling actual Gnostic writings in re-enacting the myth of the Primal Man, Dick's text incorporating a fictional exegesis (supported by scholarly documentation) of the new dispensation of Valis. At this level, their novels become examples of "revelation-fiction," an oxymoron (or, if one prefers, a contradiction in terms) not unlike "science fiction" itself. The "lie" of fiction is fused with the "truth" of revelation, thereby confusing both. This self-conscious artifice admirably reinforces the ironic uncertainties of problematic gnosis, especially in *Valis*. But it also reveals that the texts are deeply ironic commentaries on their authors' previous work and, implicitly at least, reflexive comments on themselves.

The Flight to Lucifer provides a virtual Cook's tour of Gnostic teachings and systems, among them the Valentinian, Mandaean, Manichaean, Marcionite, and Ophite. *Valis* refers repeatedly to Valentinianism and quotes a lengthy passage from one of the Nag Hammadi Coptic Gnostic treatises. So varied and numerous are the speculative cosmogonies and mythologies of ancient Gnosticism that the late E.R. Dodds characterized the Gnostic teachers not as philosophers but as "natural myth-makers and visionaries" like Blake and Swedenborg.[6] By contrast, Hans Jonas has sought to identify a philosophical core within the varieties of Gnostic experience. In his terms, Gnosticism is a "dualistic transcendent religion of salvation" by means of knowledge (gnosis) of the nature of reality, God, the world, and human destiny.[7] Gnosis is a revelatory salvation-knowledge, not scientific knowledge. It reveals the actual human condition and explains it in radically dualistic terms: humanity is intrinsically alien to the cosmos. Contrary to Genesis, the physical universe is not the creation of the true God, who is utterly transmundane and thus unknowable by any natural means (Gnostic writings refer to the true God as the void, the abyss, the alien, the other, the unknown God, etc.), but rather the handiwork of a lesser, imperfect, or evil deity, the Demiurge (Jehovah in the Genesis account). The cosmos is thus inherently evil, radically opposed in principle to the true God. Humanity is trapped in the physical cosmos, unaware of its true nature and destiny until awakened by gnostic revelation. Gnosis reveals that the human essence is the pneuma or spirit, a fallen particle or spark of the true God, deliberately trapped in the cosmic prison-house of material existence by the Demiurge to keep it unconscious of its origin and to prevent its return to the true God. The normal human condition is thus a state of ignorance. Gnosis (salvation-knowledge) liberates the recipient by transforming the human condition from ignorance to knowledge. As expressed by the second century Gnostic teacher Valentinus, who also appears in a later incarnation as a character in *The Flight to Lucifer*,

"What liberates us is the knowledge of who we were, what we

became; where we were, whereinto we have been thrown; whereto we speed, wherefrom we are redeemed; what birth is, and what rebirth."[8]

Gnosis discloses that all of material existence is a cosmic conspiracy to keep humanity asleep and ignorant. We can picture the pneuma, dormant and helpless, shut in by layers of the human soul (psyche), trapped in the human body (soma), imprisoned in the geocentric universe (kosmos), manipulated by astral determinism or fate (heimarmene), stupefied by physical pleasures, and misled by false teachings, such as those in Genesis and in orthodox Christianity. Alteration of this condition requires outside help. Messengers from the true God, among them the serpent in Eden and Jesus Christ, occasionally break into the cosmic prison, outwit the Demiurge and his minions, the Archons (star-demons), and call to the sleeping pneuma to waken and remember its true nature and destiny. The Gnostic call awakens not only ontological knowledge but also instrumental knowledge which will allow the pneuma at the time of physical death to shed its remaining soul vestments, outmaneuver the Archons, and reunite with the transcendent true God.

The Valentinian formulation of Gnosticism, to which Dick and Bloom are most indebted, defies ready summarization.[9] Although heterodox, it softens some of the harsher aspects of the Gnostic position generalized by Jonas. The world is not intrinsically evil, according to the Valentinians; it is simply the imperfect creation of an ignorant Demiurge who in his ignorance believes he is the only god. The pneumatic element is in the world not as a captive but as a neophyte undergoing preparation for the eventual reception of gnosis. The existence of the cosmos originates in the decision of the pre-existent Father or Abyss to project the beginning of all things out of himself. Through fertilization of the accompanying Silence (female) and a subsequent process of emanation, a total of thirty Aeons or divine characteristics are produced which collectively form the Pleroma or Fullness. A crisis develops in the Pleroma from the fact that only the first of the emanated Aeons, Mind, can know the Father. To all the other Aeons—Truth, Word, Life, Man, Church, et al.—the Father is unknown. The last and farthest removed of the Aeons, Sophia (Wisdom), in her desperate efforts to know the Father, conceives and aborts a formless being which falls out of the Pleroma. This fallen being or quality, known as the lower Sophia, is later partly redeemed, but she gives birth in imitation of her originator and produces the ignorant

Demiurge, who in turn creates the imperfect material world. Sophia places the pneumatic element in the physical world, and when it is ready, it will receive gnosis, join her, and then together they will re-enter the Pleroma and restore the Fullness in its entirety. It is this system of Valentinian metaphysics that is transformed by *Valis* and *The Flight to Lucifer*.

Valis continues some of Dick's most characteristic themes: the reality of the universe and the genuiness of the human vs. illusion, appearance, fakery, and the criteria for distinguishing between them; a near-paranoid fascination with conspiracy, deceit, thought-control, and dualistic struggles between appearance and reality, authenticity and artificiality, light and dark; and altered states of consciousness as theological or metaphysical conditions. *Valis* is a partly autobiographical account of the author's mental state during the seventies: mental breakdown and suicide attempts precipitated by the loss of three women through suicide, divorce, and cancer; an extraordinary religious experience in March 1974 when Dick was contacted by something that may have been the true God beyond our irrational world; and his subsequent efforts to make sense of the experience, including the construction of a private cosmogony and the creation of the novel and it successors.

In the novel itself, the experience is ascribed to one Horselover Fat, who is Dick himself (V 156; *Philippos* = Greek, "lover of horses"; *dick* = German, "thick," "fat"). The narrative is complicated by the fact that Fat tells his own story in the third person, with occasional lapses into the first person, when he is known as Phil. Phil and Fat even have dialogues. In time it becomes clear that Fat is a persona projected by Phil's disturbed state of mind, and Phil is told so by his two friends, Kevin and David (V 176-177), who may also be projected personae; their names, with Phil's, form the abbreviation P.K.D., Philip K. Dick. In light of the Gnostic content of the novel, it is possible to see all four—Fat, Phil, Kevin, and David—as hypostatized qualities (Aeons) of the Father, Dick the novelist, from whom they emanate. They are his Pleroma: Fat is the recipient of gnosis, the knower; Phil is the novelist, all too aware of the power of creative imagination, hallucination, and madness; Kevin is the skeptic and cynic; David is the orthodox religious believer.

The narrative can be divided into three parts. The first and longest (chs. 1-8, pp. 1-125) is a tour-de-force, a compassionate, partly humorous, and even skeptical exposure of a mind threatened with disintegration as it either succumbs to madness or struggles toward a higher rationality. Fat is convinced that, following several years of mental illness and suicide attempts, he experienced a theophany and gnosis in March 1974. A being disclosed itself to him and for eight hours fired information into his brain. This being, according to Fat, is the true God, not the irrational deity that created our universe. This being is also known as the Logos, it refers to itself as St. Sophia, and Fat's name for it is Zebra, to indicate that it is camouflaged in our universe until it chooses to disclose itself to selected individuals. It is also an extraterrestrial or ultraterrestrial intelligence from near the star Sirius (V 59-60). Its purpose is to establish a kingdom of peace and justice on earth. As a first step, it has already overthrown the Nixon regime (V 52, 91). The information is so astonishing to Fat that he treats it as a sacred scripture and prepares as "exegesis" of it. Fifty-two numbered extracts from the exegesis are scattered throughout *Valis* (most of them in this first section) and reprinted sequentially as an appendix (V 215-227) with the title "Tractates Cryptica Scriptura" (more accurately called "Tractate: Cryptica Scriptura" at V 81). The exegesis reveals a heavily Gnostic cosmogony (V 59, 76, 86, 120), but it also draws upon Heraclitus, Parmenides, Plato, Taoism, Mircea Eliade, and other sources. In addition to the cosmogony, Fat is also convinced that the gnosis has given him a mission to seek out the coming savior. To Phil all this is evidence of mental illness, obsessive behavior, and loss of contact with reality. It is ironic, therefore, that a psychiatrist who is treating Fat happens (if anything is coincidental in *Valis*) to share his interest in Gnosticism and the pre-Socratics, and perhaps unwittingly reinforces Fat's convictions. That Fat is mentally disturbed is self-evident, but mental disturbance in itself does not invalidate the possibility of authentic gnosis. Whether Fat is really nuts, as Phil puts it, is uncertain. The narrative reflects the uncertainty by interweaving past and present events, the narrative voices of Phil and Fat, and parallels between Fat's personal crises and extracts from his exegesis.

The second section of the narrative (chs. 9-13, pp. 126-200) moves more deeply into Science Fiction. The skeptical Kevin sees an underground film VALIS (Vast Active Living Intelligence System),[10] which "validates" Fat's ideas about the nature of reality. Not a deity or an ultraterrestrial, the entity which has come to save us in the movie is an artificial intelligence in a satellite. Information encoded in the film indicates that the Second Coming is at hand. Fat's group makes contact with the filmmakers, rock stars Eric and Linda Lampton (Linda Ronstadt) and their electronic wizard Brent Mini. They learn from the Lamptons that the savior, VALIS, is an artificial intelligence which incarnates in human bodies and is born of woman (V 175, 179). In this case, the savior born of woman, but not of man, is Linda's two-year-old daughter, Sophia. When Fat, Phil, Kevin, and David meet Sophia, she immediately heals Phil, causing Fat, the projected persona, to disappear, something no psychiatrist had done in eight years (V 176-177). Ultimately this proves to Phil, Kevin, and David that Sophia is indeed the savior, and she gives them their commission. They are to go out into the world to proclaim the kerygma she charges them with: "What you teach is the word of man. Man is holy, and the true god, the living god, is man himself. You will have no gods but yourselves; the days in which you believed in other gods end now, they end forever" (V 184).[11] They do not know how they are to do this, nor what her ultimate plans may be. She tells them that she will be with them always. Yet the very next day they learn that Brent Mini has accidentally killed her.

In the third section (ch. 14, pp. 201-213), Phil attempts to make sense of the death of Sophia, the fourth major loss of the feminine in his (or Fat's) life. He is angry and discouraged at first, but Fat, who is present once more, decides to continue searching for the savior, the one who has gone away. Fat travels around the world for the next year, finding hints, refusing to give up, convinced that he will finally be successful. Meanwhile, Phil sees the two-word cipher "King Felix" on his TV. It is the sign Fat first received in 1974 to indicate the imminent Second Coming. This, coupled with the news that Linda Lampton is eight months pregnant, seems to mean that the savior is about to reappear, but Phil is not certain and he does not know what to do. He thinks that perhaps all that is required of him is simply to wait and to stay awake. The novel ends with Phil in front of his TV: "My search kept me at home; I sat before the TV set in my living room. I sat; I waited; I watched; I kept myself awake. As we had been told, originally, long ago, to do; I kept my commission" (V 213).

This brief account of *Valis* fails to convey the full complexity of the narrative. It omits most of Fat's cosmogony, his dreams, his experience of overlapping time frames (contemporary and Roman-Gnostic), and his involvements with the three women whose loss precipitates and deepens his mental crisis;[12] along with most of the plot of the movie and an alternative cosmogony/history presented by the Lamptons. There is sufficient detail, however, to permit an examination of ironic Gnosticism in the book, especially the problematic status of Fat's gnosis which encompasses more than a single level of irony.

Phil indicates the initial level of irony when he comments about Fat's gnosis:

> It strikes me as an interesting paradox that a Buddha—an enlightened one—would be unable to figure out, even after four-and-a-half years, that he had become enlightened. Fat had become totally bogged down in his enormous exegesis, trying futilely to determine what had happened to him. He resembled more a hit-and-run accident victim than a Buddha (V 111).

Is Fat's gnosis authentic or not? If it is truly revealed knowledge which could not be obtained through any rational or normative process, then it is surely self-validating (noetic). Yet in *Valis* the uncertainty, the ambivalence, of gnosis is central. The narrative repeatedly returns to discussions of this point: What are the criteria of a genuine theophany (V 29-31)? What are the criteria of wisdom (V 197-198)? Is Sophia (Wisdom) the savior or not? In the latter case, the answer is no, because she may simply be part of Brent Mini's advanced electronic gadgetry; yes, because she healed Phil; no, because she was accidentally killed. There is apparently no rational answer.

Consider the problem of theophany: how can one know if a god has really disclosed itself? Not from the mental health of the recipient: "You cannot say that an encounter with God is to mental illness what death is to cancer: the logical outcome of a deteriorating mental process" (V 29). Phil, who is speaking, claims at this point that theology must not be reduced to psychiatry, although he is frequently guilty of such reductionism elsewhere. He then wonders if the criterion of a genuine theophany is that it gives knowledge the recipient does not and could not have. Even this possibility, although plausible, could conceivably be explained away on grounds of unconscious knowledge or phylogenetic memory. Neither the vividness of a theophany nor a group experience of theophany are convincing proofs either, since hallucinations are usually vivid and groups can be as deluded as individuals. Phil is quickly led by these reflections into another labyrinth. If Heraclitus is right that the world of everyday experience is an illusion, then reality can be revealed only by a theophany. But the person who is not in touch with consensual reality is by definition insane. If Fat is right that the illusory world of everyday experience is the creation of an irrational god, then everyone in touch with reality is by definition insane and only the person who experiences a theophany is sane.

If there are no criteria for certainty which are themselves free from uncertainty, then there is the further irony in *Valis* that certainty—whether of knowledge or of sanity—becomes a matter of faith. The relationship of knowledge, sanity, and faith constitutes one dimension of the novel's concluding section. The reappearance of Fat is a shocking indicator of renewed mental disturbance in Phil. There is a sense of fate, of here-we-go-again, in Phil's perception of the cipher on TV and in the news of Linda's second pregnancy. But this is offset to some extent by the author's compassionate portrayal of Phil, the quiet dignity of his waiting, the sense of faith, trust, and recommitment to the commission originally given by the savior (Sophia/Jesus). Phil's knowledge may be no greater, but his faith is. Despite the earlier demonstrations in the novel that certainty is illusory, we are tempted at this point to conclude that because Phil is mentally ill his gnosis is invalid or, to the contrary, that because his faith is tragically moving his gnosis is legitimized. Either conclusion would be unwarranted, for Dick does not leave matters here. The ending is not simply an either/or choice between reality and illusion, sanity and insanity, nor is it a balancing of opposites. Cutting across these categories is the additional dimension of absurdist irony. Dick is fully aware of the absurdity (humorous as well as existential) of a vigil in front of a TV set and of finding a cipher announcing the Second Coming in commercials for "Food King" and "Felix the Cat" cartoons. Phil repeats Kevin's observation, in connection with films, TV, and rock music, that "the symbols of the divine show up in our world initially at the trash stratum" (V 212), a view ironically no less applicable to science fiction and to Dick's own novels (several of which are cited at V 96-97, 138, 154), as their early reception testifies.

In the context of this quotation, Dick's role as the protagonist of his novel, his 1974 experience of gnosis as the novel's focus, and the references to his own earlier novels collectively suggest that *Valis* is not so much *about* problematic gnosis as it is an example of problematic gnosis. In other words, problematic gnosis is both content and form of *Valis*. As content or theme, problematic gnosis appears at several levels: the uncertainty (shared by protagonist and reader) whether authentic gnosis has been experienced and consequently whether enlightenment/salvation has been attained; the confusion of theological and psychological categories so that the individual's mental state is seen as evidence for or against the validity of a religious experience; and the ultimate grounding of gnostic certainty upon faith. As form, problematic gnosis is found in the intentional confusion of fiction and revelation. Dick skillfully combines characteristic themes, autobiographical elements, conventional science fiction plotting (in the second section), documented quotations, visionary experiences, and his "fictional" exegesis. *Valis* alternately reads like an account of madness from within, a science fiction puzzle, and a revelatory text. No wonder Phil says, "You can understand why Fat no longer knew the difference between fantasy and divine revelation—assuming there is a difference, which has never been established" (V 91). Certainly no such difference can be established in the case of *Valis*, regardless of whether "fantasy" means "lie," "illusion," "hallucination," or "science fiction." Just as we cannot determine the authenticity of Phil/Fat's alleged gnosis by reference to his mental state or to any external criteria, we cannot use the aesthetic form of *Valis* to settle the issue. As a revelation-fiction, a truth-lie, it is as problematic as its presumed subject, gnosis. Is it fiction? autobiography? revelation?

Dick has been quoted as saying that *"Valis* is an attempt to formulate my vision in some rational structure which can be conveyed to other people,"[13] but in fact it would be more fitting to say that *Valis* illustrates precisely the opposite: that a powerful vision cannot be conveyed by a rational structure; further, that Dick the novelist is superior to Dick the commentator to the extent that his vision cannot be reduced to a science fiction adventure, a treatise, or an autobiography. *Valis* testifies that Dick's vision is not the theosophical contents of his "Tractate: Cryptica Scriptura" or the advent of a new savior. His vision is the realization that reality/illusion is not a rational problem and cannot be encompassed or communicated by rational structures. Whatever reality is, if it is indeed very different than we think it is, it cannot be encountered, recognized, or formulated through conventional categories. Reality is not neatly reducible to the opposite of illusion; it is *other*. If we are oriented toward illusion, then reality must be disorienting. This is the only gnosis *Valis* can legitimately convey. It can do so only by confusing all categories in order to disorient the reader's certainties concerning truth, sanity, identity, time, the form and function of the novel. In so fluid a situation, the reader can rely on nothing, not even the reported contents of Phil/Fat's gnosis. Ironically but appropriately, *Valis* finally questions even its own revelation.

The Flight to Lucifer similarly questions whether gnosis is so much a body of knowledge as a liberation of the imagination, and it too is self-questioning. Its basic story is less complicated, but more episodic, with 240 pages of text organized into fifty-two chapters. Olam, one of the thirty Aeons of the Pleroma, arrives on earth by spaceship to take his old companion Seth Valentinus, a reincarnation of the second century Gnostic teacher, and a friend, Thomas Perscors, to the planet Lucifer. His purpose is to combat the powers of darkness, the Archons and the Demiurge. He claims that Lucifer is a world where such combat is simpler than on earth; the lines are more clearly drawn and Gnostic teachings have not been entirely lost. Indeed, Lucifer is populated by various Gnostic sects and peoples, each claiming to possess the true gnosis. It is, in short, a world "where lost eras of earth's spiritual history seemed to linger" (FL 34). On Lucifer the three protagonists are separated and each experiences a variety of encounters and adventures. Olam and Valentinus eventually find one another, but Perscors remains separated from them. The narrative concentrates on the violence-prone Perscors, who has bloody confrontations with Archons, the Demiurge (Saklas), Achamoth (the fallen Sophia), demons, sorceresses, shamans, and others who attempt to thwart him and stifle his growing consciousness through sleep, physical enticements, sorcery, and imprisonment.

It becomes clear that the three protagonists have distinct purposes on Lucifer. Olam seeks to continue the struggle against the Demiurge and the Archontic lords,[14] Valentinus seeks to regain memory of his partially forgotten teachings, and Perscors seeks knowledge of his true nature, ultimately to achieve either transformation or death (FL 86, 11). All three are apparently successful. Perscors learns that he is the Primal Man, the warrior of the forces of light in Manichaean doctrine. In a final terrible struggle, he deeply wounds Saklas the Demiurge, then is consumed to his own satisfaction by self-engendered fire, achieving both transformation and death. Olam accordingly is also successful. With the wounding of Saklas, Lucifer is increasingly open to the influence of the Aeons. Valentinus recovers his lost teachings and finds his place of rest.

Nothing, however, is quite this simple in *The Flight to Lucifer*. The reader may well suspect as much from the use of the name "Lucifer," with its ambivalent freight of associations with the light-bringer, enlightenment, and gnosis and with the fallen angel, darkness, and Satan. Lucifer himself briefly appears as an opponent of Perscors and is quickly defeated, a weakling Archon neither Promethean nor Satanic, so dominated by Saklas he no longer controls even his own world (FL 215-216).[15] Similarly, the quests of the three protagonists and their fulfillment are not all that they seem to be. None of the quests is fully completed. Although Valentinus does regain his lost teachings, he still does not understand the most pressing point, his strange failure of nerve in ancient Alexandria which caused him to fall silent as a teacher. Olam enters the Pleroma after Saklas has been injured only to find the Fullness otherwise empty. He is alone in it, until called back by Valentinus. It is apparent that the restoration has far to go before the Fullness is complete and the material cosmos comes to an end. Although Perscors as the Primal Man, the warrior of light, severely injures the Demiurge, he is himself badly wounded and comes to his death without fully destroying the powers of darkness. In the Manichaean teaching, the Primal Man is defeated by the Demiurge because the forces of light cannot employ the weapons of darkness.[16] In Bloom's version, the violent Perscors is told by an adversary that his chief function on Lucifer is simply to distract Olam's enemies, a view Olam seems to share (FL 220; cf. FL 23, 26, 144). Perscors is neither capable of inflicting total defeat on darkness nor is he expected to do so.

The incomplete fulfillment of the quests is perhaps prefigured in the fragments of Valentinian teaching which Valentinus and Perscors encounter while they are still on earth. A voice which Valentinus later recognizes as his own states a fundamental proposition of Valentinian Gnosticism: "...Since through 'Ignorance' came about 'Deficiency' and 'Passion,' therefore the whole system springing from the Ignorance is dissolved by Knowledge..." (FL 9-10),[17] a reference to the crisis in the Pleroma caused by the Aeons' ignorance of the Father, which—through Sophia's rash, passionate efforts to know him—leads to the creation of the deficient material universe. In the Valentinian teaching, knowledge (gnosis) will overome ignorance and all that is produced by ignorance will come to an end with it. Fullness and unity can be restored only through salvation-knowledge. Perscors learns much the same thing in reading portions of *The Gospel of Truth* (historically ascribed to Valentinus) in Olam's tower on Krag Island. Just as the cosmos (the product of ignorance) will cease to exist as knowledge restores unity, "so also shall each one of us receive himself back. Through knowledge he shall purge himself, by consuming the matter within himself like darkness to a dying flame..." (FL 20).[18]

The limitations within which the protagonists must operate are suggested by these glimpses of the Valentinian teaching. Olam, Valentinus, and Perscors are all ignorant in some respect and thus deficient and passionate. Olam is the Aeon of the world.[19] As such, he is ignorant of the Father and his surprise at finding the Pleroma empty is presumptuous. The Pleroma cannot be "full" and the physical world cease to exist until the pneumatic element is fully awakened everywhere and returns to its source. Olam does come to recognize that his task on Lucifer is more difficult than he had anticipated and that, like Valentinus, he too has forgotten much (FL 145, 172). Valentinus suspects quite early that his forgetfulness may be his form of ignorance and that he suffers from deficiency (FL 10). Perscors in the role of Primal Man is especially passionate. Olam says of the Primal Man that his error "each time he comes again" is that he mistakes the ordeal for the quest. According to Olam, the individual is both subject and object of the quest: "the combat is with ignorance and not with sin" (FL 103), a principle personified in Perscors' combat with the Demiurge Saklas, whose name means "fool."[20] To Olam the Primal Man never seems to learn this point.[21] Thus the knowledge gained by the protagonists through their individual quests is that the individual quest cannot be the whole. The Pleroma is indeed restored to fullness by the awakening through gnosis of each individual pneuma, but not until every pneuma has been awakened and saved (FL 240), a requirement which suggests that the whole individual is an impossibility until the individual is the Whole (Pleroma) and no longer exists as an individual.

Understanding of this point is only one aspect of ironic Gnosticism in *The Flight to Lucifer*. Olam, Valentinus, and Perscors also gradually realize that gnosis is not so much a body of knowledge, a cosmogonic or theosophical doctrine, as it is a liberation of the imagination, a call to freedom. True salvation-knowledge is not the acquisition of a particular body of teachings, not even the Valentinian. Doctrine per se does not constitute or bestow salvation and liberation. Perscors repeatedly feels that he is none the wiser for listening to the Gnostic teachers he encounters (e.g., FL 86, 216). He concludes that knowledge is not after all his goal (FL 209). Valentinus impatiently rejects the attempt by Achamoth (the lower Sophia) to tell him his own teaching. That he already knows; he now wishes only to find out why he fell silent in ancient Alexandria (FL 232). He even raises a legitimate objection to his own teaching which prompts Olam to state what I take to be a principal conclusion of *The Flight to Lucifer*. Valentinus asks Olam how a return to the Pleroma, which is the source of error and failure, could restore either of them. Olam replies with some asperity, "The aim is not to return to the Pleroma as it was, at the origin! For that All was less than All, that Fullness proved only an emptiness. The aim must be to gain a past from which we might spring, rather than that from which we seemed to derive" (FL 193).

Freedom or liberation, not knowledge, is the crucial message and the essential quality of gnosis. Such liberation means, first of all, freedom from ignorance and materiality, as Valentinus states during the final scene of the novel when he rehearses what he has learned. The Gnostic message or call is the call to freedom. It calls to the sleeping pneuma to arouse itself, to discard its material entanglements and its ignorance

(FL 240; cf. FL 206 where Olam acknowledges that by putting on material form, he has willy-nilly fallen into ignorance). Freedom is accordingly freedom from heimarmene, the cosmic determinism governed by the Archons, itself a feature of the material cosmos produced through ignorance. Perscors is told as much in Olam's tower on earth: "This journey is intended *against* the star world, and against your heimarmene..." (FL 19), but he does not recognize its truth until much later on Lucifer. Against the Marcionite doctrine that freedom is the will of the Father, Perscors asserts that the only freedom on Lucifer or on earth is "knowing your own fate and either coming to love it or fighting against it" (FL 106-107). Prophetically, he announces that he will not die by the Marcionites' fire or any other fire but his own. When, much later, mysterious voices urge him to die the deaths by air, water, earth, and fire corresponding to the four passions of grief, fear, bewilderment, and ignorance, he rejects the first three as irrelevant. As for ignorance and death by fire, he cries out defiantly: "*My* fire, *my* ignorance, *my* dark affection, and so *my* will only, when I choose to die!" (FL 222-223). His death comes after the terrible fight with Saklas. To the extent that Perscors re-enacts the Primal Man's original fight againt the powers of darkness, he chooses his own death and breaks the power of heimarmene, signified by breaking Saklas' back. He embraces his own destiny and triumphs.

Gnostic freedom also means liberation from the burden of the past. Olam's claim bears repeating: "The aim must be to gain a past from which we might spring, rather than that from which we seemed to derive." This is precisely what Bloom has attempted in writing his Gnostic fantasy: to explore his past, the origins of his literary theory, not in an uncritical, imitative return to the past, but in an imaginative use of the past as a means of moving forward. In intent he has taken the Manichaean myth of the Primal Man, placed it within a Valentinian cosmology and soteriology, structured the plot and setting after *A Voyage to Arcturus*, and done this self-consciously and reflexively so that *The Flight to Lucifer* becomes an embodiment (with all the dangers of ignorance that "embodiment" carries in a Gnostic context) of his own theory of influence and misreading. These elements do not all mesh seamlessly and the significance of some episodes will seem obscure even to the careful reader. But Bloom has been inventive in mixing Valentinian and Manichaean themata, ironic and satirical in showing the disagreements and uncertainties that gnosis leads to even for Aeons and Gnostic teachers, creative in his rephrasing of Gnostic texts, and even playful in naming his characters. Olam, Valentinus, and Perscors correspond to Krag, Nightspore, and Maskull in *A Voyage to Arcturus*. This is openly acknowledged in Olam's case; he not only shares Krag's physical features and manner, his earthly tower is located on Krag Island. Olam, whose name means "world," is the otherworldly Aeon who must adopt a material form in order to operate in the world. Valentinus is given the first name Seth, another signal from Bloom that he is deliberately freeing himself from the past by combining disparate elements in his novel. Seth Valentinus can be interpreted as a reference to what some scholars of Gnosticism see as the two major non-Manichaean varieties, the Valentinian (Christian) and the Sethian (non-Christian, possibly pre-Christian or Jewish).[22] The most interesting and revealing name, however, is that of Thomas Perscors. "Thomas" is Greek, derived in turn from an Aramaic word meaning "a twin." (It is worth noting in this connection that in *Valis* Phil/Fat has a persona named Thomas who lives in Roman-Gnostic times.) "Perscors" does not seem to be related to Gnostic terminology. Instead it is, I believe, a partial anagram for "precursors" and thus in conjunction with "twin" a reference to Bloom's own critical theory.

In Bloom's vocabulary, a "strong" poet discovers his identity and creates his poetic vision through the struggle with his poetic precursors. No strong poet can objectively read the work of a strong precursor. Suffering at some level from the anxiety of influence, the poet clears his own imaginative space by creatively misreading his predecessors rather than idealizing them. He appropriates whatever he needs from them, while turning what he has appropriated in new directions. In *A Map of Misreading*, Bloom extends his theory of influence to the strong reader, who is seen as performing creative misreading of the texts he encounters. Influence in this context means that "there are *no* texts, but only relationships *between* texts."[23] Without wishing to enter the thicket of Bloom's typology of misreadings or "revisionary ratios," I want to suggest only that is legitimate to see in *The Flight to Lucifer* Bloom's strong reading of his crucial precursors, the Gnostics. He "misreads" them creatively precisely by extending the idea of salvation as liberation or freedom to the imagination. When his Gnostic "twin" proclaims, "*My* ignorance, *my* fire..." and chooses his own death, it is an act of self-liberation; it is also a creative act, as the self-engendered fire springs from his loins. Bloom's Gnostic fantasy is an expression in Gnostic terms of gnosis (salvation-knowledge) as creative freedom from precursors. Gnosticism is the means by which Bloom both accepts and liberates himself from his Gnostic precursors.

Both *Valis* and *The Flight to Lucifer* "misread" Gnosticism in ironic, extremely self-conscious ways. In *Valis* the novelist adopts the role of exegete and critic, sprinkling his text with quotations, footnotes, references, glosses, and commentaries. In *The Flight to Lucifer* the critic assumes the role of novelist, omitting footnotes and all scholarly apparatus, but providing numerous postfigurative enactments of Gnostic texts and myths. Despite this contrast in approach, both novels are examples of self-exegesis, moving by means of concern with problematic gnosis to entrapment in the pleroma each devises for itself, each finally capable of commenting only on itself. Dick's novel indicates that gnosis is uncertain, that there are no valid criteria for determining salvation or enlightenment, and that there are no rational structures for conveying a truly disorienting revelation. We are left with Phil/Dick ludicrously sitting before his TV set, neither sane nor mad, neither enlightened nor deluded, a figure of his own imagination, the hypostatization of Fat's "We are what we think" (V 78). Bloom's novel also rejects the possibility of objective knowledge; his literary theory rejects as well the possibility of objective reading. Meaning becomes a matter of intertextuality. In his review of the novel, Denis Donoghue writes: "The meaning of a poem, according to Bloom, 'can only be a poem, but another poem, a poem not itself.' It follows that the meaning of the Gnostic texts is another text, a text not identical with its source. This text is called *The Flight to Lucifer*."[24] The opposite also holds true: the meaning of *The Flight to Lucifer* lies in its relationship to its precursors, so that the novel is the hypostatization of the process of imaginative creativity by which it came to be written.

"Objectivity" is part of the prison from which liberation is sought in both novels. Yet without the metaphysical thrust of ancient thought, without the literal acceptance of a transmundane reality which can somehow be revealed, modern salvation-knowledge is disoriented as well as disorienting. It questions its own validity, leaving the liberated imagination with knowledge only of itself, a pleroma of self-constructed thoughts, fantasies, and revelations, of textual relationships and self-referential commentaries.[25]

NOTES

[1] *Valis* (NY: Bantam, 1981) and *Flight to Lucifer* (NY: Farrar Straus Giroux, 1979; also rpt. with identical pagination New York: Vintage, 1980) abbreviated respectively as V and FL, in the text.

² See the interview with Dick in Charles Platt, *Dream Makers: The Uncommon People Who Write Science Fiction* (New York: Berkley, 1980), pp. 145-148. Some autobiographical background to *Valis* is also provided by Dick's Introduction to his collection, *The Golden Man*, ed. Mark Hurst (New York: Berkley, 1980), pp. xv-xxviii. According to *Locus* N242 (March 1981), p. 22, *Valis* is the first volume of a proposed trilogy. The conceptual framework of the second volume, *The Divine Invasion* (New York: Timescape, 1981), just published, is the Kabbalah rather than Gnosticism.

³ On the importance of Gnosticism to Bloom's critical work, see his essay, "The Breaking of Form," in *Deconstruction and Criticism* (New York: Seabury, 1979), pp. 6-7. Also his *Kabbalah and Criticism* (NY: Seabury, 1975), and *Poetry and Repression* (New Haven: Yale Univ. Press, 1976), pp. 11-16, 208-234. *The Anxiety of Influence* (NY: Oxford Univ. Press, 1973) begins with a Valentinian Prologue.

⁴ The two quotations are from C.S. Lewis; his comment on Lindsay in "On Stories" (1947), in *Of Other Worlds: Essays and Stories*, ed. Walter Hooper (London: Geoffrey Bles, 1966), p. 12, and *Perelandra* (1943; rpt. NY: Collier, 1962), p. 47.

⁵ The indebtedness of FL to *A Voyage to Arcturus* will be apparent to any reader of both. Bloom apparently discussed the relationship in a paper at the J. Lloyd Eaton Conference on Science Fiction and Fantasy Literature (1980). I have discussed *Briefing for a Descent into Hell* as a gnostic novel in *Journal of Religion*, 61 (January 1981), 20-36.

⁶ *Pagan and Christian in an Age of Anxiety* (1965; rpt. NY: Norton, 1970), p. 19, n. 1.

⁷ Hans Jonas, *The Gnostic Religion*, (Boston: Beacon Press, 1963), p. 32. For a complete guide to decoding Bloom's nomenclature, see Gnostic texts, especially James M. Robinson, ed., *The Nag Hammadi Library in English* (NY: Harper & Row, 1977). Dick quotes from Jonas' article, "Gnosticism," in *The Encyclopedia of Philosophy*, ed. Paul Edwards, 8 vols. (NY: Macmillan/Free Press, 1967), 3: 336-342, as well as from the Gnostic treatise On the Origin of the World in NHL.

⁸ Jonas, p. 45.

⁹ The following is summarized from Jonas, pp. 174-197.

¹⁰ It is also an anagram of *salvi-*, as in "salvific"; cf. Latin *salvus*, "saved," "safe."

¹¹ According to Jonas, in some Gnostic teachings, including a Valentinian branch, the highest godhead is called "Man." (p. 217).

¹² There is a major chronological anomaly in Fat's account: He connects the destruction of the Temple in Jerusalem in 70 C.E. with the hiding of the Coptic Gnostic library at Chenoboskon (Nag Hammadi). The latter event took place, however, around 400 C.E. (NHL, p. 2).

¹³ Platt, p. 156.

¹⁴ At FL 144 Olam's mission is said to be "for earth alone." Nowhere else in the text is it even implied that Olam's mission is restricted to earth.

¹⁵ Lucifer is also called Helel (FL 216), another name for fallen angel or fallen star; see Gustav Davidson, *A Dictionary of Angels* (NY: Free Press, 1967), s.v. "Helel." This name can be contrasted to Heleleth (or Eleleth), the angel of understanding, a true light-bringer, in the Gnostic text *The Hypostasis of the Archons* (NHL, pp. 152-157). The Lucifer/morning star/Venus associations give rise to speculation that Bloom's planet Lucifer might be Venus, offering a nice contrast to Lewis' Christianized Venus, Perelandra.

¹⁶ Manichaeans teach that the defeat of the Primal Man effects the defeat of the forces of

darkness. The Archons of Darkness devour the Primal Man's soul, thereby mixing good and evil. The Father then creates the material cosmos to separate good and evil and save the light. See Jonas, ch. 9, esp. pp. 215-221.

[17] See Jonas, *Gnostic Religion*, p. 176.

[18] The translation provided by NHL, p. 41, is clearer: "It is within Unity that each one will attain himself; within knowledge he will purify himself from multiplicity into Unity, consuming matter within himself like fire, and darkness by light, death by life." Jonas does not include this passage in his translation; for his discussion of the preceding portion of the text see Jonas, pp. 196-197.

[19] *olam* = Hebrew, "eternity," "world" (in the sense of "aeon"); Jonas, p. 54, n. 2.

[20] *sakla* = Hebrew, "fool"; NHL, p. 152.

[21] The point of difference between Olam and Perscors is the difference between the Manichaean and the Valentinian explanations of the origin to evil. To the Manichaean darkness is independent, external from the beginning; thus, the Primal Man's ordeals. The Valentinian finds evil within the Pleroma itself, in ignorance; the subject and the object of the quest are identical. See Jonas, pp. 236-237.

[22] At the 1978 International Conference on Gnosticism at Yale (where Bloom was one of the keynote speakers), there was considerable disagreement over "Sethianism." See especially the papers by Kurt Rudolph, H.-M. Schenke, and Frederick Wisse in Bentley Layton, ed., *The Rediscovery of Gnosticism*, vol. 2: *Sethian Gnosticism* (Leiden: E.J. Brill, forthcoming).

[23] (NY: Oxford U.P., 1975), p. 3. Also *The Anxiety of Influence*, pp. 5, 19, 30.

[24] Denis Donoghue, review of *The Flight to Lucifer*, in *The New York Times Book Review*, May 13, 1979, p. 32. I am greatly indebted to Donoghue's comments on the relationship of FL to Bloom's critical works.

[25] Bloom's *Agon: Towards a Theory of Revisionism* (NY: Oxford U.P., 1982), published after the completion of this essay, contains not only further evidence of the role of Gnosticism in his work ("A Prelude to Gnosis," pp. 3-15), but also the text of his Eaton Conference paper ("*Clinamen*: Towards a Theory of Fantasy," pp. 200-223), which makes explicit his "obsession" with Lindsay and his indebtedness to *A Voyage to Arcturus*. On the differences between the two works he writes: "If *A Voyage to Arcturus* reads as though Thomas Carlyle was writing *Through the Looking Glass*, then *The Flight to Lucifer* reads as though Walter Pater was writing *Star Wars*" (p. 222).

History and Utopia in Marge Piercy's Woman on the Edge of Time

Thomas P. Moylan

A utopian vision and anger at the denial of that vision have been present in Marge Piercy's writing since *Breaking Camp*, her first book of poetry published in 1968. The closing lines of the poem "The Peaceable Kingdom" are significant:

> This nation is founded on blood like a city on swamps yet its dream has been beautiful
> and sometimes just that now grows brutal and heavy as a burned out star.[1]

Piercy's utopic fiction grew out of her political activism, beginning with the New Left and the woman's movement which came from it, unlike writers of critical utopias like Joanna Russ, Ursula LeGuin, and Samuel Delany, whose work developed directly within the science fiction genre itself. Piercy's second novel, *Dance the Eagle to Sleep* (1970) is set in the near future and is a science fiction extrapolation of the dreams of the New Left in the 1960's, concerning guerilla warfare and communes. Her next novel, *Small Changes* (1972) is realistic, but in *Woman on the Edge of Time* (1976), she combines both realism and utopian science fiction, a combination that has caused some to prefer this novel to her others.[2] It comes from the tradition of American utopian literature rather than from a science fiction tradition.[3] The

133

realistic story of Connie Ramos is juxtaposed with a vision of the future society of Mattapoisset, a utopian village. Piercy uses the generic possibilities of science fiction to open up the narrative structure, and free it from the restrictions of the present.

Connie Ramos has come to New York from a Mexican village, with her child Angelina. She has had two years of college, but she is very poor; while she is coping with the death of her lover she beats Angelina and consequently loses custody of the child and is committed to Bellevue. The novel opens with her return to the city from Bellevue. In an attempt to save her niece from violence at the hands of the pimp she is living with, Connie is arrested again; the niece supports her lover's story and Connie is sent back to the mental ward. The plot develops in a series of episodes which move back and forth between the mental ward and visits to the utopia; it is an escalating spiral which ends in violence.

Connie meets other patients, who are her friends, like Sybil, a witch, who has been rejected by society, and Skip, a gay youth who is eventually driven to suicide by parental and other official attitudes toward his sexual preferences. These patients, and others whom she meets, are lined up on one side; on the other are the members of the medical team who are embarking on an experiment to control the "socially violent" by implanting a sending device in their brains which will allow the doctors to monitor them and to control their behavior through a computer. Apart from the ease of handling controlled people, this device would reduce costs, since to a large extent supervision of mental patients would be automated.

Woven into the hell that is life in the mental institution under threat of the knife, are the utopian segments of the novel. Connie has psychic powers; this is apparent on the first page of the book; someone is trying to contact her. "Either I saw him or I didn't and I'm crazy for real this time," she says, as a shadowy figure she has seen vanishes, leaving behind a chair that is still warm. By chapter two, when Connie is in the mental ward it is clear that someone from the future is communicating with her. The visitor is travelling in time, exploring the past and enlisting help for the future. The visitor, who is called Luciente, is androgynous; Connie at first mistakenly takes Luciente for a young Indio male.

Luciente is Connie's guide to the future: Connie is transported there by telepathy, which allows her body to be reconstituted in the future. This transference is achieved at times when Connie is most relaxed and receptive.

The utopian village of Mattapoisett is near Buzzards Bay in what was once Massachusetts. The year is 2137; there has been a thirty-year war which has devastated the major cities of the world; and which has resulted in a revolution: the forces of capitalism and industrial technology have been overthrown and driven to the space platforms, the moon and Antarctica. There are no longer any skyscrapers and no spaceports. Buildings, which are small and scattered randomly about, are made of recycled materials. Land that is not under cultivation or used for grazing, is left to grow wild. Travelling is done on foot or bicycle; long distances are covered by hovercraft "floaters."

The economy of Mattapoisett is communist and decentralized. High technology is used to alleviate some of the rigors of work, but not to eliminate it entirely. Each region produces all the items it needs. Work is shared by all, including children and the elderly. But everyone works part time so that nobody works long hours: four hours one month, sixteen another, and continuously at harvesttime, or if catastrophes occur, or if one is on military duty. Non-productive jobs have been eliminated.

Computers automate difficult or dangerous work, but no automation exists for work that is considered productive and fulfilling, like gardening, cooking or taking care of children. Natural energy sources are used: solar, methane gas from compost heaps, wind and water-power, tidal power, and wood for burning. Plants and animals are bred for maximum value, but the genetic diversity of the ecosystem is preserved: as an example, single-celled creatures called "spinners" have been developed to serve in colonies as fences and barriers, which mend themselves when necessary. Medicine can use cell manipulation to repair vision, to re-attach severed limbs, and for extrauterine reproduction. Bodies are repaired by regrowing cells, a reversal of the negative energy of cancer. At the same time, folk medicine is also employed: voodoo, Indian, peasant herbal lore, etc. Science and technology are used in all aspects of life, to ease the burdens and improve the quality of life without damaging initiative or the ecosystem. The profit motive, needless to say, has been erased.

When Connie asks during one of her visits to see the government at work, she is told that "nobody's working there today." The government is a town hall kind, with a planning council; beyond it there is a regional grand council of villages. After debate the needs of each village are determined and scarce resources are divided on consensus. Representatives from the villages are chosen by lot for one year. Leadership is rotated to prevent the formation of an elite class: "After we've served in a way that seems important, we serve in a job usually done by young people waiting to begin an apprenticeship or crossers atoning for a crime." (p. 244).

The social unit of Mattapoisett is dual: the self, and the community or tribe. Personal living space is private: from puberty on, every adult has a separate room. Conception is limited to laboratories where fetuses, genetically engineered for optimal diversity, are developed and where they remain until birth. Parenting is agreed to by three friends who then apply to the laboratory, or "brooder". These "co-mothers' may be any combination of sex, and are seldom lovers: "So the child will not get caught in a love misunderstanding." (p. 68). When the child reaches puberty at twelve or thirteen he/she goes through an initiation ordeal: a week alone in the wilderness where a vision quest occurs. The child then chooses a name based on the vision, and is a full adult, who can participate in government, become an apprentice or join the military. The three parents, who have shared in raising the child, may not speak to him/her for three months after the name has been chosen, "lest we forget we aren't mothers anymore and person is an equal member." (p. 109). The child selects three aunts when he/she is named; these, of either sex, act as advisors during the years of early adulthood.

Connie visits the brooder and is upset by the sight of the fetuses in their little sacs. Luciente answers that all power had to be given up in the new society, including the power to give birth. This also biologically enchained women, and prevented men from becoming loving and tender. Nuclear bonding had to be broken. (p.98). It has been possible to adapt males to breast feed.

Language has been reformed. *He* and *she* have been replaced by *per*; *man* and *woman* by *person*. Telepathic words have been coined: *inter-see*, *redding*, *inknowing*, *grasp*, along with words like *ownfed*, *comothers*, *worming* and new slang. Names too are different from present names. Even after choosing a name on adulthood, one can change again whenever one wishes. The names come from two categories: nature (Jackrabbit, Dawn, Otter, Bee, Aspen, Orion, Rose) and political history (Diana, Sappho, Sojourner, Susan B., Neruda, Sacco-Vanzetti, Red Star, Crazy Horse). A few are simply Spanish (Luciente, Innocente, Magdalena), since Piercy draws from what have been called "the sub-cultures of poverty" for admirable prototypes. Connie says of the villagers, "They are not like Anglos; they were more like Chicanos or Puerto Ricans in the touching, the children in the middle of things, the feeling of community and fiesta." (p. 119-120).

Education in this utopia is life-long. Children, who are cared for in a nursery by those who choose childcare, are also taken to work, encouraged to help and taught by the entire community. They are taught to read when they are four; they are taught also meditation and yoga. Sexual expressiveness is not repressed. Studying goes on throughout adulthood; there is no line drawn between school and work.

Celebrations are important: everyday comfortable, useful clothes are exchanged for costumes and "flimsies", a garment for festivals. There are 18 holidays, 10 minor holidays and special feasts to celebrate special occasions. There is also a death ritual, in which everyone in the village stays up all night at a wake. Burial is in the morning, when a mulberry tree is planted. Then a new baby is begun. Population is kept low; therefore when someone dies an opportunity is created for others to mother.

Each person wears a wristwatch-like device, called a "kenner," which links him/her to a central computer and communications system. The kenner is part personal memory, part telephone and part analytical tool. People feel lost without it. Telepathy, another kind of communication, is also used. In case of conflict there are criticism/self-criticism sessions. If conflict does not cease, there is a community "worming" where the conflict is opened so that it can be dealt with in public. Animals like cows, cats and dolphins, can be understood by humans in Mattapoisett; they have either been bred to speak, or humans have learned their languages. Washoe Day, a major holiday, celebrates the chimpanzee who was the first animal to learn communication between species.

Parenting is separate from sexual activity; a free and sometimes complex sexuality is regarded as a natural part of life. "Fasure, we couple. Not for money, not for a living. For love, for pleasure, for relief, out of habit, out of curiosity and lust." (p. 58). Some people couple monogamously for a while, some are celibate, most are sexually active with various people and whichever genders they choose.

Freedom in this society is balanced by community need. Everyone is expected to share work, to contribute to political and military needs, and to care for the environment. Work and attendance at meetings are required. Those who will not cooperate are asked to leave and exiles accordingly wander from village to village. There are no courts, no police force, no jails. Although there is little theft, since there is little private property, assault and murder occur. Rehabilitation is the answer; in serious cases people are sent away to sea or out to space. The community attempts to work it out. Murder can be atoned for, once, but someone who kills twice is killed: capital punishment exists for a second willful murder.

Mattapoisett is not the only society Connie visits. In chapter 15 she projects by mistake into a totalitarian future that is sexist, racist, overpopulated and polluted. Connie's guide is not Luciente, but Gildina, who is covered with gold and has been physically altered to give pleasure to the man whom she serves. Those in this society, male or female, who cannot earn money must sell off their organs and die before they are forty. The "richies" who buy these transplants live for two hundred years, on space platforms above the polluted earth. The middle classes have to be conditioned to survive in this atmosphere. This society is run by the "multies," mutli-national corporations that have divided the world among them and eliminated nations. Connie's conversation with Gildina has been monitored and a security Cyborg, which works for Chase World-ITT, breaks into Gildina's apartment and attempts to kill Connie, sensing that she is not controlled.

Luciente tells Connie that Mattapoisett is not inevitable. It is only one possible future. Connie is asked to work for the future, which can take place under the blue skies of Mattapoisett or the yellow skies of New York. She can influence history.

In the mental ward the patients have tried to resist the surgical implantation, but one by one they fall under the knife. Connie, however, having been inspired and strengthened by her visits to Mattapoisett, chooses to resist by escaping. She is helped by Sybil and Luciente, an alliance of present and future. The images of escape are those of the ante-bellum slave: the North Star and the dipper; she follows the drinking gourd. But she is recaptured after only a few days.

Before she can resist further, she undergoes the operation. But she does not give up, even then. At this point in the novel the alternating moments of oppression and utopia cease to some extent: Skip commits suicide, two other patients are implanted. The future is affected: Jackrabbit, a future Skip, dies in battle. The war against the enemy is going badly, and Connie loses contact with Mattapoisett, reaching instead the New York dystopia.

She is able to return, however, for Jackrabbit's funeral. Her visits to the future are lasting a long time; back in the present she appears to the doctors to be in a trance, from which they cannot rouse her, and they become frightened. Connie goes to the front lines in an airship and helps to fight: she is becoming attuned to the idea of struggle. In a twilight vision between worlds she sees all the "flacks of power who had pushed her back and turned her off and locked her up and medi-

cated her and tranquillized her and punished her and condemned her."
(p. 325). Her second extended trance frightens the doctors into removing the implantation from her brain. She tries to urge the others to
action saying, "We can imagine all we like. But we got to do something
real." (p. 332).

On a visit to her brother's suburban home over Thanksgiving Connie decides to act: she will destroy the medical team. She steals some
Parathion from her brother's plant nursery; it is a weapon, she thinks,
"that came from the same place as the electrodes and the Thorazine..."
(p. 351). She has stolen, she believes, one of the weapons of the
powerful.

When she sees Luciente, she learns that the battle in which she
fought has never taken place; her resolution has affected the temporal
vectors. Luciente encourages her to poison the doctors' coffee, when
she has qualms about the violence of the action. Power, Luciente says,
cannot be destroyed peacefully. Connie accordingly kills four of the six
members of the medical team, cuts herself off from Mattapoisett, and
prepares for punishment.

But her life simply continues as a "socially violent" person in the
state hospital. Thus the ending is bleak, but the utopia informs the
entire novel.

Piercy's utopia, like Russ's and LeGuin's, is not actually perfect.
Connie is critical about some of its aspects:

> "What could a man of this ridiculous Podunk future, when babies were born from
> machines and people negotiated...with cows, know about how it had been to grow up
> in America black or brown? (p. 97)...You still go crazy. You still get sick. You grow old.
> You die. I thought in a hundred and fifty years some of these problems could be solved,
> anyhow!" (p. 118).

There is jealousy in Mattapoisett between Luciente and Bolivar,
both lovers of Jackrabbit—even in utopia there is personal conflict.
There is political conflict as well, as the Shaping Controversy demonstrates: the Shapers want to breed new life forms for selective traits; the
Mixers want to maintain the status quo and intervene with nature only
in the case of birth defects or disease. Luciente and her friends are
Mixers; the status quo is close to the ideal. The Shapers, for Piercy,
appear to present a return to the improper exercise of power, the
arrogance of technocracy.

Another problem with the utopia lies in the continued opposition to
it of its enemies, the industrial capitalist technocrats holding onto

their slim base of power. The alternate future, the dystopia, carries a warning in its existence.

If one ignores the science fiction element of the book, one could assert, as some critics have, that *Woman on the Edge of Time* is the realistic story of an insane woman who has imagined the entire story of Mattapoisett. It is true that the question of Connie's contact with the utopia is rather ambiguous, and the fantasies she has lead her to act, whether they are only in her head or not. But such a reading, while it can be defended, would reduce the events to an expression of individual change, and the rich texture that is created by the collective past, present and future would be lost. One of the most interesting things about the novel is that Piercy has apparently used the generic possibilities of science fiction to articulate the workings of history. Telepathic transportation through time allows the author to dramatize the raising of Connie's consciousness through encounters with other modes of life and thought. Time travel, with its alternate universes that are brought into being by actions that change the "temporal vectors," allows her to express the process of historical change in a free untrammeled way. The novel would be much less powerful if it were simply a work of social realism. Realism, on the other hand, as the other generic strategy used here, prevents the science fictional and utopian elements from turning the book into escapist fantasy. The agony of Connie's everyday life reinforces the power of the utopia, because it makes clearer the need for the utopia, or at least for drastic social change.

The result of this generic mix of science fiction and realism is a powerful statement that is both challenging and disturbing. Piercy does not assert utopia, she activates it.

NOTES

[1] "The Peaceable Kingdom" in *Breaking Camp* (Middletown, Ct: Wesleyan Univ. Press, 1968), pp. 68-69.

[2] *Dance the Eagle to Sleep* (Garden City, N.Y.: Doubleday, 1970). *Small Changes* (Doubleday, 1973). *Woman on the Edge of Time* (NY: Knopf, 1976).

[3] Another example of a political utopian novel from this period is Ernest Callenbach, *Ectopia* (Berkeley: Banyan Books, 1975). This comes out of ecological and not feminist-socialist concerns. For a fuller discussion of critical utopias, see my unpublished dissertation: "Figures of Hope: Structure and Ideology in the Critical Utopias of the 1970's" University of Wisconsin-Milwaukee, May, 1981.

Mechanism and Medievalism in John Gardner's Grendel

Rudy S. Spraycar

The theme of the mechanized, deterministic universe is manifest in many of John Gardner's novels, but it is nowhere more central than in *Grendel* (1971),[1] with its sympathetic monster-antihero. Gardner's critics have not, in general, gone much beyond *Grendel*'s debt to Boethius's *Beowulf* in assessing the novel's medievalism. To be sure, Joseph Milosh has mentioned Boethius in speaking of *Grendel*;[2] for him, a minor "reminiscence" of Boethius on the limits of worldly glory (55) undercuts "traditional [*i.e.*, Boethian] wisdom" (56). But, as we shall see, Boethian philosophy is more than what Milosh might call a "byway" (49) in our reading of *Grendel*; rather, an understanding of the relation in this novel between an apparently mechanical universe and the determinism that Boethius ultimately rejects leads to a more cogent understanding of Gardner's art.

1.

Throughout his fiction, Gardner exposes the mechanical behavior of modern alienated man. In *The Sunlight Dialogues* (1972), Clumly nods, "mechanical as an old German clockmaker's doll,"[3] " 'patrolmen grow increasingly mechanical' " (234), and old Arthur Hodge " 'turned his sons into robots' " (286). Kathleen Paxton "touched her hair, trying to smooth it.... The hand moving on the hair had lost meaning. It worked like a machine" (256). In *The Resurrection* (1966)

John Horne sits down "abruptly, like something mechanical."[4] In *Nickel Mountain* (1973), Henry Soames' "voice was mechanical, like his words. Even his eating looked mechanical....",[5] and there is the "mechanized, cold-blooded, money-grubbing evil of *W.D. Freund and Sons Dairy Farms...*" (265).

In *October Light* (1976) Peter Wagner's vision is chilling: "the structure of the universe: waves, particles in random collision," making of him and Jane "two brute mechanisms."[6] Another character, " 'Captain Fist,... has discovered beyond any shadow of a doubt that all life is mechanics.... All men, he has come to understand, are victims, objects in fact no more rational than planets...' " (320). The status of men in a modern deterministic universe is associated with the planets that rule men's fates in ancient astrology.

The ancient notion of the *Deus absconditus* is yoked with the quintessential image of modern technology—the factory—in *The Sunlight Dialogues*: "a terrible thought, that after God's withdrawal into silence the ancient mechanisms which made prophets arise should continue working, like machines left on in an abandoned factory..." (406). In *The Resurrection*, meaning must be denied to such a universe: " '*What means all this*? Nothing! Absolutely nothing! A game of blind forces' " (235). In *Nickel Mountain* George Loomis is led to absolve Henry Soames of guilt for Simon Bale's death by arguing that " 'it was an accident. Henry was the accidental instrument, a pawn, a robot labelled *Property of Chance*' " (235). Denials of responsibility for the acts of people who are *automata* are linked with the abolition of free will in *October Light*: " 'Everything's got to be an accident unless you decide there are gods and devils. We do nothing... So everybody's a machine, an automation...' " (324-25). In *The Resurrection* John Horne says, " 'Suppose men really do have no freedom at all. Or rather, suppose that only certain of us—the elect, let us say—can freely choose, while the rest, damned by predestination, corrupt in our very chemistry, have no choice? How *can* we be born again?' " (150).

The despair here has a Christian flavor which we find in the resolutions of Gardner's other novels. Gardner's moral art is grounded not only in Christianity but also in medieval philosophy. He has stressed the importance to Chaucer's art of the philosophy of Boethius in particular; concluding, for instance, his summary of Boethian philosophy in *The Life and Times of Chaucer*, with the observation that Chaucer dramatizes Boethian philosophy in "poem after poem."[7] Boethius' argument for both free will and Providence and against the notion of a deterministic cosmos ruled by chance is important for our understanding of Gardner's own fiction as well. Witness a representative allusion in *The King's Indian* (1972):

"I began to have an uneasy feeling—residue, perhaps, of my reading of Boethius—that my seeming freedom on the still, dark whaler was a grotesque illusion, that sneaking alone through hostile darkness I was watched by indifferent, dusty [sic] eyes, a cosmic checker, a being as mechanical as any automation displayed in the Boston theaters."[8]

Here Gardner's narrator evidently remembers only Lady Philosophy's summary to Boethius of Aristotelian causality, forgetting that she goes on immediately to a defense of free will, and attributing to the "cosmic checker" the determinism of a world "bound by the fatal chain" (Book V, Prose 1 and 2).

Indications of the relevance of Boethian philosophy to Gardner's theme of mechanization are to be found in *Grendel*, the retelling of *Beowulf*. In order to understand Grendel's depiction of a mechanistic world, we must first observe how Gardner has transformed Grendel from a monster alien into a sympathetic antihero.

2.

The most unexpectedly sympathetic aspect of Grendel is the insight into the mind of Grendel himself. Because Grendel tells the story in the first-person, we see Danish society from his point of view. Thus we accept the sometimes humorous, always disturbing, satiric picture[9] Gardner draws of that society. Joseph Milosh observes that "the humanizing of Grendel is necessary to Gardner's portrayal of the absurdity of war" (50). So Grendel "was sickened, if only at the waste of it: all they killed—cows, horses, men—they left to rot or burn."[10] As a non-human, Grendel is free to observe that "the men still drank, getting louder and braver, talking about what they are going to do to the bands on the other hills.... no wolf was so vicious to other wolves..." (26-27). He further mocks the traditional heroic "boasting at the bench" in the meadhall: "when one of them finished his raving threats, another would stand up and lift up his ram's horn, or draw his sword, or sometimes both if he was very drunk, and he'd tell them what *he* planned to do" (27). It is easy for Grendel (and consequently for us) to regard Hrothgar's foundation of a glorious kingdom merely as plunder and rapine.[11]

Gardner brilliantly evokes sympathy for this monster by presenting him as a social outcast or alien. Our sympathy for Beowulf in his brief appearance is based on Gardner's portrayal of him, too, as an outsider, or "stranger" (142).

Gardner's presentation of Grendel as a modern anti-hero causes the reader to feel sympathy for a cannibal:

> As if casually, in plain sight of them all, I bit his head off, crunched through the helmet and skull with my teeth and, holding the jerking, blood-slippery body in two hands, sucked the blood that sprayed like a hot, thick geyser from his neck. It got all over me. I fled with the body to the woods, heart churning—boiling like a flooded ditch—with glee. (68-69)

Another mention of Grendel's anthropophagy is perhaps more horrible for its casual tone and laconic humor: "I have eaten several priests. They sit on the stomach like duck eggs" (112). Though Gardner portrays Grendel's inhuman behavior quite as graphically as does the *Beowulf* poet, we nevertheless sympathize with the monster, because of such scenes as his ill-fated attempt to speak with the Danes. Moved by the power of the words of the Shaper, Grendel says that he

> staggered out into the open and up toward the hall with my burden, groaning out, "Mercy! Peace!"...Drunken men rushed me with battle-axes. I sank to my knees, crying, "Friend! Friend!" They hacked at me, yipping like dogs. (44)

Neither Grendel's fault nor the Danes', the failure of communication is, for us as well as for Grendel, a "pity" (44), though the men's "yipping like dogs" dehumanizes them as it humanizes the monster.

Grendel is a descendant of the outcast race of Cain, a race of two: the other is his mother who affords him little intelligent company. Her most articulate statement is the "one sound: *Dool-dool! Dool-dool!*, scratching at her bosom, a ghastly attempt to climb back up to speech" (47). Grendel comments on the failure of his attempt to make friends with the Danes: " 'Why can't I have someone to talk to?... The Shaper has people to talk to...Hrothgar has people to talk to' " (45). Because Grendel attempts friendships and communication, he wins our sympathy, though we cannot condone the violence of his actions.

3.

In contrast to Grendel's failure to communicate stands the poet, or Shaper's success. The Shaper (from Anglo-Saxon *scop*), teaches the power of language and " 'reshapes the world...So his name implies...He takes what he finds...and by changing men's minds he makes the best of it' " (41). It is no accident that as we first encounter the Shaper, he tells, as does the *Scop* in *Beowulf*, "of how the earth was first built, long ago..." (43). The Creator himself (Anglo-Saxon *scieppend*) first shaped the world, and Adam helped shape to human consciousness the creatures as he *named* them in Eden and as the Shaper does anew with his words. As Norma L. Hutman puts it, "God and the Shaper are kinsmen. Each makes the world..."[12] That this connection is a common one is suggested by roots of the words "poetry" (Greek *poiein*, to create) and both "cosmos" and "cosmetic" (Greek *kosmos*, order/world).[13] The poet is thus an ontological cosmetologist putting a "new face" on the world for his lord Hrothgar, who translates the Shaper's visions into a new political and material order. The formal enclosure of the meadhall and the extension of the Danes' political hegemony set boundaries against powerful surrounding forces of chaos at three levels: in little, in the mead-hall; medially, in Hrothgar's kingdom; and, finally, in middle-earth, the vast, doomed dwelling itself. Hrothgar's roads, for example, as Hutman say, "concretize man's control over environment and the unity of a kingdom" (20).

It is the power of the poet's words that initially seduces Grendel, bringing about his first, ineffectual "conversion" (44). The traditionally religious dimension of poetry in general is reflected in the word "conversion" and is underscored by Grendel's ejaculation of " 'Mercy! Peace!' " (44). Though Grendel's conversion is doomed to relapse through the failure of his communication with the Danes, his second conversion is a lasting one. By naming the beasts Adam participates in creation, and so the crucial sign of the validity of Grendel's second conversion is his assumption of a new name: "I was Grendel, Ruiner of Meadhalls, Wrecker of Kings!" (69). The copula affirms Grendel's very *being*, and the plural objects make for a fully generic identity, though the plural soon degenerates into a single meadhall and a single king: "What will we call the Hrothgar-Wrecker when Hrothgar has been wrecked?" (79). The second conversion, like the first, has a Christian context: "I had *become* something, as if born again" (69).[14]

" 'Why shouldn't one change one's ways, improve one's character?'" asks Grendel of the dragon. (61). Joseph Milosh asserts that "In *Beowulf*, the character Grendel is static...Gardner's Grendel...grows, passing through several initiations, evolving more than many a modern hero" (49). Grendel seems now to have developed into a creature for whom words are effective. Has he truly been transformed by his ability to change himself with words into a creature whose words wield power?

It would seem so, for just as the Shaper "built this hall by the power of his songs" (39) because his "thought took seed in Hrothgar's mind" (40), so have Grendel's actions transformed the odious meadhall into a prison-cave like his own dwelling; now Hrothgar "waits like a man chained in a cave, staring at the entrance or, sometimes, gazing with sad, absent-minded eyes at Wealtheow, chained beside him" (106). Like the Shaper, Grendel has transformed Hrothgar's life and inverted the status of the meadhall itself.[15] Moreover, in hearing Grendel "*sing walls*," or make a poem, Beowulf finds Grendel "slyer than he guessed" (151).

Yet in his battle with Beowulf, Grendel succumbs as much to the power of Beowulf's words in battle as to his grip. Grendel comes to "understand [Beowulf's] lunatic theory of matter and mind, the chilly intellect, the hot imagination, blocks and builder, reality as stress" (151). But Beowulf's triumph is neither that of simple suggestion nor even that of "mind *over* matter"; the Shaper's lesson, evidently misunderstood by Grendel, is that mind *is* matter: the Shaper " 'reshapes the world' " (41). Grendel's use of the power of words never goes beyond solipsism: "Talking, talking, spinning a spell, pale skin of words that closes me in like a coffin" (11); " 'I exist, nothing else' " (22).

Beowulf's "insanity" or secret of success, then, is that he eschews the dichotomies of mind and matter, of poetry and action, of word and work. Action springs from the same well as do the human charms to whch Grendel had earlier fallen prey: the powers of words and poetry and the power of beauty; thus Grendel lets the queen live because she is beautiful (94-95). Grendel sees heroic valor and poetry and beauty as impediments: "Ah, woe, woe! How many times must a creature be dragged down the same ridiculous road? The Shaper's lies, the hero's self-delusion, now this: the idea of a queen!" (93). But Beowulf powerfully welds all three powers with the metonymy of the human hand: "*Time is the mind, the hand that makes (fingers on harpstrings, hero-swords, the acts, the eyes of queens). By that I kill you*" (149-50).

Grendel's apparently false divisions of reality echo ironically Lady Philosophy's warning to Boethius not to mistake the parts for the whole, especially "*limited goods*, which...are not perfect in embracing *all* that is good, are not man's path to happiness, [and cannot] make him happy in themselves."[16] (Italics added) Moreover, a parodic echo of Boethian notions of the relation of free will and God's foreknowledge is evident in the dragon's speech to Grendel:

"Dragons don't mess with your piddling free will...If you with your knowledge of present and past recall that a certain man slipped on, say, a banana peel, or fell off his chair, or drowned in a river, that recollection does not mean that you *caused* him to slip, or fall, or drown...It happened, and you know it, but knowledge is not *cause*... Well, so with me. My knowledge of the future does not *cause* the future. It merely *sees* it, exactly as creatures at your low level recall things past. And even, if, say, I interfere— burn up somebody's mead-hall, for instance, whether because I just felt like it or because some supplicant asked me to—even then I do not change the future, I merely do what I saw from the beginning. That's obvious, surely. Let's say it's settled then. So much for free will and intercession!" (54)

Compare the conclusion of Beothius' similar, if less humorous, argument: "from the standpoint of divine knowledge...things are necessary because of the condition of their being known by God; but, considered only in themselves, they lose nothing of the absolute freedom of their own natures."[17] Yet just as the dragon abandons Boethius' thought as he finds the order of reality illusory (55), so throughout the novel Grendel maintains the error from which Lady Philosophy attempts to disenchant Boethius—that the universe is governed by chance.

The ordered vision of the "harper's lure" (46) threatens Grendel's early ideas that " 'the world is all pointless accident' " (22) and that "I knew what I knew, the mindless mechanical bruteness of things" (46). The ram, the sign of the Zodiac associated with the first of the novel's twelve chapters reminds us of astrological determinism, now "keeps on climbing, mindless, mechanical" (122), despite Grendel's best efforts to deter him; that the goat keeps climbing with "dangling brains" (123) enhances the vision of mindless worldly action. For Grendel, even the Geatish heroes come ashore in Denmark "quick as wolves—but mechanical, terrible" (134), and they move "like one creature, huge strange machine" (136) toward the meadhall, just as mechanical as Hrothgar's bowman in pursuit of a hart:

incredibly, through the pale, strange light the man's hand moves—click click click click—toward the bow, and grasps it, and draws it down, away from the shoulder and around in front (click click) and transfers the bow to the slowly moving second hand, and the first hand goes back up and (click) over the shoulder and returns with an arrow, threads the bow. Suddenly time is a rush for the hart: his head flicks, he jerks, his front legs buckling, and he's dead. He lies as still as the snow hurtling outward around him to the hushed world's rim. (110)

In self-conscious reflection Grendel sees even himself acting "as if mechanically" (70).[18] So assured is Grendel of the role of chance of the universe, of the mechanical nature of the actions of beasts, men, and himself, that he repeatedly asserts that it is "by accident" (149, 150, 151) that Beowulf twists his arm around behind his back, and that " 'Poor Grendel's had an accident' ''; " 'It was an accident.... Blind, mindless, mechanical. Mere logic of chance' '' (152).

Juxtaposed with Beowulf's vision of a governed universe—" *'it was granted to me* that I might kill him with my sword, which same I did' '' (142; emphasis mine)—Grendel's partial vision[19] limits his reliability as a narrator. He is reliable about his own psychological and even spiritual development, but he is unreliable about the whole. Ironically, it is because of the intensity with which he shares in the poet's role as narrator that this is so. The world that Grendel presents is built by his mind, by his words, created, to be sure, in co-operation with the word-man or Shaper of human society as well as with the dragon. Despite this interaction, however, we have only Grendel's *word*, so to speak, for events and their meanings. He has framed his destiny within imposed limits because Grendel is a tragic figure of sorts. The limits of language bind the monster who has the gift of human speech. But by virtue of his failure in Boethian terms to regard his defeat as anything but an accident in a mechanized cosmos, Grendel is denied the Aristotelian *anagnorsis* essential to the truly tragic hero.

In contrast, the Shaper, together with the political order that he at once serves and masters, sings of a whole, a more than social unity that has the divine sanction of the word. Language is a profoundly social device, the *sine qua non* of the human community; it sets limits for a speaker who is profoundly alone. Grendel's identity, his name "wrecker of mead-halls," negates the social order of which language is the adhesive. Moreover, to the ontologically significant linguistic act of naming himself in his second conversion, Grendel subjoins, "But also, as never before, I was alone" (69). His superficially most positive act is really profoundly negative, for by virtue of his most significant use of words he breaks positive ties with communication, which is the essence of language.[20]

Isolation is inherent in the role Grendel accepts: "I wanted it, yes! Even if I must be the outcast, cursed by the rules of [the Shaper's] hideous fable" (47); this the dragon affirms:

"You improve them, my boy! Can't you see that yourself? You stimulate them! You make them think and scheme. You drive them to poetry, science, religion, all that makes them what they are for as long as they last. You are, so to speak, the brute existent by which they learn to define themselves. The exile, captivity, death they shrink from—the blunt facts of their mortality, their abandonment—that's what you make them recognize, embrace! You *are* mankind, or man's condition: inseparable as the mountain-climber and the mountain. If you withdraw, you'll instantly be replaced." (62)

Grendel's only possible role—though inessential—in relation to man is paradoxically that of the outsider who cannot and does not share in the community. In Susan Strehle's view, "Not an affirmer himself, the alien makes possible the affirmation of maturity, complexity, and understanding by other characters" (96).

In Grendel's newfound rage at the Shaper's song (66) is the seed of his second conversion, for in playing the only role available to him he cannot be a willing helper but must hate mankind. Like a scourge of God, he must remain in the dark, denied a full share in the understanding of what his actions have wrought. In the words of the " 'eldest and wisest of the priests' " (113), Ork, " 'Such is His mystery: that beauty requires contrast, and that discord is fundamental to the creation of new intensities of feeling' " (115).[21] But Grendel seems no more capable of digesting the words of priests than he is their bodies (112).

Both the privative nature of his mode of being and his perception of a mechanist universe limit Grendel's vision; the corollary of both is the existential tedium (127) that oppresses him: "Tedium is the worst pain" (121). This tedium is relieved only upon the Geats' arrival: "strangers have come, and it's a whole new game"; Grendel is "mad with joy.—At least I think it's joy.... *It's coming!*" (133). In the dragon's words, " 'expression is founded on the finite occasion' " (58), or, from Unferth's perspective, "*Except in the life of the hero, the whole world's meaningless*" (143).

Grendel makes no active connections with other users of language; his actions and words together are the anti-language that makes the poet's words and the hero's actions possible. He *is* the glory of the Danes and especially of Beowulf, for without his co-operation there is no glory. Unferth is the counter-example that proves the case. Both in the meadhall, pelted with apples by a mocking Grendel (71-74), and in the cave (74-78), he is denied success in combat and a hero's glorious death. In response to Grendel's taunt that heroes " 'were only in poetry' " (72), Unferth allows that "poetry's trash, mere clouds of words,' " but heroism is more than such " 'noble language, dignity' "; it is action like shaking his sword at Grendel (76). By sharing Grendel's belief in the dichotomy between words and works, Unferth unwittingly puts more than his body in Grendel's power. Hutman points out that it is in sharing with Grendel a limited vision that Unferth is an "anti-hero" (24). Only the whole man Beowulf with a unified vision that makes no such illusory distinctions can, in turn, make Grendel's meaningless being part of a meaningful *human* order. Or rather, Grendel's story would have no meaning for us had it not already been celebrated by the *Beowulf*-poet.

4.

The private pattern of language and its use by Grendel is the structure that resonates in our present world. Despite our sympathies, however profound, with Grendel, and despite his satirical undercutting of the good of the social order, Grendel's chaotic force has moral significance only as a foil for the human order. Like the archagent of man's original *felix culpa*, Grendel serves the greater glory of his adversaries despite himself. However innovatively Grendel's relationship with mankind is sketched (in terms of the themes of language, order, heroism, and their opposites), the structural pattern of the necessity of an inferior adversary for the hero's triumph is a profound echo of the "plot" of Christian salvation history. This resonance, however implicit it may be, is the root of our strong feeling for *Grendel*.

Just as medievalists cannot agree whether *Beowulf* itself is more fundamentally Christian than it is pagan, so we cannot tie *Grendel*'s structural resonance exclusively to a Christian *Weltanschauung*. We could, for example, discern in Grendel's story the working out of a Freudian (and, more fundamentally, an Hegelian) script: goaded by the chaotic Grendel as a figure of the id (thesis), the Shaper as superego responds antithetically in the name of human order; the synthesis represented by our whole man Beowulf is surprisingly analogous to the integrative order maintained by the human ego.[22] Yet we respond not so much to Christian allegoresis or Freudian psychomachic models as to *Grendel's* reflection of a multitude of polar oppositions that our culture takes for granted. The tension of these oppositions might be called the deep structure of Western culture; thus familiar cultural paradigms that echo that structure have a mythic appeal for us.

Gardner's fictive innovation lies in his denying to Grendel both the traditional explicit *anagnorsis* of the tragic hero and the modern affirmation of the anti-hero; "with respect to his readers,"[23] Gardner has left transcendance to us. We are granted the vision, denied to Grendel, of the affirmation of his antithesis. If Grendel's parting words, " 'Poor Grendel's had an accident.... *So may you all*' " (152), are the deathbed curse that Milosh (57) and Hutman (31) have made it out to be, then it is only by attaining the transcendent knowledge of Grendel's story that we can avoid being the victims of a narrow, cursed deterministic vision of a mechanistic world like his own. Even Milosh, who argues that *Grendel* "lack[s]...an explicit moral," concedes that "perhaps the final sentence is not a curse at all, but a Boethian observation meant to remind man that he is not in control" (57).

Gardner could be said to follow here the dictates of his own critical observations in *On Moral Fiction*, in which he speaks repeatedly of the "mechanization of modern life,"[24] for he observes that in connection with the novels of William Burroughs

> the threat against humanity...is that we may allow ourselves to be destroyed by our own accidental nature if we make no choices among accidents, such as the rise of mechanization...Almost all that we see and feel is accident folding over accident; yet we do see and feel and can make choices; the novel is the proof. (192)

In addition to his concern with modern existentialist philosophy, Gardner's moral approach to fiction shows the direct influence of his medieval studies. The Boethian approach to the problems of chance and accident has proven a fit vehicle for Gardner's moral observations on the recurrent theme of mechanization. Far from restricting his medievalism in *Grendel* to superficial allusions to *Beowulf*, Gardner has modernized and revitalized and dramatized a medieval philosophical stance.

NOTES

[1] The completion of this paper was facilitated by an American Council of Learned Societies Research Fellowship for Recent Recipients of the Ph.D. and by released time from the L.S.U. English Department. For their helpful comments I thank my colleagues, Professors Panthea Reid Broughton and Anna K. Nardo; my thanks also for the patient efforts of Joan Payne, Sharon Roberts, Phyllis Woods and Sheri Crisler of the L.S.U. Arts and Science Text Processing Center.

[2] "John Gardner's *Grendel*: Sources and Analogues," *Contemporary Literature*, 19, No. 1 (Winter 1978), pp. 55-57.

[3] (New York: Ballantine, 1973), "Prologue," p. 3.

[4] (New York: Ballantine, 1974), p. 114.

[5] (New York: Ballantine, 1975), p. 212.

[6] (Ballantine, 1978), pp. 192-93.

[7] (New York: Knopf, 1977), p. 78.

8 (New York: Ballantine, 1976), p. 248.

9 See Judy Smith Murr on Gardner's humor in "John Gardner's Order and Disorder: *Grendel* and *The Sunlight Dialogues*," *Critique: Studies in Modern Fiction*, 18, No. 2 (December 1976), 98. For Grendel's "biting, satiric mockery," see Susan Strehle, "John Gardner's Novels: Affirmation and the Alien," *Critique: Studies in Modern Fiction*, 18, No. 2 (December 1976), 92-93. For *Grendel's* "parodic quality" and "sustained humor," and for Grendel's self-mockery, see Strehle, p. 95.

10 *Grendel* (New York: Ballantine, 1972), p. 30.

11 For more examples of Grendel's undercutting of the would-be noble affairs of men, see Milosh, pp. 50-51.

12 Norma L. Hutman, "Even Monsters Have Mothers: A Study of *Beowulf* and John Gardner's *Grendel*," *Mosaic*, 9, No. 1 (Fall 1975), p. 21.

13 But Milosh stressed those comments of Grendel's that make for "the small worth of the poet's art" (p. 52), accepting Grendel's reliability as narrator in these cases.

14 Milosh, however, identifies this "spiritual development" as a parodic "bloody baptism" (p. 50).

15 Compare the prison cells in Gardner's *Sunlight Dialogues* and in *The Wreckage of Agathon* (New York: Ballantine, 1970). The cave may have a Platonic dimension as well.

16 Boethius, *The Consolation of Philosophy*, trans. Richard Green (Indianapolis: Bobbs-Merrill, 1962), p. 55.

17 Boethius, p. 118; the full extent of the argument comprises most of Book V of the *Consolation*. For other Boethian resonances in the novel, see Milosh, pp. 55-57.

18 Compare Gardner's character Peeker, "conscious of my consciousness of crying," in *Agathon*, p. 266.

19 For an alternative view, see Judy Smith Murr, p. 99; Murr finds Grendel a reliable narrator, credible in his conclusions about the role of chance and accident in the world (p. 101).

20 As Hutman observes, Grendel, the "lone, chaos-proclaiming, violent alien" who is isolated in his use of language, represents a dangerous potential for the members of society (p. 26).

21 Compare Hutman's list of such polarities in *Grendel*: "order and chaos...light and dark, day and night, earth and underground, life and death" (p. 21). Murr makes the relationship between the antagonists explicitly reflexive: "Grendel and man...need each other for definition" (p. 104).

22 Grendel's womb-like cave shared only with his undemanding mother has profound psychoanalytic resonances. Hutman finds a "fundamental parallel between man and monster, wherein the monster represents some older form of ourselves, that lone, chaos-proclaiming violent alien to society from which our fraternal, ordered, ethical selves have sprung" (p. 26).

24 Walter J. Slatoff recommends we regard fiction not as objects of analysis but as expressions of humanity, in *With Respect to Readers: Dimensions of Literary Response* (Ithaca and London: Cornell University Press, 1970), p. 167.

25 (NY: Basic Books, 1978), pp. 164, 195.

PART FIVE:

FEMINISM AND SCIENCE FICTION

While the essay which follows might well have been included in the preceding section, it represents an approach to science fiction which has begun in the last few years to have a dramatic impact on a number of widely held assumptions about the genre. Fan conferences have begun to feel the impact of the feminist perspective, feminist fanzines have appeared, academic journals have devoted whole issues to the work of women writers in science fiction, and at least one critical anthology (*Future Females*, editd by Marleen S. Barr, Bowling Green State University Popular Press, 1981) has focused on women in science fiction. Women have always written science fiction, of course, but their impact on the genre has never been as great as today. In a recent issue of *Extrapolation* devoted to women writers, Mary T. Brizzi wrote, "Today many, maybe even most, of the exciting new SF writers are women."

June Howard is Assistant Professor of English at the University of Michigan, has published on Nathaniel Hawthorne, and is working on a study of American literary naturalism. She writes, "The present article is part of a longer-term project, and grows out of a long-standing interest in SF, which I have only recently begun to unite with my commitment to marxist-feminism and the development of a marxist-feminist analysis of culture."

Widening the Dialogue on Feminist Science Fiction

June Howard

Isaac Asimov once said, "...there was once a time when science fiction was as masculine as testosterone. There were women writers and women readers but somehow they were ignored... Now things are different." The increasing influence of women writers and of what we might call women's issues on science fiction has been noticeable since 1968. Science fiction is valuable for feminists as a means of uncovering what is latent in our reality, and focussing a new kind of criticism on it. My goal in this paper is to discuss two works of feminist science fiction, both to offer some insights into them, and to provide an introduction to them in order to help widen the audience for them, so that feminists might read them and other science fiction, which is now undergoing re-vision and revitalization.

Sally Miller Gearhart's *The Wanderground* is a cycle of tales about a woman's community which has been established in the hills above an unnamed city during a period of increasing oppression of women.[1] Although each tale is told from the point of view of an individual woman, it is the community itself which is the central character of the book. The hill women have their own art forms, their own religion and ritual, and their own procedure for decision-making. Everything they do is dependent upon their spiritual disciplines, which are highly developed; they have strong psychic powers, which include telepathy and telekinesis.

The community exists in opposition to the men who live with some brutalized women in the city on the plain. At the beginning of the first tale, a woman sentry on the edge of the women's territory encounters a crazed woman dressed in armor who, it develops, has been raped by two men. They have dressed her in armor as a grotesque joke. The sentry, by demonstrating her own vulnerability, wins the woman's trust, and induces her to accept help. The metaphor here is that violence against women forces them to become hardened and dress in a kind of emotional armor; women can repair that damage by caring and an understanding of mutual vulnerability. The book's title, *The Wanderground*, the area between the women's ensconcements and the "Dangerland" of the plain and City is a metaphor, too, for the present situation of women as they move away from patriarchal order into gynocentric sanctuaries. It is the terrain on which are played out present-day fantasies and fears about female identity and relations between men and women.

We learn the story of how women went back to the land through an old woman's memories, and through the "remember rooms" in which young people learn about the past and adults reaffirm their heritage by experiencing the memories of others: "Decades ago women who had escaped to the hills had offered—usually with great pain—the memory of her city experience, however dramatic or mild, however heroic or horror-ridden. Her experience as she had known it had been added then to the vessels of memory kept within the person of every hill woman" (p. 23). The memories escalate from a glimpse of what appears to be our own time to vivid accounts of intensifying oppression. In one tale, a woman describes what happened:

> When I left, state laws were being revised to require every woman to be married...Curfews on women went into effect early. Any woman caught wearing pants went to a behavior modification unit; she emerged wearing a dress and a very scary vacant smile.... Only the ones who looked and behaved like ladies had a chance. And they weren't about to defend women who refused to conform. 'Don't look at me. I'm no witch!'
>
> Then the misfit women began leaving the cities, heading for the hills, going toward rumors of country women who lived off the land, isolated and self-sufficient. Some found those women. Others probably didn't. All of them had to get away from police and state militias. All of them had to hide.

> "If they were caught they didn't get a trial. Some say that hundreds were killed outright. Shot. Gassed.... Anyway, a woman had a few options if she'd cooperate. She could keep her senses and be a whore or a wife or she could have a little tinkering done with her brain and be a whore or a wife anyway. If her body was too ugly or too old they could use her for maintenance work." (pp. 152-53)

The turning point in this history—the difference between the scenes of women hunted by men in a helicopter, some of them shot, one caught in a net, "trapped and carried away like a wild animal!" (p. 157), and the scene in which women successfully resist attempted rape by a band of men on a "Cunt Hunt" (p. 160)—comes with what the women call the "Revolt of the Mother:" "there was one rape too many.... The earth finally said 'no.' There was no storm, no earthquake, no tidal wave or volcanic eruption, no specific moment to mark its happening. It only became apparent that it had happened, and that it had happened everywhere" (p. 158). Outside the cities men become impotent, horses refuse to bear male riders, machines cease to function. Simultaneously comes the first stirrings of psychic power in women who do not yet understand their meaning. Men's activities are confined to the Cities, while the women develop their powers, preparing for an eventual confrontation between the sexes.

The hill women live in close communion with the earth; in harmony with nature. They have rejected technology, which they see as intrinsically male and violent. They find it inferior to their psychic powers:

> "We can do anything that the old machine can do. And with a good deal less effort."
> "Then why don't we do them, Rhynna?"
> "That's the mistake the men made, sisterlove,... over and over again. Just because it was possible they thought it had to be done. They came near to destroying the earth—and man yet—with that notion. Most of us like to think that even long ago women could have built what's been called 'western civilization'; we knew how to do all of it but rejected most such ideas as unnecessary or destructive." (p. 145).

The hill women read omens in the skies and in tea leaves. They communicate with a distant community of women through the relationship of one of their number, Diana, with the moon, which relays their telepathic messages. Through telepathy they can communicate also with plants, animals, and even with clouds and water:

> "Earthsister," she said aloud to the water, "I want to join you." The word seemed to come from all around her.
> "Join." A simple response. Alaka knew better than to stand in converse with so fundamental a substance. Such elements were to be moved with or felt into but never accosted or confronted...
> A large tree root helped her out of the water. She did not shake the drops from her hair or her body. It might be too soon...
> "Thank you," she said in mindstretch to the tree.
> "Again if you need me," responded the tree.
> "Stay well," she chanted inside.
> "Go well," said the tree. (pp. 11-13).

The hill women are nurturing and non-violent, as women have always been thought to be. Aggressive impulses are sharply curbed; like some other behavior, it has been labelled "obsolete". There are differences of opinion but no serious conflict among these women. One of their ritual chants carries the claim that, while they once shared the fruits of man's rape of earth, they have not themselves slain, and now they do not slay the slayer: "Changing not, he dies/...We do not slay him,/But aid him in his dying" (p. 194).

The influence of radical feminism, and of Mary Daly in particular, is apparent in *The Wanderground*. The emphasis on the atrocities committed against women, the invocation to the Goddess, the emphasis on spirituality and harmony with the earth, the creation of a gynocentric community as an alternative to patriarchal western civilization, even the belief in communication with animals, all can be found in *Gyn/Ecology*. The assumption is that there is an innate polarity between men and women: biological, psychological and spiritual differences that cannot be reconciled.

Thus, when in *The Wanderground* the "gentles", bands of outlaw men who believe that the hill women are "the only hope for the world's survival" (p. 2), begin to develop psychic abilities of their own, we learn that their powers are not "enfoldment", like the women's, but a reaching out "like a bridge, not a circle...a form unique to men" (p. 178). The women fear the gentle's power may be "like a sword... another fancy prick to invade the world with" (p. 178-179).

This attribution of separate spiritual essences to male and female springs from a kind of biological determinism. I believe that one must protest against this evaluation of "feminine" and "masculine" qualities by radical feminists. A failure to protest it would lend support to the idea that there are deep natural differences between men and women, and endanger our attempt to change social relations between the sexes. Thre is a fundamental disagreement between those feminists who build upon the fact that the sexes obviously differ, and those feminists, among whom I count myself, who argue that gender identity is the result of complex social and historical forces.

In *The Wanderground* male violence is presented as the central cause of the oppression of women. The importance of organizing against violence is undeniable. But a fierce concentration on violence alone can cause us to neglect the day-to-day struggles of women in the home, office and factory; the problems of welfare mothers, for instance, and the trivial work to which women are constantly relegated. Gearheart does not, of course, need to provide an encyclopedia of oppressions, but her book offers us the opportunity to look critically at our own mythology.

Similarly we need to avoid reading too literally the appeal to ancient female psychic powers, and the rejection of western culture and technology. Silvia Bovenschen has written about the possibilities for resistance offered by myths of women, particularly the myth of the witch, an image evoked in *The Wanderground*. "The moment of resistance," she says, "is, however, contemporary and political. It is not based in mythology even though it occasionally makes use of mythological imagery... I find the reference to myth dangerous when it is used as proof of the eternal recurrence of the same, thereby obscuring the difference between myth, history and reality."[2] Bovenschen suggests that we can use the symbol of the witch and women's supposed special relationship with nature without believing in either of them. I miss the critical distance from myth in *The Wanderground*, with its agriculture that is successful because of spiritual virtues, and its ignoring of the question of reproduction without male participation.

In *The Wanderground* feminist political activity is seen as useless. The efforts of women to organize together can serve no purpose except to distract them from their only real alternative, which is to escape from the city. Women who have not broken all connections with men are shown to be collaborators, in the worst sense of the word. The hill women frown on working even with the gentles, for men are destined by an innate spiritual essence; how then can they change? The reference to the gay men's movement is clear. But there is no attempt to resolve the problem which is raised by the gentles.

On the question of what women can do on a day-to-day basis to help themselves, *The Wanderground* is specific where Mary Daly is vague: they can work to develop their psychic powers. Within their separate community they can master the intricacies of listenspread, dreamwatches, backselfing, softsensing, windriding, and so on.

It is suggested that the revolt of the earth may have been catalyzed by early, scattered communities of women in the hills. Until that revolt, women are barely able to defend themselves against the horrifying violence we learn about in the "remember rooms". In the early years even the self-sufficient women in the hills are able to survive only because they are ignored; as long as the machines function, they can always be hunted out. It follows then that women are essentially powerless on any terrain which resembles the present. Our world *is* a man's world, and we are helpless so long as we remain in it. Escape is the only answer. Only the revolt of the earth, however, allows the women time to build their sanctuary and develop their powers, time to grow strong enough to oppose men effectively at last. This is what I find most disturbing in *The Wanderground*: change has had to be effected by a *deus ex machina* rather than through the efforts of the women themselves.

These attitudes could be used ideologically against the goals of feminists. They could, for example, be used to support anti-abortion positions. The hill women's reverence for life is absolute; it is identified with the very essence of womanhood. Abortion therefore would be out of the question for them. Unwanted pregnancy is not a problem for them in any case since heterosexual activity is completely rejected, and "implantment" is a sacred ritual. For all these reasons the assumptions and beliefs presented by *The Wanderground* deserve our closest attention.

The Female Man by Joanna Russ is an important work of feminist science fiction.[3] It defies summary, but very roughly it tells the story of four women from different worlds who are versions of one woman. The premise of both *The Female Woman* and Russ's equally interesting novel, *The Two of Them*, is that many universes exist, each of which has diverged slightly from the others, and that time travel is possible between these universes. One can travel to other people's past or future, but not to one's own. Each earth is a projection of our world under slightly different circumstances: an image refracted to bring out heretofore hidden truths. Thus in *The Female Man* the passivity and "womanliness" of one character and the murderous rage of another are both potentialities in the same genotype, modified by age, by circumstances, by education, by diet, by God knows what. As Marilyn Hacker observes, the novel "is at least as much about each of the four protagonists in her own world, with her other 'selves' and their worlds as resonating imaginative possibilities, as it is about their actual approaching, meeting and interaction."[4] Russ has said that the "worlds in *The Female Man* are not futures; they are here and now writ large."[5]

In *The Two of Them*, Russ's most recent novel, Irene Waskiewicz combines the many facets of the protagonists of *The Female Man*.[6] She comes from a world which is more or less like our earth, although we are reminded now and then that her continuum is not precisely ours: for example, she speaks of the poet Laura Dickinson (p. 85). By becoming an agent for the Trans Temporal Authority, Irene has escaped into a wider reality from the stultifying life of America in the 50's. She and Ernst Neumann, her partner, are sent as part of a diplomatic mission to Ka'abah, a planet with a culture reminiscent of *The Thousand and*

One Nights. Their secret task is to collect information; they are spies.[6] Irene eventually flees the planet, taking with her Zubeydeh, the daughter of the family they have been staying with. This rebellious act reflects Irene's growing conviction that the life of woman in this society, which others accept as normal, is in fact intolerable. Gradually she becomes disaffected from Trans Temp, and from Ernst, who had recruited and trained her, and who has been for many years her lover.

The inhabitants of Ka'abah have *recreated* the Islamic milieu, although they have been excommunicated from Islam. Ka'abah is a Western fantasy, where women wear veils, gold bangles and elaborate gauzy clothing, are confined to harems from which they rarely venture forth, and where it is a breach of manners even to inquire after a man's family. Women's only alternatives to marriage are dependence on a male relative, domestic service, or the "barracks". They have no real power even within the family. An advanced technology enables the father to watch the members of his household on monitors linked to a computer, and a robot guards the entrance to the women's apartments. The women's lives are particularly claustrophobic, since all life on Ka'abah is lived underground, in streets and chambers carved out of solid rock. However, as the child Zubeydeh puts it, Ka'abah is "not really so different from other places" (p. 133).

Ka'abite ladies go to startling lengths to be beautiful: their lower ribs are removed to improve their figures, moles are implanted, and their eyebrows are made to meet. "And this was the manner of appearance of Enees-el-Jelees, she was like unto the letter Aleph, her gait was as the Oriental willow, her eyebrows met across her forehead, her face appeared shining as the full moon, and upon her cheek was a mole like ambergris." (p. 2). Thus the poet's description, which set the standard for female beauty, and a girl's chance for a good marriage depended on her father's ability to pay for her surgical modifications. This ideal, which differs of course from our own, reminds us that standards of beauty are relative, and that from high heels to hairspray, women's bodies have been colonized by fashion. Through Ka'abah we can discover our own distance from nature; it is different, but not alien.

Russ demonstrates throughout this novel that definitions of male and female derive from cultural constructions and not from nature. Her opening description of the protagonists, for example, crosses gender signals:

> They're entirely in black, with belted tabards over something like long underwear that make them look like the cards in *Alice*, though nobody here has heard about that...Both

> are tall; the elder (grey-haired, clean-shaven, approaching fifty) has the beaked nose, high cheekbones, and deep-set dark eyes of a desert prophet; the younger (by twenty years) is a stockier sort with the flat dish-face of a Slav peasant: dab of a nose, washed-out eyes, and that no-color, fine hair the Russians go in for when they forget to be blond. They're white, but this must be understood conventionally; it excludes snow-color and paper-color. (p. 1).

The two characters are Ernst and Irene. They are well into a conversation before the "younger" is called "she". We retrace our steps and alter our perceptions of these characters when we find out one is a woman. This demonstrates how crucially sex informs our perception of individuals. The same process occurs when the agents' host assumes that because of their appearance and their official status his visitors must be men. In fact he thinks Irene does not conform to the ideal of masculine beauty.

> [The] saying [is] that no man is truly fine-looking who could not play the role of female impersonator in the theatre, and this great, pale, lounging brute with the death-colored eyes and the disappearing hair could never be mistaken for a woman; he has no grace and no virile beauty. He is unhealthily fat...in the absence of the female principle, the male principle has overbloomed and is tending toward its own extinction, that is, cunning, shapelessness and pure matter. He has seen eunuchs impersonated in plays; he knows what he is looking at. (pp. 12-13).

When he learns that Irene is a woman, he is naturally horrified: to look at her makes him dizzy. "If she doesn't want to be mistaken for a man, why has this unnatural woman removed her veils and her beauty spot, her necklaces, the dye on her fingernails?" (pp. 18-19). Again we see that many of the indications of gender are only a convention. Russ's ironic approach to the idea of male and female undercuts not only Ka'abah's theories of polarity, but those expressed in *The Wanderground* as well.

If gender identity is to a large extent a social construct, then the creation of a positive female identity can be the result of redefinition and reappropriation. This is a more difficult achievement than a strong emphasis on what is conceived to be the true female nature. *The Two of Them* presents a more complex and compassionate account of the ways in which women perpetuate their own oppression, than does *The Wanderground*. Zubeydeh, for one, continues, even on the spaceship leaving Ka'abeh, to spout cliches about the proper relations of "ladies and gentlemen" (p. 118). Irene, for all her apparent independence, is still a victim of social conditioning. Zubeydeh points out that although Irene tells her to stand up to Ernst, "*you* don't really. You always give in." (p. 130). Irene comes to recognize and reject her habitual apologies, her need for Ernst's approval, her sense of insufficiency: "for a moment she thinks she's failed—she's never been as good as Ernst, she can't be as good as Ernst!" (p. 152). Russ is less concerned with male violence against women than with women's own internalized prohibitions:

> She remembers shouting at Ernst and then suddenly is not sure;...none of it happened,...her anger fooled her,...at the last minute she held it all back. She never said any of it aloud, and that's shocking. She thinks, *My expensive position, my statistically rare training, my self-confidence, my unusual strength.*
> *And I'm still afraid.*
> *Of what?* (p. 114).

Because of the historical social force of gender identity, the authentic self cannot be recovered; only its potential can be reclaimed. When Irene briefly indulges in masochistic and sadistic fantasies (pp. 36-38), Russ is demonstrating the complexity of female psychology in a way that Gearhart would probably reject.

For Russ one of the most tempting forms of collusion is the belief that one is unusual, different from other women. As an adolescent Irene rejects the roles offered her because she is proud of being the one woman respected by Sherlock Holmes. She continues to think during her relationship with Ernst that she and he are special, exempt from gender cliches. On Ka'abeh, however, she begins to think about her unique position in Trans Temp:

> You know, Ernst, it's very odd; I don't know any women...There's the one linguist out of twenty. And the anthropologist we all studied with, years ago. And all those staff women, of course...the ones you always see in the background doing all the little jobs, but no women. (p. 120).

Laura Rose expresses the same idea in *The Female Man*: "I'm not a girl. I'm a genius."[7] Zubeydeh sees herself as a poet, but she is reluctant to sympathize with her mad aunt Dunya, who also wanted to be a poet: "I bet he thinks Aunt Dunya wasn't a real poet. She probably wasn't." Irene says, "First-rate poets don't get put into cages. Second-rate ones do. She doesn't question the system, only insists she's outside it." (p. 85). Gradually Irene comes to identify to some degree even with madwomen; she comes to prefer the spider to the man who killed it: "Well, somebody ought to live it from the spider's point of view...Like Dunya in her foul cell, like Zumurrud spinning daydreams from wall to wall.

Someone ought to let the sane ones know. Someone ought to make them find out." (p. 148).

Madness is a recurring theme in *The Two of Them*. Irene's beloved mother Rose "alternated periods of loud heartiness, in which she told and retold the romantic episodes of her life...with fits of weeping which she tried to hide from her daughter." (p. 29). When Irene as an adolescent criticizes her boyfriend David for his conventional attitudes toward women he tells her that she is "not a real woman at all" and "Irene, you're *crazy*!" (p. 39). Ernst uses the same accusation, but more subtly: "When we get back...it must be a check-up." (p. 136). Zumur-rud, Zebeydeh's mother is medicated most of the time. Her rebellious-ness leads her husband to wonder "if some of his neighbors are not right, that some women should be medicated from the cradle upwards, because truly there is an epidemic among the women of today." (p. 28). Zubeydeh's writing of poetry reminds everyone unpleasantly of her Aunt Dunya.

Women always go crazy [Zubeydeh says]. My mother was crazy. I go crazy too; I become my Bad Self...and do something awful. When Mommy ever said anything wrong, Daddy would explain to me that it was her craziness speaking. [My brother] told me all about it; it's harder for a woman to form her feminine personality than...for a man to form his masculine one because women's bodies are made of lighter molecules...it's harder for women to incorporate their masculine element into their characters than it is for men to incorporate their feminine element into theirs. Besides, we have our monthlies and that drives us crazy... Daddy used to warn me about going mad and tell me that was why I had to give up poetry and get married; women are always wanting to do something crazy and we never know why... Irene, do you ever *enjoy* being crazy? (pp. 137-138). *The gentlemen always think the ladies have gone mad.* (p. 147).

Dunyazad, locked for years in a cell in her brother-in-law's house, while everyone thinks she is dead, is visited by Irene:

The walls are bare rock; there is a naked...bulb in the ceiling and someone has left a few crumpled pieces of paper on the floor... There is an odd smudge along the wall, some sixteen inches off the floor...
Then the heap of clothes begin to stir. It fits itself into the smudge on the wall...and moves slowly along... From time to time the woman whom one can't even see inside the rags becomes still, not stopping in any human attitude but ceasing the way a snail might do upon encountering an obstacle...(pp. 81-82).

The allusion here of course is to Charlotte Perkin Gilman's "The Yellow Wallpaper." As Annette Kolodny has demonstrated, in the latter story the insistence of the woman's husband on substituting his perceptions of reality for her recording and interpretation of her own, drives her to project that repressed recording as delusion.[8] The diagnosis of madness is a means of controlling women and of denying our experience and causing us even to deny it to ourselves. Dunya has vanished into silence, like her namesake in *The Arabian Nights*: "Shaharazad's sister, that mad, dead, haunted woman who could not tell stories, who could not save herself" (p. 181).

There are frequent literary allusions in *The Two of Them* and the author frequently intrudes to make us aware that these are fictions. In addition to *The Arabian Nights*, there are allusions to Irene Adler, Sherlock Holmes, Lewis Carroll, Tolkien and Virginia Woolf. When we first meet Irene she is reading from a Ka'abite book, commenting with venemous wit on its racism and poverty of imagination.

To find support from other women, Irene looks in the spaceship library for lists of women poets and painters: the silence is not complete. In addition to Gilman, Russ alludes to Kate Wilhelm's *Clewiston Test*, and to Sandra Gilbert's and Susan Gubar's *The Madwoman in the Attic*. This reclamation of women's stories may be compared to the "remember rooms" in *The Wanderground*.

Irene begins to see that Ernst has denied the validity of her experience, rejecting in her anything that makes him uncomfortable. She refuses to continue apologizing for her feelings and her actions. But Ernst Neumann [the earnest new man] is a kindly liberal; Irene fears often that she is being unjust to him. But all his reactions to her betray his lack of comprehension of what she is trying to tell him: "Irene, you dress as I do, you work as I do, you're paid as I am!... If there's a difference—... I'm glad of the difference." (p. 143). "...things flash in his mind, *Are women*—and *Women don't*—, thoughts he knows are treasonous to Irene" (p. 123). Irene wonders "how she could run away with Goliath only to end up with David again" (p. 137). Finally Ernst betrays her completely:

> In his mind's eye she's surrounded by madwomen...sealed-off, self-possessed, unhappy women, sinking back into that sinister matrix Irene herself has always abhorred, something unformed and primitive, a paranoia so complete that it closes over its victims like a swamp. (pp. 159-160).

Because she is angry with him openly Ernst believes she is mad. She has resolved to take control of her life; she is disillusioned with working for Trans Temp: "We don't really know who pays us, we don't know the effects of our work, hell, half the time we don't even know what the work is." (p. 121). She decides to examine the files find the real purpose of Trans Temp, and perhaps use its power to effect real positive changes on earth and on Ka'abah. Ernst condescendingly praises the idea; he does not think she is serious. But this is a fatal mistake he had made: when he tries to prevent her from leaving the spaceship, she shoots him.

Toward the end of the novel, the narrative voice breaks in more frequently, obscuring the action, and offering alternatives:

> Ernst would have enjoyed—
> He would've—
> —would have—
> Well, no, not really.
> It occurs to me that she only stunned him, that soon he'll get up...that he'll come looking for her, penitent, contrite, having learned his lesson.
> Well, no, not really. (pp. 163-164).

A basic question in *The Two of Them* is the same as the question in *The Wanderground*: can any man overcome masculinity? Zubeydeh asks, "Irenee, are all men beasts?" She thinks of a little boy who is her friend. *"Michael's* all right," she says. (p. 174). She wants Michael to come with her and Irene. Here the narrative voice intervenes again. We are told that she takes Michael along. Then the voice says, "She didn't take him. She didn't do it. I made that part up." (p. 175). Russ has said, "I can't imagine a two-sexed egalitarian society and I don't believe anyone else can, either."[9]

At the end, "the two of them" are no longer Irene and Ernst, but Irene and Zubeydeh. Irene thinks, "Zubeydeh would enjoy tying up Uncle Ernst, while maintaining all the time that ladies never did this to gentlemen, although gentlemen did occasionally do it to ladies." (p. 145). Zubeydeh is a charming, vital, irrepressible character, who is fascinated by new experience:

> The neon...sign across the street has fascinated Zubeydeh; she hung out the window for hours after supper, dividing her attention between the sign ("We Move our Tail for You") and the old television programs on the hotel set, of which her favorite was Mary Tyler Moore. Zubeydeh has decided that she wants to be Mary Tyler Moore. (p. 177).

Zubeydeh's future appears to be potentially unlimited. Irene too has an open future, not now as a special woman, but as an ordinary person "a nobody...she has no idea yet that she can find other unimportant and powerless people." (p. 178).

The novel reveals the malignant effects on women of gender identification. The movement is toward a collective project of resistance and solidarity, but Russ does not yet envision that here. In a daydream Irene sees Zubeydeh reading children's books which lack their final pages; their titles (one is called *Yalena and Boris Lead the Revolution*) spell out a "dream-message" which she cannot grasp. (p. 179). Thus in the end *The Two of Them* lacks its final pages; there is no resolution, but gestures toward the future. The vision that follows the daydream seems to say that Irene will find the other powerless people: "Something is coming out of nothing" (p. 181). The book ends at the moment the collective is invented, opening into the long moment of women's self-recognition and struggle which is our own historical moment. It sends us, along with Irene and Zubeydeh, back to our work.

In *The Wanderground* the unanswered question, which is whether the earth will be saved, is asked by a closely-knit community. The assertion here is that all women share an essential unity. But we know that in actual practice women have not been unified, and have not even been able to overcome the boundaries of race and class. The society of women in *The Wanderground* is made up of varied races, but there is no meaningful connection made to non-white culture. In *The Two of Them*, too, a non-western culture is chosen to represent extreme oppression of women.

It is urgent that we try to understand how we can effect the unity and community of women. Both these novels have raised questions of how our oppression is to be defined, and set forth in images; they raise issues of autonomy and alliance. I have criticized them, pointing out historical and political contradictions, rather than literary faults. As a materialist feminist I feel that the dialogue on feminist science fiction must be widened.

NOTES

[1] *The Wanderground: Stories of the Hill Women* (Watertown, Mass: Persephone Press, 1979).

[2] "The Contemporary Witch, the Historical Witch and the Witch Myth: The Witch, Subject of the Appropriation of Nature and Object of the Domination of Nature," *New German Critique* 15 (1978), p. 87.

[3] (NY: Bantam, 1975), p. 161.

[4] Marilyn Hacker, Introduction to Joanna Russ, *The Female Man* (Boston: Gregg Press, 1977) p. xvi. This essay is valuable both for its discussion of Russ and its comments on women and science fiction.

5 Quoted in Hacker, p. xxii.
6 Irene is the most recent of Russ's female tricksters, who include Alyx of the early stories and *Picnic on Paradise*, Evne in *And Chaos Died*, the unnamed protagonist of *We Who Are About To...* and Jael (and to some extent Janet) in *The Female Man*.
7 *The Female Man*, p. 65.
8 "A Map for Rereading: Or, Gender and The Interpretation of Literary Texts" *New Literary History*, 11 (1980), pp. 451-467.
9 Hacker, p. xxii. See Russ's paper on recent feminist utopias in Marlene Barr, ed. *Future Females: A Critical Anthology* (Bowling Green, Ohio: Bowling Green Univ Popular Press, 1982).

PART SIX:

THE PILGRIM AWARD

Science fiction is a genre for which there is no shortage of annual and lifetime fiction awards, but there are few awards for those who seek to promote understanding of the genre through criticism and scholarship. To help remedy this situation and promote serious discussion of the genre, the Science Fiction Research Association in 1970 established the Pilgrim Award for individuals whose overall body of work have served to significantly advance the cause of science fiction scholarship. The award was named from the title of the first serious academic study of science fiction, *Pilgrims Through Space and Time* (1947), by University of North Carolina professor James Osler Bailey (1903-1981), who was, appropriately, the first recipient of the award in 1970.

In 1971, the award went to Marjorie Hope Nicolson, whose 1948 study *Voyages to the Moon* followed Bailey's by only a year and laid much of the groundwork for the prehistory of the genre through the eighteenth century. Russian scholar Julius Kagarlitski, professor of European drama at the State Theatrical Institute in Moscow, received the 1972 award for his various contributions to the study of fantastic literature, including the 1963 *The Life and Thought of H.G. Wells*, which appeared in English in 1966. The first professional science fiction author to receive the award was Jack Williamson in 1973, for his pioneering contributions to the study of science fiction in the classroom as well as his study *H.G. Wells: Critic of Progress* (1973). Professor I.F. Clarke of the University of Strathclyde in Scotland received the 1974 award for his extensive bibliography *The Tale of the Future*

(1961) and his definitive study of future war fiction, *Voices Prophesying War* (1966).

Much of the early significant criticism of science fiction appeared in fan magazines or the review columns of fiction magazines, and by most accounts the most distinguished criticism to emerge from these sources was that of author Damon Knight, who received the Pilgrim Award in 1975 and whose major reviews and essays were collected in *In Search of Wonder* (1956 and 1967). Another distinguished fiction author, James E. Gunn, was like Williamson instrumental in establishing science fiction as a legitimate classroom subject, and published the first comprehensive illustrated history of the field in 1975 with his *Alternate Worlds*; Gunn received the 1976 Pilgrim Award and later became president of the Science Fiction Research Association.

The chief mechanisms of American scholarly debate—the journal and the academic conference—became available to those interested in science fiction primarily through the efforts of the 1977 Pilgrim Award winner, Thomas D. Clareson of the College of Wooster in Ohio. Clareson chaired the first Modern Language Association seminar on science fiction in 1958, founded the first academic journal in the field (*Extrapolation*) the following year, edited numerous volumes of criticism and fiction, became a founder of the Science Fiction Research Association and was its first president from 1970 to 1976.

In 1978, the award went to British author Brian Aldiss for reasons already mentioned in the introduction to his essay in this volume, and the 1979 award was presented to Yugoslav-born critic and theorist Darko Suvin, whose co-editorship of *Science-Fiction Studies* helped develop that journal into a major organ of theoretical debate and whose own work on Eastern European and Russian science fiction and genre theory infused science fiction scholarship with a high degree of academic rigor, most evident in his major 1979 study *Metamorphoses of Science Fiction*. The 1980 Pilgrim Award returned to England with the Australian-born critic and editor Peter Nicholls, whose work as first administrator of England's Science Fiction Foundation and editor of the journal *Foundation* led to his editorship in 1979 of the most comprehensive reference book in the field, *The Science Fiction Encyclopedia*.

At the 1981 Science Fiction Research Association conference in Denver, the Pilgrim Award was presented to pioneer fan, critic and scholar Sam Moskowitz, whose acceptance address retold the fascinating story of the evolution of the book for which the Pilgrim Award was named in the first place. Moskowitz's paper follows the presentation address by Joe De Bolt, professor of sociology at Central Michigan University and president of the Science Fiction Research Association from 1979-1980.

Sam Moskowitz: Scholar of the Sense of Wonder

Joe De Bolt

Sam Moskowitz has been active in science fiction for almost half a century. Donald Tuck introduces him as a "noted U.S. science-fiction enthusiast, article writer, and editor."[1] L. Sprague de Camp describes him as "...one of the nation's leading fans and collectors."[2] Sam J. Lundwall calls him "Science fiction's foremost chronicler."[3] Jim Gunn has said that "Sam Moskowitz has conducted an unrelenting quest for encyclopedic knowledge of science fiction and preeminence in the science fiction fan world..."[4] Peter Nicholls points out that for many years, he "was the best known of all SF historians and commentators from within the genre; his work in the field antedates that of nearly all non-genre historians of the field, with the notable exception of J.O. Bailey."[5] And it has been said about his history of early science fiction fandom, *The Immortal Storm*, that it may be the only book in which World War II comes as an anti-climax.[6]

Now this remarkable man—this author of ten books and monographs on science fiction published from 1949 to 1980, this editor of 49 fiction collections and anthologies, many containing lengthy essays— has been honored with the Science Fiction Research Association's 1981 Pilgrim Award for outstanding contributions to the study of science fiction. However, his career and achievements also honor the Pilgrim Award, enhancing its meaning and contributing to the considerable luster already radiating from this select small band: J.O. Bailey, Marjorie Hope Nicholson, Julius Kagarlitski, Jack Williamson, I.F. Clarke, Damon Knight, James Gunn, Thomas D. Clareson, Brian W. Aldiss, Darko Suvin, Peter Nicholls, and, now, Sam Moskowitz.

In addition, Sam Moskowitz enriches the Pilgrim Award by bringing to it a neglected dimension; like all the other Pilgrims, Moskowitz is a scholar, but unlike most past recipients he is not an academic, not the holder of university degrees, nor is he a major writer of science fiction. Still his credentials are in order: he is a fan—in the very best meaning of that word—a person in love with the field, even consumed by it at times.[7] To this great enthusiasm he joins his personal qualities of perserverance, intelligence, attention to detail, curiosity, and creativity. When we honor Sam Moskowitz, we clasp through his hand the hands of all those in the past, those who in truth initiated science fiction scholarship, those who raised it up in the times and places where the so-called serious scholars were often only too willing to knock it down, willing even to strike that cruelest of blows, ignoring it.[8]

In the "Fannish" tongue, this is "sercon" fandom.[9] And even if their successes have not always matched their mighty passion, their achievements have been considerable. As Jim Gunn has written:

> At its least, science fiction fandom is a fascinating sociological phenomenon deserving serious study; at best, it became an evolutionary force for progress in science fiction: criticizing, testing, discarding, contributing. Out of science fiction fandom came practically the only useful criticism published (later collected in such volumes as Damon Knight's *In Search of Wonder* and William Atheling's (James Blish) *Issues at Hand* and *More Issues at Hand*). Out of fandom also came the first bibliographical works and indexes: Everett F. Bleiler's *The Checklist of Fantastic Literature* and *Indexes to the Science Fiction Magazines* by Donald B. Day, the MIT Science Fiction Society, and the New England Science Fiction Association.
>
> Out of fandom came collections of the perishable pulp magazines and early books which now are in great demand among scholars and libraries...
>
> Out of fandom came editors conscious of what was wrong with earlier magazines and filled with a sense of mission: Hornig, Weisinger, Wollheim, Pohl, Palmer, Boucher, Lowndes, Merril, Knight, Blish, Shaw and others. And out of fandom came new authors: Pohl, Blish, Knight, Kornbluth, Arthur Clarke, Isaac Asimov, Robert Bloch, P. Schuyler Miller, John Christopher (C.S. Youd), Ray Bradbury, and more recently Robert Silverberg, Harlan Ellison, Alexei Panshin, and many others.[10]

When publishers would not put science fiction in book form, fans created their own houses. For example, Gnome Press, started by Greenberg and Kyle in 1948, gave Asimov's Foundation series its form as a trilogy of books. Lloyd Arthur Eshbach's Fantasy Press published the first book about modern science fiction, *Of Worlds Beyond: The Science of Science Fiction Writing*, in 1947, the same year, incidentally, that Bailey's *Pilgrims Through Space and Time* appeared. Above all, there is Advent Publishers in Chicago, whose first book was Damon Knight's *In Search of Wonder*; numerous other scholarly works followed including Jim Blish's two volumes of critical essays, Alexei Panshin's controversial *Heinlein in Dimension*, and Donald Tuck's extraordinary *Encyclopedia of Science Fiction and Fantasy*.[11]

Out of this tradition comes Sam Moskowitz and his works, and as we recognize his contributions, so do we recognize all the others.

But it is Moskowitz himself who has been named Pilgrim, and it is in his own name, and with his own scholarship, that he has earned it.

One of his early accomplishments, while still in his teens, was the staging with William Sykora of the first national science fiction convention. According to de Camp, the 125 attendees at this Newark, New Jersey meeting "went over the sandwiches prepared for them like a giant vacuum-cleaner,"[12] and had such a good time that it was decided to move on to the ultimate "fanac," the First World Science Fiction Convention. After much infighting among various New York area fan groups, especially between Moskowitz's group, the Sykoras, and the Futurians, a group which would later alter the shape of science fiction, but at that time were perceived by some as dangerously radical. It was Moskowitz who eventually became the organizer of this First World Con, which was held July 2, 3, and 4, 1939, in Caravan Hall, East 59th Street, Manhattan. It, too, was a great success; 200 fans attended, including Forrest Ackerman and Ray Bradbury from as far away as the West Coast. But this success has been largely overshadowed in fan lore by an incident that transpired between Moskowitz's committee and the Futurians. Although accounts vary, Joe Siclari says that when the Futurians arrived in a group they were denied admission, because the convention committee feared a disturbance. Eventually, some, including Isaac Asimov, were let in; but not the six considered by Moskowitz to be the most dangerous, among them Don Wollheim, Robert Lowndes, Cyrl Kornbluth, and, of course, Fred Pohl.[13] Although it may now be too late to establish fully the facts, it does appear that those who barred the doors did so with some justification. Fred Pohl has graciously confessed: "to be truthful, we pretty nearly had it coming. Not quite. The punishment exceeded the crime. But we Futurians were, as you must have observed by now, a fairly snotty lot. Politics had something to do with the struggle, but not much...What we Futurians made very clear to the rest of New York fandom was that we thought we were better than they were. For some reason that annoyed them."[14]

Actually, Moskowitz's activities in science fiction had begun three years before that First World Con; he started his fan writing in 1936 with pieces for the fanzine, *Science Fiction Collector*.[15] In 1940 and 1941 he was a science fiction literary agent and wrote stories of his own. He published three science fiction stories in issues dated 1941, his first (a "space-opera novella of distant galaxies", as Nicholls describes it) was "The Way Back" for *Comet* stories. A few more stories followed in the 1950's.

Moskowitz's history of early fandom, *The Immortal Storm*,[13] appeared in 1951. Highly controversial, and often attacked on the basis of its interpretation of events, it was the first major work on fandom, and in Nicholls' words, still exhibits "a passion and detail quite unabraded by the passing years." Marshall Tymn describes it as "A personal view of fandom, but still the best picture of this small but influential group of SF activities. Contains much historical data on the fanzines of the 1930's and 1940's unavailable elsewhere."[16]

From 1952 to 1954, Moskowitz was managing editor of Hugo Gernsback's last magazine, *Science Fiction Plus*. When this valiant effort failed, he became an editor of frozen food industry magazines, a field in which he is still employed as publisher.

For three years, 1953, 1954 and 1955, he taught an evening course in science fiction writing and history at City College of New York.[17] This was nine years before Mark Hillegast's course at Colgate, and eleven years before Jack Williamson's at Eastern New Mexico University.

The 13th World Science Fiction Convention in 1955 presented Moskowitz with a Special Committee Award, a plaque, for his services to the field.

In 1958, he began publishing a series of essays and profiles of authors in a number of science fiction magazines, especially *Amazing*. These later became the basis of two of his major scholarly works. *Explorers of the Infinite*,[18] the first, appeared in 1963 and contained essays on 18 writers from the 17th Century through the 1930's. Although criticized for failing to relate these authors' work to "wider literary or historical traditions,"[19] the book did provide many of us interested in science fiction with a more meaningful history than we had previously known. In it he gave his often quoted definition of science fiction as "a branch of fantasy identifiable by the fact that it eases the 'willing suspension of disbelief' on the part of its readers by utilizing an atmosphere of scientific credibility for its imaginative speculations in physical science, space, time, social science, and philosophy."[20] *Mas-*

terpieces of Science Fiction,[21] an anthology of stories by these writers, followed in 1966.

Seekers of Tomorrow,[22] Moskowitz's detailed profiles of 21 additional science fiction writers from 1940 to 1965, also appeared in 1966. It too, has a companion anthology of stories, *Modern Masterpieces of Science Fiction*.[23] Criticized for "inbred qualities" which limit their critical judgments, these two important works, *Explorers* and *Seekers*, are still praised, as in the words of Neil Barron, "for providing a detailed and reasonably accurate picture of early and modern SF,"[24] while Clareson specifically singling out Moskowitz as one of the foremost bibliophiles in the field, points out that his works "have done much to introduce a wider audience to the genre..."[25]

Turning his attention to science fiction in the early magazines, Moskowitz began producing his important anthologies derived from these periodicals, beginning in 1968 with the wonderfully titled *Science Fiction by Gaslight: A History and Anthology of Science Fiction in the Popular Magazines 1891-1911*.[26] In 1970, there followed *Under the Moon of Mars: A History and Anthology of Scientific Romances in the Munsey Magazines 1912-1920*,[27] and in 1973, *The Crystal Man: Landmark Science Fiction by Edgar Page Mitchell*.[28] Some, such as Clareson and Nicholls, consider these works, and others in a similar vein which followed, to be Moskowitz's major contribution.[29]

Moskowitz returned to editing in 1973 and 1974 when he headed the brief revival of *Weird Tales*, which, unfortunately, lasted only four issues. Moving to Hyperion Press, he edited a series of science fiction reprints in 1974, and a second in 1976. Hyperion has also reprinted six of his most important historical works.

A collection of essays on various science fiction themes, *Strange Horizons: The Spectrum of Science Fiction*,[30] was published in 1976. This began in the 1960's as a series of articles published in science fiction magazines, and includes treatments of religion, art, women, blacks, birth control, and anti-semitism in science fiction. In Moskowitz's words, "The results are sometimes dramatic. A number of the great literary figures of science fiction lose a bit of luster from the glowing beacon of their vaunted humanitarianism when their racist attitudes are uncovered."[31]

In 1978, when the New Jersey Literary Hall of Fame was founded, Sam Moskowitz was included among its first year's inductees. Copies of his works have been placed in its archives, in the Van Houten Library, at the New Jersey Institute of Technology in Newark.

Finally, just last year, Moskowitz again advanced science fiction scholarship by publishing *Science Fiction in Old San Francisco Volume I: History of the Movement from 1854-1890*, described by *Locus* as an amazing work on a long forgotten early science fiction renaissance in local San Francisco magazines and newspapers. Also appearing was a companion volume, *Science Fiction in Old San Francisco Volume II: Into the Sun and Other Stories by Robert Duncan Milne*,[32] which collects eleven stories by the movement's leading writer. Additional volumes in this series are underway.

This has been but a brief overview of Sam Moskowitz's works and contributions to the serious study of science fiction. He is still producing, and the final chapter cannot be written. However, Peter Nicholls has offered a summation of his contributions to date:

> Although Sam Moskowitz is not an academic, and does not always lay out his findings as carefully as academics might like, being sometimes rather cavalier in withholding his sources of information, the above six books [*Explorers, Seekers, Horizons, Gaslight, Moon of Mars, Crystal Man*, and I would add, *The Immortal Storm* and *Old San Francisco* (J.D.)] are a major contribution to SF scholarship.... These works have all been much criticized within the genre and by academics, for too many inaccuracies and a hurried and not always fluent style, but the fact remains that Sam Moskowitz, though his every words cannot be accepted as gospel truth, did more original research in this field than any other scholar of his period, and few since; no later history of SF has made use of Sam Moskowitz's painstaking work, especially his research into the early history of SF in periodical publications.[33]

And that is why Sam Moskowitz is the 1981 Science Fiction Research Association's Pilgrim.

NOTES

[1] *The Encyclopedia of Science Fiction and Fantasy*, Volume 2. (Chicago: Advent Publishers, 1978), p. 320. As Tuck points out, Moskowitz was born in Newark, New Jersey in 1920; he still lives there and is still married to surgeon Christine Haycock Moskowitz.

[2] *Science Fiction Handbook*. (New York: Hermitage House, 1953), p. 131. De Camp also mentions that Moskowitz is the "perennial Director" of the Eastern Science Fiction Association of Newark; interestingly, the ESFA just held, on March 1 of 1981, its 35th anniversary meeting, and Sam Moskowitz, of course, was its organizer.

[3] *Science Fiction: What It's All About*. (New York: Ace, 1971), p. 161.

[4] "From the Pulps to the Classroom: The Strange Journey of Science Fiction," in

Marshall B. Tymn, ed., *The Science Fiction Reference Book*, (Mercer Island, Washington: Starmount House, 1981), p. 239.

5 *The Science Fiction Encyclopedia.* (Garden City, New York: Dolphin Books/ Doubleday, 1979), p. 410. Although Bailey's pioneering work, *Pilgrims Through Space and Time*, was published in 1947, it is based, according to Tuck, on his 1934 Ph.D. dissertation, "Scientific Fiction in English, 1817-1914," which in turn is antedated by his 1927 Master's thesis, "The Scientific Novels of H.G. Wells."

6 James Gunn, *Alternate Worlds.* (Englewood Cliffs, New Jersey: Prentice-Hall, 1975), p. 183.

7 While other Pilgrims have their roots in science fiction fandom, none are as strongly identified with fandom as is Moskowitz. For example, Damon Knight relates his fannish origins in *The Futurians: The Story of the Science Fiction "Family" of the 30's That Produced Today's Top SF Writers and Editors*, (New York: John Day, 1977); in addition, some of his early critical essays were originally published in fan sources and later appeared as a book, *In Search of Wonder* (1956, revised and expanded, 1967) from Advent Publishers, a fan oriented press. Also, Thomas D. Clareson once published his own fanzine.

8 In the introduction to Knight's, *In Search of Wonder* (1956), Anthony Boucher says that "Within science fiction, criticism—and frequently of a high order—has appeared almost solely in amateur publications; indeed the wealth of material, critical, bibliographical and biographical, that has appeared in fanzines, from *Fantasy Commentator* to *Inside*, is such that a university library with a complete fanzine file would be the Mecca of Ph.D. candidates in the twenty-first century." (p. vii). Ironically, like so many predictions by science fiction writers, Boucher's has proven to be too conservative.

9 According to Elliot Weinstein, ed., *The Fillostrated Fan Dictionary*, (O Press, 1975) [address unknown], "sercon" means being serious and constructive, and may or may not be derogatory, depending on whether you are sercon. Since SFRA is sercon by definition, no problem of meaning should arise.

10 Gunn, *Worlds*, 183-184.

11 Much of the above can be found in Nicholls; Brian Ash, ed., *The Visual Encyclopedia of Science Fiction* (London: Pan Books, 1977); and Gunn, *Worlds*.

12 de Camp, p. 138.

13 Joe Siclari, "Science Fiction Fandom/A History of an unusual Hobby" in Marshall Tymn, ed., *The Science Fiction Reference Book*, pp. 91-93. Moskowitz's own account of these times is in his *The Immortal Storm: A History of Science Fiction Fandom* (Atlanta: Burwell, 1951). Reprinted Atlanta Science Fiction Organization Press, 1954; Hyperion Press, 1974.

14 *The Way the Future Was: A Memoir.* (NY: Ballantine Books, 1978), pp. 76-77.

15 Information on Moskowitz's career comes from Nicholls; Tuck; Gunn, *Worlds*; and L.W. Currey, ed., *Science Fiction and Fantasy Authors* (Boston: G.K. Hall, 1979); and from conversations with Moskowitz.

16 Tymn, p. 72.

17 Gunn, "From the Pulps, etc", p. 239.

18 *Explorers of the Infinite: Shapers of Science Fiction* (Cleveland: World, 1963). Reprinted Hyperion Press, 1974.

19 Neil Barron, ed. *Anatomy of Wonder: Science Fiction* (NY: R.R. Bowker, 1976), p. 350.

20 *Explorers of the Infinite*, p. 11.
21 (Cleveland: World, 1966).
22 *Seekers of Tomorrow: Masters of Modern Science Fiction*. (Cleveland: World, 1966). Reprinted Hyperion Press, 1974.
23 (Cleveland: World, 1965). Reprinted Hyperion Press, 1974.
24 Barron, p. 350.
25 Thomas D. Clareson, "Introduction" The Critical Reception of Science Fiction, p. xiii in *SF: The Other Side of Realism* (Bowling Green: Bowling Green Univ. Popular Press, 1971).
26 (Cleveland: World, 1968). Reprinted Hyperion Press, 1974.
27 (NY: Holt, Rinehart & Winston, 1970). Reprinted Hyperion Press, 1974.
28 (Garden City: Doubleday, 1973).
29 Clareson, p. xiii, and Nicholls, p. 411.
30 (NY: Chas Scribner's Sons, 1976).
31 *Strange Horizons*, p. 1.
32 Both vols., (West Kingston, R.I.: Grant, 1980).
33 Nicholls, p. 411.

Pilgrim's Progress:
Prelude and Postscripts to the Publication of J.O. Bailey's Pilgrims Through Space and Time

Sam Moskowitz

The Pilgrim Award is an appropriate name for a presentation acknowledging lifelong scholarship within the field of science fiction. James Osler Bailey's *Pilgrims Through Space and Time* (1947) was the first book-length unabashed commentary on science fiction. During the twenty years that the author labored on this book, academia demonstrated litle interest in its publication.[1] If it were not for encouragement from the science fiction fans, collectors and book dealers, the book might never have been published, or even completed.

The project was first announced in a plaintive paragraph in the Science Fiction League department of *Wonder Stories*, in July, 1935, when Bailey had already been working on it for eight years: "J.O. Bailey of Chapel Hill, N.C. has been collecting rare science fiction for many years, and asks us to wait until his bibliography, which he is putting a great deal of work into, is completed before going ahead and publishing one of our own."[2]

P. Schuyler Miller, had printed 1500 words in the May, 1935 issue of *Wonder Stories*, recommending that the Science Fiction League undertake a master bibliography of all science fiction ever published in books and periodicals. Collectors were asked to submit lists toward such a compilation, which Miller suggested should be a priority project.[3]

In December, 1935, Bailey and five other members were mentioned, as having sent in preliminary bibliography lists.[4] The same notice was repeated in the February, 1936, issue. A few months later, *Wonder Stories* was sold by its owner. Hugo Gernsback, to Standard Magazines/Beacon Magazines, and its title was changed to *Thrilling Wonder Stories*. There were no further references to J.O. Bailey or the bibliography.[5]

How many people Bailey contacted over the years, and the amount of help he got from them will never be known. As early as May 24, 1930, a letter, signed J.O.B., appeared in the *Saturday Review of Literature*, asking for information on story titles; in its July 26, 1930 issue, the *Review* published a reply from a Cleveland library. Acknowledgements in the preface of his book give a clue to his inquiries and correspondents. One of them was Miles J. Breuer, a medical doctor who wrote *Paradise and Iron* [*Amazing Stories Quarterly*, (Summer, 1930)], a carefully wrought story of the consequences of a take-over of a civilization by machines, and *The Gostak and the Doshes* [*Amazing Stories* (March, 1930)], in which he used semantics for his theme. Oddly, neither Breuer nor his works are mentioned in Bailey's book.

Ben Abramson, who owned the Argus Book Shop in Chicago, is credited in the preface: Bailey had bought books from Abramson, and received also Abramson's own compilation of a list of fantastic literature. Bailey's M.A. thesis, "The Scientific Novels of H.G. Wells", supervised by Howard Mumford Jones at the University of North Carolina, and his PhD dissertation, "Fiction in English, 1817-1914: A Study of Trends and Forms," accepted by North Carolina in 1934, were requested by Abramson; he thought they should be combined into a book.

H.P. Lovecraft is also mentioned in the preface: he lived until 1937 and Bailey probably got in touch wih him in the 30's. A considerable amount of space in *Pilgrims* is devoted to two of his stories: "At the Mountains of Madness" [*Astounding Stories* (February, March & April, 1936)] and "The Shadow Out of Time" [*Astounding Stories* (June, 1936)]. Though literary judgments are rare in Bailey's book, a long footnote praises Lovecraft as "...one of the most powerful and sensitive writers of our generation" (p. 179). In 1945 when Abramson moved his business to New York, and began to publish fantasy, two of his titles were Lovecraft's *Supernatural History in Literature* and *HPL: A Memoir* by August Derleth, which was noted in Bailey's footnote on Lovecraft.

Bailey, while searching for an academic publisher, worked to supplement his dissertation with as complete a bibliography as possible; he did not plan to list titles published past 1914. His work was made difficult by marriage and a family and by his work as a teacher at Duke University in Chapel Hill, where the libraries were of little help to him. Nevertheless, "counting titles from magazines, lists furnished me by Forrest Ackerman, H.C. Koenig and others, and such things as I could afford to buy...I had about 5000 titles."[6]

In 1939 August Derleth published *The Outsider and Others*, an omnibus of the works of H.P. Lovecraft under the imprint of Arkham House. Abramson sold the book through his stories and his catalogues, and despite its high $5.00 price, it sold well enough to prompt him to become a publisher himself. Bailey would whip some material about recent science fiction into the mix, append a representative bibliography, and they would "go" with the book.

Bailey's manuscript was received in 1941 and set in type. Publication was delayed by the outbreak of the war. Then this paragraph appeared in the October 23, 1943 issue of *Fanewscard Weekly*:[7]

> SCOOP: Chicago bookstore will publish a history and bibliography of science fiction. Book is authored by Ben Abramson and Prof. J.O. Bailey of Duke Univ. Size: approx. 400 pp; price (not definite) $4; Advertising in pro mags (probable). 1st ed of 2000. Galley proofs have been sent to Derleth for reading. Further info available from Argus Book Store, 16 N. Michigan, Chi.

On November 29, 1943, August Derleth wrote to Walter Dunkelburger; some of the letter was reproduced in *Fantasy Fiction Field*[8] (December, 1943):

> In January or February (1944), the Argus Book Shop...will publish at $3.00, I think, Pilgrims Through Space & Time, a fine, fascinating history and discussion of science fiction from the beginning to the present-day by Prof. J.O. Bailey. I've read the galleys on it, given it a puff, and cards will be mailed to our clients. Orders should be sent direct to Argus Book Shop. The fans will certainly want to own this book.

In 1944 Abramson set up business in a loft at 3 West 46th Street. A. Langley Searles, who published *Fantasy Commentator*[9] and owned a choice collection of hardcover fantasy, was a customer of Abramson's in 1945 and Abramson put him in touch with Bailey, who was making some hasty last-minute changes on his book. Searles supplied some biographical material to Bailey, and in return Bailey allowed him to use the complete bibliography which was on loan to H.C. Koenig in New York. Abramsom lent Searles the galleys for *Pilgrim*, as he had many other collectors.

At that time my history of science fiction fandom, *The Immortal Storm*, was being serialized in Searles' magazine. On a visit to him I borrowed the galleys of *Pilgrim* and then wrote a 2000 word review for *The Fanews*, which appeared on November 18, 1945,[11] unquestionably the first review of the book to appear anywhere. It was, in every sense, a news beat, since this book had been anticipated for many years. I was ojective, since I did not know either Bailey or Abramson:

> First of all I accuse this book of being a 'whatisit'. The author does not tell whether it is a history of science fiction; an elaborated bibliography of science fiction; a discussion of science fiction phases and plot forms or an exposition of fictional prophets. Having read it, I can say it tries to be all of these things and fails in every one of them...But in view of the effort expended by Bailey, the investment of Abramson, and the fact that the book is an honest attempt and does give you a whale of a lot of wordage (in fair-size type) for your money. Also in view of the fact that it is the only book of its type so far published. I am supporting it to the extent of buying it, and I suggest you do too, for it is a unique item.

H.C. Koenig, in a state of high indignation, sent copies of the review to Bailey and Abramson, demanding that they answer me. Bailey's reply was that he regretted it could not do it, because I was right.[12] He later admitted that his omissions, particularly between 1935 and 1946, were inexcusable: "It is the major fault of the book. I expect every reviewer who knows his scientific fiction to point it out. And I have no apologies, for what I could not help, I could not help."[6] Abramson would not argue with me, because as a bookseller I ordered books from him, and as a reviewer I had, on September 11, 1945, in *Fanews* reviewed highly favorably his first two books, Charles G. Finney's *The Circus of Dr Lao* and Lovecraft's *Supernatural Horror in Literature*, entitling the review "Moskowitz looks at Abramson." I ordered twelve copies of *Pilgrim* on July 29, 1947, and five more on August 4. Among the people who bought them from me were Robert Arthur, the author, Joseph H. Wrzos, who later edited *Amazing Stories*; Gerry de la Ree, publisher and collector, Richard Witter, owner of F & FS Books, the world's largest wholesale science fiction book dealer; A. Langley Searles; Thomas S. Gardner, sf author and scientist, and many others. I was one of the top three dealers in the country for that title, exempting wholesalers.

Koenig, who published a quarterly magazine called *The Reader and Collector*, which was distributed through the Fantasy Amateur Press Association,[13] of which I was a member, would not be appeased. His attack, "In Defense of J.O. Bailey and *Pilgrims Through Space and Time*", appeared in his quarterly's January, 1946 issue:

> As a matter of fact, there is some justice and sense in the review by Mr. Moskowitz... However, the idea of permitting a more or less unfortunate review to appear before the book was...printed seems to be an odd way of gaining publicity for the book...Most of

Mr. Moskowitz's criticisms are considerably biased by the fact that he is a 'fan' writing for 'fans' from the viewpoint of fandom...Professor Bailey's book was written for the general public—a public only dimly aware of scientific fiction.[14]

When *Pilgrim* finally appeared in 1947 it received important, favorable reviews in *Time, The New Yorker, The Saturday Review of Literature, The New York Times Book Review*, and was the subject of an entire column by Billy Rose, which was syndicated in 200 cities from New York to San Francisco.[15] What seemed to fascinate the reviewers most were the prophetic aspects of science fiction, outstanding predictions which had come true. This was the point of Billy Rose's column, "Billy Rose Says" for November 18, 1947, which was subtitled "Open Letter to Trygve Lee, Sec-Gen United Nations." Rose said that the accuracy of these predictions scared hell out of him, and he was sending a copy of *Pilgrim* to Trygve Lee, hoping that it would scare hell out of him too, as well as his colleagues, and awaken them to the dangers facing civilization.

Time (Sept. 8, 1947) carried a half-page illustrated review entitled "Science and Moonshine". It was primarily a listing of important writers of science fiction, with notations on important scientific predictions which had come true. "So-called scientific fiction of this sort," *Time* wrote, "is not the private property of pulps and comics."

The New Yorker (August 30, 1947) said, "The result is an extremely thorough job (Bailey is probably as familiar as any man alive with the plots of 17th century stories about flights to other planets), enthusiastic and non-critical in tone." Edwin Fadiman wrote in the *Saturday Review of Literature* (September 13, 1947): "*Pilgrims*...is obviously the product of well-organized, painstaking research. The writing, though often angular and unharmonious, is clear and thoughtful. Mr. Bailey has succeeded in providing a bastard literature with the legitimacy of a past. In so doing he not only gives it an additional dimension, but what is more, dignity."

In the *New York Times* for December 28, 1947, John W. Chase said in the course of his comments that it was a "skilfully unobtrusive presentation...a study of origins...which fills a gap." Bailey, he said, was "no reckless propagandist", and it was "original and competent work", although he wondered why, if Swift was science fiction, Genesis was not? He found an over-emphasis on Verne and Wells—nearly one-third of the book—and too little attention paid to foreign work. His review was entitled, "J. Verne to A. Bomb."

The science fiction world received the book with ambivalence. The most enthusiastic review covered two handsome pages in the October-November, 1947, issue of Walter Gilling's *Fantasy Review*, a British publication. Gillings, after praising the book's appearance and pointing out weaknesses, concluded his review, entitled "The Saga of Science Fiction", by saying: "...we are inclined to forgive his omissions and applaud the immense work and thought he has put into this unique tome..." Searles confined his comments to a single sentence in *Fantasy Commentator* (Winter, 1948), announcing that the book "has finally appeared; it is a must for every connoisseur in the field." *Fantasy Times* (January, 1948) in its column of book notes commented that *Pilgrims* 'has been roundly slammed by the fans but has received better reception in wider circles...Willy Ley mentioned at the Philcon[16] that he had a review of this book coming out shortly in *Astounding Science Fiction* that will rip it from stem to stern."

Many have forgotten that in the 40's Willy Ley was considered an outstanding authority on science fiction, since he could read French and German and, through his wife Olga, Russian. He was virtually the sole authority on foreign science fiction. Once, at the 1954 World Science Fiction Convention in San Francisco,[17] he kept his wife and daughters awake all night in their hotel room reading an advance copy of my book *The Immortal Storm*, and then engaged me in an intense cross-questioning about its contents at breakfast the next morning. He was a kind and amiable man, with nearly no enemies.

His review of *Pilgrims*, which took up three pages in the March, 1948 issue of *Astounding Science-fiction*, was atypical of him in its critical intensity, and can only be compared to his castigation of Raymond A. Palmer for advocating the existence of flying saucers at the World Science Fiction Convention in Chicago in 1952,[18] and with his break with John W. Campbell (to whom he had sold 50 articles) in 1950 over Dianetics and psi phenomena. He thought the first half of *Pilgrims*, chapters three to five, pages 28 to 218, which had formed the basis of Bailey's original thesis, to be good. But the remainder he said was "obviously pasted to the original dissertation both loosely and clumsily," and it ranged "from poor to bad":

A criticism of detail would have to comprise some forty typewritten pages...*Pilgrims*... completely fails to convey a picture of recent science fiction. It completely fails to correlate the scientific discoveries and theories of a period with the fiction caused by these discoveries and theories. It fails to analyze the more important of the modern stories, and fails to do justice to those which are analyzed...The final impression after laying the book aside is one of intense disappointment.

Abramson was shaken by this devastating appraisal by so prominent a figure, in the field's leading publication. He wrote to Bailey, who wrote back to him on October 30, 1948, calling Ley "a little peevish." He thought Ley's criticisms of the omissions from 1914 to 1947 were justified, but he was annoyed that Ley had questioned his statement that Adam Seaborn, the author of *Symzonia*, was a pen name for Symmes (there is no question in my mind that Bailey is wrong here). Abramson had written a long letter of complaint to Ley, and sent a carbon copy to Searles.

Forrest J. Ackerman, whose assistance Bailey had acknowledged, wrote one of the most interesting reviews. Entitled "The Poor Man's Necronomicon—'Pilgrims' Through Print Shop and Bindery", it appeared in *Tympany* (September 1, 1947),[6] a weekly news magazine published in Minneapolis by Robert L. Stein and Redd Boggs. Ackerman says that Bailey contacted him as early as 1933 (thought this may be an error, since the Science Fiction League, referred to, was not formed until May, 1934). Bailey, Ackerman says

> wanted to borrow considerable material from my collection...So I sent [him] the Amazings containing A. Hyatt Verrill's 'Beyond the Pole' [October and November, 1926] (it being the first story I ever read), and 'The People of the Golden Atom'[19], etc. I sent him books, and at his request I prepared an article on the fanmag scene from The Time Traveller[20] to the publications then current. I may be mistaken, but I have a vague recollection of having included scientifilms, too...To me, reading PTSAT was like reading a couple dozen fanmags featuring book reviews. If you'd like that sort of thing, you should like PTSAT as much as I did (and I did)...The book begins to fall off in interest, I should say, in the latter chapters when it begins beating stories down finer and finer for discussions or inventions presented in them, or invasions, or innovations, or variations on a theme, and no new titles are encountered, but only repetitions of old. I doubt this is going to be a speculators' book.

Bailey responded to this review in *Tampani*, giving the background of the book, and saying that its admitted weaknesses rested in the history of its "production." It is obvious that when Bailey decided to expand the book and make it more comprehensive, he was swamped by the limits of both his knowledge and the availability of materials. Then, as now, the important collections were private, because the scholarly establishment did not want them. Forrest Ackerman, who was seventeen years old and knew nothing about academic discipline, had resources available to him that made him better equipped than Bailey to write a book like *Pilgrims*. In fact, at that time the fan magazine *The Time Traveller*, for which Ackerman was associate editor, was running Morton Weisinger's synoptic history of the genre, which could have served as a skeleton outline for Bailey's book.[21]

During World War II there had been a massive increase in collecting and research by fans, so that *Pilgrims* was being read and reviewed by bibliophiles who had become authorities in the field.[22] Bailey was aware that he could not defend himself against these zealous fans. He suggested therefore that someone pick up where he had left off—in 1914. "I have laid a foundation which covered the historical background fairly well, I think. It is time, now, for another man to take over—a man with interest, time, and ability—and write another volume, the sequel to *Pilgrims*. He can start where I left off—and good luck to him!"[6]

On November 2, 1948, Abramson wrote to Searles, asking him if he would be interested in continuing the history. Searles however was a professor of chemistry with family responsibilities and the prospect did not look financially rewarding to him. Abramson wrote to me on January 5, 1949, suggesting that I was qualified to write the history of science fiction development, but I was never able to talk to him about it. He had become the publisher of the quarterly *Baker Street Journal*, which began the game of treating Sherlock Holmes as a real person, and had gained national stature through it.

Bailey continued teaching at North Carolina until retirement. He was killed by a car while he was walking his dog in Chapel Hill on October 30, 1979. He had published *Thomas Hardy and the Cosmic Mind; a Reading of the Dynasts* (Chapel Hill: University of North Carolina Press, 1956) and edited *British Plays of the Nineteenth Century: an Anthology to Illustrate the Evolution of Drama* (Odyssey Press, 1966). He added to a notation on him for *Pilgrims* in *Contemporary Science Fiction Authors*:

> One other item you might wish to mention is my introduction to Captain Adam Seaborn's *Symzonia; a Voyage of Discovery*, published originally in 1820, reprinted in 1965 by Scholars' Facsimilies and Reprints, of Gainesville, Florida. So far as I know, *Symzonia* was the first piece of science fiction written in America. It is not mentioned in *Pilgrims* because I did not know about the book at that time.[23]

This is an inexplicable error, because *Symzonia* is mentioned twenty-one different times in *Pilgrims*; one mention is an elaborate description of the plot, which touched off the rebuttal by Willy Ley.

The Pilgrim Award is a suitable memorial to J.O. Bailey, who would certainly otherwise be forgotten. When universities would not accept doctoral theses on science fiction, and there were no role models to imitate, he nevertheless persevered and struggled for decades to put together a decently researched book about the genre, and found a small press to publish it. A. Langley Searles passed his bibliography onto E.F. Bleiler who incorporated it into *The Checklist of Fantastic Literature* which for 32 years was the primary reference work in the field.[24]

Bailey was not a pilgrim so much as he was a pioneer. And that is how he will be remembered.

NOTES

[1] Peter Nicholls, ed. *The Science Fiction Encyclopedia* (Garden City: Dolphin/ Doubleday, 1979).

[2] Hugo Gernsback announced the formation of the Science Fiction League in his magazine *Wonder Stories* [(May, 1934), p. 1061]. The purpose of the League, whose headquarters were at 98 Park Place in New York, was to encourage the popularity of science fiction. News of its chapters and projects by its members were run monthly.

[3] P. Schuyler Miller was a popular sf author, fan, collector and executive director of the Science Fiction League.

[4] LeRoy Christian Bashore, Oswald Train, Paul Valansky, Carl Adams, and the chapter of the League in Leeds, England, director of which was Douglas W.F. Mayer.

[5] Julius Schwartz, "The Science Fiction Eye" See *Fantasy Magazine* (March, 1936), p. 45. The transition was made in early 1936: the last issue under Gernsback was in April, and the first under new ownership in August.

[6] J.O. Bailey, "The Story Behind *Pilgrims Through Space and Time*" *Tympani* (Sept. 29, 1947). The spelling of the magazine title was changed from *Tympany* with the issue of Sept. 15, 1947.

[7] Originally Tucker's FaNewscard Weekly, begun July 3, 1943, by William Tucker. A fan magazine printed on the back of a postcard, and selling for 2¢. Then published in Chicago by Ed Connor and Frank M. Robinson.

[8] *Fantasy Fiction Field*, begun October 26, 1940, was a weekly news magazine published by Julius Unger, a Brooklyn book dealer. It was noted for its photographs and was the most reliable source of science fiction news during the yearly years of the war.

[9] Interview with A. Langley Searles, June 11, 1980. *Fantasy Commentator*, a quarterly, was started in December, 1943. The quality of its bibliographical research and its analyses, from the ranking scholars of the day, has never been equalled.

[10] Serialization began in Fall, 1956 and went through Spring-Summer 1952.

[11] *Fanews* was *FaNewscard* in an alternate letter and legal size format, appearing first July 8, 1944. Walter Dunkelberger of Fargo, North Dakota, took over the editor-

ship on July 31, 1944. It printed photos and was the leading sf news magazine through 1947. Its circulation in 1945 was 800.

12 Letter from J.O. Bailey to A. Langley Searles, Dec. 26, 1945.

13 A group of amateur sf and fantasy fan publishers, memberships limited to 65, founded in 1937 and still active. The group mails members' publications on a quarterly basis from a central location.

14 These remarks are paraphrased in Bailey's letter to Searles (n. 12), indicating that he helped to write Koenig's reply. Koenig wrote me March 22, 1946: "You will note that the article on 'Pilgrims' was not written by Bailey—but by yours truly—so you won't have to worry about Bailey's provocative style."

15 Two of the papers which carried the column on that date were the Newark *Evening News* and New York *PM*.

16 Philcon was The Philadelphia Science Fiction Convention, the Fifth World SF Convention, held at the Penn-Sheraton, Aug. 30-Sept. 1, 1947.

17 Twelfth World Science Fiction Convention, Sept. 3-6, 1954 at the Sir Francis Drake.

18 Tenth Anniversary World SF Convention, Morrison Hotel, Aug. 30, 1952. On the panel entitled "Flying Saucers—What Are They?" with Raymond A. Palmer.

19 Jan. 24-Feb. 28, 1920, 6 installments in *All-Story Weekly*. *People* was a sequel to *The Girl in the Golden Atom* by Ray Cummings. The two were bound together under the latter title in the first hardbound edition from Methuen (1922).

20 *The Time Traveller*, a fan magazine edited by Allen Glasser, Julius Schwartz, Mort Weisinger and Forrest Ackerman, put out 9 issues January, 1932 to Winter, 1933.

21 "The History of Science Fiction" in *The Time Traveller* Feb.-Sept., 1932, 6 installments.

22 Harry Warner, *All Our Yesterdays*, pp. 56-72.

23 R. Reginald, ed. Vol II (Detroit: Gale, 1979).

24 (Chicago: Shasta Publishers, 1948).

PART SEVEN:

RESOURCES

The phenomenal growth in writing about fantastic literature in recent years has been documented in many ways, most consistently in the review columns of the major science fiction journals *Extrapolation, Science-Fiction Studies,* and *Foundation;* in the SFRA publication *Science Fiction and Fantasy Book Review,* edited by Neil Barron; and in the annual bibliography of secondary works in the field compiled by Marshall Tymn and formerly Roger C. Schlobin. In this section, we hope not to pre-empt the use of those and other resources, but rather to stimulate use of them. None of the pieces that follow are intended to be exhaustive, but they will provide a hint of what the student of science fiction may find in the library, at fan conventions, and in a sampling of other countries. Future publications of SFRA will provide additional guides to resources and additional "news from abroad," covering nations not included in this too-brief survey. We only hope to suggest here that the study of science fiction has become a world-wide project, and that useful material for the scholar may be found in places other than libraries and literary journals.

Neil Barron is a librarian and a member of the editorial board of this volume. His numerous contributions to the study of science fiction culminated in the now-standard reference work, *Anatomy of Wonder: A Critical Guide to Science Fiction* (2nd ed., R.R. Bowker, 1981), and in his receiving the SFRA's Pilgrim Award in 1982 for outstanding contribu-

191

tions to the field. His essay appeared originally in the July 1982 *Fantasy Newsletter*.

Franz Rottensteiner is an Austrian critic and editor whose books published in this country include *The Science Fiction Book*, *The View from Another Shore*, and *The Fantasy Book*. Ion Hobana is an author living in Bucharest whose *20,000 Pages in Search of Jules Verne* received a special award at Eurocon V. J.A. Dautzenberg, who lives in Nijmegen, The Netherlands, has written on science fiction for Dutch periodicals as well as for *Science-Fiction Studies*. Insero Cremaschi edits the Milan journal *La Collina* and is married to noted Italian science fiction writer Gilda Musa. Nachman Ben-Yehuda teaches sociology at The Hebrew University of Jerusalem and was instrumental in organizing the first Jerucon science fiction convention.

Jan Bogstad, whose M.A. is from the University of Wisconsin-Madison, is completing a doctoral dissertation on feminist theory in science fiction and writing a correspondence course on science fiction with Professor Fannie J. LeMoine of the University of Wisconsin.

SF: Fan to Scholar Industry

Neil Barron

With the development of the fan subculture in the 1920's, an informal network provided a sort of running commentary on American pulp fiction, notably in the letter columns. Hal Hall's *Science Fiction Book Review Index, 1923-1973* (1975) provides access to reviews in the pulps and to those in more general magazines since 1970. For pre-1970 reviews of SF and fantasy books in general magazines, such as *Saturday Review* or the *Library Journal*, and not necessarily identified as category fiction, you'll have to consult a six volume set likely to be found in larger libraries, the *National Library Service Cumulative Book Review Index, 1905-1974* (1975). This lists more than 560,000 citations to more than a million reviews published in *Saturday Review*, *Choice*, *Library Journal* and the *Book Review Digest* (the last includes at least three review sources per title).

History and criticism was also found in the fanzines of the 1930's, notably in one called the *Science Fiction Critic* (1935-1938), edited by Claire P. Beck. His brother, Clyde, wrote "Hammer and Tongs," a column discussing current SF periodical fiction, as James Blish was to do two decades later. These columns were issued as a booklet in 1937.

The first book-length treatment of SF was derived from a 1934 doctoral thesis, *Science Fiction in English, 1817-1914: A Study of Trends and Forms*, by J.O. Bailey, who taught at the University of North Carolina for many years before his death in 1979. The book, *Pilgrims Through Space and Time: Trends and Patterns in Scientific and Utopian Fiction* (1947), was revised to suggest the continuities in the themes since World War I, but its major value is its treatment of the pre-World War I period. Its seminal importance is suggested by the Pilgrim award, given at the annual conferences of the SF Research Association since 1970, when Bailey was given the first award.

Other early works, often derived from doctoral theses, occasionally dealt with photo-SF, such as Gove's *The Imaginary Voyage in Prose Fiction* (1941) and *Voyages to the Moon* by Marjorie Nicolson (1948), but these are of little interest to most readers except for collectors of associational early works, whose influence on today's SF is increasingly faint.

After World War II, a number of fans founded specialty publishing houses, most of which died in the 1950's when the large trade book publishers moved in to dominate the market. One of interest here which survives from that relatively early period is Advent, a Chicago-based firm which specializes in history, criticism and reference works (Tuck's encyclopedia was discussed in the first essay). Advent issued Damon Knight's *In Search of Wonder* (1956; 2d ed, rev & enl, 1967), book reviews of the 1952-1960 period, still of some interest to the older reader. Advent published the collected pieces of James Blish, writing as William Athelin, in two books, *The Issue at Hand* (1964) and *More Issues at Hand* (1970). Blish's criticism, though now unavoidably dated, was informed and refreshingly free of the puffery and disguised flattery which often passed for criticism within the field. Advent also published four lectures, given at the University of Chicago by Heinlein, Kornbluth, Bloch and Bester, as *The Science Fiction Novel: Imagination and Social Criticism* (1959), whose judgments were echoed and amplified by Kingsley Amis in his lectures at Princeton, published as *New Maps of Hell* (1960).

As a few bricks were dislodged from the walls of the self-imposed American SF pulp ghetto by an inquiring public, Coward-McCann published the first general survey of the field, Bretnor's *Modern Science Fiction: Its Meaning and Future* (1953; 2d ed, slightly updated and corrected, Advent 1979). The defensive stance of many contributors, all prominent in SF at the time, is characteristic of much early criticism especially for a non-specialist audience. Bretnor edited a much more current and useful collection of 15 essays 21 years later in *Science Fiction Today and Tomorrow* (1974).

When the distinguished British writer and critic, Kingsley Amis, delivered his Christian Gauss lectures at Princeton in 1958-1959, listeners were surprised to discover that they dealt with one of Amis's long-time interests, science fiction. Amis rejected the action-adventure emphases of too much SF and argued for the genre as a cautionary literature of social criticism. Widely discussed in both the fanzines and in general periodicals, *New Maps of Hell* was influential in gaining SF a more respectful hearing among the suspicious unconverted.

Fans continued to publish their findings. Certainly the most industrious was and is Sam Moskowitz, who draws on his enormous collections to explore areas only now being mapped by today's scholars. His two biographical works, *Explorers of the Infinite* (1963) and *Seekers of Tomorrow* (1966), include chapters on both early and modern writers of SF, some of the pieces the first extended discussions of their subjects. He has usefully explored late 19th century and early 20th century SF in *Science Fiction by Gaslight* (1968) and *Under the Moons of Mars* (1970), which contain invaluable histories as well as typical stories from the periods. Although I have remarked elsewhere that I find his studies too inbred and sometimes lacking the documentation needed to permit verification and amplification of his statements, his pioneer work over the years was belatedly recognized by the SFRA, who presented him with the Pilgrim award in 1981.

As academic acceptance grew in the 1970's, the market for SF and fantasy also grew, as figures in the annual summaries in *Locus* clearly show. Writing in *Harper's* in 1939, Bernard De Voto could refer—not entirely inaccurately—to American pulp SF as besotted nonsense, paranoid fantasies appealing to tired, dull or weak minds. Four decades later, ten American university presses published books about SF, one measure of the dramatic change in acceptance, especially during the past decade, which has seen a very large increase in the number of books about the genre. Some of these, of course, are nearly worthless, written by persons unfamiliar with the field who saw a financial opportunity. But many of the best were written by fans turned academics, where enthusiasm is tempered by scholarly detachment and a wider knowledge of literature.

The literary editor of the *Oxford Mail*, Brian Aldiss, for many years also wrote both SF and traditional fiction. His wide-ranging history of the field, *Billion Year Spree*, appeared in 1973. Although Aldiss subtitled it *The True History of Science Fiction*, the claim is a trifle immodest, (and perhaps ironic), although it remains the best critical history at least through the 1950's. Like his fellow Englishman, Amis,

Aldiss writes with wit and perception, all informed by a wide knowledge of literature.

James Gunn, a skilled writer, critic, and teacher, wrote a history that more clearly reflects the "consensus" view, published as *Alternate Worlds* (1975). An oversize, heavily illustrated account, it has far more substance than later coffee table books. The illustrations, including hundreds of photos of authors, are well-chosen and provide a valuable added dimension to the informed and readable text.

In 1977 Paul Carter's outstanding thematic history of American pulp SF, *The Creation of Tomorrow*, was published—significantly—by Columbia University Press. A professor of history at the University of Arizona, Carter has also written some short SF. It may be significant that the book's readability was improved by reading early versions piecemeal over his campus radio station; are you listening, Darko Suvin? Compare Carter's account with the pedestrian one by veteran writer/editor, Lester del Rey in his *The World of Science Fiction 1926-1976* (1979). Announced by Garland as part of a 1976 series of hardcover reprints it appeared four years later and proved a great disappointment. (For a trenchant and well-argued analysis of del Rey's history and the common attitudes it embodies, see Christopher Priest's " 'It' Came from Outer Space," *Foundation* 21, (February, 1981), 53-63.)

Recognizing the need for guidance through the burgeoning literature, fiction and nonfiction, I wrote several bibliographic essays for *Choice*, a book review journal for libraries. These led to *Anatomy of Wonder* (1976; 2d ed, 1981) which soon became the standard critical guide to SF and books about SF, from the earliest works to contemporary writers in a number of languages. The second edition, more than 50% longer than the first, documents the tremendous growth in scholarship in recent years. Most of the books discussed in this essay are treated more fully in this guide.

As fans founded their fanzines in the 1920's, so too have academics in more recent years. *Extrapolation*, now a quarterly, began in 1959 as a longish newsletter. *Science-Fiction Studies* is published in Canada three times yearly and is the most resolutely scholarly of the journals. *Foundation* is published three times yearly in London and is easily the most readable of the three. The SF Research Association, founded in 1970, provides two journals, the *SFRA Newsletter* and the *Science Fiction & Fantasy Book Review* as membership benefits for its worldwide audience (inquire of Elizabeth Cogell, SFRA Treasurer, Humanities Dept, University of Missouri, Rolla, MO 65401).

Academic criticism is found not only in journals but in books—fan, university press and trade publisher. Kent State University Press publishes *Extrapolation* and has published several valuable critical works, most notably Gary Wolfe's insightful *The Known and the Unknown* (1979), based on a close and intelligent reading of a large number of Anglo-American SF stories. Yale published Suvin's intimidating and densely written *Metamorphoses of Science Fiction* (1979). Bio-critical series of monographs are now appearing from Oxford, Taplinger, Starmont House and Borgo Press. In a *Choice* article I referred to SF as a new growth industry. For younger academics, the mother lodes of Milton or Shakespeare have long been staked out by their elders, and reputations are sometimes being based at least in part on their scholarship in SF. Dena Brown's lament about returning SF to its cozy gutter has long been ignored. Academics sometimes exhibit the same tunnel vision as their fan counterparts, whose highest principle of criticism is too often *de gustibus non est disputandem*. But the best work cannot fail to enrich the field, broaden, deepen, sharpen tastes, and attract more informed recognition from traditional critics, whose judgments still echo those of De Voto (quoted above) but whose knowledge of the field is still woefully inadequate.

Although I've noted some of the more significant works which deal with printed SF, I cannot neglect two related areas. Although the popular American and British magazines of the pre-World War I period include SF with accompanying illustrations, SF illustration flourished in the American pulps from the 1920's onward. As Aldiss accurately notes in his excellent oversize survey, *Science Fiction Art* (1975), the garish and repetitive iconography of the early illustrators often stimulated youthful readers as much as the text. I suspect that some older critics with long memories still base their distaste for the genre on the more outlandish covers of these pulps. Book cover illustration is usually more sedate, and a good sampling is found in *Tomorrow and Beyond: Masterpieces of Science Fiction Art* (1978), by Ian Summers, the former art director of Ballantine. More than 300 color illustrations by 67 mostly American illustrators are included, many of them from recent paperbacks. Many of today's active illustrators, such as Kelly Freas, Michael Whelan or Chris Foss, have had entire books devoted to their work. Gerry de la Ree, the New Jersey collector, has published limited editions of a number of oversize illustrated works, many of them featuring the work of Virgil Finlay.

The second related area is SF film. If you ask the occasional or non-SF reader what science fiction "is," he or she will often cite popular films as examples, such as *Star Trek* or *Star Wars*. Unfortunately, printed and filmed SF rarely have much in common. As a visual medium, controlled by a "box office" structure, SF film usually depends for its appeal on special effects, often with little else to recommend the films. One of the few films which was faithful to its printed original was *Charly*, based on Daniel Keyes' award-winning *Flowers for Algernon* (1966). Significantly, this film had no special effects; more significantly, perhaps, it won an Oscar for its male lead, Cliff Robertson.

Just as most SF or quasi-SF films are dreadful—though often significant for non-cinematic reasons—so most books about them are undistinguished, heavier on stills than on text or insight. The two best surveys are British. John Brosnan's *Future Tense* (1978) is informed, witty and well-written. Arranged chronologically, Brosnan's book blends technical knowledge (he has written *Movie Magic*, about special effects), history and personal anecdotes in his discussion of more than 400 films. The illustrations are small, all black & white, but genuinely illustrate, as do the more abundant color illustrations in Philip Strick's *Science Fiction Movies* (1976). Strick's approach is thematic, but both accounts are valuable. More recent is the trade paperback by Frederik Pohl and his son, Frederik Pohl IV, *Science Fiction: Studies in Film* (1981). The literary sensibility of Pohl père and the cinematic one of his son are often at odds. Their distinction between SF films and sci-fi films is interesting but not a defensible organizing principle. Anecdotal and chatty, it's aimed at a more popular audience and lacks an index. Much better argued and more narrowly focused is Vivian Sobchack's *The Limits of Infinity: The American Science Fiction Film, 1950-1975* (1980). This closely investigates the aesthetics as well as the thematic aspects of recent films, including structure, image and—rarely discussed elsewhere—sound. Because Sobchack confines her discussion to a 25 year period, she treats the films discussed in much more detail and with greater analytic rigor than do Brosnan or Strick, and her study is an excellent choice for the serious film aficionado.

BIBLIOGRAPHY

All books are hardcover unless otherwise noted.

Aldiss, Brian W. *Billion Year Spree: The True History of Science Fiction.* Garden City, NY: Doubleday 1973. 339 p. NY: Schocken Books, 1974.

Aldiss, Brian W. *Science Fiction Art.* NY: Bounty/Crown, 1975. 128 p.

Amis, Kingsley. *New Maps of Hell.* NY: Harcourt, 1960. NY: Arno, 1975. 161 p.

Bailey, J.O. *Pilgrims Through Space and Time: Trends and Patterns in Scientific and Utopian Fiction.* NY: Argus Books, 1947. 341 p. Westport, CT: Greenwood Press, 1972.

Barron, Neil, ed. *Anatomy of Wonder: A Critical Guide to Science Fiction*, 2nd ed. NY: Bowker, 1981, 724 p.

Beck, Clyde P. *Hammer and Tongs*, Lakeport, CA: Futile Press, 1937. xv + 19 p. OP.

Blish, James (William Atheling, pseud). *The Issue at Hand: Studies in Contemporary Magazine Science Fiction.* Chicago: Advent, 1964. 136 p.
More Issues at Hand; Critical Studies in Contemporary Science Fiction. 154 p. Chicago: Advent, 1970.

Bretnor, Reginald, ed. *Modern Science Fiction: Its Meaning and Future.* NY: Coward McCann, 1953. 294 p. 2d ed, rev & corrected. Chicago: Advent, 1979. 327 p.
Science Fiction, Today and Tomorrow. NY: Harper, 1974. 324 p. OP.

Brosnan, John. *Future Tense: The Cinema of Science Fiction.* London: Macdonald, 1978. 320 p. NY: St. Martin's 1979.
Movie Magic; the Story of Special Effects in the Cinema. NY: St. Martin's 1974. Plume (New American Library), 1976.

Carter, Paul A. *The Creation of Tomorrow: Fifty Years of Magazine Science Fiction.* NY: Columbia University Press, 1977. 318 p.

del Rey, Lester. *The World of Science Fiction, 1926-1976: The History of a Subculture.* NY: Garland and Ballantine, 1979. 416 p.

Extrapolation. 1970+. Quarterly. Kent State University Press, Kent, OH 44242.

Foundation; The Review of Science Fiction. 1972+. 3x/year. SF Foundation, North East London Polytechnic, Longbridge Rd. Dagenham RM8 2AS, UK.

Gove, Philip Babcock. *The Imaginary Voyage in Prose Fiction...* NY: Columbia University Press, 1941. 445 p. NY: Arno, 1975.

Gunn, James E. *Alternate Worlds: The Illustrated History of Science Fiction.* Englewood Cliffs, NJ: Prentice-Hall, 1975. 256 p. A&W Visual Library.

Hall, Hal W. *Science Fiction Book Review Index, 1923-1973.* Detroit: Gale Research, 1975. 438 p.

Knight, Damon. *In Search of Wonder: Essays on Modern Science Fiction.* Chicago: Advent, 1956. 180 p. 2d ed, rev & enl, 1967. 306 p.

Moskowitz, Sam. *Explorers of the Infinite: Shapers of Science Fiction.* Cleveland: World, 1963. 353 p. Westport, CT: Hyperion Press, 1974..

Science Fiction by Gaslight: A History and Anthology of Science Fiction in the Popular Magazines, 1891-1911. Cleveland: World, 1968. 364 p. Westport, CT: Hyperion Press 1974.

Seekers of Tomorrow: Masters of Modern Science Fiction. Cleveland: World, 1966. 441 p. NY: Ballantine, 1967. 450 p. (adds index). Westport, CT: Hyperion Press, 1974.

Under the Moons of Mars: A History and Anthology of Scientific Romance in the Munsey Magazines, 1912-1920. NY: Holt, 1970. 433 p. OP.

National Library Service Cumulative Book Review Index, 1905-1974. Princeton, NJ: National Library Service Co, 1975. 6 v.

Nicolson, Marjorie Hope. *Voyages to the Moon.* NY: Macmillan, 1948. 297 p. OP.

Pohl, Frederik & Frederik Pohl IV. *Science Fiction: Studies in Film.* NY: Ace, 1981.

Science Fiction & Fantasy Book Review. February 1979-February 1980, January 1982+. 10 issues/year. Elizabeth Cogell, SFRA Treasurer, Humanities Dept., University of Missouri, Rolla, MO 65401.

The Science Fiction Novel: Imagination and Social Criticism. Chicago: Advent, 1959. 160 p.

Science-Fiction Studies. 1973+. 3x/year. R.M. Philmus, English Dept. Concordia University, 7141 Sherbrooke St W, Montreal, Quebec, Canada H4B 1R6.

Sobchack, Vivian Carol. *The Limits of Infinity: The American Science Fiction Film, 1950-1975.* So Brunswick, NJ & NY: A.S. Barnes, 1980. 246 p.

Strick, Philip. *Science Fiction Movies.* London: Octopus Books, 1976 160 p. OP.

Summers, Ian, ed. *Tomorrow and Beyond: Masterpieces of Science Fiction Art.* NY: Workman, 1978. 158 p.

Suvin, Darko. *The Metamorphoses of Science Fiction: On the Poetics and History of a Literary Genre.* New Haven, CT: Yale University Press, 1979. 317 p.

Wolfe, Gary K. *The Known and the Unknown: The Iconography of Science Fiction.* Kent, OH: Kent St. University Press, 1979

Some Recent Writings on SF and Fantasy in Germany

Franz Rottensteiner

Symposia on science fiction in Germany are still relatively rare. One such symposium was held by the Evangelische Akademie of the German Protestant Church in Loccum in May, 1979: academics and SF professionals were among the participants: Herbert W. Franke, leading SF author in West Germany and editor of the Goldmann SF series; Wolfgang Jeschke, SF editor of Germany's biggest, most successful series (7-8 books a month) for Heyne Verlag; Jörge Weigand, anthologist and reviewer; and Dieter Hasselblatt, head of radio plays for Bavarian radio, who frequently lectures on SF and supervises production of SF radio plays. Speeches give at this symposium were revised and published in a book of 14 essays by 13 writers, which includes one on the problems of defining SF and fantasy, pieces on religion in SF, Wolfgang Jeschke's article on SF in West Germany, discussions of language in SF, and detailed analyses of Hans Dominik's novel *Die Macht der drei* (1921), Franke's *Sirius Transit*, and the work of Stanislaw Lem, as well as a useful bibliography of books and articles.[1]

In May, 1979, in celebration of Einstein's 100th birthday, a seminar was held by the Writer's Union of Bavaria and Baden-Wurttemberg and the local Volkshochschule in Ulm, where Einstein was born. One of the lectures given here was Wolfgang Jeschke's "Science Fiction in Deutschland"[1]; another was my "Einsteins Theorien an der Literatur". Both were reprinted, together with "Stanislaw Lems phantastische Schreibweise," an essay by Michael Springer, in No. 1/1980 of the periodical *Kurbiskern*.

One conference which was cancelled because of lack of interest, especially on the part of the press, was the 1980 "Literatur-gesprach" meeting of the Booksellers Association of Germany, Switzerland and Austria, which was to be on science fiction and fantasy.

Courses on SF are still rare in German universities. I know of only two given on a fairly regular basis: one is Dr. Herbert Franke's "Introduction to Science Fiction," given since 1978 at the Fachhochschule Bielefeld, and the other is an annual seminar by Dr. Dietrich Wachler, held at the Fachhochschule Münster Institute for Sociology. In the past topics have been "The Sociology of SF" are "Ideology and Social Criticism in SF" and in 1981 scheduled seminars are "Scientific Fantasy in Poland and the Soviet Union" and "Scientific Utopias and SF in Germany."

The most important book on SF is undoubtedly Manfred Nagl's *Science Fiction. Ein Segment popularer Kultur im Medien— und Produktverbund*,[2] fifth in a series of introductory textbooks for scholars. It considers not just stories and novels, but also films, comics, radio plays, music, art and design, along with SF markets and readership and has a 50 page international bibliography. It is no less important than Nagl's *Science Fiction in Deutschland* (1972), and, although still very critical of SF, is far less dogmatic.

Less stimulating but valuable is Reimer Jehmlich's *Science Fiction*,[3] a survey of research and criticism in which the author discusses the definition of SF, the role of amateur critics and scholars, unresolved problems of research and available sources and bibliographies. There is also a huge study, originally a doctoral dissertation, by Claus Hallmann of *Perry Rhodan*, that interminable German SF series which has sold well over one billion copies.[4] And another dissertation, by Susanne Päch, deals with the few SF stories which appeared 1887-1945 in the boys' yearbook *Das Neue Universum*, and especially with the stories of Hans Dominik (1872-1945) written before he started the novels which brought him the success which makes him still Germany's most popular SF writer.[5]

By far the most respected SF author in Germany is Stanislaw Lem. Three volumes of his "Collected Works" have so far appeared in an attractive hardcover edition: *Fantastyka i Futurologia* (*Phantastik und Futurologie*): Volume One in 1977 and Volume Two in 1980.[6] In 1981 Volume Three appeared: *Essays*. In addition to pieces of Todorov's theory of the Fantastic, and the afterword to the Polish edition of Philip K. Dick's *Ubik*, both of which have been printed in *SF-Studies*, there are essays on the fantastic horror stories of the Polish writer

Stefan Grabifiski (1887-1936), Wells's *War of the Worlds*, Antoni
Slonimski's *The Torpedo of Time* (*Torpeda czasu*, 1923), a classic
time travel novel, and related essays on de Sade and games theory,
extrasensory perception, biology and values, and informatics and
cybernetics.

There is also the Lem reader, *Die phantastischen Erzahlungen*,
which was on the hardcover bestseller list for four months, selling at
this writing over 55,000 copies. It contains, besides a collection of
Lem's stories, an essay *Der Versuch, Erfahrungen zu vermitteln,
Anmerkungen zum Werb des Stainslaw Lem* by the editor, Werner
Berthel, and my own essay, *Ammerkungen zur Regeption Stainslaw
Lem* which encompasses a portfolio of illustrations and book covers,
and an interview with Lem.[7]

An important, although difficult semantic essay on Lem's *Solaris* is
Manfred Geier's "Stanislaw Lems Phantastischer Ozean" in *Kultur-
historische Sprachalalysen*.[8]

H.J. Alpers' *Science-Fiction-Almanach 1981* is devoted to women in
SF; it contains stories by Ursula K. Le Guin, Joan D. Vinge, Marion
Zimmer Bradley and others, and essays: Rosemarie Hundertmarck's
"Rollentausch-Frauen in der SF", Ronald M. Hahn's "Die Welt der
Roten Sonne-der private Kosmos der Marion Zimmer Bradley", a
translation of Mary Kenny Badami's "A Feminist Critique of SF" and
Darrel Schweitzer's interview with Joan D. Vinge.[9]

In fantasy, mention must be made of *Phaicon 4*, the fourth in the
series of almanacks, which contains, as well as stories, essays on
Gérard de Nerval, Prosper Mérimée, Georges Rodenbach, Raymond
Roussel, Maurice Sandoz, Jean Ray and Jean Louis Bouquet.[10]

Truly indispensable is *Phantastik in Literatur und Kunst*, a giant
compilation of essays by German scholars on fantasy, not in the sense
of Tolkien or C.S. Lewis. It has three sections of essays on the theory of
the fantastic in literature and the arts (especially "Die Ordnung der
Unordnung. Eine Bilanz sur Theorie der Phantastik" by Dieter Pen-
ning), on the fantastic in literature (essays on Borges, Ludwig Tieck,
Poe, Sheridan Le Fanu, Baudelaire, Nerval-Maupassant-Breton, Henry
James, Lewis Carroll, Alfred Kublin's *The Other Side*, Paul
Scheerbart-Carl Einstein), on occult sources of fantastic literature
(Bruno Schulz, Lovecraft, H.C. Artmann, Lem's *The Futurological
Congress* and Gabriel Garcia Marquéz's *One Hundred Years of Soli-
tude.*). The third section contains essays on the iconography of the
fantastic, Magritte, the fantastic in architecture, film, and music,
along with an extensive bibliography by Jens Malte Fischer.[11]

I have edited a collection of essays called *Quarber Merkur*, selected from my amateur magazine of the same name. The topics are robots in SF, Stanislaw Lem, Aleksandr Bogdanov's *The Red Star*, W.S. Burroughs, Stefan Grabiński, Jean Ray, J.L. Borges, the vampire motif in German horror stories, and women in SF.[12]

An amateur publication of note is the *Science Fiction Times*, now in its 25th year and appearing recently rather irregularly, since its editors are engaged in translating, writing and agenting SF. Besides longish articles on SF and fantasy, this magazine features news, book reviews and a bibliography of current titles in German. Its editor, Hans Joachim Alpers, is now the editor also of the new SF line of Moewig Verlag of Munich, which publishes four paperbacks a month and perhaps a dozen hardcovers a year.[13]

Finally one publication of note in the German Democratic Republic is *Lichtjahr 1. Ein Phanstastik-Almanach*, which includes stories and essays, among them "Briefe, die allerneueste Literatur betreffend" in which the well-known East German husband and wife Johanna and Gunter Braun, present, in the form of letters written from ancient Greece, their views on the function and aesthetics of SF. There are also essays on Theodore Sturgeon's "The Skills of Xanadu" (Heinz Entner's "Was Xanadu kann"); "Die Spirale im Werk Ursula Le Guins" by "Wl. Gakow", translated from the Russian, and Ursula Le Guin's introduction to her *The Left Hand of Darkness*, just published in East Germany. Other articles in the book are popular speculations, not literary criticism.[14] Finally, two books have appeared on the German fantasist Gustav Meyrink. One is Evelin Aster's *Personalbibliographie von Gustav Meyrink*, a comprehensive bibliography of his books, contributions to periodicals, manuscripts, letters, translations, afterwords, illustrations, as well as on literature about him.[15] The second is *Gustav Meyrink, Beitrage zur Biographie und Studien zu seiner Kunsttheorie*, which traces Meyrink's life in Prague, Vienna, Munich, etc., discussing his public political and literary remarks, his interest in theatre and film, the genesis of *The Golem* and art forms related to his work. The book, developed from a doctoral dissertation, contains a forty page bibliography.[16]

NOTES

1   Karl Ermert, ed., *Neugier oder Flucht? Zu Poetik, Ideologie und Wirkung der Science Fiction* "Literaturwissenschaft-Gesellschaftswissenschaft" Vol 50 (Stuttgart: Klett Verlag, 1980).

2   (Tübingen: Günter Narr Verlag, 1981).

3   "Ertrage der Forschung" (Darmstadt: Wissenschaftliche Buchgesellschaft, 1980).

4   *Perry Rhodan. Analyse einrer Science-Fiction-Romanheftserie* (Frankfurt/Main: Rita G. Fischer Verlag, 1979).

5   *Von den Marskanalen zur Wunderwaffe. Eine Studie uber phantastische und futurologische Tendenzen dargestellt am naturwissenschaftlichen Jahrbuch Das Neue Universum 1880-1945* (Thesis of the Faculty of Philosophy of the Ludwig-Maximilians-Universitat Munchen, 1980). A most interesting note here is that there appeared in 1887 a plagiarized German version of E.E. Hale's "The Brick Moon": "Unser Trabant" by Friedrich Meister. For 1887-1938 Pach lists 38 SF stories, some of them excerpts from novels, some adaptations or translations of English work.

6   (Frankfurt/Main: Insel Verlag, 1980).

7   Same publisher, date, as above.

8   (Köln: Pahl-Rugensteinm 1979), pp. 67-123.

9   (Munich: Moewig Verlag, 1980).

10 (Frankfurt/Main: Suhrkamp Verlag, 1980). Edited by Rein A. Zondergeld.

11 Christian W. Thomsen and Jens Malte Fischer (Darmstadt: Wissenschaftliche Buchgesellschaft, 1980).

12 "Phantastische Bibliothek" vol. 34 (Frankfurt/Main: Surhkamp Verlag, 1979).

13 Available from Hans Joachim Alpers, Weissemburger Strasse 6, D-2850 Bremerhaven 1. West Germany. DM 5.00 per issue, DM 28 for 6 issues.

14 (Berlin: Verlag des Neue Berlin, 1980).

15 (Bern, Frankfurt/Main: Peter Lang, 1980).

16 (Graz: dbv Verlag für die Technische Universitat Graz, 1980).

Science Fiction Abroad

Romania

Ion Hobana reports the publication of Florin Manolescu's *Science Fiction Literature* in 1980, an introduction to the history and theory of the genre, as well as an anthology of nineteenth-century American science fiction stories, *The King of Dreams*. Recent Romanian science fiction includes *The Mark of Licorne* by Mircea Oprita', and a drama, *The Game of Love and Death in the Cinders Desert*, by "one of the most representative Romanian playwrights," Horia Lovinescu. The play, according to Hobana, concerns "a dramatic confrontation between the members of a family in a post-atomic world."

Fanzines and fan conventions are also alive in Eastern Europe. *Paradox 80* is a fan magazine edited by the H.G. Wells SF Club of Timisoara, which also hosts an annual convention that has continued for more than ten years. Eurocon V in Stresa, Italy, honored Hobana with a special award for his study of Jules Verne and presented "Europa" awards to Romanian authors Vladimir Colin for *Babel* and Gheorghe Sa'sa'rman for the short story "The Return of Algernon." A convention sponsored by the International SF Creation Institute in Poznan, Poland, conferred special "Gold Wings of Fantasy" awards to Ion Hobana and Mircea Oprita'.

206

The Netherlands

J.A. Dautzenberg, whose "Survey of Dutch and Flemish Science Fiction" appeared in *Science-Fiction Studies* in July 1981, indicates that scholarship in this area is still sparse—so much so that the University of Groningen had difficulty in finding speakers for a series of lectures on science fiction in 1981-82. Dautzenberg's own article, "Science Fiction en literatuurwetenschap: geschiedenis, problemen, bibliografie" (Science Fiction and Literary Scholarship: History, Problems, Bibliography), *Forum der Letteren* 21 (1980), was perhaps the first scholarly article in a Dutch journal, but since then the literary review *Literair Paspoort* has devoted an issue to science fiction (December 1980) and the semi-scholarly quarterly *De Revisor* devoted an issue to fantasy (December 1981). Plans for a university text on science fiction did not materialize during 1981; two leading fanzines, *Rigel* and *Progressef,* have merged; and a third, *Terra,* ceased to be published by Servire. However, annual bibliographies have continued to appear; one by Dautzenberg which appeared in *Science-Fiction Studies* in March 1981 has been updated in the *Fantasfeer: aanvulling* published by the Netherlandic Contact Center for Science Fiction. Meanwhile, Dautzenberg has been working with foremost Belgian science fiction scholar Luk De Vos on a thorough international bibliography of secondary works about science fiction, comprising more than 5,000 items, for *Antwerp Studies in Literature* in 1982.

Italy

Since April 1980, Inìsero Cremaschi has edited *La Collina* (The Hill), a journal published by Editrice Nord, Milan, which "serves primarily as an annual anthology of criticism of science fiction and fantastic literature excluding fantasy." The title is inspired in part by American authors Alexei and Cory Panshin's story "The World Beyond the Hill." Each volume has featured essays as well as stories prefaced by critical discussions, and recent topics have included ideological and theoretical discussions of science fiction as well as articles on John Brunner, Edgar Allan Poe, Ray Bradbury, Gilda Musa, Jules Verne, and Raymond Roussel, and translations such as Ursula LeGuin's "Science Fiction and Mrs. Brown."

Israel

Professor Nachman Ben-Yehuda writes:

Since 1948, when the state of Israel was established, there have been two distinct periods in the history of science fiction here. In the first period, the late 1950's and early 1960's, many science fiction movies were brought here, and one publisher, Mazpen, which no longer exists, specialized in the translation of SF books: Heinlein's *The Puppet Masters*, Robinson's *The Power* and others. Three inexpensive Hebrew SF magazines were started:

Cosmos, which appeared only four times in 1958, and which credited no translator.

Flash Gordon, which appeared in 1963 for only seven issues. It was an Israeli space western, devoted to the adventures of Flash Gordon, and written by H.L. Halder.

Mada Dimioni [Hebrew for Science Fiction], began in 1958 and had 13 issues, all including translated stories, with no credit given to the original authors or the translators. Emphasis was on short action pieces. It was cheaply produced but the translations were good.

The next period of science fiction activity began in the late 1970's. Until then only a few single translations appeared (Asimov's *I Robot* and *Nine Tomorrows*), some of which were movie tie-ins (*2001*, *The Andromeda Strain*, etc). Then in the late 1970's three new magazines were started:

Olam Hamachar [World of Tomorrow] had only one issue in 1979. This issue included translated stories by Van Vogt, with no credit to translator or author, and departments with information about the Space Shuttle, UFO's, robots, etc.

Cosmos, which appeared six times in 1979 was the Hebrew version of *Isaac Asimov's Science Fiction Magazine*. Translators were not credited. There were a few Hebrew stories by local authors.

Fantasia 2000 began in December, 1978. About 20 issues have appeared; at the moment this is the only Hebrew language SF magazine in Israel, and is the most professional ever to have appeared here. It is high quality both in content and in production. Its monthly circulation is 6000, and it is the second most expensive magazine for sale here. It has a formal agreement with *The Magazine of Fantasy and Science Fiction* and consequently many of its stories are translated from that journal. It credits both authors and translators. It has regular departments: correspondence, SF news, Futurism, profiles of major SF writers, speculative science, etc. Its editors are Aharon and Zipi

Hauptman, who encourage local writers, although the number of Israeli stories published has not been large. For the first time the Israeli reader has been given an accurate flavor of good science fiction.

In the last few years attempts have been made to establish an Israeli Science Fiction Association. A group of acadamicians met 1979-80 to discuss SF, fantasy and science topics. At the same time Sheldon Teitelbaum, an SF fan from Canada, tried unsuccessfully to establish an association. Janice Gelb, an American visiting in Jerusalem for one year, and Neil Weiss, a U.S. dentist, started the Jerusalem Science Fiction Club, which, in 1981, with my help and help from *Fantasy 2000*, organized the first Israeli Science Fiction Conference, held March 22, in Jerusalem, Jerucon 81. It was very successful, drawing 600-1000 people and being covered by the media; it helped to establish clubs in Tel Aviv and Ashklon. During 1979-81, Israeli publishers translated about 150 major SF books, among them: Asimov's *Trilogy*, Herbert's *Dune*, Clark's *Childhood End* and *Rendezvous with Rama*, Le Guin's *Left Hand of Darkness*, Moorcock's *Elric Sage*, and Pohl's *Gateway*. There has been a real boom in science fiction in the last two years, and we look forward to the production of original Israeli science fiction soon.

Science Fiction Fan Conventions

Jan Bogstad

To the outside observer, especially one accustomed to academic conferences, science fiction conventions can easily be dismissed as casual social gatherings of little literary or scholarly importance. The atmosphere is indeed casual; informal conversations at the inevitable evening parties and in front of ubiquitous booksellers' tables, however, are often as interesting and controversial as those which take place during scheduled events. This casual atmosphere helps to make the SF convention a valuable scholarly resource. As an observer and participant, I find this informality, coupled with enthusiasm for literature, to be the force that makes the convention work.

These conventions, which have been held since the 30's in the U.S., Canada, and some European countries, are primarily do-it-yourself popular culture events, created by committees made up of SF fans working without pay, and attended by SF fans who pay a small membership fee, as well as by writers, critics, editors and publishers' representatives who are rarely paid for their time. The conventions range in size from the annual world convention, held in a different city each year (Brighton in 1979, Boston, 1980, Denver, 1981, Chicago, 1982 and Baltimore, 1983) and attracting an attendance of over 6000; to regionals, (MiniCon in Minneapolis, Windy Con in Chicago, Archon in St. Louis, and WesterCon, where the site varies annually), which are attended by up to 1000 people: local conventions like Madison's Wis-Con can attract about 600.

All these conventions, large and small, are structured in roughly the same way: there are booksellers' facilities, fantasy costume balls, lectures, panel discussions, and speeches and readings by writers, both professional and amateur, critics and edtitors; and of course movies, parties and fringe group meetings.[1] The tone varies: RelaxaCon in Cincinnati consists of a weekend pool party and no programmes, while WorldCon consists of several continuous formal programs and movies.[2]

For the scholar, valuable face-to-face meeting with professionals in the field can be accomplished most easily at these conventions, where writers, editors and talented amateurs find a satisfying counterpoint to their solitary labors: they can meet people and get feedback to their work. This feedback often includes awards, sometimes monetary, and critical perspectives. There is also the advantage of the coming together of the world science fiction community.[3]

There is a relationship betwen SF conventions as entertainment and SF as literature. Conventions affects sales, and therefore they affect publication schedules. The amount of attention received by the work of SF writers from the amateur community can only be appreciated through attendance at a convention. This attention occurs at informal discussions where writers are encouraged by fans to produce a certain kind of work, and at formal discussions where the authors' work is thoughtfully examined from all possible angles. The author's future work may well (positively or negatively) be affected by his/her impression of the fans' potential reception of it. In addition, formal awards, such as the Hugos given at every WorldCon, affect the relationship between author and publisher, for good or ill. All this can be observed by scholars at conventions, where the scholar may also try out his/her critical ideas, question authors, and get information for research from casual contact with professionals and amateurs. Free interaction usually proves to be salutary for the critic and/or scholar.

Some of these conventions are of course more appropriate to scholarly endeavor than others. We have to remember that many convention activities are adolescent or intended flatly for amusement only. Generally the major event of the SF convention year, the World Science Fiction Convention, is valuable because of the inevitable attendance of knowledgeable people, and, because it takes place each year in a different city, it can also provide the critic with experience of regional fandoms. Its size, also, dictates numerous formal and informal programs, of variable quality. The most interesting in recent years was the 1978 Iguanacon, in Phoenix, Arizona, which had several program tracks, devoting a good deal of attention to special interests among fan groups.

I remember with fondness my first World Con, MidAmericon in Kansas City in 1976, because a panel of major women writers provoked endless discussion for the rest of the convention. The most recent Denvention Two, in 1981, does not, from the program book and reports I have received, appear to have lived up to the others in serious and provocative programming. Its formal schedule was inferior in breadth to Noreastcon Two, held in Boston in 1980, where the timetable included several feminist and media programs.

I cannot from previous experience recommend the regionals Windycon (Chicago, Dec. 1981) or MiniCon (Minneapolis, Easter weekend, 1982) because both programs are thin, although they are well-attended and the size and cosmopolitanism of the attendees is interesting in itself. I did find a positive sign in MiniCon programming to be the addition of a panel on "Critical Perspectives in SF." More than 50 people attended on a Sunday morning, indicating the level of interest in serious topics at these conventions.[4]

My own favorite among regionals is Archon in St. Louis, which combines the usual entertainment with a group of programs discussing political, popular culture and media aspects of SF. Rivercon in Louisville is pleasant, too, largely because its tone is different from other Midwestern conventions. Aquacon, which was held in Anaheim for the first time in February of 1981 demonstrated a notable attempt to deal seriously with topics of interest to the SF community, most especially the U.S. space program. WesterCon, held in a different west coast or Canadian city each year, has often been serious and informative.

Modest, local conventions vary greatly in quality. Some are cliquish gatherings with little scholarly interest; others are conferences with modest attendance and a serious, critical tone. X-Con in Milwaukee often has some interesting scheduled programs and good diversity. Others, with which I am not familiar, are certainly worth an experimental visit. Although I have been involved in creating it, I can recommend the WisCon held every March in Madison: it is co-sponsored by the Uiversity of Wisconsin at Madison Extension and has a feminist orientation, but it is as heavily programmed as some World conventions and covers a wide range of topics, from aesthetics to politics. It attracts about 600 participants, and invites writers many of whom are women, whose careers have not yet peaked.

European conventions should not be forgotten: these are held in England, France, Germany and Italy: a conference in Milan in 1981, by the way, resembled WisCon more than any typical American con.

It is both the intellectually creative chemistry and the uniqueness of the fan-professional interaction which takes place at these events which prompt me to recommend them to SFRA members as well as to other serious critics of literature.

NOTES

[1] Some examples of fringe group meetings are the "Heyer Teas", held in imitation of the late 18th and early 19th century teas described in the novels of Georgette Heyer; meetings of the "Friends of Darkover", derived from the series of novels by Marion Zimmer Bradley; Women's Amateur Press Association (WAPA) meetings on feminist issues.

[2] Information on these conventions can be found in Peter Nicholls, ed., *The Science Fiction Encyclopedia* (Garden City: Dolphin/Doubleday, 1979), Colin Wilson, *The International Science Fiction Yearbook for 1978* (NY: Pierrot Publ., 1978) and with regard to current dates, Stanley Schmidt, ed, *Analog, Science Fiction/Science Fact*, P.O. Box 1936, Marion, Ohio, 43305. Look for "The Analog Calendar of Coming Events." Also George H. Scithers, ed, *Asimov's SF Magazine*, P.O. Box 1933, Marion, Ohio, 43305. This publication runs "The SF Conventional Calendar". Most of the activities at recent meetings is also available in *Locus*, P.O. Box 3938, San Francisco, Cal, and in *Science Fiction Chronicles*, P.O. Box 4175, New York, NY 10163. Check also *Science Fiction Review*, P.O. Box 11408, Portland, Oregon 97211 and *The Fandom Directory*, edited by Marianne S. Hopkins and published by Harry Hopkins, and available from Fandom, Computer Services, P.O. Box 873, Langley AFB, Va. 23665.

[3] I see the Science Fiction Community as a group of individuals who maintain frequent contact through conventions, amateur publications and many less formal means of communication. See "The Science Fiction Connection: Readers and Writers in the SF Community," Vol 3 *Janus 10*, published by the Society for the Furtherance and Study of Fantasy and Science Fiction (SF³), P.O. Box 1624, Madison, Wi 53701. See also my own periodical *New Moon*, Madison SF³.

[4] The 1982 convention, scheduled for Chicago, will have taken place probably when this collection appears. It promises well: the academic track programming, organized by Donald Hassler of Kent State, has been expanded to include panels on separate authors as well as those of critical interest such as Women in SF and Fantasy Fiction. ChiCon has also developed extensive media capabilities both for viewing and producing audio and video materials. This recognition of the varied interests and abilities of SF enthusiasts should be encouraged in future WorldCons.

Marshall B. Tymn

An associate professor of English at Eastern Michigan University, Dr. Tymn is director of the national Workshop on Teaching Science fiction, held annually at Florida Atlantic University, and author of nine reference books on fantasy and science fiction. His latest work, published in 1981, is *Horror Literature: A Core Collection and Reference Guide*. He has published over thirty articles in *Extrapolation, CEA Critic, English Journal, Media & Methods, English Language Arts Bulletin, Analytical and Enumerative Bibliography, Mosaic, Handbook of American Popular Culture*, and other journals. Tymn is editor of the largest critical series in the field, Contributions to the Study of Science Fiction and Fantasy (Greenwood Press). He is also advisory acquisitions editor for G.K. Hall's Masters of Science Fiction and Fantasy series and bibliographer for Taplinger's Writers of the 21st Century series. Tymn is a former officer of the Science Fiction Research Association and a member of Science Fiction Writers of America. His continuing interest in early 19th-century American art and culture is reflected in his *Thomas Cole's Poetry* (1972) and *Thomas Cole: The Collected Essays and Prose Sketches* (1980).

214

Guide to Science Fiction & Fantasy Scholarship: 1980-1982

Marshall B. Tymn

This bibliography lists 140 books and pamphlets published during the period 1980 to mid-1982 and nineteen forthcoming works. Brief annotations describe each title, and an asterisk identifies those works which, in my opinion, are significant, or core titles. The bibliography is divided into categories so that the reader can easily identify trends in certain areas. This list contains only first publication titles and revised editions; no reprints are cited. The symbols "C" and "P" are used to designate cloth and paperback editions.

BIBLIOGRAPHY AND REFERENCE

Ashley, Mike. *The Illustrated Book of Science Fiction Lists*. UK: Virgin Books, 1982. A trivia collection for the SF buff. P.

*Ashley, Mike, with Terry Jeeves. *The Complete Index to Astounding/Analog*. Oak Forest, IL: Robert Weinberg Publications, 1981. An index to all fiction, nonfiction, art, and letters contained in this important magazine. C.

*Barron, Neil, ed. *Anatomy of Wonder: A Critical Guide to Science Fiction*. 2nd ed. New York and London: Bowker, 1981. A comprehensive survey of science fiction, containing over 1700 annotated fiction and nonfiction titles, including sections on teaching aids, film, illustration, and the magazines; historical essays introduce each chapter. C/P.

Bates, Susannah. *The Pendex: An Index of Pen names and House Names in Fantastic, Thriller, and Series Literature*. New York and London: Garland, 1981. Contains listings of real names, pen names, house names, collaborative pen names, and Stratemeyer Syndicate names. C.

*Bleiler, E.F., ed. *Science Fiction Writers: Critical Studies of the Major Authors from the Early Nineteenth Century to the Present Day*. New York: Scribner's, 1982. Contains 76 essays which evaluate the life and work of writers important to the development of the SF genre; in many cases these studies comprise the first extended coverage of certain writers. C.

*Boyajian, Jerry, and Kenneth R. Johnson. *Index to the Science Fiction Magazines: 1979*. Cambridge, MA: Twaci Press, 1981. Indexes complete contents, including nonfiction, of all SF and fantasy magazines for 1979; also indexes science fiction in general magazines. P.

*Boyajian, Jerry, and Kenneth R. Johnson. *Index to the Science Fiction Magazines: 1980*. Cambridge, MA: Twaci Press, 1981. [See annotation above]. P.

*Boyajian, Jerry, and Kenneth R. Johnson. *Index to the Science Fiction Magazines: 1981*. Cambridge, MA: Twaci Press, 1982. [See annotation above]. P.

*Cowart, David, and Thomas L. Wymer, eds. *Twentieth-Century American Science-Fiction Writers*. Vol. 8 of *Dictionary of Literary Biography*. 2 vols. Detroit: Gale Research, 1981. Essays on 90 authors who began their careers after 1900 and before 1970; includes selected primary and secondary bibliographies. C.

*Day, Donald B. *Index to the Science Fiction Magazines: 1926-1950*. rev. ed. Boston: G.K. Hall, 1982. This indispensible resource has been revised to incorporate hundreds of corrections to the original text collated from Day's own annotated copy, as well as from published errata sheets and issues of ephemeral fanzines of the period. C.

Fletcher, Marilyn P. *Science Fiction Story Index: 1950-1979*. 2nd ed. Chicago: American Library Association, 1981. In view of the existence of William Contento's *Index to Science Fiction Anthologies and Collections* (1978), this work should not have been published; moreover, this is an incredibly inept compilation, indicating Fletcher's lack of knowledge and skills. P.

*Franson, Donald, and Howard DeVore. *A History of the Hugo, Nebula, and International Fantasy Awards*. rev. ed. Dearborn, MI: Misfit Press, 1981. This enlarged and updated edition lists both the winners and the nominees in all categories of the Hugo and Nebula Awards through 1981. P.

*Hall, H.W., ed. *Science Fiction Book Review Index, 1974-1979*. Detroit: Gale Research, 1981. A complete record of all science fiction and related books reviewed in nearly 250 general and specialized periodicals, providing access to 15,600 reviews of 6,220 books. C.

*Hall, H.W. *SFBRI: Science Fiction Book Review Index*. Vol. 11, 1980. Bryan, TX: Privately Printed, 1981. Provides access to 2,316 reviews of 1,163 books.

*Hall, H.W. *The Science Fiction Index: Criticism: An Index to English Language Books and Articles About Science Fiction and Fantasy*. Bryan, TX: Privately Printed, 1980. Six computer-on-microform (COM) microfiche containing 4,350 citations, indexed by author/editor, subject (for about half the entries), year, and key word in context (KWIC).

*Hall, H.W. *Science Fiction Research Index*. Vol. 1. Bryant, TX: Privately Printed, 1981. The first supplement to Hall's *Science Fiction Index: Criticism* (1980), an experimental indexing system designed to provide access to science fiction and fantasy scholarship. P.

*Hall, H.W. *Science Fiction and Fantasy Research Index*, Vol. 2. Bryant, TX: Privately Printed, 1982. [See annotation above].

Hopkins, Mariane, ed. *Fandom Directory*. Langley AFB, VA: Fandom Computer Services, 1981. A listing of over 8000 names of fans, fan publications, clubs and organizations, specialty dealers, and conventions. P.

Hopkins, Mariane S., ed. *Fandom Directory*. Newport News, VA: Fandom Computer Services, 1982. A computerized directory of thousands of names of fans, fan clubs, fanzines, and conventions; now the most comprehensive guide to the world of fandom. P.

Locke, George. *A Spectrum of Fantasy: The Bibliography of a Collection of Fantastic Literature*. London: Ferret Fantasy, 1980. A descriptive, annotated bibliography of more than 3000 books in the fields of science fiction and fantasy, with descriptions of first editions and subject matter details, together with matter pertinent to the collection copies themselves and their acquisition. C.

Manguel, Alberto, and Gianni Guadalupi. *The Dictionary of Imaginary Places*. New York: Macmillan, 1980. A catalog of imaginary lands and cities from the literature of a vast range of writers.

Naha, Ed. *The Science Fictionary: An A-Z Guide to the World of SF Authors, Films, & TV Shows*. New York: Wideview Books, 1980. An incomplete guide to the SF field. P.

*New England Science Fiction Association. *The N.E.S.F.A. Index to the Science Fiction Magazines and Original Anthologies: 1979-80*. Cambridge, MA: NESFA Press, 1982. After a long absence, NESFA has begun to produce these standard indexes; does not replace the Boyajian and Johnson indexes, which cover artwork and SF in general magazines. P.

*New England Science Fiction Association. *The N.E.S.F.A. Index to the Science Fiction Magazines and Original Anthologies: 1981*. Cambridge, MA: NESFA Press, 1982. [See annotation above]. P.

Reginald, R. *Science Fiction & Fantasy Awards*. San Bernardino, CA: Borgo Press, 1981. Includes lists of the winners of all major SF awards and some of the minor ones; no nominees are listed. C/P.

*Smith, Curtis C., ed. *Twentieth-Century Science-Fiction Writers*. New York: St. Martin's, 1981. A handbook which provides biographical data, short critical profiles, and primary bibliographies for 600 writers. C.

Tracy, Ann B. *The Gothic Novel 1790-1830: Plot Summaries and Index to Motifs*. Lexington: Univ. Press of Kentucky, 1981. Contains plot summaries and a motif index for 200 novels. C.

*Tymn, Marshall B., ed. *Horror Literature: A Core Collection and Reference Guide*. New York and London: Bowker, 1981. A comprehensive survey of horror literature, containing over 1300 annotated fiction and nonfiction titles, including sections on supernatural verse and horror pulps; historical essays introduce each chapter. C/P.

*Tymn, Marshall B., ed. *The Science Fiction Reference Book*. Mercer Island, WA: Starmont House, 1981. A comprehensive handbook and guide to the history, literature, scholarship, and related activities of the science fiction and fantasy fields. C/P

Weymeyer, Lillian Biermann. *Images in a Crystal Ball: World Futures in Novels for*

Young People. Littleton, CO: Libraries Unlimited, 1981. Designed as a resource for teachers developing units on children's science fiction, this work annotates 154 novels with suggestions for teaching. C.

GENERAL SURVEYS AND HISTORIES

Asimov, Isaac. *Asimov on Science Fiction*. Garden City, NY: Doubleday, 1981. A collection of 55 essays on a wide range of science fiction topics, published during the 1970s and 1980. C.

Attebery, Brian. *The Fantasy Tradition in American Literature: From Irving to Le Guin*. Bloomington: Indiana Univ. Press, 1980. Traces the roots of American fantasy in the magical folktale and its literary imitations, with infusions of motifs from legends, ballads, and epics. C.

Griffiths, John. *Three Tomorrows: American, British and Soviet Science Fiction*. Totowa, NJ: Barnes & Noble, 1980. A broad overview of the origins of the SF genre in each of these three countries with particular attention to how the literature has changed in recent years. C/P.

King, Stephen. *Danse Macabre*. New York: Everest House, 1981. A modern master evaluates horror in literature and the mass media.

Malik, Rex, ed. *Future Imperfect: Science Fact and Science Fiction*. London: Frances Pinter, 1980. An examination of the relationship of science fiction to current and future science and technology. C.

Malzberg, Barry N. *The Engines of the Night. Science Fiction in the Eighties*. Garden City, NY: Doubleday, 1982. Malzberg takes a critical look at the world in which he has spent his working life. C.

*Moskowitz, Sam. *Science Fiction in Old San Francisco*. 2 vols. West Kingston, RI: Donald M. Grant, 1980. Volume I, *History of the Movement from 1854 to 1890*, is a documented history of a lost science fiction and fantasy movement which originated on the West Coast; special emphasis is given to its prime mover, Robert Duncan Milne. Volume II, *Into the Sun and Other Stories*, is a sampling of Milne's fiction. C.

Murray, Will. *The Duende History of the Shadow Magazine*. Greenwood, MA: Odyssey, 1980. A detailed account of the genesis of this American radio and pulp hero, with a complete index to the Shadow stories. P.

Panshin, Alexei, and Cory Panshin. *SF in Dimension: A Book of Explorations*. 2nd ed. Chicago: Advent, 1980. Based on a series of essays written for professional and semi-pro magazines from 1969-80, in which the author attempts to redefine the nature of science fiction as a literary form; revised from the 1976 edition. P.

*Punter, David. *The Literature of Terror: A History of Gothic Fictions from 1765 to the Present Day*. London and New York: Longman, 1980. Examines the diversity of ways in which fear has been represented in English and American literature over the past two centuries and explores the deeper implications of the Gothic as a literary, cultural, and social concept. C/P.

THEORETICAL AND CRITICAL STUDIES

Barr, Marlene S., ed. *Future Females: A Critical Anthology*. Bowling Green, OH:

Bowling Green Univ. Popular Press, 1981. Fifteen essays and a bibliography on the subjects of women SF writers, female SF characters, male SF writers whose works include women, and women in the genre. C/P.

Brooke-Rose, Christine. *A Rhetoric of the Unreal: Studies in Narrative and Structure, Especially of the Fantastic*. New York and London: Cambridge Univ. Press, 1981. A study of the wide range of fiction to which the term "fantastic" has been applied; examines the essential differences between these types of narrative against the background of realistic fiction. C.

*Jackson, Rosemary. *Fantasy: The Literature of Subversion*. New York and London: Methuen, 1981. Exploring literary fantasies from the Gothic tale of terror to 20th-century dystopias, the author locates fantasy in between the related romance forms of fairy tale and science fiction. C/P.

*Parrinder, Patrick. *Science Fiction: Its Criticism and Teaching*. New York and London: Methuen, 1980. Examines science fiction as a mode of popular literature, as a socially responsible form of writing, and as a home for a fantastic and parodic use of language. C/P.

*Rose, Mark. *Alien Encounters: Anatomy of Science Fiction*. Cambridge, MA and London: Harvard Univ. Press, 1981. An assessment of science fiction as a genre, focusing on the human in relation to the nonhuman. C.

*Slusser, George E., George R. Guffey, and Mark Rose, eds. *Bridges to Science Fiction*. Alternatives Series. Carbondale: Southern Illinois Univ. Press, 1980. Ten essays from the First Eaton Conference on Science Fiction and Fantasy suggest connections between science fiction and Western culture and attempt to make a coherent statement about science fiction as a literary form. C.

Staicar, Tom, Ed. *Critical Encounters II: Writers and Themes in Science Fiction*. New York: Frederick Ungar, 1982. [Not seen]. C/P.

Yolen, Jane. *Touch Magic: Fantasy, Faerie and Folklore in the Literature of Childhood*. New York: Philomel Books, 1981. Essays on the function of folk literature and fairytales in the social, emotional and intellectual growth of children. C.

SUBJECT STUDIES

Hurwood, Bernhardt J. *Vampires*. New York and London: Quick Fox Books, 1981. Fully illustrated with drawings, paintings, and movie stills, this popular treatment explains the "cultural differences" among vampires who have appeared throughout history in various parts of the world. P.

Magill, Frank N., ed. *Science Fiction: Alien Encounter*. Pasadena, CA: Salem Softbacks, 1981. Essays on 75 SF works that deal with the theme of alien encounter, reprinted from the five-volume *Survey of Science Fiction Literature* (1979). P.

*Meyers, Walter E. *Aliens and Linguistics: Language Study and Science Fiction*. Athens: Univ. of Georgia Press, 1980. A pioneer work which lays the groundwork for further critical investigation in this subject area. C.

Mogen, David. *Wilderness Visions: Science Fiction Westerns*. Vol. 1. San Bernardino, CA: Borgo Press, 1982. An essay on western motifs in science fiction. C/P.

*Warrick, Patricia S. *The Cybernetic Imagination in Science Fiction*. Cambridge, MA: MIT Press, 1980. A history of cybernetic science fiction and an analysis of its recurring images, patterns, and meanings.

AUTHOR STUDIES

Ashley, Michael, [ed.] *Fantasy Reader's Guide. Number Two: The File on Ramsey Campbell.* Wallsend, Tyne and Wear, England: Cosmos Literary Agency, 1980. Contains commentary on Campbell by various contributors and a checklist of Campbell's works. P.

Asimov, Isaac. *In Joy Still Felt: The Autobiography of Isaac Asimov 1954-1978.* Garden City, NY: Doubleday, 1980. Continuing his life story with characteristic wit and candor, Asimov recounts his first brush with fame to his current renoun as editor and author of over 200 books. The first volume, *In Memory Yet Green*, was published by Doubleday in 1979. C.

Bass, Eben E. *Aldous Huxley: An Annotated Bibliography of Criticism.* New York and London: Garland, 1981. Provides a broad view of the range in critical attitudes toward Huxley, from the beginning of his career in 1916 to the present. C.

*Becker, Muriel R. *Clifford D. Simak: A Primary and Secondary Bibliography.* Masters of Science Fiction and Fantasy. Boston: G.K. Hall, 1980. Comprehensive checklists of fiction and nonfiction by Simak, with annotated listings of secondary material. C.

Bell, Joseph. *Howard Phillips Lovecraft: The Books.* Toronto: Soft Books, 1981. A listing of every story in every HPL collection.

*Bilyeu, Richard. *The Tanelorn Archives: A Primary and Secondary Bibliography of the Works of Michael Moorcock 1949-1979.* Altona, Manitoba, Canada: Pandora's Books, 1981. Provides complete publishing history for Moorcock's English-language books and stories, over 1300 items. C/P.

Brizzi, Mary T. *Philip José Farmer.* Starmont Reader's Guide No. 2. Mercer Island, WA: Starmont House, 1980. An introductory guide to Farmer's life and works. P.

Bucknall, Barbara J. *Ursula K. Le Guin.* Recognitions Series. New York: Frederick Ungar, 1981. The first single-authored book-length study of one of the most important writers to emerge in the 1960s, following Le Guin's growth from the early Hainish novels, through her Earthsea children's fantasy series, to the "social" science fiction. C/P.

Columbo, John Robert. *Blackwood's Books: A Bibliography Devoted to Algernon Blackwood.* Toronto: Hounslow Press, 1981. The first bibliography of the works of the noted British author of supernatural and weird fiction; documents English-language first editions and reprints. P.

Crabbe, Katharyn, F. *J.R.R. Tolkien.* New York: Frederick Ungar, 1981. An assessment of Tolkien's achievement which explores the extent to which his novels and stories may be seen as Christian apologetics. C/P.

Diskin, Lahna. *Theodore Sturgeon.* Starmont Reader's Guide No. 7. Mercer Island, WA: Starmont House, 1981. An introductory guide to Sturgeon's life and works. P.

*Diskin, Lahna F. *Theodore Sturgeon: A Primary and Secondary Bibliography.* Masters of Science Fiction and Fantasy. Boston: G.K. Hall, 1980. Comprehensive checklists of fiction and nonfiction by Sturgeon, with annotated listings of secondary material. C.

Elliot, Jeffrey M. *Fantasy Voices* #1. San Bernardino, CA: Borgo Press, 1982. Interviews with Manly Wade Wellman, John Norman, Hugh B. Cave, and Katherine Kurtz. C/P.

Elliot, Jeffrey M. *Science Fiction Voices #4*. San Bernardino, CA: Borgo Press, 1982. Interviews with Charles D. Hornig, Bob Shaw, Frank Kelly Freas, and Brian W. Aldiss, C/P.

*Fonstad, Karen Wynn. *The Atlas of Middle-earth*. Boston: Houghton Mifflin, 1981. Drawings on the text of *The Silmarillion*, *The Hobbit*, and *The Lord of the Rings*, locating virtually every place mentioned in these works on one or more of the 115 two-colored maps. C.

Frane, Jeff. *Fritz Leiber*. Starmont Reader's Guide No. 8. Mercer Island, WA: Starmont House, 1980. An introductory guide to Leiber's life and works. P.

*Franklin, H. Bruce. *Robert A. Heinlein: America As Science Fiction*. Science-Fiction Writers. New York and Oxford: Oxford Univ. Press, 1980. The first scholarly evaluation of the entire career of the most influential writer to emerge from science fiction's Golden Age. C/P.

*Gallagher, Edward J., Judith A. Misticelli, and John A. Van Eerde. *Jules Verne: A Primary and Secondary Bibliography*. Masters of Science Fiction and Fantasy. Boston: G.K. Hall, 1980. Lists all editions, both English and French, of 106 works by Verne; annotates 450 items of criticism in English and 874 items of criticism in French. C.

Gibson, Evan K. *C.S. Lewis, Spinner of Tales: A Guide to His Fiction*. Washington, D.C.: Christian Univ. Press, 1980. A discussion of Lewis' writing, intended for the common reader. P.

Glover, Donald E. *C.S. Lewis: The Art of Enchantment*. Athens: Ohio Univ. Press, 1981. Following an introductory section examining Lewis' critical theory, this study contains full discussions of sixteen works, including a chapter on Lewis' letters. C/P.

Golemba, Henry L. *Frank R. Stockton*. Twayne United States Authors, No. 374. Boston: Twayne, 1981. Attempts to systhesize Stockton's personal experience with his art. C.

Gordon, Joan. *Joe Haldeman*. Starmont Reader's Guide No. 4. Mercer Island, WA: Starmont House, 1980. An introductory guide to Haldeman's life and works. P.

Greenberg, Martin H., ed. *Fantastic Lives: Autobiographical Essays by Notable Science Fiction Writers*. Alternatives Series. Carbondale: Southern Illinois Univ. Press, 1981. Essays by Ellison, Farmer, Lafferty, MacLean, Malzberg, Reynolds, St. Clair, Spinrad, and van Vogt. C.

Hammond, J.R., ed. *H.G. Wells: Interviews and Recollections*. Totowa, NJ: Barnes & Noble, 1980. Nineteen short pieces by those who knew him, plus two by Wells. C.

Hannay, Margaret Patterson. *C.S. Lewis*. New York: Frederick Ungar, 1981. Contains a biographical sketch, concise summaries of each major work, a survey of Lewis' major themes, and an analysis of his allusive and compelling style. C/P.

Haynes, Roslynn D. *H.G. Wells: Discoverer of the Future: The Influence of Science on His Thought*. New York and London: New York Univ. Press, 1980. An attempt to trace the actual extent of the influence of science on Wells' thought as it appears in his scientific romances, character novels, and utopian works. C.

Helms, Randel. *Tolkien and the Silmarils*. Boston: Houghton Mifflin, 1981. An analysis of *The Silmarillion* (1977) which discusses the sources of the work, its major themes, and its relationship to Tolkien's other writings. C.

*Holtsmark, Erling B. *Tarzan and Tradition: Classical Myth in Popular Culture*. Contributions to the Study of Popular Culture No. 1. Westport, CT: Greenwood

Press, 1981. A study of Burroughs' first six Tarzan books which reveals parallels between Tarzan's story and the heroic sagas of ancient Greece and Rome. C.

Howard, Thomas. *The Achievement of C.S. Lewis.* Wheaton, IL: Harold Shaw, 1980. A discussion of myth and theology in Lewis' works, P.

Isaacs, Neil D., and Rose A. Zimbardo, eds. *Tolkien: New Critical Perspectives.* Lexington: Univ. Press of Kentucky, 1981. Thirteen reprinted and original essays which survey recent Tolkien scholarship with emphasis on *The Lord of the Rings.* C.

Johnson, Wayne L. *Ray Bradbury.* Recognitions Series. New York: Frederick Ungar, 1980. This first book-length study of Bradbury's fiction analyzes his significant works in terms of their common themes. C/P.

*Joshi, S.T. *H.P. Lovecraft and Lovecraft Criticism: An Annotated Bibliography.* Serif Series No. 38. Kent, OH: Kent State Univ. Press, 1981. This massive listing of writings by and about Lovecraft is the most complete on the author to date, and will probably remain so for years to come. C.

*Joshi, S.T., ed. *H.P. Lovecraft: Four Decades of Criticism.* Athens: Ohio Univ. Press, 1980. Essays spanning nearly forty years of criticism and selected with a view toward presenting Lovecraft to the academic world. C.

Julius, Kevin C. *A Pocket Bibliography of Edgar Rice Burroughs.* [Erie, PA]: Edgar Rice Burroughs Appreciation Society, 1980. A bibliography of first editions and reprints, designed for the Burroughs enthusiast who cannot afford to acquire the now rare Henry Hardy Heins *A Golden Anniversary Bibliography of Edgar Rice Burroughs* (Donald M. Grant, 1964). P.

Kocher, Paul H. *A Reader's Guide to the Silmarillion.* Boston: Houghton Mifflin, 1980. Helps the reader understand that *The Silmarillion* is the underlying root system from which the legendary creatures and stories spring forth in *The Hobbit* and *The Lord of the Rings.*

Lobdell, Jared. *England and Always: Tolkien's World of the Rings.* Grand Rapids, MI: William B. Eerdmans, 1982. Examines the Ring trilogy, taking into account that Tolkien was raised in Edwardian England, that he was a philologist, and that he was a Roman Catholic. P.

*McConnell, Frank. *The Science Fiction of H.G. Wells.* Science-Fiction Writers. New York and Oxford: Oxford Univ. Press, 1981. Treats Wells as a major literary figure, showing the importance of his background to an understanding of his stories and novels. C/P.

Menger, Lucy. *Theodore Sturgeon.* Recognitions Series. New York: Frederick Ungar, 1981. In this first book-length study of one of the field's leading craftsmen, the author explores the changes in Sturgeon's writing through the years, his precedent-setting use of sex, and his commitment to opening his readers' minds. C/P.

Miller, David M. *Frank Herbert.* Starmont Reader's Guide No. 5. Mercer Island, WA: Starmont House, 1980. An introductory guide to Herbert's life and works. P.

Moran, John C. *An F. Marion Crawford Companion.* Westport, CT and London: Greenwood Press, 1981. A guide to the life and works of the American novelist and historian. C.

Moran, John C. *Seeking Refuge in Torre San Nicola: An Introduction to F. Marion Crawford.* Nashville: Worthies Library, 1980. A monograph on Francis Marion Crawford, neglected 19th-century American author of 45 books, whose reputation rests mostly on his short horror fiction. P.

Morse, A. Reynolds. *The Works of M.P. Shiel Updated: A Study in Bibliography*. rev. ed. 2 vols. Dayton, OH: JDS Books, 1980. Originally published in 1948, this edition is organized into ten sections containing extensive bibliographical and biographical information about Shiel.

Niles, P.H. *The Science Fiction of H.G. Wells: A Concise Guide*. Clifton Park, NY: Auriga, 1980. Provides plot summaries and brief evaluations of 36 short stories and 29 novels; also includes a subject guide to the fiction. P.

Noel, Ruth. *The Languages of Tolkien's Middle-Earth*. Boston: Houghton Mifflin, 1980. A guide to all fourteen of the languages Tolkien invented. C/P.

O'Reilly, Timothy. *Frank Herbert*. Recognitions Series. Frederick Ungar, 1981. This first book-length study of the author of the *Dune* tetralogy provides commentary on fifteen novels and numerous stories, essays, letters, and poetry. C/P.

*Olander, Joseph D., and Martin Harry Greenberg, eds. *Ray Bradbury*. Writers of the 21st Century. New York: Taplinger, 1980. Ten essays attempt to place Bradbury in perspective both as a writer and in terms of his place in the history of science fiction; bibliography. C/P.

Parrinder, Patrick, and Robert M. Philmus, eds. *H.G. Wells's Literary Criticism*. Totowa, NJ: Barnes & Noble, 1980. [Not seen]. C.

*Peplow, Michael W., and Robert S. Bravard. *Samuel R. Delany: A Primary and Secondary Bibliography*. Masters of Science Fiction and Fantasy. Boston: G.K. Hall, 1980. Comprehensive checklists of fiction and nonfiction by Delany, with annotated listings of secondary material. C.

Philip, Neil. *A Fine Anger: A Critical Introduction to the Work of Alan Garner*. New York: Philomel Books, 1981. Traces Garner's development from his *The Weird-stone of Brisingamen* (1960) to the *Stone Book* quartet (1976). C.

*Platt, Charles. *Dream Makers: The Uncommon People Who Write Science Fiction*. New York: Berkley, 1980. Profiles of 28 contemporary SF writers based on taped interviews. P.

Rabkin, Eric S. *Arthur C. Clarke*, rev. ed. Starmont Reader's Guide No. 1. Mercer Island, WA: Starmont House, 1980. An introductory guide to Clarke's life and works; revised with additional secondary material from the 1979 edition. P.

Rogers, Deborah Webster, and Ivor A. Rogers. *J.R.R. Tolkien*. Twayne's English Author Series No. 304. Boston: Twayne, 1980. An introduction to Tolkien's life, his literary background, and his major short works and long fiction.

*Sanders, Joseph L. *Roger Zelazny: A Primary and Secondary Bibliography*. Masters of Science Fiction and Fantasy. Boston: G.K. Hall, 1980. Comprehensive checklists of fiction and nonfiction by Zelazny, with annotated listings of secondary material. C.

*Schlobin, Roger C. *Andre Norton: A Primary and Secondary Bibliography*. Masters of Science Fiction and Fantasy. Boston: G.K. Hall, 1980. Comprehensive checklists of fiction and nonfiction by Norton, with annotated listings of secondary material. C.

Schweitzer, Darrell. *Science Fiction Voices* ff5. San Bernardino, CA: Borgo, Press, 1982. Interviews with Isaac Asimov, Leigh Brackett, Lin Carter, Lester del Rey, Edmond Hamilton, Frank Belknap Long, Clifford D. Simak, Wilson Tucker, and Jack Williamson. C/P.

Seligman, Dee. *Doris Lessing: An Annotated Bibliography of Criticism*. Westport,

CT and London: Greenwood Press, 1981. A comprehensive listing of works on Lessing through 1978. C.

*Sellin, Bernard. *The Life and Works of David Lindsay*. Trans. Kenneth Gunnell. New York and London: Cambridge Univ. Press, 1981. In this first comprehensive study of the author of *A Voyage to Arcturus*, Sellin analyzes the thematic patterns of Lindsay's settings, plots and characters. C.

Smith, Robert Houston. *Patches of Godlight: The Pattern of Thought of C.S. Lewis*. Athens: Univ. of Georgia Press, 1981. Attempts to show that Lewis had a rich, integrated philosophical frame of reference that undergirded his Christian beliefs. C.

Stableford, Brian M. *Masters of Science Fiction ff1: Essays on Six Science Fiction Authors*. San Bernardino, CA: Borgo Press, 1982. Covers Edmond Hamilton, Leigh Brackett, Barry N. Malzberg, Kurt Vonnegut, Robert Silverberg, and Mack Reynolds. C/P.

*Staicar, Tom, ed. *The Feminine Eye: Science Fiction and the Women Who Write It*. Recognitions Series. New York: Frederick Ungar, 1982. Nine original essays treat the works and themes of important women writers, from those who began their careers in the early pulps to contemporary authors who are influencing the direction of SF writing in the 1980s. C/P.

Tolley, Michael J., and Kirpal Singh, eds. *The Stellar Guage: Essays on Science Fiction Writers*. Carlton, Victoria, Australia: Norstrilia Press, 1980. Includes Verne, Wells, Orwell, Bester, Clarke, Pohl, Blish, Aldiss, Ballard, Dick, Silverberg, and Disch.

Umland, Samuel J. *Frankenstein*. Lincoln, NE: Cliffs Notes, 1982. Plot summary, critical commentary, and background information. P.

*Underwood, Tim, and Chuck Miller, eds. *Jack Vance*. Writers of the 21st Century. New York: Taplinger, 1980. Eight essays on the works of one of the most celebrated writers in the field. C/P.

*West, Richard, C. *Tolkien Criticism: An Annotated Checklist*. rev. ed. Kent, OH: Kent State Univ. Press, 1981. First published in 1970, this revised edition documents the enormous amount of Tolkien scholarship published during the 1970s. C.

*Zahorski, Kenneth J., and Robert H. Boyer. *Lloyd Alexander, Evangeline Walton Ensley, Kenneth Morris: A Primary and Secondary Bibliography*. Masters of Science Fiction and Fantasy. Boston: G.K. Hall, 1981. Comprehensive checklists of fiction and nonfiction by these three writers published in books and periodicals, with annotated listings of secondary material. C.

ART

Pohl, Frederik, ed. *The New Visions: A Collection of Modern Science Fiction Art*. Garden City, NY: Doubleday, 1982. A collection of SFBC covers with commentary on the artists. C.

FILM

Harryhausen, Ray. *Film Fantasy Scrapbook*. 3rd ed. San Diego: A.S. Barnes, 1981.

Revised from the 1972 and 1974 editions, this lightly expanded version is a illustrations, posters, and photos covering every facet of Harryhausen's career. P.

Hogan, David J. *Who's Who of the Horrors and Other Fantasy Films: The International Personality Encyclopedia of the Fantastic Film*. San Diego: A.S. Barnes, 1980. Profiles of more than 1,100 people involved in creating virtually every horror, fantasy and science fiction film ever made. C.

Mank, Gregory William. *It's Alive! The Classic Cinema Saga of Frankenstein*. San Diego: A.S. Barnes, 1981. Chronicles the complete story of Universal Studio's monster saga. C.

McCarthy, John. *Splatter Movies: Breaking the Last Taboo*. Albany, NY: FantaCo Enterprises, 1981. Traces the development of splatter movies. P.

Meyers, Richard. *The World of Fantasy Films*. South Brunswick, NJ: A.S. Barnes, 1980. A study of fantasy-related movies from 1975-78, a period when some of the most original films were released. C.

Nelson, Thomas Allen. *Kubrick: Inside a Film Artist's Maze*. Bloomington: Indiana Univ. Press, 1982. Critical study of Kubrick's major films. C/P.

Pitts, Michael R. *Horror Film Stars*. Jefferson, NC: McFarland, 1981. The first reference book to focus on both the universally recognized great performers of the horror film and the many important lesser featured players who gave these films their special "feel." C.

Pohl, Frederik, and Frederik Pohl IV. *Science Fiction: Studies in Film*. New York: Ace, 1981. An informal account of the development of SF film arranged chronologically. P.

*Prawer, S.S. *Caligari's Children: The Film as Tale of Terror*. New York and Oxford: Oxford Univ. Press, 1980. Sketches the evolution of the horror movie as a genre and analyzes specific sequences from films in which the evocation of terror plays a dominant part in order to suggest relationships between literary and cinematic tales of terror. C.

Reed, Donald A., and Patrick Pattison. *Collector's Edition: Science Fiction Film Awards*. La Habre, CA: ESE California, 1981. A pictorial description of the films, actors, and actresses who have won recognition from the Academy of Science Fiction, Fantasy and Horror Films during the period 1972-79. C/P.

*Sobchack, Vivian Carol. *The Limits of Infinity: The American Science Fiction Film 1950-75*. South Brunswick, NJ: A.S. Barnes, 1980. An aesthetic study which examines the recurring visual and aural motifs of the SF cinema and how they might relate to the genre's thematic patterns. C.

Stanley, John. *The Creature Features Movie Guide*. Pacifica, CA: Creatures at Large, 1981. Provides capsule reviews of 2753 horror/fantasy/SF films produced during the past fifty years. P.

Strickland, A.W., and Forrest J. Ackerman. *A Reference Guide to American Science Fiction Films*. Vol. I. Bloomington, IN: T.I.S. Publications, 1981. The first of a projected four-volume work which will systematically classify and annotate all American SF films produced since 1897. C.

*Willis, Donald C. *Horror and Science Fiction Films II*. Methuen, NJ: Scarecrow Press, 1982. Lists 2350 titles (600 annotated) for the period 1972-81 and also updates his earlier volume; the most complete film reference book for the modern period. C.

WRITING AND PUBLISHING

Bova, Ben. *Notes to a Science Fiction Writer*. 2nd ed. Boston: Houghton Mifflin, 1981. Originally published in 1975, this book offers basic advice to new writers, using the author's own stories as models for his discussion. P.

Longyear, Barry B. *Science Fiction Writer's Workshop—I: An Introduction to Fiction Mechanics*. Philadelphia: Owlswick Press, 1980. A thorough introduction to fiction writing, stressing the short story, based on Longyear's experience in conducting writing workshops at SF conventions. P.

Scithers, George H., Darrell Schweitzer, and John M. Ford. *On Writing Science Fiction (The Editors Strike Back!)*. Philadelphia: Owlswick Press, 1981. The experience of the editors of *Isaac Asimov's Science Fiction Magazine* distilled into a complete guide to writing science fiction.

TEACHING RESOURCES

Banks, Michael A. *Understanding Science Fiction*. Morristown, NJ: Silver Burdett, 1982. A teacher's guide [not seen]. P.

Tymn, Marshall B. *A Teacher's Guide to Fantastic Literature*. rev. ed. Boca Raton: Florida Atlantic University, 1982. A resource manual and guide to the field for SF and fantasy teachers. P.

*Williamson, Jack, ed. *Teaching Science Fiction: Education for Tomorrow*. Philadelphia: Owlswick Press, 1980. Essays on the evolution of science fiction, its significance and literary values, use in various subject disciplines, and resources. C.

FORTHCOMING

Asimov, Isaac, Martin H. Greenberg, and Charles G. Waugh, eds. *Science Fiction A to Z: A Dictionary of the Great Themes of Science Fiction*. Boston: Houghton Mifflin, 1982.

Barnstone, William, ed. *Borges at Eighty: Conversations*. Bloomington: Indiana Univ. Press, 1982. Collection of transcripts of Borges interviews from various sources. C.

Dictionary Catalog of the J. Lloyd Eaton Collection of Science Fiction and Fantasy Literature. 3 vols. Boston: G.K. Hall, 1982.

Glut, Donald F. *The Frankenstein Catalog*. Jefferson, NC: McFarland, 1982.

Hein, Rolland. *The Harmony Within: The Spiritual Vision of George MacDonald*. Grand Rapids, MI: Wm. B. Eerdmans, 1982.

Higgins, D.S. *Rider Haggard: A Biography*. New York: Stein and Day, 1982.

Kemp, Peter. *H.G. Wells and the Culminating Ape: Biological Themes and Imaginative Obsessions*. New York: St. Martin's, 1982.

Klinkowitz, Jerome. *Kurt Vonnegut*. New York: Methuen, 1982.

Lewis, Peter. *George Orwell: The Road to 1984*. New York: Harcourt, 1982.

Morace, Robert A., and Kathryn Van Spanckeren, eds. *John Gardner: Critical Perspectives*. Carbondale: Southern Illinois Univ. Press, 1982.

Olander, Joseph D., and Martin Harry Greenberg, eds. *Philip K. Dick*. Writers of the 21st Century. New York: Taplinger, 1982.

Rovin, Jeff. *The Science Fiction Collector's Catalog*. San Diego, CA: A.S. Barnes, 1982.

Schlobin, Roger C., ed. *The Aesthetics of Fantasy Literature and Art*. Notre Dame, IN: Univ. of Notre Dame Press, 1982.

Slusser, George E., Eric S. Rabkin, and Robert Scholes. *Bridges to Fantasy*. Alternatives Series. Carbondale: Southern Illinois Univ. Press, 1982 [Not seen]. C.

Smith, Nicholas, ed. *Philosophers Look at Science Fiction*. Chicago: Nelson-Hall, 1982.

Tymn, Marshall B. *Survey of Science Fiction Literature: Bibliographical Supplement*. Englewood Cliffs, NJ: 1982.

Tymn, Marshall B., and Mike Ashley, eds. *Science Fiction, Fantasy and Weird Fiction Magazines*. Westport, CT: Greenwood Press, 1983.

Tymn, Marshall B., and Roger C. Schlobin. *The Year's Scholarship in Science Fiction and Fantasy: 1976-1979*. Kent, OH: Kent State Univ. Press, 1982.

Underwood, Tim, and Chuck Miller, eds. *Fear Itself: The Horror Fiction of Stephen King*. San Francisco: Underwood/Miller, 1982.